THE CURIOUS CASE OF THE CONJURE WOMAN

An Appalachian Detective Yarn

THE CURIOUS CASE OF THE CONJURE WOMAN

An Appalachian Detective Yarn

JERRY PEILL

Creekview Press

The Curious Case of the Conjure Woman

Copyright © 2014 by Jerry Peill

1st Edition published in 2014 by Creekview Press
ISBN 13:   978-1502313461
ISBN 10:   1502313464

Book design by Tom Crockett
tomcrockett@mac.com

Photo of Tom Watson: Courtesy of the IBM Corporate Archives. ©International Business Machines Corporation (IBM) 1956

Printed in the United States of America

Contents

Dedication

For Algernon Percy Elkins, my father,
who made me brother to those angry young men;
playwrights John Osborne and Harold Wesker,
and my favorite novelist, Kingsley Amis.

Tom Watson, PhD
Caney Forks, Virginia
November 5, 1968

Tom Watson
(the other one)

Chapter 1

Anger Management

I would never have met my conjure woman but for my father's infatuation with IBM.

Kingsley Amis' son believes that you should stop blaming your parents after you turn twenty-five. What does he know? That milestone is already four years behind me, yet my father's culpability is as comprehensive as ever. He saw IBM's rapid growth under its aging CEO as the future not just of our planet but of the entire solar system. Had I been born before this beastly corporation had taken over his mind, he would hardly have christened me Tom, after their CEO. My name in itself is of no great detriment. There are legions of harmless Toms. But my father couldn't leave it at that. He changed my family name to Watson, to make his point unequivocally clear. Then, as I grew up, the old bore relentlessly steered my social and educational activities toward the arid world of computing machines.

Let me ask you; what is a machine beside a folk song? After I discovered the songs collected by Cecil Sharp there was never any contest in my mind. My hero, not my father's! And Cecil not Tom, you'll notice. My father could find no way to imagine my new star affording me the lucrative and secure future offered by the mighty IBM. Under the visionary leadership of the real Tom Watson, of course. Our mealtime talk grew so bitter that I finally abandoned the family table altogether. I learned to live in cheap cafes on milk and sausage rolls. Later my tastes graduated to beer, Scotch eggs and crisps in the plentiful pubs of stodgy Surbiton.

Inspired by Cecil Sharp I won a scholarship to Balliol College, Oxford. There I read English folklore and popular culture. Yes culture. This was the perfect field for me; as far from IBM as I could contrive to get. Better yet there was nothing my father could do about it. He wasn't willing to fork out the funds for whatever computer-riddled courses smelled strongly enough of IBM.

With time my studies became less satisfying and, to my regret, more demanding. I felt relief when, in the final year, my tutor, Derek Farnsworth, began to review my post-graduate options. He lamented that folklore in the British Isles had abandoned its roots to go wherever the money was: festivals, agricultural shows, village Morris dances, TV shows, recording studios, those very pubs that had nourished me. In a word singers and musicians alike had turned professional. I had been uneasily aware of this problem in Britain, but not, as he then told me, that it had spread plague-like throughout Europe.

Had I thought this dilemma through I would not have been the least surprised by his proposed solution. He asked whether I would consider working in America, where I would find unspoiled traditions still flourishing. This seemed highly unlikely to me, until he explained that he was referring to Appalachia.

I knew that Cecil himself had visited the Southern Appalachians, during the First World War. Sadly he was much hampered there by poor health and the oppressive climate. His young assistant, Maud Pauline Karpeles, when not nursing him, had done some collecting on her own account. Her work has since been laid open to question because of her insistence that folk music is the 'pre-literate emanations of mankind.' As I write, she is preaching this theory in Kensington, of all places. She is even feuding with the venerable Fiddle & Bow Society, for heaven's sake!

Derek emphasized all the work that Cecil had left undone or also open to question. He assured me the Appalachian peoples still kept alive the music of their Scotch-Irish forebears, from Tennessee, to the Carolinas, Kentucky, and both Virginias. Derek worked with me to identify what he termed virgin territory. Using U.S. census data we pin-pointed a mountain community in which every family name, bar one or two, was indisputably Scotch, or Irish, or both. If my grant writing succeeded I could be the sole Anglo Saxon among three dozen mountain Virginians in the southwest of their state.

Or is Virginia a commonwealth? If the latter, I should feel far more at home.

The grant writing was a dreadful grind, but at last I got it done and submitted.

While awaiting the outcome, I brooded on the lack of opportunity in Britain, and the consequent necessity of dealing with dubious American material that would probably be no better than third-hand. And in that most Philistine of our former colonies, no less.

I ask you; how would you feel? Derek had warned me how the Appalachian people are clannish; not in a Scottish sense so much as in their taciturn suspicion of visitors from beyond their mountains and hollows. Worse yet, once you do get them talking, they are, of all the English-speaking peoples, perhaps the hardest to understand.

For the first time, despite myself, I began to wonder if I wouldn't be better off had the old man never got that IBM bee in his bonnet. At least when the grant finally came through it did keep me fully occupied, preparing for my year's exile in the middle of nowhere.

I tried to forget my phony name and clung to warm thoughts of dear old Cecil Sharp.

Chapter 2

Nowhere

There's nothing for it; it's time to start my diary. Here am I; a hot, damp, newly minted folksperson mere miles from his first field assignment. My U.S. government green card tells me I am a resident alien. Bosh! It's this rotten place that's alien. Cecil was dead right about the climate. I feel like a customer of the Bosphorus Steam Baths, Ltd. (Cherwell Road branch, Oxford). I resent these endless tree-clad slopes that shut out the sun, most of the sky and anything else resembling life as I have previously known it. Where's the relief? In England you only have to turn the corner or climb the hill. Alright, alright, I suppose I must make allowances. After all, this is America. More specifically my rail ticket says it is...yes, Meadowview. So does the sign on this unpainted, so-called depot, more like an old barn. The conductor says... hang on a minute...let's hope that battered old pick-up truck isn't from my hostess.

Unfortunately, it only too unavoidably is. Ben Cochran, it transpires, is the Caney Forks handyman sent to meet me by my landlady and mountain mentor, the widow Flora MacTaggart. He stares at me with piercing blue eyes. Nothing else about his looks inspires confidence. His battered felt hat and vast, silvering beard belong in an old-time stage melodrama. A confusion of patched denim clothes his lanky frame. So why is this sartorial last-gasp frowning at my new anorak and corduroys? I explain this is mountain gear. He looks the other way. Thank God for small mercies.

Now in what passes as a passenger seat, I shift my feet to accommodate various unlabeled empty bottles. Mr. Cochran has to crank his chariot to get it started! With a violent grating of gears we jerk forward. This vehicle seems to have no shock absorbers, indeed appears to have been constructed before their invention. Mr. Cochran evinces no curiosity for my world, only to know what possessed me to book into such a small community as his for a whole year. Evidently Flora has said nothing to brief him.

To what have I sentenced myself for these twelve months? Mr. Cochran is no help. In a nasal whine he talks malevolently about the failings of the machine jouncing us over the rough country roads that would appear to be our inescapable lot. I try asking him which are his favourite songs. As far as I can translate his reply, he has none. His gravelly voice may be sufficient explanation. He does not recognise Cecil Sharp's name, so familiar to the rest of the world. Shall I be totally wasting my time over here?

Social gloom thus amplifies the all-encompassing murk of these densely forested mountain slopes. I begin to wonder if the mountaintop removal I understand to be so passionately protested by those new tree huggers might not in fact be a good thing. It would brighten up the place no end. And speaking of ends, according to my churlish chauffeur, our tortuous journey is mercifully approaching its own.

As the last light fades we bump over abandoned rail tracks and lurch into a hollow lined with humble frame homes of indeterminate age. The dusty road is soon peopled with a gauntlet of staring, stone-faced hillbillies, mostly female. I wonder, are the latter called "billies" too, or "nannies" perhaps? This appellation works for goats, which are so well adapted to mountains; why not for these people, too?

My chauffeur hauls on his hand brake outside one of the better-preserved dwellings. He extracts a raucous triple raspberry from his klaxon. Stiffly, we dismount. I am left free to contemplate a porch, bare except for a pair of wooden rocking chairs flanking a plain little table. It's mission in life is evidently to support a big chipped, glass ashtray.

After a more than decent pause the screen door on this porch twangs open to reveal a stiff-necked old lady. She identifies herself as Granny MacTaggart. I must say that her appearance inspires more optimism than my driver's. Her kindly face is sharp-featured, her eyes shrewd. Her white hair is neatly arranged, her faded blue cardigan and skirt spotless. Good show, Miss Flora MacTaggart. She instructs Mr. Cochran not just to bring up my luggage but to look sharp about it. A welcome paragon in this wilderness.

She speaks slowly and is not so hard to understand.

Flora urges me inside her home, to unpack, freshen up and partake of a typical supper with her. I come downstairs, tired but hungry. We draw up to a small table in a clean but cut-price Victorian setting, distressingly devoid of folk furniture. Flora has clearly gone to no little trouble assembling a meal illustrative of various aspects of Appalachian life. She gives me a running commentary upon this as we eat. Despite her good intentions the white red eye gravy remains a mystery, as do her fatback and shucky beans. And she refuses to sing a note for me, hinting at some problem with her teeth. She has nothing to say of the great Cecil Sharp. When asked about other researchers, she tells me there have been TV scouts in the area on two occasions, both looking not for music, but moonshiners. A disappointing start to my twelve months' stay.

I am frankly relieved to escape to my room for the night, nursing the assorted aches in my travel-weary body and mind. Am I in what they call culture shock? And what on earth kind of animals can they be, howling so discordantly in the distant dark?

After cajoling me downstairs next morning, Flora serves a meal that she insists constitutes breakfast in these parts. What is hominy? What are grits? What she calls biscuits are actually limp tea scones, and the coffee appears to be made from chicory. While I experiment with appropriate caution, she tells me she has prepared a set of rules for my conduct among her community. Oh my hat! I do my best to look unfazed.

"Take care ye don't offend them black Arsh." Already I am tuning in to her brogue.

"I have visited Ireland more than once, Miss MacTaggart, and there is no such thing,"

"Ye may could know 'em as black Dutch." I shake my head firmly.

"Why, ye've surely heared tell o' Melungeons then, Mr. Watson? They're a bunch ye mus' pay special mind."

"You have the advantage of me. Could you invite one around for my inspection?"

"No, Ah sure cain't, Mr. Watson. The ver' ideah! Them folks is a gaum o Africans, West Indians, loose whites and eastern Cherokee."

I shudder at the thought of the monotonous drumming and wailing associated with these peoples in general. Flora must have noticed, as she warns me, "Don't ye ne're hold yer face jus' so fer a Melungeon! They're sure ta take offence! Show 'em some respec', Mr. Watson, an' they'll treat ye fair. Don't forgit ye're not but an outsider y'self!"

Yes, and an angry outsider, here as well as back home, but I can't admit it to Flora.

"Same as ye mus' show respec' fer the snake handlers over acrost ta our meetin' place. Jus' as ye would fer the copperheads an' the bars..."

"I think I know what a copperhead is and believe me, Miss MacTaggart, I would give it a wide berth. But are you asking me to foreswear alcohol for a whole year?"

"Ah ain't said nothin' 'bout hit, Mr. Watson. Ah'm a-tellin' ye hightail hit if 'n ye sees a bar. They come down nights an' root about in our plantin's. They act plumb ornery if 'n they're interrupted. More so if 'n hit's a Momma bar." Now I understand her. I sigh and mumble my thanks. I worry more at the mysteries of her speech than its subjects.

"Now, Mr. Watson, thar's sartain topics ye mus' ne're

breathe a word on. Thar's the War atween the States, the Pinkerton Agency, them Hatfields an' McCoys, the Scopes trial, the Blue Ridge Parkway land theft, revenooers, hair conditionin', the Piggly Wiggly..." I would, in fact, welcome some discussion of air conditioning, but for the rest, I simply cannot maintain focus for such gross impediments to my important work. Their tenor reminds me of nothing so much as those Kremlin photographs with an obvious blank for each purged figure the Politburo wants forgotten. Yet this is America. I can hardly research effectively when so much material is proscribed.

Nothing Flora has said so far works for me. I do my best to act with restraint in expressing this irrefutable fact. Flora takes it on her pointy chin. She explains that I had been 'kinda misty' to her when forming her plans for my time here in Caney Forks. So it had been plain good sense to prepare an alternative program for my stay. Plan B!

Apparently this consolation prize entails my serving as an intern with a certain Shirley M'Gonaughy. From Miss M'Gonaughy I can evidently count on learning far more than I can possibly imagine. I do hope Flora is right. Time will tell. There are three hundred and sixty four days to go.

Flora, suddenly swelling and looking intensely impressive, emphasises that Miss M'Gonaughy is a conjure woman and a private eye. Helpfully, she explains that so-called conjure men and ditto women possess magical powers. Up to that moment my sole exposure to the term "private eye" had been as the title of a highly irreverent English satirical publication. Registering my unabated bafflement, she translates 'private eye' for me. Apparently it means a detective. My sainted aunt! Derek never prepared me for this. It is arrant nonsense, certainly not worth crossing the wide Atlantic for. Sorry about that. Ending the sentence with a preposition, I mean. It's simply not done...must be the strain of this appalling place.

"Does Miss M'Gonaughy sing?" I am clutching at straws.

"Our Shirley she'll curl yer toes, Mr. Watson. Better'n

singin' she fiddles anymore.

"Now, once't Ah done tidied up these breakfas' bits, we'all kin walk on over out fer Miss M'Gonaughy's. An' as we'all like ta say, 'kill us two birds wi' one dornick'. Shirley lives a fair piece out'n town. We'all cain't help but meet folks along our way. Ah want 'em feelin' all safe an' comf'able when ye axe 'em fer help wi' yer special research. D'ye see how Ah have got yer day all cut out fer ye?"

I nod. Gorm? Dornick? I try to look optimistic. What else can I do?

"Did ye write me down 'bout the birds, Mr. Watson?"

I ignore that. All right, the fiddling part offers a glint of hope, but as for this being a town, that's absolutely ridiculous! Overall, things still look about as black as the inside of a coal mine.

Please note that I choose this simile fully conscious that there should be plenty of old mine shafts around here for reference.

Chapter 3
Somewhere?

I hand Flora down from her porch onto the dusty and un-marked road. A fitful breeze stirs its surface into what she ex-plains are dust devils. In my capacity of sightseer these prove annoying to encounter. Flora leads left, among randomly spaced, unpainted houses devoid of any architectural orna-ment, but not without occasional flower boxes. In sparse-ly weedy, beaten-earth front yards, ancient and abandoned pick-ups and cars, sit sunk aslant. Others perch on concrete blocks, shorn of their wheels. Most appear to be serving as chicken coops, dog kennels or tomato storage.

"Miss MacTaggart, why would people put tomatoes in their old vehicles?"

"D'ye mean 'maters, Mr. Watson? If 'n so they're thar ta dry."

"But all those hens, they can't be there drying." Flora stares at me doubtfully.

"Hain't ye heared o' chicken hawks, Mr. Watson?" I see I had better keep quiet.

The occasional cow stares at us from what Flora terms side yards. Set well back from the road gnarled old apple trees mark homes that have disintegrated, she tells me. "Life is chancy," she adds. And gloomy. At every step the everlast-ing trees block the sun; cast their dark, broken shade. Is this why we hear no birdsong? I don't count the occasional crow of a rooster, and certainly not last night's distant, mournful howling.

"Can we skip Ben Cochran?" I plead. "That blighter really does take the biscuit."

"Blighter, Mr. Watson, what kinda word might could thet be? An' lan' sakes, what d'ye mean 'bout biscuits? Ah hope ye ain't foun' no fault wi' mine."

Fortunately the approach of an elderly woman lets me off the hook. Flora introduces her as Granny Phipps; on her way, she says, not in the least abashed, to have her daily gossip with my hostess. I am introduced as 'the man makin' notes on our mountainy ways'. This new Granny stands still as an Egyptian mummy. She looks me up and down three times before declaring that she would recognise me if she saw me again. "Ah be a-waitin' f 'ye ta come agin frum yer gallivantin'," Miss Phipps tells her gossip partner with a long, meaningful stare.

"Yonder big place on yer right, hit's Obadiah Spade's," resumes my guide. " He does the buryin' fer Caney Forks. By happenstance he's real busy right now, a-readyin' ta put Sally Holdaway in the ground. But we kin take us a peek an' see if 'n he ain't in."

We peek indeed and find, in its capacious, bare interior, a well-fed, older man of mournful countenance, dressed almost in rags. These he makes haste to characterize as his working clothes. That distraction disposed of, Flora introduces me with the same bare-bones phrase she had used to Granny Phipps. I make a note to speak to her about this failing, in private, of course. Obadiah Spade behaves much like a stand-in for Miss Phipps. Rooted to the spot he looks me up and down, up and down, only to pronounce a quite different finding. "Six foot one bah a half, Mr. Watson?"

What? Oh! "You are...absolutely right, Mr. Spade," I sputter, quite at a loss until I recall his livelihood, "May I converse with you in depth at a more convenient time? I feel sure you can supply me with further information of perhaps greater interest."

"Ye may could, ye may could, Mr. Watson, soon's we'all done seed our dear Sally safely inta the groun'."

I confess that I am so overcome by his co-operative spirit, I grasp his pudgy hand with a warm enthusiasm. My mentor in turn looks almost pleased. We step outside.

"Now, acrost thar hit's Rosie Ross...she who's pullin' up weeds. She'll be welcomin' a break." Rosie straightens up with undisguised relief. She is a plumpish, middle-aged brunette in coveralls. She has a friendly, weather-beaten face and looks eminently sensible to me. I perceive a black arm-band on her sleeve, no doubt for the soon to be interred Sally Holdaway. Flora says her piece.

"What do you raise in your garden, Miss Ross, apart from all the flowers?" I inquire.

"A bit o' sorghum, cabbage, leaf lettuce, sweet 'taters, black-eyed peas, ramps. Mah beans is Kentucky Wonders. Nex' year Ah plan on tryin' asparagus, Mr. Watson."

"Sparrow grass!" I can't stop myself from exclaiming.

"Sparrow grass?" echoes Flora. "Why d'ye say sparrow grass?"

"It's what the right people call it in Blighty."

"Right people, Mr. Watson? Ah do b'lieve ye's puttin' on hairs! An' jus' whar, pray, is this Blighty place? Don't ye go tellin' me hit's whar them blighters live!" Why does Flora sound so upset?

Rosie defuses the situation with a shy smile. "Mah gran-maw use ta say spar grass. Ah know she would of had hit on granpaw's grave. Hit was the custom those days. We'all ain't so far apart, Flora. Ah'll be plum glad ta answer yer questions, Mr. Watson, when ye have the tahm." Great Scott! A volunteer! And friendly too.

Turning away from this encouraging woman, we find ourselves in the path of a fierce, bent little figure in a long, dowdy dress. She looks frail and gray. In her train three grinning, barefoot children ape this old woman's scuffling gait as a honey-coloured puppy gambols in circles around them.

"This is Meg M'Sweeney," Flora announces. Meg, this heah's Mr. Watson." The old crone glares up at me through thick-lensed spectacles.

"Looks no better'n one a them Tee Vee fellers. Y'all knows how we deals wi' them fools." She tosses this Parthian shot over her meagre shoulder as she darts around me like a lizard and shuffles off.

"Who does she think she is?" I ask Flora in dismay. "What an old trout!"

"Trout? She sure ain't frum Caney Crick down thar." Flora points to our left.

I bite my lip and think for a minute before telling her, "That's the term we use to signify an annoying, bad-tempered old person; especially when applied to a woman."

"Thet's powerful innerestin', Mr. Watson. We calls Meg the scald crow o' Caney Forks. She looks arter the snakes fer our visitin' preacher man. Whate're ye mought think, don't fergit mah warnin' 'bout showin' 'em proper respec'! Ye'll git more out'n her than ye reckon. An' ye'll ketch more flies wi honey than vinegar." She looks grim.

A textbook old trout! There's Flora's Creek alright, but where's the eponymous Fork?

The modest houses are already thinning, the trees and debris between crowding right up to the road. Ahead, in a clearing to our right, lies a graveyard. I point at it, asking Flora where the church is. She smacks my arm down. "Ne're point at a graveyard, less'n ye want bad luck! Ah don't b'lieve so mahself, mind, but Ah fret fer sech a new fur'ner as y'self."

Chastened, I observe a small, dark man digging in leisurely fashion what will no doubt soon be Sally Holdaway's last resting place. Flora halloos to him.

"Festus Fraser, heah's Mr. Watson. He wants a word wi' ye when the buryin's o'er an' done." The gnarled figure raises his head, grunts, lifts a knobbly arm to wipe his glistening brow, then stoops back to his task without a word.

"Thar's another'un wi' more ta tell than ye mought like ta think," says Flora severely. For myself, I wouldn't bet a halfpenny on this grumpy, self-effacing old grave digger.

Something else has been troubling me for a while. "Miss MacTaggart, I can't help noticing we have skipped a lot of houses. Some had chickens in the yard, or in old vehicles. Surely they're not all unoccupied. I'll need a lot more than seven people to do what I hope to do."

"Rest aisy, Mr. Watson. The only empty'un hit's the Holdaway place. Mos' a the others are mens' an' they're off away workin'." I am stunned by this sudden vision of Caney Forks as a commuter suburb.

"What kind of work would that be, for example, Miss MacTaggart?"

"Them as have bottom land, they're a-tendin' thar corn crop or thar cane.. Them as don't are up ta the woods, cuttin' an' splittin', an' stackin' an'..." Her voice trails off. I hesitate to voice what I'm thinking. As I'm not allowed to mention revenuers, I let it slide. Flora looks relieved. Could it be that we have a hollowfull of moonshiners?

"More'n the homes belong ta womenfolk gone day-visitin' o'er in the nex' holler. Mayhap a few on o'er ta Hutchins. If 'n hit 'ud make ye feel ary better, Mr. Watson, Ah kin call off the folks we'll be a-meetin' when they're back. Ye write 'em down now."

She closes her eyes to concentrate: "Thar's Jimmy Fanaghy—with a g---Andy Goggin...Earl Casey...Robby Burns...Rory Sullivan...Owen Brien...Kenny Irving...Dan Sullivan...Tom Houlahan... Let's see who-all ilse; yes, Eddie MaCafferty...Charlie Rattigan...Donny Dwyer...Peter Duffy an' Joe M'Cabe, Lyney an' Birty McEvoy an'... Red Reardon," she concludes in triumph. I scribble hard to catch up with her recital.

I dimly recall many of these names from the far-off days of our census researches.

"Then thar's them visitin' women; Alice Knox...Rosy Hennessey, Cat Kane...Nancy Mullins...Cherry O'Flaherty...an' Jean Tierney."

"Surely not Gene Tierney the film star?"

"No, ye silly boy, jus' plain Jean Tierney, J...e...a...n!" She gives me a disapproving glare. But Flora's recital has reconfirmed the rightness of my research choice. Caney Forks is a hotbed of Scotch-Irish. My copying complete, I tally the score.

"You certainly know your onions, Miss MacTaggart!" I want to show her how much I appreciate her feat of social memory. This could never be equaled by anyone I know back home in England.

"Mah onions, Mr. Watson? Ah know whar they're at. What more should Ah know?"

"I apologise. That just slipped out. It means that you are in top form...right up to snuff..." I am floundering. Maybe none of that is any clearer over here. I resolve to be more careful what I say in Caney Forks. Aha! Here is a fork in the road.

We veer along it, past a lone mailbox onto a narrow track through dark laurel thickets crowned with gloomy conifers. We splash through a ford and traipse on until we see a tiny log house. Leading the way through its neatly kept front yard, Flora knocks on its rough door. This opens to reveal a startling young vision, whose rich amber hair is a complete mess. It curtains her face, falls over her plain brown dress, is tangled in its buttons. I can look at nothing else. She claps a hand to where her mouth is hiding.

"Mah Lawd, Flora, Ah plumb forgot. Mah only one excuse is Ah have me a new flatland customer. He's visitin' this ver' mornin'. Ah'm not neah ready, as y'all kin see." She parts her fine-spun auburn curtain to peer at me with an appraising eye. "An' you'll be Mr. Watson, Ah reckon. Won't y'all step on in? We'all kin sit a li'l spell."

We do as she bids. There are only two chairs in the barely furnished one-room interior. I am still standing when Miss M'Gonaughy tells me, "Ah see you have your notebook all ready, Mr. Watson. An' your ink pen." Startled, I wonder how she knows. I have kept both discreetly hidden behind my back.

"You're reflected in that window glass," she laughs. She points to it with a slender finger. "Why y'all done walked on ovah when Ben could a driven y'all?" I realise her survey has also taken in my dusty shoes, though Flora's are hidden beneath her long skirts. That's the sort of thing detectives do, I suppose.

"Ah deal wi' many diff'rent folks in mah line o' work, Mr. Watson. Ah rely on askin' a whole heap a questions. Flora an' Ah done figgered how you might could come along a me ta note down mah questions, an' the answers as given. Might could you don't care ta do it?" Her green eyes can still flash disarmingly through their amber veil. Only after a long moment, combining masculine and syntactical paralysis, can I nod my eager agreement with what I fervently hoped her question was.

A conjure woman and a private eye. Isn't that how my mentor described her? Yes, and what devastating eyes they are. Is this why my toes feel to be curling already?

Seemingly unaware of my filleted condition, Flora withdraws to fulfill her next assignment, with Granny Phipps. "Supper at seven," she calls to me from the door. Thus recalled to harsh reality I hope against hope that this evening's meal will be substantially different from my welcome supper; or at a minimum more identifiable.

Chapter 4
My New Tutor

No sooner is Flora out the door than Miss M'Gonaughy issues my instructions for the day, brushing her flaming, unruly hair aside this time to give me the sweetest smile. Though there are enough chairs now, Miss M'Gonaughy overlooks this fact in her hurry:

"Ah'm no ways set for mah client, Mr. Watson. He may could arrive anytahm an' for sartain he's a-comin' bah car. The minute we heah the motor Ah want for you ta scoot behin' this screen. Perch on that stool an' be ready ta take your notes. You mus' be quiet as a mouse. Kin you do that for me?" I can only nod wordlessly.

"That's him," she cries almost immediately, beckoning me wildly onto the hidden stool. I am putty in her hands. I almost stop breathing for the duration of the ensuing interview although at first I am distracted by the unsought attentions of a black cat that appears out of nowhere, only to run off in haste.

"Hold your water, Whassup. Ah'm a-comin', mah deah." This assurance from Miss M'Gonaughy does nothing to lessen a furious scratching at the sagging, never-painted front door of this humble cabin. Whassup. What a strange name for a cat. I can just hear Miss M'Gonaughy brush her cascading hair away from her eyes, then scurry to the door to release the importunate Whassup. She later tells me that he embarrassed her by rubbing against the fancy pants of her new client, poised to rap on the door. I hear the following exchange:

"Miss M'Gonaughy, I presume?" The new voice sounds frightfully upper-crust.

"Yes indeedy, sir, 'cept nobody heah'bouts calls me so. An' who mought you be?"

"Jack Forsythe, with an e. Related to the Lees of Virginia, whose family emblem we share; a squirrel rampant." His tone is clipped and commanding.

"Them dang squorr'ls, if 'n you'll pardon mah French, Mr. Witherknee. Though they do make mighty fine eatin' in a hard winter. Oh please excuse mah prattlin'. Might could you tell me your purpose in callin'?"

"To be frank with you, Miss M'Gonaughy, I have it on the highest authority that you possess an unparalleled gift for solving mysteries. Tell me, pray, is this so?"

"Just gimme a couple shakes, Mr. Witherknee. Ah'll be back momently." Finger to lips, she materializes beside me. Bending to gaze into a cracked wall mirror, she pins her wayward tresses with a wild assortment of plastic tortoiseshell combs in the Spanish style. Their effect is transformative. Giving her imprisoned locks an admonitory pat, she skips out and I hear the door creak wide to admit her well-spoken visitor.

"Why thank you," I hear him stammer. "Are you related to the lady with whom I have just been conversing? You... er..."

"Don't trouble your noodle, Mr. Witherknee, "Ah'm she, but Ah'm she with her combs in. This ain't mah reg'lar style, less'n Ah'm fixin' ta head inta town. Now, let's easy up some. You're welcome ta call me mah nickyname. Ever' livin' soul in the holler calls me 'Combs'. Shirley Combs at your service, Mr. Witherknee."

Hmmm...why does her name sound familiar? It bounces around in my head like a persistent fly. Although I feel mesmerised by it's sound, I manage to push it aside. I can't afford to miss any important points for notation. Of these I have as yet all too few.

"Very well, Ms. Combs it is. Can you please answer my question as to your gifts?"

"Why sure, Mr. Witherknee. It's simple 'nuff figgerin' out mos' ever'thin' as foxes folks 'round heah. Flatlanders too. 'Deed Ah've not heard one single complaint atall. Anyone in the holler 'ull tell you so."

"Then may I inquire, Ms. Combs, whether you would be willing to take on a matter which has brought me to my wits end, and of which I can make no sense whatever?"

"Set y'self down on this hickory-split, Mr. Witherknee. It's the best Ah kin offer. Now jus' you fire away 'til you have tol' me ever' las' thing that's a-botherin' you so."

As she speaks I detect evidence of Whassup's re-entry. From Jack's angry exclamations I gather that this importunate animal is now investigating his custom-made wingtips.

Nevertheless, Jack begins, his voice tight with powerful emotions. "I have been happily married to Ermyntrude for three years now, Ms. Combs...until...her manner changed literally overnight...cold and distant as any stranger's.

"I should advise you that she was a widow when we met. Her first husband worked in Brazil. They had a child together, named Carter. Then both were torn from her by Yellow Jack. I have seen their death certificates with my own eyes, Ms. Combs."

Whassup emits a long, indeterminate sigh which Jack echoes, then carries on wearily:

"Disenchanted with Brazil, Ermyntrude sailed for America, richer by her husband's R65,000 estate. On landing she made her way to Wytheville, where I chance to have a business. There we met and became fast friends. Our relationship blossomed and I soon made a knee before her. She accepted warmly. We were wed in a small, private affair, for she seemed to have no friends in this country.

"Soon after we settled in Marion. Such was her love and trust that she insisted I accept her Brazilian inheritance. Imagine my surprise when, out of the blue, she asked me for $100. She promised to tell me what is was for one day, but said she could not do so now."

Whassup lets out a most peculiar noise. That cat is a bloody nuisance. He is making Jack sound more upset than ever.

"Now to the cause of our disharmony, Ms. Combs. A week ago a moving van came to an empty house almost opposite our happy home. Curious who our new neighbours might be, I observed the unloading. Before long I felt keenly that I myself was under scrutiny. Scanning the house front I became aware of a frightening yellow face at the upper window. This face suddenly pulled back out of my view. Greatly disquieted I crossed the road and knocked on the front door. This was opened by a harsh-faced woman with a rough voice. She rebuffed my neighbourly offer of help with a brusque; 'We'll ask when we want it'.

"My wife refused to discuss these strangers with me. Worse yet, she stole out of our home that night when she thought me fast asleep. On her return, she looked pale and anxious. Again she refused to answer my questions.

"The next day, returning early from Wytheville, I saw her leaving the mystery house. She would only say that she had called to offer her assistance. I told her she forced me to enter it myself, to get to the bottom of the matter. She implored me not to do so until my heart relented. I promised to trust her on condition that there should be no more such doings. In return I would let her preserve her secret. Could any man say fairer than that, Ms. Combs?"

I thought Shirley was going to ask the questions. This man does go on.

"'Deed not, Mr. Witherknee, no more'n y'self could an' did."

"Three days later I came home early again, to find my wife out. With a sinking heart, I sat at our front window to keep watch on the hateful house until, as I suspected, Ermyntrude emerged. I ran to her. She went into loud hysterics, but I had taken as much as I could bear. I entered and searched the house from cellar to attic. There were signs of very recent occupancy, but not one living soul to be found."

Shirley then comes to her senses; "Have you ever seen a photy on her fust husband?"

"No. There was a fire in her lawyer's office. All her papers were lost."

"But you done tol' me 'bout seein' those death papers."

"Yes. She sent for duplicates after the fire, on account of our pending marriage."

"Did you ever meet anybody who'd a-known her in Brazil?"

"No."

"Or get ary letters frum over thar?"

"Never."

"Well, Mr. Witherknee, this affair it calls for a good, long think. If 'n the birds have flown for keeps it makes us a problem. But if 'n they do return, Ah kin surely reckon it out direc'ly with thar help. If 'n you like, they'all don't need ta know Ah'm actin' for you."

"And if the house is still abandoned tomorrow, Ms. Combs?"

"Then Ah shall visit it...if 'n you'll be kind 'nuff ta drive me on over."

"Should that prove to be the case I shall call on you in the morning, Ms. Combs. At nine, say. Meanwhile I bid you good evening." He doesn't sound too confident. Wait. Evening? I consult my watch for the first time today. There is just time to make my supper appointment. But Shirley stops me, explaining that she needs to debrief me first.

"Did you write ever'thin' down for me?"

"Every answer he made to your questions. I could fill out the rest tonight if you like. How do you want me to write Mr. Forsythe's name? I ask because you kept calling him Witherknee."

"That's jus' mah teasin', Mr. Watson. All his huffin' an' puffin' 'bout the Lees an' them squorr'ls! He prob'ly got hisself a squorr'l hood ornyment on his Cadillac car. Be honest now, din't you feel he needs takin' down a peg or more?"

23

"That's well and good...but...er...what am I to call you now Miss M'Gonaughy?"

"Oh, Shirley 'ull do fine," she says, giving me another warm smile. "Now les' jus' think out loud a minute. We have us a bad case o' the willies heah. Thar could easy be blackmail in it. Ah do have a theory, Mr. Watson, but Ah ne're say a word 'til Ah have all the fac's. Ever' one. Whassup knows it but he forgets how curiosity kills cats."

'Meouwwww', howls Whassup impatiently, perhaps signaling his willingness to take that risk. No! What am I thinking?

"Mr. Watson, you need ta unnerstan' how Whassup? comes along on all mah cases. His instinc's are plumb canny. An' Ah mus' tell you his name ends in a question mark. Jus' watch him signalin' questions bah nose an' whiskers. Then too he kin tell a bunch jus' frum the tone of a person's voice. He din't cotton ta that Mr. Witherknee one bit. Ah kin read his body language like a book, Mr. Watson."

"I am ready to take your claims for him on trust, Shirley," I lie, "and while we are talking of names, I must honestly confess that my own name has been compromised.

"I am really an Elkins, but my father changed it to Watson for reasons of his own. No more am I a Mister either, but a qualified doctor."

Shirley claps her hands in delight. "That's a blessin'. Thar ain't no other doctor anyplace neah heah." "Unfortunately I am not a doctor of medicine. I am a doctor of philosophy. You will have to decide what to call me, Shirley."

"Ta tell you the flat-out truth, what sits best wi' me is you be Dr. Watson."

"Everyone here knows me as Mr. Watson," I point out. Then a bell rings deep in my mind. Dr. Watson and...and...and...no, no, absolutely not! Perish the thought.

"Now you better run on home, Dr. Watson. Have your supper an' finish them notes.

"Mahself, Ah shall play awhile on mah fiddle. Never once't din't it holp mah thinkin'.

"'Far as nex' mornin', Ah want you ta have Ben let you sit in his ol' pick-up truck. Y'all mus' foller behind us if we drive on bah. Ben cain't mistake that Cadillac car. When it stops, make Ben park well back a him. Then jus' hop out an' find y'self what Ah call a listenin' post. Anyplace in back a that troublesome ol' house."

Bemused, no longer a free agent in any sense of the term, I take my leave. Soon the strains of a jolly but fading fiddle tune put life into my homeward steps. If I weren't English, I'd probably be hopping and skipping by now. This particular jinking melody slyly weaves itself into my sub-conscious un-til...I stop dead in my tracks. My giddy aunt! Doc Watson! Isn't there a legendary mountain musician of that name?

Who am I? What is this place doing to me?

Conjure woman Shirley could hardly be a more different mentor than Flora or Derek Farnsworth. She has me abso-lutely and completely flummoxed.

Trudging back to Flora's home, I acknowledge how primitive my new surroundings are. That completely unengi-neered ford on Shirley's lane, the abandoned rail tracks and all these trees, trees, trees! Shall I be able to survive here for more than a week?

From somewhere above me a hound bays, deep and long. It produces a rolling, blood-curdling echo, the way I have always imagined the hound of the Baskervilles to sound. His baying had devastating effects on its unfortunate auditors. I remind myself repeatedly how that hound was a work of pure fiction. Only through this mantra am I able to compose my over-taxed mind for another unavoidable encounter with my all too predictable landlady and her mountain meals.

Chapter 5
The Fiddle's Mettle

"Well?" asks Flora, at her porch door. The howling of now numerous hounds in the woods behind her place is making any conversation a tall order, but I soldier on bravely.

"Miss M'Gonaughy is the bee's knees, Miss MacTaggart. I am deeply in your debt."

"Bee's knees, Mr. Watson? Whate'er d'ye mean by hit? Is hit more'n yer oniony sayin's?

Damn, I've done it again. "It means that Shirley is the tops...in top form." I stall out. "What I mean to say is that she is just the right person for my work here. Your plan B is most excellent."

"Then quit yer prattlin', Mr. Watson. Come on in, set down an' feed y'self up. Ye look too skinny, fer Caney Forks even. Tell me 'bout yer day atween mouthfulls."

This I do, but add how much note-writing I still have to finish before turning in. Then I ask if she can arrange for barmy Ben to play his part the next morning. She promises to see to this and give me an early breakfast. To be on the safe side, as she puts it.

I don't turn off the light until past 2:00 a.m., hours after the hounds had called it a night. Only four hours later I am awakened by Flora's urgent summons to table, for more grits and so forth.

By 6:30 I am ensconced once more on the torn passenger seat of Ben's rusty old rattletrap. I wonder when the sun will reach the road, and whether the old grouch will appear before the Cadillac comes by. I need not have worried. By 7:00 he squirms into place, in glacial silence, whereas the Cadillac takes another two hours to show up. Ben dutifully pulls out, soon muttering crossly about having to push his machine to its limit to keep our quarry in sight.

Ben's chuntering ceases only when the Cadillac draws up at its destination. There, as per instructions, he stops well back. He sits brooding until Shirley, Jack and Whassup? are safely inside the mystery house, and I can flit to the back of it. The house is poorly maintained. I soon find a discreet spot for monitoring all client/consultant conversations unseen. There is even a crack providing a narrow view of what has to be the kitchen.

"Tahms a-wastin', Mr. Whitherknee," I hear Shirley whoop, then clatter upstairs, crying, "Foller me!"

"Hold on, Ms. Combs," I hear Jack's breathless reply. "I had no idea you have staircases as steep as your mountains."

"They ain't steep, Mr. Witherknee, so much as the steps are close together. It costs less thataway."

Then I hear him stop and gather his breath, not to acknowledge Shirley's information, but to say, "Now tell me please what you have found."

"Looky heah, Mr. Witherknee, thar's not but a few clothes in this chifferobe, an' they're all gal's. If 'n your wife had only the one boy, it's jus' you an' Ermyntrude now."

Jack seems to have lost his voice.

"Now let's see what's below."

I hear her skittering down those steep stairsteps, like a tomboy on a toboggan. She shouts up from the kitchen, "Come look at all this squorr'l crockery in the sink! Your wife only did what any good mountain woman 'ud do. Those new neighbours must a axed her ta lend 'em crockery an' cutlery. Borry a cup o' sugar heah, a cup o' flour thar, an' a cup o' sorghum sirop, say. She jus' run over wi' ever' durn thing that housekeeper done called for. An' Ah reckon too your wife likely staked 'em that $100 for vittles."

I can hear Whassup? purring, with no audible objection from Jack.

"Well, if you say so, Ms. Combs, I'll accept your explanation, even if, to say the least, it does leave me more than a trifle embarrassed. But how do you explain why my dear wife and that rude housekeeper wanted to keep me out of the house at any cost?"

"You'll have ta wait for thar maybe return ta know it sure as shootin', Mr. Witherknee. Howsomever Ah'm ready ta bet mah best boots that poor young'un was kep' locked up on doctor orders. Who could be yeller as you said an' not be real sick? Ah b'lieve your poor wife was a-skeered out'n her mind you'd ketch whatever it was an' sicken like that poor mite. She likely feared you might up an' die, jus' like her fust man."

There goes Whassup? unmistakably purring again. This is so hard to take.

Jack speaks in a new voice, filled with relief, "You are a wonder," he breathes. You have given me back my life! Tell me who you really are, Ms. Combs."

Shirley says nothing, but must have done something. The last thing I hear from Jack is, "Me oh my!" This is followed by the faint whisper of folding money changing hands. I catch a glimpse of Whassup? prancing out, his tail held high.

As soon as I hear them leave, I cautiously come out of hiding to remount Ben's terrible transportation. We drive in all-encompassing silence back to Shirley's. On our arrival, the first thing she wants to know is if my notes of her conversations with Jack are complete. I tell her there is very little left to fill in, which I will complete right away. I put a question of my own to her: "What did you give Jack that made such a stiff fellow as him say, 'Me oh my'?"

She fishes around in her faded blue dress and shyly proffers a grubby, dog-eared, visiting card. I read:

SHIRLEY "COMBS" and WHASSUP?
Mountain Investigators
221B Whistle Pig Lane, Caney Forks
Y'all stop on by

While I ponder on the incongruity of Whassup?'s title, another aspect strikes me; her address. I look hard at her. "Yours is the only dwelling in this lane, Shirley. Where does the 221B come from?"

"Oh, that 'ud be tellin', wun't it?" she replies, her bright eyes twinkling.

Am I dreaming? In any event, it is a provoking conundrum. It occupies my thoughts all the way back to my Mac-Taggart headquarters. It even displaces the unsettling memory of the hellhound to trouble my sleep that night.

Chapter 6
A Bothersome Bequest

Next morning I am allowed to breakfast late. I am working off its ill-effects in the parlor when I hear Granny Phipps greeting my hostess and mounting the porch to sit in the other rocking chair. Evidently it accommodates her daily. Should I eavesdrop? Is the Pope Catholic?

"Ah swan Ah ne're seed Caney Forks so gaumed up. Not in all mah borned days! All on account a thet no-good flat-land woman. Them flatlanders ne're do bring nothin' but trouble." This is unmistakably Miss Phipps seeking affirmation of her judgment from Flora, who is quick to agree.

"Ye gits no argyment thar. She's crazy as a coot an' high fallutin sump'n tur'ble."

They are interrupted by the faint sound of scuffling feet. Both of them fall silent until a familiar, unwelcome voice grates on my ear:

"Ah guess Ah knows jus' who y'all a-gossipin' on, ladies." It's that blasted Ben again. So Ben does have a tongue in his head. Not unexpectedly he receives no invitation that I can hear to join the ladies on the privileged porch.

"Sweet Jesus! Shet yer foolisness, Ben Cochran. Who talks 'bout ary'un these days but Beatrice? 'Less'n hit's Mr. Watson, granted. Ye know yer galluses be half undid?" Flora's disdain is all too audible. But is it for Ben or for me?

"Y'all got me thar, mah deahs, fair an' square. But is y'all smack up ta date 'bout our mutual frien'?"

"Is thar some new awfulness, Ben?" Granny Phipps can

no more help asking than a rabbit hynotized by a snake.

Ben is quick to answer; "Eliza Jane done seed thet flatlander runnin' back'ards out'n her Aunt Sally's place, a-sneezin' fit ta bust an' a-swottin' her own haid wi' all two han's, like she's in a cloud o' bees. 'Cept thar warn't none. Then she stops dead in her tracks, an' runs right on back indoors, a-shakin' her head like a mad dog.

"If 'n only Sally Holdaway ne're took sick an' died on us, we'd not had ta put up wi' her crazy niece." That's Granny Phipps again, stating the superfluous.

"Yes," allows my mentor. "Beatrice 'ud be jus' another Roanoke fashion-fly, an' we'all 'ud be spared her catawampus doin's."

"Does y'all grant the fust sign o' trouble done follered the readin' o' Sally's wull?"

"Ain't thet jus' how hit goes, Ben?" That's my Flora again, so admirably practical.

"But warn't hit the ver' nex' day Beatrice done nail shet her ver' own new back door? Tell me why'd she do hit? Yup, indeedy, Nex' thing we knowed she pops out'n her front door an' throws a hen's aig clean up o'er the rooftree."

There ensues a heavy silence, broken only by the deep bass croaks of what I take to be a bullfrog. Compared to the howling hounds his is an entirely tolerable intrusion.

Knowing those two porch rockers face the road, I can't resist taking a peek. Flora's jar of wildflowers will give me some cover if either gossip should turn around. To my amazement, my highly respectable Flora is puffing away at a pipe, the barrel of which can only be...a corncob! Granny Phipps is spooning some dark matter into her mouth from a squat jar, whose label reads, let's see...'apple butter 9/68'. What in God's name is apple butter? And why on earth is the preternaturally taciturn old Cochran codger such a fountain of speech today? Could it be he only goes mute on me?

"Thar's some on us 'ud tell ye hit's a sure fire way ta git shet on bad luck," suggests Granny Phipps. Her superior lets this contribution pass unacknowledged. "Though Ah'd sure like ta know whar's the bad luck inheritin' a nice place liketa Sally's?" Flora's adjutant is making a fair attempt at damage control.

"Then what does she do but make the rouns on ever' durn hog in the holler, pullin' thar tails, settin' off sech a sqealin' as ye gits at hog killin' tahm."

There is no audible hint from either listener whether this particular intelligence comes to their ears fresh or stale. The invisible Ben presses on gamely, "Then she done shet ever' winder in the homeplace up tight an' kep' 'em so, rain or shine." His claim reminds me how much more shine we have had than rain.

"City folks do have some real strange ways," Flora offers mildly, as though she were addressing a slow child. Granny Phipps nods vigorous assent, her gum-clenched spoon wagging up and down in time.

"Well then, d'y'all know as Beatrice hain't ne're spoke one word ta ary'un since the readin' on the wull? Nor ne're so much as done looked at nobody?"

"If'n ye walked aroun' actin' like Beatrice, wud'n ye have trouble lookin' ary'un in the eye, Ben?" Flora is really coming down hard on him. I love it.

Rebuked, Ben falls back on his trump card. "Rosie's nose, hit's so out'n joint, she done sent ta Spring Crick fer thar preacher man ta come x or size Antie Sally's house!"

The two gossips rock silently, to my mind implying that exorcism is the obvious next step for anyone with half a brain. The mournful howl of a dog up in the hills asks to be answered. It is. I hear these dogs, but why do I never see one in the hollow?

"Remember how y'all done heared hit fust frum me." Ben can be heard shuffling away, seething, I feel confident, with curmudgeonly discontent.

Note to self: are all flatlanders so demonstrative compared with mountain folk?

Although I have now begun my interviews with the residents, they are unsatisfactory. The pending exorcism of the

Holdaway place is on everyone's mind. Only once is it briefly supplanted, when Rosie, hears her neighbour digging in her backyard one moonless night. Beatrice is cursing under her breath as her implement hits rock, root or boot. Rosie, whose equanimity had impressed me so at our meeting, has reportedly been too upset to sleep since. She asks all and sundry, "Is Beatrice a-buryin' some'un herself?" I begin to feel more like a crime reporter than a researcher.

On the morning of the exorcism, the preacher finds himself repeatedly waylaid by frightened residents. They want to be absolutely sure he is fully informed of every strangeness that concerns them. They dog his progress to the Holdaway place, then cluster in the road before it. Their fears are clearly troubling to the borrowed preacher. When at last he ducks under a bower of honeysuckle to cross the Holdaway threshold the trepidation he must feel is palpable. But he is hardly inside the house for two minutes before he comes out into the bright day with a smile on his bony features.

"Thar's no evil heah, mah good people," he assures the agitated crowd. "Ah don't jus' know what's at work heah, but y'all have my word hit's surely not Satan nor ary on his minions. Ah say ye employ the services on a secular expert ta lay this matter ta rest. Les' bring relief quick as we'all kin ta our sorely afflicted frien', Miz Beatrice."

An immediate buzz breaks out among the onlookers as they struggle to come to terms with this unexpected finding. In each little knot of people that forms, I hear the talk going round and round, returning always to its beginnings. Ben Cochran is ignored and, perhaps as a result, he is the first to adjust. "Ah's goin' out o'er ta Whistle Pig Lane." Good thinking, in my opinion. I run to catch the blighter and beg another ride.

Chapter 7
Shirley's New Client

Finding Ben at her door, bursting with the importance of his self-appointed mission, Shirley sees she must first cool him down. "Why don't we'all set in mah dooryard a spell, Ben? This is too fahn a day for wastin' inside, don't you agree, Dr. Watson? Why don't y'all set on these log cuts, an' Ben kin tell us the fac's a the matter. Ah done heard a rumour or two mahself, but Ah never pay much heed ta gossip. Jus' let me get y'all comf'able fust."

She retreats into her log cabin, returning soon with three jars of clear fluid, "In case y'all have the drooth on," she explains. "Now, Dr. Watson, if 'n you don't cotton ta our local drink, Ah do b'lieve Ben 'ud be glad ta help you out." She bestows one of her most beguiling winks on that shameless rapscallion, then glances under a mulberry bush. I look and spy Whassup? taking his ease in its shade. Satisfied, she opens the meeting: "Now, Ben, give us ever' bit you know in your own words. Take your tahm an' be sure an' sartain you leave nothin' out."

Without prompting, I pull out notebook and pen.

Ben nevertheless rushes to retell every rumour with which he has regaled the two grannies, and a few more he must still have had up his sleeve when they shamed him away from the MacTaggart porch. Shirley only has to interrupt him with a couple of questions before he runs dry. I note these questions down.

"Ben, Ah sure do like your idea 'bout all her troubles

startin' wi' the readin' o' Sally's will. Did she leave Beatrice her house alone? Was thar anythin' more, far's you know?" I take that down too, my interest piqued.

"Yup, thar was a twist o' bills fer Obadiah's buryin' fees, wi' a mite lef' o'er, an' thar was too a li'l bitty ol' envylope. Hit had 'privy an' confidenshul' writ on hit. Kin ya figger what-all's in thar, Miz Shirley?" I scribble away.

"'Deed Ah don't know, Ben, but Ah'll bet it holds our answer. We kin call it a day. Now, y'all have ta pass the Hold-away place, so why not stop bah an' make a call date for me an' Dr. Watson? Tell Miz Beatrice nine tomorrer mornin'. Kin you do that Ben?"

All too plainly delighted to be right at the center of things, Ben gives Shirley his promise. Ten minutes later, he makes good on it. Beatrice, her countenance a map of worry, nervously agrees. Ben's commission is complete.

"Ya kin walk frum heah on in, Mr. Watson," he grunts. To keep the peace, I tell the blighter there's no problem. Where would I be without my chauffeur?

Chapter 8

A Secular Solution

I try putting myself in Beatrice's shoes. With all her new neighbours shunning her daily, she must feel uncertain how to get ready for her morning visitors. If she were only back in her Roanoke home, her preparations would be second nature. But she is not, and, as I have found, all the rules here are so very different. In the end she has probably put a kettle on the hob and set out cups, biscuits—definitely biscuits—butter and plates. The usual Flora set-up.

Probably pacing the floor, unable to sit down in her worry, Beatrice is at the door within seconds of Shirley's knock, and edges it open a bit. Overcome to find a friendly face smiling at her, Beatrice swings her door wide, beckons us in and gestures at her kitchen chairs. But Shirley remains on the threshold, her eyes taking in the inexplicable disorder of the big kitchen, dining space and inglenook hearth. Dust motes swarm the air. Jewel-like ladybirds crawl on every surface. Balls of matted hair litter the floor, their colour matching Beatrice's own fiery locks. The closed windows make the atmosphere unbearably stuffy. Scatters of pale powder smear the floor and furniture. Even the left sleeve of Beatrice's otherwise smart green blouse; a blouse which could easily pass muster in London. What in heaven's name can all this conceivably mean?

Beatrice interrupts Shirley's survey: "It's been so very hard to keep all the new rules.

"I just don't know how you all manage..." She pauses, watching anxiously as Whassup? wanders in, whiskers a-quiver, nose twitching, staring wide-eyed everywhere. With regulation feline caution he approaches a drift of powder on the floor then lets out three back-to-back sneezes. He gives Shirley a hurt look.

"Ah'm so sorry, Miz Beatrice. Ah plumb forgot mahself. You know this gentleman is Dr. Watson, but this heah's Whassup? He goes ever'place Ah do. He's a tee-total needcessity ta me in mah work. Don't you mind him any, you heah. Now, may we set down? Ah hate ta see cool biscuits an' your'n look liketa real fine eatin'."

Clearly relieved, Beatrice follows Shirley's example and sits herself at the kitchen table. She is now acting more like the practiced hostess that she must be at home in Roanoke. I steel myself for another round of Caney Forks non-biscuits.

Some of us munch away. "Could you mayhap share your receipt for these delicious biscuits, Miz Beatrice?" Shirley asks. Our hostess cracks a shy smile, nods her assent.

Receipt? Why would Shirley need a receipt? They are Beatrice's expense, not her's.

Is this an old mountain custom? I make a note to seek her explanation.

In this and other ways Shirley continues her efforts to put our client at ease, until Beatrice impulsively reaches across the table and warmly presses her guest's hand. "You can't know how much your visit means to me," she says. "I pray that you can help make my life even the tiniest bit easier in this dreadfully demanding place."

I second that. I know exactly what she means.

"It ain't so difficult once't you know the ropes. An' Ah do b'lieve there might could be a short cut for you, Miz Beatrice. It hangs on the contents o' that li'l confidential envelope Ah heard your Antie Sally done lef' you."

"Yes, oh yes, that is the trouble." Beatrice's cry startles Whassup? out of his reverie. "You must see for yourself what I mean." She rises to open a dresser drawer, taking from it a little, well-worn envelope. This she hands shakily to Shirley.

Shirley lifts its flap, draws out and unfolds a single sheet of notepaper. It is covered in a tiny, spidery hand. Shirley begins to read this, her face betraying mounting surprise. Suddenly she stops. "Ah'm a-goin' ta start this ovah agin, mah deah; readin' out loud, an' speakin' mah thoughts."

Rather sternly Shirley starts quoting: "If a bird flies in an' out of an open window, someone in the house will die." She pauses, then comments, "True 'nuff, but it might could cost you sixty year a-waitin'. D'you see that, Miz Beatrice?

"'It is bad luck ta leave a house by a different door than the one you came in bah.' Mayhap so, Miz Beatrice, but isn't it worse luck if'n you lock y'self out entarly? Might wouldn't you call it more'n a mistake ta nail your own back door shut? Hmmm?

"Next: 'If you pull a hog's tail you kin break a spell o' bad luck." Shirley giggles at this and shakes her head. "You do that, Miz Beatrice, an' you'll upset ever' hog farmer in these hollers. Then jus' wait an' see what they charge you for fat back, mah deah.

"Right: 'It's bad luck ta kill a ladybug!' Well, excuse mah smirkin' but we'all got over that ol' chestnut way back when, mah deah. Tell me, what bad luck have you seen neahabout, savin' your own?"

Ladybug? Not ladybird! I add that to my burgeoning, nearly illegible scribbles.

Shirley's eye runs ahead on the paper; "No more'n you need throw a soft-shell hen's egg over your roof ta rid y'self o' bad luck. Or keep birds frum a-flyin' inta your rooms, or gather your comb har, less'n you go plumb crazy. Ah have more comb har than all the womenfolk in Caney Forks laid end ta end. Now how crazy do Ah soun' ta you, Miz Beatrice? An' don't go tellin' me 'bout not lookin' any'un in the eye who has a stye, less'n you get one too. Think on it: how you a-goin' ta know jus' who has a stye or not 'less'n you peek in the fust place?"

This has all been moving too fast for me. I feel the onset of writers' cramp. On the other hand, my toes are relaxing.

But Shirley's not done yet.

"You've a great long list heah, o' good things as'll happen if 'n your nose itches, or your right palm does, or your foot, or left ear, or lips an' sech, on an' on. Next you'll be tellin' me you've bin a-tryin' itchin' powder ta make the good tahms roll. Don't you see how you have a real big piece o' good luck already? Your inheritance, Miz Beatrice. Mos' folk heah truly need ta feel a better chance at good luck. Tho' Ah'll admit, mah deah, as some older folks do take special notice on itches ta this day.

"Do Ah need ta say the only sort o' luck in runnin' back'ards is when you pay no heed whar you're a-headin' ? Out heah we need sech reminders. It's sixty mile o' rough roads ta the neares' doctorin'."

"Then, too, if 'n you mus' plant 'taters, Miz Beatrice, thar's no call ta put 'em in bah a dark moon, whate'er your aunt done wrote heah. How you goin' ta find 'em agin?"

Thank goodness that Shirley stops reading and commenting to turn the paper over, scrutinising it minutely. "Judgin' bah the age o' this notepaper, Ah bet it hales frum your Antie Sally's Momma. Might could be further back yet. Ah reckon Sally lef' you it more'n a family harloom than a set o' rules for holler livin'. Nothin' Ah see heah 'ud seem strange ta us folk, but most on us don't bother anymore wi' but a few. Like those itches, say. They're no differen' than a State lott'ry ticket, but they're free. Kin you blame 'em? Mah deah, your only bad luck is ta be tee-totally over-citified."

Shirley is too polite; I'd say this highly impressionable client needs a full-time keeper.

Shirley eyes Beatrice carefully: "D'you see how pretty you're sittin' now? Plumb in the catbird seat." Whassup? glances up. Shirley appraises the answering expression on our client's tired face. "May Ah tell our Caney Forks folks how you're ready for callers? Soon's you have your new place all redded up."

I drop my pen. For his part Whassup? must feel satisfied. He stands and stretches luxuriously, then trots jauntily out over the newly sanitised Holdaway threshold. I heartily second his sentiments.

In case the ladies need to talk some more I assure Shirley that today my notes are all complete. I bid Beatrice good day and start walking back to my home from home, untroubled for once by the quavering notes of the unseen hound from Hell.

Chapter 9
My Day Off

A furious drumming awakens me before daylight. Melungeons? I haul myself from bed to window to reconnoitre. A cold, gray rain teems down. The road is streaming and steaming, but otherwise empty. This is no day to be outside, whoever you are.

If I haven't mentioned it previously, most of the houses along the road have tin roofs. The rain unleashes a full-throated roar on Flora's tin panels. The creek has to be flooding! Raindrops ping sharply against my lone window. I return to my narrow, iron bed. Do I have a schedule today, or not? If I do, surely it will have to be canceled.

The best use for my time, I decide, will be to make a fair copy of my unavoidably headlong notes. Scanning the opening pages, I find I now have two quite separate sets of them. There are those notes for which I have Flora's tuition to thank, and there are the meeting minutes, so pressingly requested by Shirley. The former are more or less what Derek and I envisioned prior to the commencement of my researches. The latter represent a horse of a different colour. Shirley has yet to explain their high importance to her. As presented, the ladies' so-called Plan B hardly covers the case.

What is really going on?

Despite the discouraging weather, punctual as ever comes Flora's call to 'breakfast'. This morning I do appreciate one quality in it. Everything is hot. Across the table I tell Flora about my plans for salvaging this unobliging day. She stares at me in profound disappointment.

"How'd ye come bah sech a notion, Mr. Watson? D'ye reckon a li'l rain keeps us shet away? Leastways, all but the menfolk. They cain't do nothin' in the woods when hit's a-soakin' down like today. It's them we'alls a-goin' ta vis-it this mornin' ta fill out yer list. Thar's umbrellies fer the both'n us a-standin' bah mah front door."

"Well, I'll be jiggered!" There I go again, thinking out loud. Flora freezes.

"Jiggered, Mr. Watson? Are ye talkin' likker now?" She gives me a hard, searching look, rises grimly to carry the breakfast remains over to her sink and returns with what looks like a diary in her hand. She places this on the table-cloth and gives it a pat.

"When we'all are done fer the day, ye're a-goin' ta spell out fer me the meanin's on all these strange sayin's o' yer'n. T'ain't right atall ye're the only one as takes notes, Mr. Wat-son. Ah'm not too ol' ta larn new meanin's."

She rises and goes to the door. "Ugh, hit's airish 'nuff fer mah mackinaw! Grab y'self thet big umbrelly ta squire me on out." Flora certainly knows how to pile on the pressure. Me, I can't wait to see what a mackinaw is...oh, it's nothing but a rubbery, Melton coat. Then is my umbrella-holding only for show? Gusts of wind are already trying to wrest it from my grip.

Within minutes Flora is knocking on the door of the most ramshackle house I have seen so far. When a half-dressed, weather-beaten old, gray haired man opens it she starts right up: "How ye doin' this fahn mornin', Andy? Heah's Mr. Watson. He's some kind a scholar. He's gath'rin' hinformation 'bout the way we live in Caney Forks. Mr. Watson, this heah's Mr. Goggin. Kin we'all step on inside, Andy?"

Our target, looking as if he has no choice in the matter, waves us into his rather large, only too plainly multi-purpose living space. Is that a coffin in the corner? A welter of wood splinters, shavings and chips lie about us on all sides...well almost. Mr. Goggin retires to the room's solitary chair. He plants himself firmly on its debris-free surface, takes up a knife from the table alongside and picks up an unfathomable carving. This he calmly proceeds to whittle. He starts to hum a tune I know so well, but cannot name.

Mr. Goggin, his eyes steady under bushy, gray eyebrows, is watching me watching him. "Turkey in the Straw," he whispers.

"Stop teasin' the poor man," my protector orders him sharply.

"Ye ne're done seed a turkey call befowah, Mr. Watson?" Without pausing for my answer he delves into a frayed trouser pocket and pulls out another strange object, It is carved from a darker wood than the first. Cupping both horny hands around this artifact he blows into it. Startled, I look around the room for a gobbler on his TV, so lifelike is the call.

"Gotcha!" crows Mr. Goggin, winking at Flora, and loosing an unbroken series of celebratory turkey gobbles, until I cry uncle.

"Where did you learn that?" I ask, readying my notebook.

"Frum mah Daddy, an' him frum his Daddy befowah him, but jus' try find y'self a Caney Forks man as cain't make 'em in thar sleep. Ye'd grow old a-waitin' Mr. Watson."

"Thankee, Andy," says Flora. "Ah b'lieve ye done himpressed Mr. Watson more'n ary'un we'all met today." What? This is our first call. Oh, I think I have it; Flora must be teasing on her own account: Mr. Goggin will learn the truth soon enough.

She turns to leave. With a nod and a smile to this cheery carver, I follow her out. As I loft our capacious bumbershoot over her trim head a couple of hen turkeys turn tail and with long strides flee from the Goggin yard into the dim safety of the rain storm. Flora takes not the least notice. I'll bet this was pre-arranged for my benefit.

Two doors along, we splash into a puddled yard under dripping dogwoods. This unpainted house stands on bricks, safe from another foot or more of floodwater. "Ye're about ta meet Robby Burns," Flora tells me impressively. I shake my head to clear it.

"Any connection with...well...you know; Rabbie Burns?" I babble. What is it about names here that makes them seem so significant? And so very confusing.

"Mos'ly no. A li'l yes. Ye'll see fer y'self."

A wiry young man with unusually long, fair hair answers her knock, smiling with pleasure; including me in his warm, welcoming, brown gaze. "You'll be Mr. Watson, Ah don' doubt," he says, beckoning us, dripping, inside. This tidy room also takes up the whole first floor of the house. In place of wood fragments, it is stocked with all kinds of notepaper; on the central table and on shelves occupying one entire wall. An old fiddle lays on top of this shelving, lending me silent encouragement.

Tacked to the wall above these shelves is a poster. I move closer to read it: 'If any of you are secret poets, the best way to break into print is to run for the Presidency.'

Robby Burns looks pleased to see my interest. "Eugene McCarthy. He'll get mah vote in the primary. But honestly, Ah hope he strikes out. A President has no tahm ta write poetry, an' little enough ta read it. Mr. Watson, have you by chance read his 'Cool Reflections'?" I shake my head in demonstrable regret.

"He calls it 'poetry for the Who, What, When, Where and especially Why of it all'. Do you hear that, Mr. Watson? It's jus' what real songs are about. Ah have set ever' one piece on it ta music." My pulse races. Excellent! But how can I spend time with a man who is away at undisclosed locations every day except in pouring rain?

"I very much want to hear your songs, Mr. Burns, but I understand that you work long days in the woods. How shall we arrange to meet?" Flora doesn't look any too pleased with my oblique reference to his livelihood, but confines herself to a promise of arranging a suitable appointment. Content with this progress, she is clearly ready to move on. I bid Mr. Burns 'aurevoir'.

Outside, under our giant gamp, and with no turkeys in sight, Flora admonishes me to be more discreet concerning what goes on in the woods. "Mr. Watson! Ye'll be the death on me if 'n ye ain't a heap more keerful! An' who is 'oh ru-vwah'?"

I look as contrite as I can. To my chagrin I begin to feel that way too.

Our morning runs all downhill from this high point. And that's without counting the close approach of booming thunder and jagged lightning flashes.

The next three Caney Forkers could be triplets. Men in their forties, each of them sprawls identically at home by a jar of almost certainly illicit liquor, deep in an old recliner, helplessly studying the flickering 'snow' on their TV sets. To a man they are thick-set; burly all over, generously beard-ed, clad in matching faded blue coveralls and camouflaged hunting caps. Jimmy Fanaghy is visiting silently with Earl Casey. Neither man so much as blinks at Flora's standard introduction. Earl, I think it is, allows me a vestigial nod. His attention is fully occupied by the unchanging screen in the corner. Score nil all round. We move on from this trying twosome with relief.

Tom Houlihan is also at home. He adds nothing to our morning; a scowling clone of Jimmy/Earl. Only Red Rear-don, at our last stop, sets himself apart from the triplets. He actually speaks. As I scrutinise the muddy Harley-Davidson gracing his living space, searching in vain for its licence plate, he turns his head to comment: "Ah sees yer likes mah motor sickle, Mr. Watson." 'Yes sir, that's mah baby,' he hums am-biguously.

Even if there is this hint of music in him, it is hardly of collecting calibre.

"Arythin' yer has ta know heah an' now?" Red is display-ing renewed interest in his own afflicted TV screen. I deduce that, whatever I might want, he prefers to see our backs. I re-spond accordingly. Flora and I head for his leaky door. Again no turkeys.

"Please wait!" I tell Flora. "At least until I can get this bumbershoot up."

"Hit's bumbershoot now, is hit? Mr. Watson. "Well at least Ah don't need ta axe what ye mean this tahm."

Outside, I resume my doorman duties and we retreat homeward. From under the big brolly, I wonder if it is this drenching rain that so impairs TV reception in our hollow, or do I perhaps detect in the problem another plus for mountain top removal?

"Now stop yer lookin' cross, Mr. Watson," says Flora. "Thar's sump'n ye mus' know. Red he's over-age." She can't mean for drinking. What else answers? "Them Three Bars ain't. They're draft dodgers. Ary other day they'd be on up in the hills, hidin' out, mayhap doin' a little cuttin' or splittin'. Ye'd a ne're gotten ta meet 'em atall."

I interrupt: "They deserve no notice or notes. They are not worthy of you. I shall lump them under the heading of 'redneck intelligentsia' and forget all about them."

Chapter 10
A Scholarly Interlude

Those 'Three Bars' have cast such a pall over our morning that Flora decides we should go home for an early dinner. There she discovers that her boots have let water. She declares we're done for the day, since they are her only pair. That's alright by me. 'Rain stops play', as they say at Lords' cricket ground. All too often, come to think of it.

Flora doesn't sound the least unhappy about falling behind schedule. "We'all kin finish meetin' up wi' the rest on 'em tomorry. Hit's a-goin' ta fair up fer sure becaise hit's Sally's buryin' day, Mr. Watson. Ye're a-goin' ta see how nothin' don't bring holler folks out like a good buryin'." She beckons me to table. Her diary still lays conspicuously by her place. "Now Ah'm free ta start writin' up mah own notes. 'Bout them strange English sayin's o' yer'n," she reminds me with the ghost of...a smirk, "soon's we'all have done eatin'.

The plate she sets before me includes a new feature. Greenish, it looks like a hybrid of fat sparrow grass tips and runner beans. I have to ask...

"Why, thet's okry, Mr. Watson. Ain't ye ne're et okry befowah?"

"Okry, Miss MacTaggart? How do you spell that?"

"O... k... r...a. Ain't nothin' simpler, nor tastier, nor aisier ta cook. Now quit yer fussin' an' eat hit up like a sojer."

My caution proves well-founded. As I cut and spear an exploratory fragment of okra, a glutinous, clear, elastic filament links my morsel to its main body. This refuses to break no matter how far I stretch it. Mountain etiquette must include a way to deal with this embarrassment. How am I to discover it without more fussing? After due consideration, I settle for twirling. I twirl and twirl while Flora stares. Our early dinner develops into one of the tensest meals I have ever experienced. When at last I lay down my knife and fork, I am prostrate. Did Cecil Sharp have to endure such trials? Aside from the climate, my tutor had mentioned no specific causes of his ill health.

Flora pushes her plate away and draws her diary to the fore. She opens it at a slip of paper and announces, " Ah done set down yer sayin's in alphabet order, Mr. Watson. Ah lef ' me plenny a extry space becaise Ah fully expec's ye ta use more'n 'em.. Now, yer fust sayin' 'bout bees' knees. Tell me how ye mean hit."

"We don't really think about these things," I tell her, feeling like a hooked roach, blushing and struggling, "but my best guess is that as bees store pollen under their knees, this feature of their anatomy is celebrated for its crucial importance." Flora is writing in a careful copperplate. It takes her a while to finish. She nods at me.

"Ben takes the biscuit, ye done tol' me. Jus' what d'ye mean bah thet?"

"It is a derogation, Miss MacTaggart, the origins of which are unknown to me. However, please be assured that the reference is to English biscuits, which are quite different from your own, in every significant respect."

"Well, thet's a blessin', Mr. Watson. An' what about 'Blighter'? What d'ye mean bah hit, Mr. Watson?"

"That is a term reserved for cads, Miss MacTaggart." Flora duly makes a note, turns to the next page, makes another brief entry and turns back.

"Blighty, Mr. Watson?"

"A term of affection used of, and I quote: 'this royal throne of kings, this blessed plot, this earth, this realm, this England...' "

"Mister Watson! Ye knows well 'nuff how yer kings done

treated mah own forebars. A term on haffection ye call hit? Ah'm jus' a-goin' ta write: 'England'." She does this, with more than the customary reserve in her contemplative expression.

"I should stress my personal views on this topic, Miss MacTaggart. The highland clearances occurred centuries before my time, of course, as did the Crown's oppression of the Irish and the Welsh, yet I feel a deep sense of shame about these events. Indeed I do likewise for the later callous treatment of London's East Enders by the avaricious business class. In reaction, as you may be aware, the Cockneys devised a language of their own, a rhyming slang, incomprehensible to outsiders. Your people created the wondrous music I am here to study." Flora studies me long and hard, then moves on.

"Are ye sure 'bumbershoot' ain't a name all made up bah thet Walt Disney feller?"

"No, it is real enough, Miss MacTaggart, and you might call it a term of affection too.

"Like brolly and gamp, which serve equally to protect us from the rain forever falling into our English lives. You won't catch my fellow countrymen singing in the rain like your Gene Kelly. Or, for that matter, ignoring it as you so ably demonstrated today." A compliment seems due after all.

"Very well, Mr. Watson, nex' word down heah is 'jiggered'."

"That's another term we use without thinking; in this case to express astonishment. Originally the word meant broken or damaged. In that sense it has been superceded by an expletive entirely unsuitable for your ears, Miss MacTaggart." I could tell she was tempted but she made her note in restrained silence.

"Ye know how puzzlin' Ah find yer sayin' as ta knowin' mah onions—mah ingerns as we'all rightly say. What do Ah write down?"

"To tell the truth, it just signifies knowledgeability, Miss Mac Taggart. For example, like knowing the ropes, knowing your stuff, being in the know. Speaking personally, I suspect that it derives from the paramount necessity, for some people, to distinguish between onions and garlic bulbs." I have always found garlic intolerable.

"Liketa ingerns an' ramps, mayhap, Mr. Watson."

"Ramps, Miss MacTaggart? I am unfamiliar with the word except in regard to boat ramps and motorway ramps neither of which lend themselves to confusion with onions."

"Nobody cain't live with no ramps, Mr. Watson. They're li'l' onions with a long top. Early in spring, they sprout an' grow higher afowah grass. Folks feed 'em ta thar boys ta clean winter out'n 'em. They smell wors'n garlic so we'all close school fer a couple weeks. Hit keeps the peace. Ye've no sech remedy in Blighty then, Mr. Watson?"

"Perish the thought, Miss MacTaggart." I cannot repress a shudder.

"Tell me, Mr. Watson, is 'top form' same as 'tops' or do Ah need mahself two entries?"

"Two would be appropriate, Miss MacTaggart. 'Top form' refers to the recent record of a successful racehorse. It infers further wins or places in the short term. 'The tops' derives from a feature of the highest quality milk, as indicated by a gold foil cap on the bottle. It is still a source of wonder to me that, before my mother brought the bottles in from our doorstep each morning, birds would have pecked through the gold foil caps to get at the cream below. They knew perfectly well to ignore the red and silver caps on the respective homogenized and skim milk bottles."

"Birds an' beasts are smart, Mr. Watson," remarks Flora sagely as she writes. Her dictation retention appears quite excellent. So far she has not asked me to repeat a single word.

She turns another page and reads out, "Up ta snuff".

"Ah, that is a horse of another colour." She is writing already. "No, that is not the meaning. In fact there are both positive and negative implications. I believe I employed it in the positive sense. As John Poole wrote in parody of Shakespeare: 'He knows well enough the game we're after. 'Zooks he's up to snuff.' In other words, up to scratch. In turn this means toeing the line—a line formerly scratched in the ground, marking the start of a race or a fight. Personally I favour the derivation associated with the high degree of decoration deemed appropriate on boxes made to accommodate snuff, at the height of its fashion." Flora is writing assiduously. She finally looks up.

"Ah already done set down what ye tol' me 'bout ol' trouts. Nex' thar's all yer new sayin's terday. What d'ye mean bah 'cad'?"

"Cad is the direct opposite of a gentleman, Miss Mac-Taggart. Ben Cochran forms a good example." Flora refrains from noting this down.

"Ye're lackin' in sympathy, Mr. Watson. Listen ta me. Ben was crossed up in love. He ain't got hisself o'er hit yet, forty years on. 'Horse on another colour'?"

"I meant to say that the snuff metaphor was a quite different case, although I might better have said, a more complicated one. If you will pardon the inference, the Irish are fond of disguising horses by the judicious application of dyes, whether for purposes of altering the animal's racing odds, concealing a theft, or simply to secure a better price.

"I would have liked to spare you the embarrassment, Miss MacTaggart, but you did ask."

"Is hit Arsh ye think Ah am?" Flora is practically shouting at me. "Ah'm Scots an' don't ye ne're forgit hit!" The high colour flooding her face acts on me like a traffic light. I wait for it to change before readying my notebook and venturing my own requests:

"What is the meaning of 'catawampus'?"

"Whar did ye heah thet, Mr. Watson?" Ears burning, I realise that it was during my eavesdropping session she herself had used the term, and in less than complimentary tones. I shrug and raise my arms in what I hope is a disowning gesture. "Knocked askew, sigogglin'" says Flora grimly, "an' all whopperjawed."

Beatrice had certainly given every impression of being

knocked askew. I therefor decide to settle for that graphic interpretation rather than risk opening a possible new can of worms. Nor do I explain that our equivalent expressions are 'skew whiff,' and 'widdershins'. "Can you explain why Shirley would request a biscuit receipt from Beatrice, Miss MacTaggart?"

"Shirley done tol' me Miz Beatrice's biscuits are the best she's tasted in a coon's age, Mr. Watson. If 'n Beatrice be wil-lin' ta share her secret, why would'n 'Shirley want a receipt, ta make harself more'n the same?"

"Oh, I see; you meant to say 'recipe'."

"Ah did not, Mr. Watson, Ah done meant ta say 'receipt', an' Ah did."

Well that hasn't got that sorted out. As the great Sir Winston Churchill put it: 'Britain and America are two na-tions divided by a common language'. I move on; "And what exactly is a 'scald crow', Miss MacTaggart?"

"Ye mus' know the nature o' crows, Mr. Watson. They're either a-chasin' each other, or a-talkin' an' a-laffin' 'bout us, or they're a-scoldin' us. In the ol' tahm, 'scald crow' done stood fer a hooded crow, or a witch. But Meg's jus' an ol' crow a-given ta scoldin'. Ye've seen hit y'self. We say 'scald', meanin' 'scold'." Me, I'd vote for 'witch'. And a hood would be ideal.

"Tell me about gorm, please. I only know 'gormless', which means brainless."

"Is ye talkin' g..a..u..m, Mr. Watson? Hit jus' means a mess." I make a note.

"You spoke of a dornick in connection with your three birds."

"Dornick signifies a stone, Mr. Watson, plain an' sum-ple."

"Drooth, Miss MacTaggart?" It reminds me of Chaucer, but why?

"Drought, Mr. Watson, but Ah ne're done spoke hit ta ye." Ah yes; 'Whan that Aprille with his shoures soote the droght of March hath perced to the roote'. A six centuries old word here in Caney Forks!

"No, Shirley did. She also used the adjective tee-total as an adverb."

"Tee-totally means same as completely. Ah'm surprised ye din't know, Mr. Watson."

"How about red as a verb then? Shirley said it to Miz. Beatrice."

"Two 'd's. Ta redd sump'n means a-cleanin' hit, Mr. Watson, like Ah do fer mah house ever' week."

Now we come to a definite watershed: the topics that I have been forbidden to raise. Can it hurt if I voice one in private to Flora? One that really has me excercised. Not without trepidation I ask her what exactly she has against air conditioning. Cecil Sharp was here far too soon to experience its benefits, but I would certainly welcome some relief from the hollow's jungle heat and humidity. Flora looks shocked.

"Hair conditionin hit's work o' the Divil, Mr. Watson! If 'n ye could only see the hinjury hit does city folk, ye'd ne're a axed the question. Mah porch is important ta me. Ye know Granny Phipps an' Ah spen' a deal o' tahm on hit. Thar's others too. We don't jus' talk wi' each other. We talk wi' mah neighbours, on thar porches ta either side an' on acrost the road. Out ta Roanoke they're all on 'em gotten hair conditionin'. Now they'all jus' stay indoors! Tell me how they a-goin' ta keep up wi' news frum thar, indoors, Mr. Watson? Tell me thet. Hit ain't possible. They're pris'ners, Mr. Watson, pris'ners bah thar own choosin' Pris'ners! Don't ye talk ta me 'bout hair conditionin' agin. Ne're." Flora has turned red. I have never seen her so angry.

Chastened, I shrink into my seat. At least I have expanded my research notes a bit and Flora's diary rather more, in a fair exchange. She retires for a nap. I go out on her porch. Here I sit contemplating its social functions, eyeing the distances to its closest fellows. Yes, I decide, voices can easily carry between them. Thus any private matters all too readily become public. I see how their stifling would jointly earn the General Electric Corporation and the Carrier Company hollow folks' heartfelt disapproval.

Whatever my father may think, I am certainly not an anthropologist for nothing.

And I have assuredly earned the rest of the day off. Flora is in no position to stop me.

Chapter 11
Sally Holdaway's Funeral

Burying day dawns overcast, and stays that way. Flora calls it fitting to the occasion. "'Tis dog days. Folks 'ud a whole bunch rather stan' in rain than sun this tahm o' year." With no home air conditioning to return to, their preference seems perfectly natural to me. Caney Forks is as quiet as the Balliol library during exams. The mandatory howl of a dog, and the inevitable answering howls only add to the pervasive air of solemnity.

Breakfast is spartan; part of the obsequies I suppose. I am not about to ask Flora, in case her heart has simply not been in its preparation this morning. We eat in silence. She clears the table in silence. Her diary is nowhere in sight. I feel adrift until Flora leaves the room and returns, a dark rag in one hand.

"Heah's a harmband fer ye, Mr. Watson." Flora ties it on for me, stepping back to check if it's plumb perhaps, or just to make sure I am otherwise presentable enough for a mountain funeral. I am agog to see what the locals will wear today.

"If 'n ye're ready, Mr. Watson, we kin go set on mah porch. Ah bide mah tahm an' join the cemetery percession along about the middle." I am still considering the various and sundry constructions one might put on her preferred positioning when the first potential mourner ambles into view. This man is unknown to me. "Is that...?"

"No, he's a-headin' the wrong way. Eddie MaCafferty, he was born wrong-headed. Ah see no call fer innerductions.

Less'n ye want ta take whate're he says an' turn hit slap upside out." He sounds exceedingly tempting. I feel more inclined to make this man's acquaintance than not. Perhaps I can manage to meet him in private. After all, there's no sense in offending Flora.

"Heah come the Three Bars, Mr. Watson, an' Red. They're a-headin' fer Obadiah's. Ain't nobody in town kin match 'em fer totin' a casket." I am shocked, shocked to the core by this intelligence, and that's only the half of it.

"It may not be likely but, supposing the military police were to show up while they are toting, as you put it, Miss MacTaggart..."

"Mr. Watson! What gave ye sech a wicked thought, at a solemn tahm like this?" I have put my foot in it right up to the knee. There's nothing to do but maintain radio silence until called upon to speak. Rescue arrives sooner than I could have hoped:

"Heah's Robby Burns. Thar's Andy Goggin, Molly Mulcahy, Daisy Devlin an' thet rascal Peter Duffy. Stir y'self, Mr. Watson, so's we kin git yer innerductions done lickety split...like three birds an' one dornick. D'ye recall mah own sayin' 'bout thet?"

We step down to join the aforementioned mourners. Robby Burns, fiddle in hand, waves his bow in friendly greeting. Andy gives me a wink. Shall we have turkeys at the burying? Flora bears down on the ladies. She launches into her usual speech. Dark-haired Molly, toting a tambourine, drops a curtsey, of all things. Pretty Daisy, all dressed in white, seems to be inviting comment. What can I say? What should I say? She looks like a bride, not a mourner. Flora is quick to sense my dilemna:

"Young folk is a-turnin' frum black ta white at buryin's. Hit signifies resurrection, Mr. Watson. Ye kin see Daisy's one a our youngest."

"Yes. How do you do, Miss Devlin? We haven't previously had the pleasure, owing to yesterday's heavy rain...but please call me Tom...er..." Miss Devlin's giggles save me from digging myself an even deeper hole. I am putting my feet in everything. Miz. Mulcahy takes Daisy in hand so that I may be introduced to the grinning Peter Duffy:

"Tom, is it? D'you play the pipes, Tom?" I am gratified by his question, his use of my first name, his outgoing attitude, but Flora at once intervenes:

"Ah tol' Mr. Watson how ye like ta joke. Ah'll tell him right now how hit's not a proper question ye're axin'. He's no piper's son, Peter Duffy, an' he sartainly doesn't steal hogs. The very ideah!"

Peter Duffy keeps right on smiling. I cannot help liking his free spirit in this tightly tradition-bound community. Robby Burns falls into step with us. "Peter plays the tin whistle," he tells me. "He'd play the pipes himself if he could afford a set, but none on us heah has the money to spare. Lucky folk like me inherit their instruments. The only set o' pipes in Caney Forks fell into the wrong hands that way." I wait to hear to whom these wrong hands belong.

"Robby's too soft ta name the culprit," Peter breaks in, "But Ah ain't shy ta tell you as it's Ben Cochran. He never plays with any'un else, an' when he does play, it ain't naught but dirges."

Why am I not surprised?

The graveyard is coming into view. Festus Fraser stands by its entrance in a much used black suit, greeting each arrival with a quick, wordless nod. Granny Phipps, Rosie Ross, and Shirley are grouped by Festus' handiwork. The unmentionable Meg M'Sweeney stands aloof behind them, nursing a large, lidded basket. Flora drops anchor just inside the entrance. "We kin ketch us some more new folks as they come," she explains, holding me back by the arm as Robby and Peter walk on through.

"Now heah's Miz Mary McRory," she says as an older woman in black hobbles in from the general direction of Shirley's cabin. "Mary, Ah want ye ta meet Mr. Watson. He is heah ta record our way o' life an' Ah know ye has tales ta tell 'im. Mary she lives out'n town a far piece, Mr. Watson.

Ye'll need ta be the visitor. We ne're did see much on her heah."

In like manner I am introduced to Alice Knox, Cathy Kane, Rory Sullivan, Nancy Mullins, Dan Shanahan, Owen Brien, Cherry O'Flaherty, Lyney McEvoy (but not his cute dog), Kenny Irving, Eliza Jane, Charlie Rattigan, Joe M'Cabe and Jean Tierney. Jean has a lot of work to do if she is ever to become the film star her name evokes.

"Ye done met 'em all ever' one now, Mr. Watson. Din't Ah tell ye so?" She is pleased and I feel free to relax.

Except...who is the pale, underfed young man sidling in? He looks like someone without a ticket who wants to catch the show anyway. Flora follows my gaze.

"He's Howie Long, adopted son o' the exorcisisin' preacher ye done met. His step-paw sends him on o'er frum Spring Crick fer practisin', an' he's free. Howie's like the ol' circuit riders." Flora can explain that later. Right now I'm focused on the present, not the past. This Howie chap keeps aloof. He mounts a tiny platform under a large, bleached umbrella, and seems to switch off. Meg the witch edges closer to him.

Muted before, every conversation now abruptly ceases. Al heads swivel to watch the road. Here comes Obadiah, pacing in Dead March tahm, slowing the muscular progress of the Three Bars and Red Reardon. They are bearing Sally's coffin aloft as though it were a feather on the breeze. Who needs six pallbearers when four will do?

Impatient, the four toters accelerate past Obadiah. They soon gain the graveside.

Close behind steps Beatrice, all in black, with lowered head and the saddest mien.

Further back down the road another dark-clad figure labours toward us on a weaving bicycle. Flora grabs my arm; "Hit's Mike Collins," she shouts. Who else but me would need to know? The 'Three Bars' lower Sally's coffin gently but expeditiously. Red's corner is the last to ground, even as the draft dodgers gallumph into the woods. They take three separate and widely differing courses. A tiny terrier bounds after them in an explosion of shrill yelps.

Mourners gape, struck dumb, as a ponderous, uniformed constable pedals wheezily between the burial markers to abandon his bike at a respectful distance from the open grave. He bends low, hands on knees, to catch his alarmingly laboured breath. At last he recovers the power of speech. He addresses Beatrice:

"Ah'm so ver' sorry fer bein' all behin', Miz Beatrice. "We had us a hovernight flat. In the back tire. The tire thet really counts, d'ya see? Ah sure do hope ya kin find it in yer sorrowin' heart ta forgive a poor sinner like me."

Now this is mountain solidarity. Well done that man. But why does he say 'we'? Does he have a twin?

Miss Beatrice gives Mike Collins a strained smile and a half-hearted pat on the arm. Me, I wonder how long each 'Bar' will take to stop running, feel safe in reporting to their undisclosed woodland locations, and resume their classified work.

Free preacher Howie is still at his chosen spot, but Meg is not. She hobbles up to him, whipping the lid off her basket. As though in a trance, Howie reaches a bare arm deep inside, and in slow motion, raises on high a tangle of snakes. This action snaps his lethargy. He jigs madly up and down, to the rhythm of the tambourine that Molly Mulcahy is now beating against the heel of her left palm. That's when he drops one of his charges. It slithers off into the grass. With one accord, the grieving Caney Forkers race in the exact opposite direction, leaving Howie and Meg isolated again.

Only when a sharp-eyed man—Lyney McEvoy I believe—spies the rattler at the very bottom of the open grave and spreads the good news do the mourners warily filter back.

Howie embarks jerkily on the briefest of eulogies and returns the remaining snakes to Meg's safekeeping. He leads the singing of 'Abide with me,' looking fixedly at Red. No doubt to remind him of the technical hitch about to occur in the order of service. Red gives a start. He moves among the mourners, tapping Joe M'Cabe, I think, then Charlie Rattigan and Owen Brien to replace the 'Three Bars' at the coffin's other corners.

There ensues a protracted and unavoidably public debate on how to lower Sally's coffin into the grave respectfully, without simultaneously offering the means of escape to an alert rattler. Every man has his own theory and is sticking vocally to it. The ladies confine their contributions to looking scandalised. They add no new ideas to the pot. Obadiah does his best to act as referee, but in vain. The resulting deadlock, I am proud to say, is broken by Flora. She announces, with admirable firmness, that the choice must be made by the current casket toters, and ratified by Constable Collins.

As we all wait, Robby Burns tunes his fiddle and launches into a feeling rendering of 'I'll fly away.' Peter the joker pulls a penny whistle from his pocket to provide a soulful accompaniment. I pull out my notebook. Three tunes later the pallbearers break from their huddle. They send Dan Shanahan for the post office flagpole and Kenny Irving for a tub of 'hog grease'. Speculation runs wild. The instigators remain tight-lipped.

When the foragers return, they lean the flagpole up against a tall, sandstone marker. My armband is requisitioned to apply the lard liberally to all but its extreme ends. In the meantime Joe M'Cabe and Owen Brien pick up the free ends of the two ropes laying under Sally's coffin. They bring these together, tie them off and grease their full lengths. Red Reardon and Charlie Rattigan now carry the flagpole to the coffin and gingerly slip it under these rope loops. A burst of applause breaks from the enthralled mourners. Red-faced, the now sweating men ignore it. They are not done yet.

Joe joins Red and Owen joins Charlie. On a count of three they raise the suspended coffin, jockey it over the grave's mouth, then lower it at speed, except for the last few, careful inches. The instant it comes to rest, they draw the flagpole out of the loops. The rattler makes no re-appearance. This time, wreathed in smiles, the toters bow and wave to their admiring audience.

This has all been too much for Obadiah. He is clearly still out of the running. In his stead the rascally Peter steps forward, proffers an arm to Beatrice and escorts her to the grave's edge. Here she gathers herself enough to take a pinch of Caney Fork earth from Festus' hard-won heap. She sprinkles it on her aunt's coffin in the true, time-honoured fashion. All present bow their heads in silent prayer. Amen.

In less than an hour today I have learned more about mountain life than in all those previous days, laid end to end, as Shirley puts it.

Chapter 12
The Reception

All the mourners look far more lively now than upon their arrival. This transformation turns out to be caused not so much by the unscheduled antics we have just witnessed as by their anticipation of the imminent reception, as Flora calls it.

"Hit's our custom ta gather at Obadiah's fer sociabil'ty arter a buryin'. The Arsh element call hit a 'wake'. Ah prefer 'reception'. Hit's more fittin'. Now we'all best hurry along. Obadiah looks fair catawampus, ye might could say." Flora gives me a sly glance. "Ah ne're done seen sech a gaumed up buryin' as this'un. He is goin' ta need all the holp we kin provide if 'n he's ta reach the end o' the day right side hup." Flora has my elbow in a bony grip as she bustles towards Obadiah's place.

"Miss MacTaggart, may I ask you to explain why we have yet to visit your post office, and why we have not previously met that constable? Unless I'm much mistaken, he was not included in your list of resident names, which you said was complete."

"Ah don't b'lieve Ah done tol' ye mah list was complete, but hit is too, Mr. Watson. Mountain folks make a point on invitin' outsiders ta buryin's. Ye'd not be heah y'self but fer our custom. Constable Collins's homeplace hit's the nex' holler, along o'er thar. An' thar's other folk frum his holler too who done beat him heah ta Sally's buryin'.

"As fer the post office hit's the ol' cabin wi' the flag pole up front. Well normally ye'd say, jus' not right now." Flora is still pointing to Mike Collins' holler. All I can see are the omnipresent trees.

"Does your postmaster live in another hollow, too, Mis MacTaggart?"

"Bless ye, no, Mr. Watson. Do ye think we kin afford us a postmaster? Thar hain't bin a body in thet office since '42, when the big war took sech a deal on our menfolk. Frum then since hit's served us as school house, in season.

"As fer mail, ain't ye noticed our boxies? Jeppie Pringle he hales frum the same hollow as Mike Collins. He brings us our mail daily, 'cept Sundays. He picks up ever' one piece we leave in them boxies too. 'Long as they're stamped. Mike an' Jeppie they share thet bisickle, turn an' turn about."

Life in Caney Forks' is a non-stop lesson in economy. I am beginning to see why.

"Ye need ta do a heap more noticin', Mr. Watson. Take buryin'. Did ye notice the grave markers 'longside more'n a few o' the homes we already done visit? If 'n ye did, ye ne're axed one thing 'bout 'em. Ah'm a-goin' ta tell ye right now; they're family graves. They're frum back when thar warn't no community cemetery. Ere them days, immigrant families done buried thar dead trailside. Them graves went unmarked, Mr. Watson. Nobody wanted them Indians ta know when our menfolk numbers done fell. Ye see ta what hard tahms yer own ancestors done drove us?" She gives me the longest, hardest look yet, then grabs my elbow:

"Now Ah want fer ye ta be real nice ta Eddie M'Cafferty, Mr. Watson."

"Eddie...isn't he the man you just told me is so wrong-headed, Miss MacTaggart?"

"'Deed Ah did. But now Eddie's special' set on a-showin' ye his houn's."

"His hounds! Surely you can't mean at this reception?"

"We'll jus' have ta wait an' see. Some folks 'ud say 'Lay in the weeds', Mr. Watson. Now Ah ne're done made me a bet mah whole life long. Keepin' in mind who our Eddie is, Ah hain't about ta start."

This should be good. And it should be soon. Flora's hustle has brought us to the double doors at Obadiah's, tastefully hung with black crepe paper. We bustle in.

Flora steers me into a kitchen of sorts. She indicates trays of wide ironstone platters piled with unfamiliar funeral meats. "Mr. Watson, take these out ta the tables, would ye." I do so until the first mourners start to file in. Flora finishes up with a final two heaped platters of mysterious mountain comestibles and stands quietly by. It seems we are officially cleared for action.

Here comes Beatrice, amid a cluster of supporters. That decent Rosie Ross has a hand on her shoulder, steering her to a folding chair. She asks what Beatrice would like on her plate. Her order placed, Beatrice hastens to confess she barely knew her aunt, had never visited her here and says her present misery is mostly over these omissions.

"Hush yer noise, an' eat up," Rosie advises her. "Ye cain't change what's done, so mopin' ain't a-goin' ta help ye none. 'Sides we'all is heah ta celebrate Sally wi' music an' song. Why don't ye jus' party along?" Beatrice manages a crooked smile, just like the one she gave Shirley for putting Aunt Sally's heirloom in proper perspective. Just in time too. The clang of metal chairs, the clinking of plates and the hum of talk is quickly overlayed by rollicking sounds. It's Robby's fiddle, Molly's tambourine, friend Peter's tin whistle and... yes...Andy playing a home-made flute. Their tune is a Highland reel. Chairs scrape back, plates thud down on table tops and the erstwhile mourners become instant, gleeful dancers.

Ben Cochran offers a hand to Beatrice. At first she stares at him, uncomprehending.

Then she realises he wants to dance, and that he is the very man who set up the meeting with Shirley which put such a speedy end to her distress. She rises and this odd couple joins the whirling Caney Forkers on Obadiah's squeaking, creaking, bendy floor.

Here comes the all-white Daisy Devlin, tripping daintily. "Mr. Watson, if you want ta learn 'bout mah own way o' life in these mountains, what say we cut us a shine?" Is she asking me to dance?

Several wallflowers are watching us. Is Daisy doing this for a bet? It's a moot point. Do I really have a choice? I take Daisy in hand. She steps out, dancing like summer lightning, red hair flying. I am breathless in no time. It is of little consolation to reflect on Flora's comment that Daisy is one of the younger folk. What am I then?

I manage to keep my head: "Do you play any instruments, Miss Devlin?"

"Mrs. Mulcahy is kindly teachin' me the tambourine, Mr. Watson." A beginner then.

"Do you have a favourite song?"

"Why Ah surely do, Mr. Watson. It's 'Lucy in the sky with Diamonds'." I am taken aback. "Do you realise the underlying meaning of the lyrics , Miss Devlin?

"Oh, 'deed Ah do. If you doubt me, check wi' Shirley." A bit of a shock to my system there. I actually reel.

At last the players stop. I stagger to the nearest chair. Here I get my head down and do a fair imitation of Constable Collins recovering his wind. But in no time they strike up again. The tune is Andy Goggin's Turkey favourite. I could dance to it with Shirley, but she isn't here. She didn't come from the burying. I do hope she's...

"Jean Tierney," a voice reminds me, "Would ye care fer a caper, Mr. Watson?"

The non film star conserves her energies in a most commendable fashion. While she does keep time with our band her movements are so limited as to be more like twitches. This allows me to restore my own sorely depleted energy. It permits a rudimentary exchange. "Is ye musical y'self, Mr. Watson?" Jean wants to know.

"Not exactly, Miss Tierney, more of a student of the folk category. Indeed, that is why I am here."

"Kin Ah tell ye ary thin' partic'lar, Mr. Watson?"

"Well, since my arrival I have come across two fiddles, one tambourine, plus the flute and tin whistle to which we are dancing. I have also been told that Ben Cochran is a piper. Are there any other musicians you know of in Caney Forks?"

"Ye got me plumb on the spot, Mr. Watson. Ah kin only tell ye as thet Lyney McEvoy he knows sump'n. Now, if 'n ye'll excuse me, Ah'm more'n ready ta rest mah bones a spell. Thankee fer givin' this ol' widder lady a nice dance, Mr. Watson."

I retire equally thankfully to a vacant chair. Scarcely am I settled on it than who should walk up but the man who knows sump'n. "May kin Ah set heah?" Lyney asks me with a discomfited air. I beckon him into place. He sits, twiddling his thumbs, then lets it all out in a rush: "Ah don't know what ta say 'bout Terry's bad behaviour back thar. He ne're did the likes on hit afowah. Him sendin' them 'Three Bars' a splungin'. Kin you forgive 'im?" I am stumped.

"Terry, you say?" A third name that's not on my list.

"On over yonder," says Lyney, pointing, "partnerin' mah wife, Birty. Her in the grey dress an' the black sash." I look in the indicated direction and, sure enough, there is the lady described. Her partner is clasped to her bosom, taking a lively interest in all the activity around them. But he is no regular dance partner. He is a dog. And not only a dog, but a strangely familiar one.

Manfully I struggle to keep a straight face. "Terry is a most apt name for a terrier. I grant you that he did make a bit of fuss at the funeral, but he was only doing what Mother Nature intended. You certainly can't blame him for that. But I really must say your concern does you credit." Mr. McEvoy looks more or less mollified. I use the pause as an opportunity to advance our comversation.

"You know my purpose here, Mr. McEvoy. I am very interested in whatever you might know in the music line." He leans close to me. His caution seems extreme, in view of the extraordinary noise levels being attained by our lively quartet.

"Ah plays no instrument, Mr. Watson, but Ah does love mah music." He hesitates.

"Is that all you have to tell me?" I prompt him.

"Well, thar's sump'n more as nobody 'ud dare tell ya. If 'n Ah tells ya, ya mus' promise faithful ne're ta let on, not nowise." I can hardly wait:

"You can trust me."

"Ben Cochran has him a set o' elbow pipes, Mr. Watson, an' Eddie MaCafferty runs a pack o' coon houn's. The two on 'em is a-tryin' ta teach them houn's singin'. What d'ya think o' thet?" Well, I think Cecil Sharp never discovered anything remotely as radical.

"Mr. McEvoy, you have my solemn word that your confidence is safe in my hands. As we say, an Englishman's word is his bond'." I offer my hand to seal our agreement. Lyney, looking somewhat uncertain, nevertheless extends a calloused hand. We pump stoutly until he smiles. Even so, he must still be pretty tense. He jumps in his seat when two strangers slam Obadiah's entrance doors open, and stand proudly in the doorway. One welcoming yell turns into many. "Who are those two?" I ask Lyney.

"Why they're frum up on over the mountain," he tells me. "Fred White an' Jess Tulley. Fred has the five string banjo. He picks hit sump'n wild. An' he'll have a harmonica in his pocket, 'long on a mouth harp too."

"Does Jess have his instruments in his pockets? Mr. Mc'Evoy?"

"No, Mr. Watson, "but jus' ya wait an' see what-all Jess has in his feet. He's sump'n real special." Jess is barefoot. As I look for that special something he pulls a pair of polished black leather shoes from a sack and slips them on. At that the mourners' riotous welcome subsides. The two visitors step inside, wending their way through back-slapping couples to where the expectant band members wait. They trade handshakes with Andy, Robby, Molly, and Peter, who then retreat to the wall behind. Fred adjusts his banjo sling and plunks artlessly until Jess moves front and centre.

In a flash the pair galvanise: Fred knocking out a mad plunky rhythm and Jess's feet flashing and tapping in intricate patterns of sound. His slower moving arms suggest a puppet. He looks suspended. His feet just reach the floor. Amazing! Could this be a buck dance with flat-footing thrown in? Whatever it is, Fred is making reels and sword dances look like Obadiah's Dead March. No-one is dancing now. Everyone is clapping madly in time. Me too. The banjo and tap shoes synergy is irresistible.

How could I ever have thought I was wasting my time over here? Never have I seen the likes of this mountain reception. Oh for my tape recorder. To my idea of funerals, bringing it along had seemed socially inept. Well damn my over-done sensibilities! I begin to review the oldest Caney Forkers and consider who is most likely to pop off next. Or... if I run all the way to Flora's and back, might I still be able to get some of these two on tape?

I ask Lyney to excuse me and head surreptitiously for the door. Outside I stoop to check my shoelaces. "Mr. Wats'n," says an unfamiliar voice, "Ah'm Eddie MaCafferty an' thar's sump'n ya gotta see. Right now!"

Chapter 13

The Hounds of Heaven

Wasn't Eddie MaCafferty the man Flora had just told me to be nice to? Yet right before the funeral she had described him as wrong-headed. Is he dangerous? He had in fact framed his request in a most imperious manner, and my tape recorder *is* rather cumbersome. I recall Falstaff's decided preference for discretion over valor. I may be bigger than Eddie, but don't madmen possess the strength of ten?

"Let's go then." I hide my researcher's grief as best I can.

He strides maniacally up the wooded slope away from the fading sounds of merriment. The only flat bit is where we meet and cross that old rail line Ben had bumped me over.

"Could you please...wait for me, Mr. MaCafferty? I'm still...winded from...dancing. I can't afford to...to get lost. I have never...been up these...slopes before."

"Make durn sure ya keeps it so," replies my ruthless guide, barely breaking his long stride, "or ya'll be in real hot water." Of course, the last thing I want is to meet any secret commuters up here. I could get grounded by Flora. It could spell the end of my work. But I haven't the breath to reassure this over-mastering mountaineer. I stagger onward and upward, lungs burning, legs shaking, head swimming.

"Stop right thar! Ah's a-goin' ta tie yer eyes." What a blessed relief this halt! As he pulls out a rag and ties it around my head, I keep telling my captor that I can still see a bit here, a bit there, then elsewhere, until my lungs are my own again. An uninvited whiff of woodsmoke creeps into them. I listen hard for the 'Three Bars'.

"Grab a-holt," he orders. I grope for his loose denim jacket. "Now step out smart, Mr. Wats'n." If you have ever been blindfolded on a steep slope, with trees all around, you will know that MaCafferty's request was easier made than met. After some minutes stumbling he reluctantly slows his pace. From that point of compromise it might have been no more than ten minutes before a relentless howling starts up, uncomfortably close by. I freeze.

"Ya hearin' Blue, Mr. Wats'n. He allus acts real suspicious 'til he gits a-sniffin' ya up an' down an' roun' about. Ya needn't fear him atall. Blue's right smart. Why don't ya take a good look at 'im fer y'self?" I am considering how to do this when the rag is torn from my head. I am appalled. What can I say? 'Thank God he is tied to a tree', seems too inauspicious. Instead I try, "That is one handsome hound, Mr. MaCafferty. Do you call him Blue on account of his howl?"

"Check him close, Mr. Wats'n. His black an' white mottlin', hit looks dark blue ta us mountain folks." I hesitate to get any closer for personal reasons, but Blue does exactly as MaCafferty predicted He comes padding over through the carpet of dead leaves at the limit of his rope to give me a long, silent and thorough olfactory inspection. Only when he looks up and wags his tail do I feel safe in moving, or in speaking, for that matter.

"If you don't mind my asking, why did we have to climb so far?"

"We gits complaints," is all MaCafferty would say.

"Miss MacTaggart told me today that you wanted to show me your hounds. Where are the rest?"

"Le's not hurry thungs, Mr. Wats'n. Ben's a-joinin' us bah an' bah. He'll have him his pipes an' a couple more'n mah houn's. They're Red an' Walker; a red bone an' a treeer," he adds vaguely. "Fer now, Ah jus' wants ya ta see mah houn' singin' method.

"Ah got me the ideah frum watchin' tourists a-throwin' sticks fer Blue. If 'n a teasin' flatlander e're done kep' a-holt on the stick, Blue he'd howl." MaCafferty stoops to pick up a piece of fallen branch, draws his arm back, snaps it forward, but doesn't let it go. As forecast, Blue lets out an all too familiar deep howl.

"Sumple, hain't hit? Jus' ya figger when Ben an' Ah has a pair or more'n 'em a-lined hup. We makes a false throw fer ever' song note, an' each houn' he jus' sings his part. Ah grant ya hit took some practicin' ta git 'em all trained up. Thet's whar Ben come in.

"Ah took a notion the wail o' them elbow pipes was close ta Blue's voice as makes no matter. We'd a-line up mah houn's, an' Ah'd not throw sticks fer Ben, if 'n ya gits mah meanin', Mr. Wats'n. He'd pipe a note fer ever' durn not-throw. Mah houn's is so smart, they'all cotched on real quick. In three-four months they'all had hit nailed.

"Listen up now. Ben's early. Kin ya heah them other'uns a-headin' hat us?" Blue, too, hears them before I do. He sets to his howling. As our new arrivals come into sight through the trees, I see an orange-brown hound that has to be Red, and another looking like an English foxhound, but rangier. He must be Walker, the mysterious tree-er. Ben looks like Ben, old blue and silver, but definitely not so glum as usual.

MaCafferty and he set the hounds in a well spaced-out line and back off, clutching their not-to-be-thrown sticks. They draw these back and on the customary count of three, mimic their throws, once, twice, thrice and so on. The choir's howls and barks are right on cue and distinctive. Red has a drawling, booming bark; Walker, a clear, ringing bugle tone. They're not the Balliol chapel choristers, but I am dazed, astonished. When the choirmasters lower their sticks...no, these are truly batons, both turn to look at me in justifiable triumph.

"I am bowled over by your achievement. I never expected...(careful now)...I know the tune, but of course I couldn't recognise the words..." Unaccountably, they both double over, slapping each other and yelling with coarse laughter. Ben recovers first:

"Why, they're bin a-tellin' ya; 'Ah hain't nothin' but a houn' dawg'.

"Ya cain't no ways beat the King, Tom Watson." This from the man who didn't have a favourite song when I first asked him. Yet these two misfits have made an historic breakthrough! Mad MaCafferty is a classic genius. It is all too much for this hide-bound Brit.

If you will bear with me in my confusion, I have to draw a curtain across the rest of this surreal episode.

Chapter 14
Brain Fever

Flora cannot tell me how I arrived on her porch. She found me slumped in the Phipps rocker, out to the wide. Unable to rouse me, she sent one of the barefoot boys over to Whistle Pig Lane. Thus I later learned that a real conjure woman's repertoire includes the preparation and administering of herb, bark, root and tonic remedies, the laying on of healing hands, and the making of house calls. In Surbiton most doctors gave up on house calls a year or two after the war.

If Flora is to be believed, after a quick examination of yours truly, Shirley said she would try her 'laying on of hands' first. In my case, this evidently took the form of a half dozen sound smacks. Perhaps I had these coming to me anyway. Then, in the best maternal fashion, she reportedly laid a hand on my forehead, confirming what Flora had surmised: that I had a high fever. They say I rambled a lot about hounds and blindfolds.

This fever comes and goes, spikes and subsides, obfuscating and clarifying.

I struggle more and more to distinguish fact from fable in this invariably irregular community. Flora claims that Shirley borrowed her old motorbike to race back home, prepare a poultice, and rush back. From all the stories I subsequently heard, the most likely by far was that although the bike had been left to her by her late husband Mack, Flora had forever refused even to mention it, let alone lend it out. One wonders about the age and condition of the petrol in its tank. More to the point, one wonders about the full extent of a bona fide conjure woman's capabilities.

All this speculation constitutes my principal occupation while enduring bed rest as prescribed, until my condition returns to normal. And there you have my most urgent question: what is normal in Caney Forks? Who is qualified to provide a meaningful answer? How shall I know if it is meaningful? This is the over-arching conundrum.

I turn this riddle over and over in my febrile mind; now a seething soup of scalded crows, mackinaws, rattlers, red bones, Melungeons, grits and wrong biscuits.

A life preserver suddenly bobs up on the soup's raging surface. I strive to read the ship's name lettered around it... no...not a name...an elusive phrase... what... when...who? Yes, it's 'THE WHY OF IT ALL'; Eugene McCarthy's poetry, in his 'Cool Reflections'.

And who planted that seed in my mind but his disciple, composer Robby Burns?

If Flora has set visiting hours, maybe he can come in the evenings.

I fight to cling to that hope as reality recedes and once more my delirium descends.

Chapter 15
My Lone Visitor

Flora, it seems, has not been expecting any great onslaught of concerned citizens. She has posted no visiting hours.

"Ah tell ye fer a fac' ye hain't exack'ly the mos' pop'lar man." Flora is delivering my first breakfast since my fever broke. This is hardly the kind of moral support a sick man expects. Enfeebled as I am, I protest. She gets on her high horse.

"Mr. Watson, fer a scholar an' researcher, ye have larned mighty li'l' livin' 'mong us. Ah have made sure ye done met ever' woman an' man jack on us at ever' blest hoppertun'ty. Ye think ye're too durn good fer us. Thet's the heart on the case. When ye meet up wi' a miracle like them singin' houn's, why, stands ta reason ye jus' cain't handle hit. Small wonder yer mind is all broke ta pieces."

Not for the first time in this hollow, I am dumbfounded. I see what a great deal I have to think about. I review my behaviour, from my first sight of Ben Cochran, to my misjudgment of Eddie MaCafferty. I hang my head. I make a dent in my grits, lest I offend Flora even further. I swallow a spoonful, and then my pride.

"I do believe I needed your reproach, Miss MacTaggart. If I have misinterpreted so much before, at least now, in my present weakened condition, I can understand and take to heart what you are telling me. I shall use my convalescence to consider all the changes I should make, as a grateful guest in your home and community." I feel as though I am a sick child again in Surbiton, and Flora the mother I have seen so little of since going up to Oxford, a world away and more.

"Thet's a purty speech, Mr. Watson. We shall see what ye do 'bout hit. 'The road ta Hell hit's paved in good intentions.' Mah granmaw use ta tell me so. Now eat up an' gimme yer bowl. Ah have plenny ta do absent ye an' yer games." She sweeps out, erect and proud, her mission accomplished; accomplished that is, if I am any sort of a man. I withdraw to my room to brood.

I am awakened by the approaching natter of a small engine. Working engines of any kind are in short supply here. Even Ben's only works after a fashion. But am I being unkind to think this? How would I have got from Meadowview without the services of his old pick-up truck...or to Jack Forsythe's Marion house, and back? Could Eddie MaCafferty's hound choir members ever hit the right notes--however approximately-- without his piper's wail to tune them?

I may have been too hard on this love-lorn, bitter, old bachelor. He even laughed up on the mountain, didn't he?

But what became of that little engine? I can't hear it now. Probably broke down...or ran dry. You know how it is in this place. Wait! 'It' isn't any more, is it? I must learn to look at such oddities more as an insider. I must stop my carping. I must hope that the Caney Forkers notice. And I must hope that I can keep to the straight and narrow.

"Are ye decent?" calls Flora up her staircase.

"I am busy reforming, Miss MacTaggart, if that's what you meant."

"What Ah mean is, are ye presentable fer a lady?"

I make a few essential adjustments. "Now I am. Who is calling?" Silence.

A familiar clatter of racing feet almost deafens me. There in my doorway stands Shirley, with her combs in. She contemplates me with a searching, diagnostic eye. "Ain't nothin' ketchin' is it?" I am about to reassure her when the penny drops. Sure as sixpence, she is teasing me just as though I were that stiff old Jack

"Ah figger that for a 'no', Dr. Watson. Tho' look at me, will you, a-teasin' the ver' same doctor as Ah mahself done cured o' brain fever. Life in the holler kin be plumb confusin', don't you reckon?" Here Shirley gives me an entirely different kind of look. Has Flora been conspiring with her to aid and abet my reformation? Whatever the case, I shall play along. Life with Shirley is anything if not invigorating.

"Kin Ah come on in?" Oh boy, do I have a long way to go, forgetting something as simple as this common courtesy.

"Please do, Shirley, and I must apologise for being so backward in my invitation.

"That is the only chair, as you can see." Why am I so tongue-tied in her presence?

"Ah know it well, Dr. Watson. Ah have set on it many hours, when your fever was tormentin' you ta beat all, holdin' cold cloth herbweed poultices on your poorly brow."

I hide my face with both hands. "How could I forget to thank you, from the bottom of my heart? Miss MacTaggart told me what happened when I was in a coma, then in delirium. You were my ministering angel, in a place where I have no other friends, and the lack of them all my own doing."

"T'ain't no hurt, Dr. Watson. Leastways not ta Flora, nor me. An' you do have y'self a few frien's out thar, if 'n Ah'm any judge of it."

"Miss MacTaggart has set me straight about the damage I have done to myself and my cause. I am resolved to reform. Do you think people will forgive me?"

"Why bless you, Dr. Watson. You did no damage ta me. Indeed you done holp a fair deal. As for Flora, you cain't neahly know how she frets 'bout you not eatin' a single one o' her plates clean. But it's true mos' neighbour folk find you distant as a stranger. Jus' like Mr. Forsythe done described the change in his wife. Do you recall?"

"I do, but what is it I most need to do to change, when I can get up and out?"

"Well you might could start bah figgerin' as mos' folks heah know a bunch more'n you 'bout holler life, an' the best ways ta live it. That's how you'll learn the mos'. Not bah treatin' 'em like you're a census taker, or one o' them TV reporters we'all run plumb out'n town.

"Ah have no new client yet, Dr. Watson, but when Ah do, you mus' be fit 'nuff ta pick up whar we'all done lef' off. Missin' nothin' an' writin' it down for me; ever' li'l bit." I desperately want to know why, but now is not the time to ask. Instead I assure her: "I shall start eating up whatever Miss MacTaggart puts in front of me, Shirley. I shall start to exercise. In conversation, I shall mind my Ps and Qs..."

"Your what, Dr. Watson?"

"Oh, these things pop out naturally, you understand. Flora is intrigued by them. She has started a notebook of her own, to accommodate my translations. You will please her, Shirley, by passing on what it means to say, 'mind your Ps and Qs'.

"In our English pubs, darts players used to compete for drinks, rather than money. You can still see the chalkboard doors used to record players' scores. When a player won a game, the scorer would enter a P or a Q to indicate whether the victor was owed a pint of ale say, or a quart. Or two of them, or even three. In England, Shirley, we have bigger pints and quarts than yours. Bigger by a whole twenty per cent."

"Ah shall pass it on ta Flora, as you axed, but do you get how you're a-boastin' agin? What does it signify your English pints are bigger? You're heah, not thar. That's what matters. Jus' keep a good holt on y'self nex' tahm that boastin' feelin' tries ta break out." I am embarrassed, and in this failing too, like Jack Forsythe. There is more than meets the eye in this conjure woman thing. What can I say? I know:

"You humble me, Shirley, but you also show me how to mend my ways. Please keep up the good work."

"Do you realise how you're a-talkin' down ta me now this ver' minute, Dr. Watson?" Damn! Condescending now, am I? This is going to be harder than I thought.

"Now please don't think I am trying to change the subject, Shirley, but is it true that Flora has lent you her motor-bike?"

"That ain't the half of it, Dr. Watson. Flora always thought it a discomfittin' way ta get aroun'. She was lettin' him go all ta rust. Now she has flat-out given me that motor sickle, so Ah kin reach urgent cases quick. Cases like your own. He even came along 'bout full up o' gas. Thar's a mountain lesson for you, if 'n Ah may could say."

Why 'he'? I suppose a motor bike would seem masculine to my Shirley. Anyway, so much for changing the subject. I am now thinking of my new tutor in a wholly different light than when we first met. Her unmarried status is no longer the least surprising to me. As to that, some possible causes for my lack of success with the ladies are starting to jump up and wave about, demanding my urgent attention.

My reformation project is beginning to take a larger and more tangible shape.

Conjure woman Shirley knows exactly when to leave. She rises to do so. It is only now that I notice the absence of Whassup?

But on her way out she casts a smile at me that is positively feline.

Chapter 16
The Why Of It All

The afternoon sun is angling low into my room when Flora calls up her stairs, "Are ye fit ta be seen, Mr. Watson?"

"How do you mean, Miss MacTaggart?"

"Ah mean are ye presentable? Ah jus' cain't think why, but ye have a new visitor."

I effect some token upgrades—it can't be Shirley--and call down, "All fit now."

The tread on the staircase is measured, so different from Shirley's clatter. Who can it be? Obadiah, come to check his eye-estimate? No, it is the man I most desperately need to see; Robby Burns himself. He must have knocked off work early on my behalf.

"Ah jus' learned about your fever, Mr. Watson. Is Flora right you are on the mend?"

"Yes, she is right, and in more ways than one. I am so pleased that you have come. Have a seat...may I call you Robby?"

"Deed you may, on condition thet you be Tom from heah on out."

"Well Robby, this wretched fever I had sat in my mind, making me delirious. My cumulative experiences here be-came too much to make any sense, indeed filled my head with whirling nonsense. I think my mind refused to take any more. But out of my delirium came a life-saving memory of 'Cool Reflections'. I have wanted to ask you ever since about 'the why of it all' in particular.

"Why do your people behave this way or that; talk as they do; leave me so confused? I'm sorry to let it all tumble out like this, Robby."

"Eugene's poems tell me our answers lie within. Folk may look ta the outer world; ta parents, friends an' neighbours, fellow workers, preachers, teachers, children. In turn, they look ta us. But ta find thar meanings an' our'n we'all must search ourselves.

"Jus' look how your academic method has sent you off smack in the wrong direction. Throw it out, Tom. You need try ta sympathise wi' Ben's sorrows, Eddie's oddities, Flora's difficult widowhood, Obadiah's precarious living, the guilty feelings o' the 'Three Bears' an' plenty more of the same. Then you'll likely find your missing answers. You'll know why we are the way we are, Tom. You'll be one of us.

"Ah admire what you're tryin' ta do, Tom, but if it's ta be good for us us all, you must do it the right way. The right way for you too. Now what do you say, Tom?"

"Robby, you are building on what Flora and Shirley have advised me today. You have given me the confidence I need to turn my wrong-headed efforts around. Thank you for being such a friend; for telling me unvarnished what I need to hear."

"Good, Tom. Now kin you take a harder piece of advice yet?" I nod my head. 'In for a penny; in for a pound' is a sound maxim.

"You are so downright English, it's hard ta foller your meanin'. Of 'en your English thinkin' jus' doesn't apply heah anycase. You need ta be heah full-tahm. Forget about 'thar' for the rest o' your yeah with us. It won't neah be easy. Think you kin do that?" I nod again, pulling my mental belt in yet another notch. Ouch.

"Take heart, now, Tom. You kin be part o' mountain life. A li'l' history 'ud help ta finish you up, tho' old tahms are jus' a detail, alongside o' Eugene's method. You might could ask Flora 'bout our history. She kin fill you in better'n anyone. B'lieve you me it 'ull be like rippin' off a blindfold. Thet's a promise."

"Robby, may I just settle a question that's been puzzling me in my delirium? I have seen Caney Creek often enough, but where are the forks?"

"One it's bah the old Fork Mill. The other'n is that trail fork ta Shirley's place on Whistle Pig Lane. Wet an' dry, d'you see, Tom? It might could sound a bit chancy to you but it's all one ta Caney Forks folks". Is he serious? Am I delirious again?

"Kin Ah take mah leave now, Tom? Ah have work lef' ta do. Ah wish you well now in makin' your new start."

Robby goes downstairs. But I don't hear the porch door's tell-tale squeal. Instead I hear Flora and him in whispered conference. Sharing his joke about forks? Comparing notes? Deciding what sedative to put in my 'coffee'? Preparing Plan C?

Oh, aren't I a troublesome fellow?

Chapter 17
Practice, Practice, Practice

Flora allows me up for supper that night. "Ah done prepared us a special meal, ta put some flesh on yer sick bones. Thar's mah ol' layin' hen roasted up, pickled ramps, fried dumplins an' dried green beans boilt wi' a ham bone. Ah want ye ta know as we call the bean dish 'leather britches'. Lawd, hit's only a term of affection, Mr. Watson."

I draw up my seat and steel myself accordingly. If I can't pass this test, my goose is cooked. I take a modest forkful of 'leather britches' and chew on it thoughtfully.

"This is a new one indeed," I tell Flora superfluously. "I do believe it suits me." I carry on exploring my plate.

"Ye ain't said nothin' 'bout mah roast hen, Mr. Watson."

"It is really delicious," I tell her and I mean it too. "It has restored my appetite, Miss MacTaggart." I mean that as well. I don't have to work hard at all to clean my plate. When Flora finishes I rise to carry both of our plates to her sink. She looks secretly pleased.

"Now set y'self back down an' git ready fer yer big reeward. We call hit stack cake." Flora gets up and crosses to her icebox. Opening its door she bends to draw out a high, towering plate of cake, with the utmost care.

Close up on the table it looks strangely familiar. Why it's a Swiss roll turned sideways. Damn it, it's not a Swiss anything, is it? It's Flora's mountain cake. Robby would be pleased how quickly I caught my slip, and how I keep it to myself.

"Them li'l flapjacks are spice cake, Mr. Watson. Atween 'em they're dried slices of apple." She lifts off the first inch or so and sets it on my plate. It smells mouth-watering. "Now eat hit up." I don't need telling. Before Flora calls a halt, I have put away some four inches worth. I have never been averse to bribery of the right kind, and Flora's face is a picture. Never have I seen her looking so happy.

I perform my busboy routine again and invite her to stay in her seat, if she will tell me where the chicory is. I plan to make the 'coffee' this evening, and to ask her about the history of mountain life. Flora plays along. I succeed in making two hot, passable mugfuls. I carry these out to the porch and set them on the table. Flora looks rather disoriented, either by my coffee making, or choice of venue. Seating herself cautiously she looks to me for a lead. "Are you by chance a reader, Miss MacTaggart?"

Stirring a spoon of molasses into her mug, she pulls open a small drawer in her ashtray table. She hands me a slim, much-thumbed paperbound volume. "This be the only book wuth readin', Mr. Watson. Hit's a moon calendar fer gard'nin', fishin', best days, receipts an' forecasts. Hit's all thar.. Hit's the 'Farmers Almanac." Yes, well...

"Mah Almanac, hit's historic; frum 1819 hit says, but hit's our real hist'ry ye want. Ah tol' ye 'bout them migrants headin' west, an' thar trailside burials, Indian skirmishes an' all. When Ah was a li'l' girl, mah Daddy once't rode me up o'er the mountain ta see a gurt ol' totem pole. Ah often wunners if'n hit's standin' yet arter all these years.

"Now some o' them western migrants, a-weary o' travelin', camped bah some crick, found 'em a fruitful valley, hunted well, took a shine ta what they saw an' voted ta stay. But they had 'em a lonely life on hit, wi' no hard roads nor nothin' like we'all have now.

"In the last century, them big minin' barons brung o'er immigrants bah the boatload. Scots, Irish, Germans, Welsh,

Hungarians an' Poles. Nobody knows everwho anymore. Magyars even, Ah bin tol'. D'ye recall how Ah done warned ye 'bout the Black Arsh an' Black Dutch, an' Melungeons too? Black Arsh, they're frum yer Spanish Armady.

"So's ta have thar workers neahbout thar coal seams an' ore beds, them barons had roads run, iron rails laid, depots an' settlements built; houses, stores, schools an' even a few churches. They filled 'em wi' ever' kind of immigrant foreners they done shipped in an' got 'em started a-minin'. Grandaddy was a coal miner an' mah Daddy too.

"Now think on hit, Mr. Watson. 'Feature y'self a-comin' ta sech a place frum some old-tahm Europe country. How ye goin' ta talk wi' mos' arybody? Ye haven't the Gaelic, the German, the Polish, or Hungarian, les say. Hit was liketa the same fer 'em all.

"Hit turned out, thar war more immigrants speakin' English than other tongues. So what comes of it but a sumple kind a English takes a-holt. Hit grew, an' serves us ta this day. Ah once't heared a perfesser call our style o' speakin' amalga-mated. Fancy that!

"Now mind what Ah'm tellin' ye nex', Mr. Watson, 'cos ye're a part o' the problem. Flatlanders they laugh at us fer speakin' so slooow. They think we'all's dumb, but do ye see hit jus' ain't so, Mr. Watson? Right frum the git-go, we mountain folk have allus spoken slow. Slow out'n feelin' fer the foreners among us. Ye need ta larn the code o' the hills, Mr. Watson. The sooner the better, Ah say."

And these would be the same foreign folk she warned me about on Day One. I have no intention of rocking the boat now that Flora is calming down. I shall wait for a natural opportunity to ask for further clarification.

You see what a good boy I have become? Little Jack Horner in person.

Chapter 18
Peter's Invitation

Flora lets me sleep in the next morning to recover from the exertions of my sudden re-entry into Caney Forks' society. Her decision proves most fortuitous. Over our late breakfast she relays, with undisguised disapproval, a most welcome verbal invitation from the Peter Duffy family for me to join them at noon.

"Peter Duffy has a family?" I ask Flora in surprise.

"He does, Mr. Watson, but hit stretches mah patience more'n Ah kin say. He lives wi' Molly Mulcahy, but she ne're done changed her name. We'all's left a-guessin' are they married? They have two girls an' a boy atween 'em, Mr. Watson! Fiddlesticks!" Flora spits this out through pursed lips.

Flora's expression leaves no doubt as to how deeply scandalised she is. Putting it mildly, I thought such households were all the rage here. I am about to assure her that cohabitation is by no means unusual back home when I bite my tongue. 'I am here, not there', 'when in Rome', etc.. But Peter is so much fun I simply must go. I change gears.

"I am shocked, Miss MacTaggart. I must carefully consider the wisdom of further association with Peter. However, I should not wish to ostracise Miss Mulcahy to the same degree, and their children certainly carry no blame. Let me think the matter over, to see if there is some way in which this invitation can be handled with propriety."

I rise to gather the breakfast plates and return to my room. I cudgel my brains for a means to accept the invitation, while remaining in Flora's good graces. After a good half hour, with no solution in sight, my head is starting to feel fevered again. This is a disaster. I can't have Flora accusing me of a relapse. She will send me straight back to bed. Then where shall I be? Wait...I could tell Flora how my head feels and return to bed voluntarily. From here, let's see, I could squeeze out through the upper hall window onto the roof of her lean-to kitchen, reach into the tree behind it and climb on down.

I call out, "Are you there, Miss MacTaggart?" Flora calls up to ask If I have made my decision. "Yes, I have. Unfortunately all this thinking has made my head feel strange again." There is nothing like the truth. "I am going back to bed, to see if I can sleep it off. Can you give me a few hours, please, to see if it works?"

"Ah'm sorry at hearin' hit so, Mr. Watson, but Ah say ye're smart ta run no risks. Take all the tahm ye need. God willin', ye might could be right agin' bah nightfall."

Fully dressed, I climb into bed, truthful so far, to wait for Granny Phipps' arrival to draw Flora out onto her porch. My starting gun will be the unfailing squeal of that commendably unoiled door. Waiting, I contemplate the irony of my impatience for Granny Phipps' normally boring proximity. In fact it is she, not the hinges, I hear first, scraping her boots on the porch step and calling Flora's name. I am off to the races!

I find that I must exit that upper hall window feet first in order to establish a firm footing. Finding a serviceable tree branch proves more difficult than I had foreseen, but does promise to be easier in reverse, on my return. Silent acrobatics are not my forte. Reaching the ground noiselessly makes my head hurt afresh. I lean out of sight against the far side of the tree trunk to regain my composure. Instead my blood runs cold as I realise I have no idea where Peter lives.

Under the circumstances there is no-one I can ask for directions. My idea had been to dodge from tree to tree, Indian style, until I attained the Duffy's back yard. 'Steady the

Buffs', I tell myself. It's an old cavalry command. It works. I decide to take matters one step at a time.

Step one: did Peter come by us to Sally's funeral from the right, or the left? Surely only Eddie MaCafferty came from the left. I picture to myself how Flora waited for the first group of mourners to come by before we joined the procession. They were, in order of appearance, my good friend Robby Burns, the smiling Andy Goggin, the white and flirtacious Daisy, then Molly Mulcahy and Peter together, of course. And Flora had dubbed him a rascal immediately, hadn't she? So they live somewhere to our right.

Step two: we walked to the right on that rainy day of introductions. Flora took me to the homes of...let's see; the first was Andy Goggin's, then she skipped the next house before we called at Robby's, followed by Earl Casey's, Tom Houlihan's and lastly, Red Reardon's. Why did she skip Andy's neighbour? Oh, that's a rhetorical question if ever I heard one. Flora was already determined to keep me away from the unspeakable Duffy menage. Case solved.

What a shame I can't tell Shirley.

Now that my destination is fixed, I check my watch. I have time to spare.

First putting more distance between myself and the road, I start my dodging tactics, going from tree to tree. No question but that I am a artful dodger. Note that I use this cognomen generically to forestall any possible legal action by Charles Dickens' heirs and successors. I make sure to keep a glimpse of the houses in view, and count them off as I dodge. Duffy's is now the third from here. Flora will be all tuned in to Granny Phipps. This expedition is a piece of cake.

Here we are: number three. No call for stealth now. I come into the Duffy's open back yard. A wild outburst of shrill barks makes me jump in panic. The bark is one that I recognise. It belongs to...the back door is opening. "Andy is hit? Robby then?"

Lyney's voice is as familiar as Terry's. Throwing caution to the winds, I advance.

"Holy Moses, Tom, ye gimme sech a start. Is ye comin' on in then?"

To tell you the honest truth, Lyney, I thought the Duffys lived here."

"They ne're did, Tom. The Duffy place is acrost an' three along on yer right. Peter's Daddy's hit was, an' his Grandaddy's afowah him. Allus the Duffy's hit was."

Lyney had given me just enough thinking space to see a way out. "Your tip about the MaCafferty hounds was worth its weight in gold. They are flat-out phenomenal. They are peerless and priceless. Eddie is a genius. They are bigger than anything I had dreamed of before I came to America. Of course I gave you my word not to disclose my source. I have not, and I never shall, Lyney. So I wonder if you can you do me a similar favour?" Lyney could be seen mentally weighing my request.

"Sim'lar, ye says, Tom?"

"I count it the same, Lyney. As with your revelation, any risk is all mine". He nods.

"Peter Duffy invited me over and I wasn't about to let Miss MacTaggart's unshakable prejudice against the family stand in my way. Accordingly, she believes me to be back in bed, attempting to allay a relapse. You wouldn't blow the whistle on me now you know, would you?" Lyney shakes his head, grinning madly. He sticks out a hand so we may shake on it,

"Ah ne're done thought ye had hit in ye ta be sech an Arshman." He slaps my back. "We'll make ye a mountain man yet." Suddenly it seems I am finally attaining the ambitions held for me, not just by Shirley and Robby, but by Flora herself. Not quite through the reforms they had proposed, but by uncovering new capacities hiding within me. "I calculate you and I are pretty much blood brothers now, Lyney."

"Ah cain't a said hit better mahself, Tom. Now don't ye be late ta Duffy's."

Back into the woods, flitting tree to tree, then out behind the real Duffy place, I have to knock at their door louder than I would like. They will be expecting a gentleman such as I to report at the front.

Peter opens the door. His eyebrows rise: "Tom, we were waitin' on you at two o' the clock." He turns around to face into the house. "Molly, Tom's heah already."

"Oh, stop yer teasin', Peter, or the poor man may ne're come agin." She steps closer to murmur, "We call him 'Peter an' the Wolf' now, but he warn't this way atall afowah we married. Come on in, Tom." Aha; they are a married couple. So much for Flora.

I have not until now entered a Caney Forks home through its kitchen. This one smells most enticing. I try not to stare, telling Molly, "I can see you're a dab hand at the stove."

"Well, Tom, you haven't long ta see for sure. Ah'll have dinner on the table in five minutes. Why don't you follow Peter through thar an' meet our children?" Peter leads the way into a front room. It is much like the others, but far tidier. Two girls and a boy sit tongue-tied on a wide sofa. From six to ten, I estimate their ages. Their faces say more than their tongues, betraying inner struggles of varying degrees.

"This is Mr. Watson, children. Tom, our li'l girl heah is Maybelline."

"Mmmph," says Maybelline.

"Our boy is Ozell." The boy glowers, his mouth clamped tight shut. "An' las' but not leas', Tom our eldest'un she's Tigerli'ly."

"No, Ah am not," shouts Tigerli'ly. "Ah'm Milly, an' Ozell is Ian an' Maybelline is Jenny, ain't you, sugar?"

"And who is your delightful puppy, Peter?"

"He's Jonks," says Milly forestalling her father. Jonks wags his tail in response.

"Well, now we'all has our li'l' problem out'n the way, pr'aps you ought a tell 'em your real name, Tom."

"Since you ask, Peter, it would give me great satisfaction to do just that. I am Tom, as you say, but I am not Mr. Watson. I am Mr. Elkins. Or I am Dr. Watson. It all depends on who you ask." Peter does not seem as amused as he should.

"Let me explain the apparent confusion some other time, Peter." Molly is bringing the first dish in and beckoning us all to sit down.

Her food is much tastier and more appealing than Flora's. I tell Molly so in a low whisper, adding that I give her this information in the strictest confidence. "It's rude to whisper," says Ian to the table at large. I explain that I am doing so to protect a secret. "I know a secret," shouts Ian at once. "Thar's a whale lives at the bottom of our well."

"Daddy's two hunnert 'leven year old," pipes Jenny, not to be outdone.

How should I react? I must not disappoint these children. I applaud. All three look expectant rather than pleased. Only Peter looks happy. "Ah'm tryin' out tall tales on these three. See if'n Ah cain't outsharp 'em. Jenny, tell Mr. Watson how you kin be sure Ah'm jus' as old as you tol' him."

"You mus' roll up that sleeve, Daddy," says Jenny, pointing to his left arm. Peter rolls it up obediently. "What you see thar, Mr. Wasson?" asks Jenny.

"I see a kind of pucker in the bicep, Jenny; a deep indentation of a kind completely unfamiliar to me."

"You cain't know what it is, Mr. Wasson. Daddy says that's whar the musket ball hit him in our revolution war."

"Thank you, Jenny, This is most interesting. Now it's your turn, Ian. Tell me how you know there is a whale at the bottom of your well."

"You only need lean far 'nuff in ta hear him anytahm, Mr. Wasson."

"And when did you last check on him, Ian?"

"Ah cain't recall the day, Mr. Wasson. When Ah bend over almos' far 'nuff, mah sisters always say they gonna push me in."

We adults have managed to keep eating during these exchanges, but the children had all downed tools the moment Ian put me in my place. Molly reads my mind. "Don't fret, Mr. Watson. This happens ever' meal savin' breakfas'. We eat thet'un on the go. 'Deed those three eat breakfas' goin' ta school mos' days, though they're on vacation now."

"Does that mean they are ready to leave the table?"

"It does. You kin get on down an' go play now, children."
They rise noisily and run out shouting, "Whar's your whale
today, Ian?"

I had come to hear Peter talk about his tin whistle and
Molly about her tambourine and teaching. But a whole new
field of research had come out of the mouths of the Duffy
'babes and sucklings'. We begin to delve into it over Molly's
stack cake—of more variegated content than Flora's and just
as likely to put flesh on my bones.

Our conversation soon turns to tall tales traditions. Peter
asks me how I might tell if a story comes from the north or
south. I have no inkling. "Yankee tales start, 'Once upon a
tahm...' Our'n start, 'Y'all ain't ne're goin' ta b'lieve this...'"

Time passes very quickly, so engrossing are Peter's and
Molly's examples. Perhaps the most helpful news comes
from Peter. He tells me that the oldest and best mountain
stories are known as Jack tales. They feature a sort of ubiq-
uitous Jack , who can be of any era, age, social standing and
merit. At this point I notice that the sun has gone from the
hollow. I have to see clearly enough to dodge from tree to
tree, and, to re-enter Flora's place arborealy. Me, an English
Tarzan in America.

Thanking this enlivening couple for their warm hospitality and engaging stories, I say my fond farewells and creep
into the shadowy woods. Jolly Jonks chases me a short distance then turns back. But soon, on and off, I am alarmed to
hear short, stealthy sounds close by. I freeze behind the nearest trunk every time, until at last I reach Flora's unmolested.
I climb her tree and squeeze back through her convenient
window safely.

This question of Jacks engages my mind.

As to Shirley's Jack—the Forsythe one—his early appearance in my exile here now seems too remarkable a coincidence to credit. Tom I may be, but I am beginning to feel
like part of a tall tale myself.

Chapter 19
A Rude Awakening

Flora's call to breakfast jerks me from my dreams with its note of alarm. Before I can even dress and descend she warns me there is a prowler in town. "Thet Jimmy Fanaghy done seen 'im, smack in back o' his place. He grabs his rifle gun an' runs on out. But whene're Jimmy ketches the least sight on him an' draws a bead, thet man jus' fades away, like a hant."

"A hant, Miss MacTaggart?"

"A ghost. Now ye well know, Mr. Watson, as Ah don't hold wi' no ghosts. Ne're did in mah entar life. But ye needs take what Jimmy done seen fer real, Mr. Watson. Stay out o' them woods 'til the divil's cotched" Trapped before, I now seem lucky to be alive, or at a minimum, not riddled with buckshot.

"Come right along o' me, Mr. Watson. Hit won't hurt none ta show ye how Jimmy din't see no hant." She leads me to her back window and points to the ground outside. "See them bark scraps yonder? See them li'l broke twigs, all green leafed? They're all on 'em out'n mah pignut hick'ry, knocked down fresh. Mah Grandaddy planted hit fer shade, an' fer hits sweet nuts. Hit's mah pride an' joy. Thet durn prowler done came thisaway, Mr. Watson. He done showed mah hick'ry no respeck' atall. A hant indeed!

"Ah hain't a-skeered, but ye ought be. Leastwise 'til ye larns thinkin' like a true mountain man." She has her chin up, her lips pinched. This is serious.

My involuntary expression of fear seems to satisfy Flora

for the moment, though my actual fear is that I shall be found out. On the plus side, if I had presented such an elusive target to Jimmy, he could hardly have recognised me. And with the hold I have over Peter, through our original pact, he is highly unlikely to finger me. I shall just have to live in hope that no one else witnessed my comings and goings yesterday.

A childhood tune breaks out in my relieved mind. Without thinking, I begin to hum along. As the lyrics sift into my consciousness, I sing:

"If you go down to the woods today, you're in for a big surprise.
If you go down to the woods today, you'd better go in disguise,
For every bar that ever there was will gather there for certain because..."

"Mr. Watson, is ye a-teasin' agin?" Her tone suggests mortal offence.

"Heaven forbid I should do such a thing, Miss Mac-Taggart. My mind does play tricks on me, but I believe it is warning me that the other two 'Bars' could be patrolling the woods with Jimmy. Either this morning before work, or this evening. I feel an even stronger impetus for giving the woods a respectable berth, until you shall advise me that all is clear. When outside, I shall keep strictly to the middle of the road."

"Ah git ever' piece o' thet, Mr. Watson, but why din't ye jus' say so fust place? Why were ye singin' thet tune? Ye's the provokin'est man." She has coloured up nicely.

"Those words come from a nursery song, Miss MacTaggart. I have recalled it from my earliest days. I meant no harm by it. Please accept that it rose to my lips quite unconsciously, entirely of its own volition." Flora sniffs, stares at me.

"If 'n ye say so, Mr. Watson, Ah shall consider yer explanation. When Ah'm good an' ready, Ah shall say if 'n or not Ah accept hit. Now let's eat, an' decide how ye might could spend yer day safe. An' no more foolishness, ye heah?"

It may only have been her affronted mood, but Flora now claims she has no time to chaperone me on visits to any of the ladies still to be interviewed, and disapproves of too many of the men. "Do you suppose that Mr. Spade might be sufficiently recovered from the Holdaway burying by now, Miss MacTaggart?"

Flora is ready to clutch at any respectable straw. "He may kin be, Mr. Watson.

"Fetch y'self on o'er an' see. But none o' yer imposin' on the poor man if 'n he ain't prop'ly up ta snuff yet. Did Ah git thet right, Mr. Watson, 'bout the snuff?"

"You did indeed, Miss MacTaggart, to perfection. You may trust me to be judicious in the matter. Furthermore I shall keep to the middle of the road in all senses of the phrase."

This seems enough to mollify Flora. "Then be off wi' ye, Mr. Watson, an' let me start on mah mendin'. They're a pile a-waitin' an' mah fingers hain't what they use ta be."

I head out and into the middle of the road. At Obadiah's my luck is in. He is out. To implement my new plan I head for 'Three Bars' territory, keeping strictly to the middle of the road.

Flora wants me to be safe.

Chapter 20
The Hunt Is On

As I hoped, Jimmy is home. Seated on the loose concrete blocks that serve as his front steps, he looks more sullen than ever. "Off ta work, they is. Said thet durn prowler he's dahn ta me. Make ya'self a hero, they says. Three hour in the woods taday an' Ah ain't cotched no sight on 'im noplace. Ah needs thar holp ta hunt proper." I let him stew, hot aggrieved and needy. I edge into his yard, well beyond Flora's line of sight. She said she wants me to be safe, didn't she?

"Ya hain't no hunter, Mr. Dubya?" He catches on pretty quick for a 'bar'.

"I am not, Mr. Fanaghy, but I am willing to learn. If you will show me what to do, I will try my best. Always providing that you have the necessary firepower to spare, of course." His face fails to light up with joy.

"Ah hain't paid ya no nevermind afowah, Mr. Dubya. Bah mah lights ya's frum a college world as don't nohow fit wi' our'n. How'm Ah ta know ya won't go a-shootin' up no road signs or winder glass, say?"

"Mr. Fanaghy, I can't do any damage if you don't give me a gun. There must be other ways I can help. For example, could I spot from a different angle than you?"

His scowl lightens a fraction.

"Ya might could beat fer me."

"What would that entail, Mr. Fanaghy?"

"Ah ties a big red cloth on ya fer safety. Ah shows ya whar ta run about, a-crashin' an' a-yellin' an' a-cussin'. Ah tracks ya frum on uphill. Ya flushes the bastard. Ah fixes his waggon." His eyes glint with cold anger.

Jimmy's proposal falls sweetly on my ears, so very, very far is it from the IBM mindset than anything else which has crossed my mountain path to date. I set aside the question as to who is likely to believe my eventual report. "I'm your man. When do we start?"

"Stop right thar, Mr. Dubya. Ah'll git the kit." He lumbers into his home, to return with shotgun, cartridge box, red cloth as advertised, and round his thick neck, a whistle on a grubby lanyard. "Holt all still." He drapes me with the cloth and ties it off. It makes me feel rather like one of Garibaldi's 'Hunters of the Alps'. I mention this to him. "Now thar's one good ol' boy fer a fer'ner," Jimmy responds with surprising spirit. "His band o' mountain men done rassled back chunks on Hit'ly stole bah them Hostrians. Then what does mah Garibaldi do but give ever' chunk ta them Eyetalian Piedmonters. Eyetalian, Mr. Dubya, but still an' all Piedmonters, like us. He's mah hero."

Amazed and gratified by this example of Jimmy's extra-Appalachian knowledge, I ask if he knows anything about the origin of the red shirts worn by his hero's followers.

"Ah heared tell they're frum his days in Montevideo, Mr. Dubya. A fact'ry thar done run 'em up fer slaughter houses. Them rebels fancied 'em, an' done holp tharselves. Thet's what rebels does, Mr. Dubya. We helps ourselves.

"But fer Jimmy heah, thet's jus' the beginnin'. Garibaldi got hisself hitched ta a Uruguay gal. She was aces on a hoss. She done larned 'im the Gaucho way on life. Now Miz Mac-Taggart said ya heah ta figger out our mountainy ways, Mr. Dubya. Mah way hit's jus' like them Gauchos. D'ya see how Ah has ta live free? D'ya see how mah motor sickle is mah hoss?" I have only seen Red's motorbike. Maybe they share, like Mike and Jeppie. Who am I to quibble?

"I do, I do, Mr. Fanaghy, and I can't tell you how impressed I am." The last thing I want to do is get Jimmy any more over-excited than he already is. Flora wants me safe.

"Then le's roll," says Jimmy, pushing me toward the road. "We'all gotta crost fust."

"Can we keep to the woods for a while, and cross later?"

"Hit don't make no matter ta me, Mr. Dubya. S'long as ya don't shy at crossin' then. Nor at turnin' right neither. Ah done drawed the woods on mah side this mornin', along far's the buryin' ground. Yestiddy Ah done chased the bastard o'er on the far side. Ah give up fer want o' light an' no pardner. Hit won't do no harm ta cross o'er whar the homes runs out, an' make us a sweep 'til we'all come out acrost frum Festus' territory."

I couldn't have planned this campaign better myself.

We head deeper into the woods then trudge parallel to the barely glimpsed homes on our right until these peter out (no pun intended). Jimmy gives the order to cross over. In no time we are confronted by Caney Crick. Jimmy just wades over, leaving me no choice but to get soaking wet up to my knees. That could certainly prove awkward.

Once we are well into the woods, Jimmy explains my role. "Ought a be real easy. Jus' act like any city hunter, all gaumed up. Curse kinda low, ta show ya lost. If 'n our prowler he's aroun' yet he'll hightail hit uphill out'n ya way. Thet's whar li'l Jimmy 'ull be. Ready an' waitin'. Safety orf. Bang! Bang! Any questions?"

"How can you be sure no-one else is hunting this hillside?" Flora wants me safe.

"They're all at work, Mr. Dubya. 'Sides, even mah good buddies thinks mah prowler's jus' a hoot in the wind. Then too, ya has thet big red cloth ta keep ya safe frum fools an' ejits. Git along now."

Jimmy heads uphill like an Indian until I can no longer see him. I start my slovenly progress, guided by glimpses of homes below. My curses are half-hearted, so intriguing is this new game. I have to make chuckles of pleasure sound like furious expletives. Try it someday. It demands absolute concentration.

Looking back, I suppose this is why I panic at the sudden

sight of a bent figure shuffling toward me through the trees. It carries some kind of a staff or gun, luckily pointed at the ground. The alarm bells this sets off practically deafen me. To flee uphill is out of the question. To flee downhill will expose my Garibaldesque figure to public view. To flee whence I had come would bring Jimmy's plan to naught. I freeze behind the nearest tree. I fight desperately to bring my gasping lungs under control.

My nemesis approaches with infuriating langour. It is still bent, looking in fact like nothing so much as an elderly retiree sweeping a beach with a metal detector. The figure's posture serves me well for taking quick peeks undetected, until I can be sure the intruder is a woman. Hardly the prowler then, but someone unaware of his threatening presence. A high-pitched whistle cuts the air. That would be Jimmy, no doubt, but what does his whistle mean? My intruder has the same question, looking up sharply, and catching me in mid peek.

"What ye hidin' out fer, Mr. Clever Boots?" It is the anti-social Meg M'Sweeney. "Cain't a soul gather nuts in peace but folk aroun' start a-cussin' fit ta bust?"

"Er, do you have any of your charges with you this morning, Miss M'Sweeney?"

"Charges? What ye mean bah charges?"

"Well, snakes, to be honest." Flora wants me safe.

"Why would'n ye be honest, Mr. Clever Boots? No, Ah don't. Why 'ud Ah bring them poor critters out heah?"

During our uneasy exchange I have been scrutinising Meg's weapon. It is a stick with a small wire cage at the lower end. It holds several nuts. A little door on this cage is connected to, and activated by, a trigger beneath the handle. So this is how elderly Caney Forkers gather their nuts in comfort. Or in May for that matter.

"Did Andy Goggin happen to make your wonderful nut collector, Miss M'Sweeney?"

I am doing my best to spread oil on troubled waters.

"Ah mought kin answer thet, Mr. Clever Boots, if 'n ye

tells me why ye's all dressed up like a Red Ridin' Hood."

Although I had no choice in the matter, this was probably the most judicious moment for Jimmy to materialise, just uphill of us. He absorbs the situation at a glance, striding over to detach my red wrapping and saying, "Shoot far! Excuse us, Meg, but Ah mus' be at work an' Ah do b'lieve Mr. Dubya has hisself a dinner date." His guileless glance at me is refreshingly free of threat, disappointment or malice.

Seizing this opportunity with both feet, I head downhill to the centre of the road. I step out along its very middle, ever obedient, advancing as daintily as a tightrope walker, toward Obadiah's.

They don't paint centre lines on the roads around here.

Chapter 21
Obadiah Tells All

If Obadiah had not been present for my second call, I would have had great difficulty in recounting my morning to Flora on my return. After all, nothing had happened yet remotely suitable for publication. Fingers crossed, I hope against hope that muttering Meg M'Sweeney will not spread any rumours about little Red Riding Hood. But what can you expect? She is a true-blue, dyed in the wool Old Trout. If she spills the beans, people will surely label me as the prowler. If she does, and they do, how will I ever get another interview from anyone in this hollow? Or even in the next.

My speculation is interrupted by Obadiah, looking mournful as ever. He has opened his door to me. "Why, Mr. Watson, heah's a fahn coincidence. Ah jus' done closed the books on our dear departed Sally Holdaway. Come on in an' set y'self down bah mah desk. May kin Ah offer ye a jar?" Ben Cochran had left me little chance to sample the jar Shirley put before me, so I remain curious about the local beverage.

"I don't mind if I do, Mr. Spade. At least that is how we accept back in England. I do hope you will join me now that your labours are complete." Obadiah waddles off and is soon back with our drinks. "May I offer you my compliments for the highly professional fashion in which you kept Miss Sally's burial service on track amidst what must surely have been a wholly unprecedented series of mishaps." I raise my jar. Obadiah takes a firm grip on his, but doesn't lift it one millimetre:

"Mishaps? They warn't no mishaps, Mr. Watson. If ye had mah experience, ye'd know them blunders fer what they are. The fruits o' the Divil: lack o' faith an' disrespec' fer the law. The Caney Forks ye see is not what hit use ta be. No siree. Ye has come ta us late in the day, Mr. Watson—too late if 'n ye're not well directed by those as kin still be trusted." At this he throws up his arm and swallows his drink like the most hardened of topers. I am shocked into silence.

"Sally Holdaway she was one sech," he resumes with a sob. "Nary a year gone bah, ye could a larned much frum her. Sally done unnerstood the ol' ways. Sally lived bah 'em too. How otherways d'ye reckon she made a hunnert an' five, Mr. Watson? Ah know hit warn't them seegars o' her'n. Nor her drinkin' neither."

"Ben Cochran he's another 'un. Ye met him; Ah needn't say no more. Then thar's Meg M'Sweeney. Our Meg she's a pillar o' faith. She's more'n hit in her li'l' fingernail than thet whippersnapper Howie Long has in his tee-total beanpole body. He ain't no chip off'n ary ol' block as Ah knows on, Mr. Watson. He's how our world is a-changin'. May kin Ah fetch ye a jar more?" Horrified, I can only nod. My curiosity about the local beverage has been painfully satisfied, but now I really need one.

Obadiah shuffles back, sets down both refilled jars, and resumes his seat in a heavy silence. He has told me of two old-timers whom I can trust, plus one who is now beyond mortal reach. Is his the voice of clinical depression? Even if it is, Obadiah is an integral part of Caney Forks life. I pull out my trusty notebook and pen.

"Who else meets your standards of rectitude, Mr. Spade?" He sinks his solace in a single gulp, offering no answer; not even clearing his throat. He shakes his head in despair.

"What about Miss MacTaggart, for example, and Granny Phipps, and Rosie Ross, and Andy Goggin, and Robby Burns, Mr. Spade?" Has he black-balled Festus Fraser, too, counting him among the faithless?

"And what about Sally's casket bearers, not to mention

those who stepped into their shoes after Constable Collins arrival?" Obadiah just keeps staring silently at a red stain on the tabletop before him, though he does let out a wordless sigh. Then another, but still not one word of explanation. He drops his head on his folded arms, a picture of misery in the midst of our 'happy coincidence'.

His woeful extremity brings Robby Burns' exhortation to mind. How did it go? Umm, I must learn to sympathise with Caney Forker's troubles. In Obadiah's case, Robby had said it was his 'precarious living'. But don't all these people have precarious livings, to one degree or another? I am in no shape to offer him a loan. What comfort can I offer?

"Does anyone know your troubles, Mr. Spade? Would you like to share them with me? I promise you faithfully to keep any secrets." Here I shut my notebook and drop it on the floor. I surrender my pen to him for good measure. Obadiah stirs. He bends to retrieve my fallen notebook, sets it face down on the table and begins to doodle on the back cover. I crane, searching for clues in the patterns he traces.

At the foot of the cover crude stick figures multiply, large and small. Behind them grow what appear to be the outlines of Christmas trees. It is a child's drawing, yet I know he is a bachelor. In a sudden paroxysm he scribbles wildly across his picture, moaning as he does and striking the table with the flat of his hand. This is too easy:

"You hate death, don't you, Mr. Spade, yet you make your living from it. You only have to walk the road to see family burial plots, made before your time and without your help or charges. But I saw for myself how your reception set free all the happiness which sadness had locked up in the hearts of your friends and neighbours. Through your efforts, Mr. Spade, I saw the people in your community clearly and knew each of them properly for the first time since I came to Caney Forks. How can I thank you?"

Obadiah straightens up. He flips my notebook over and slides it across to me, putting my pen beside it. "Might would ye write down what all ye jus' done tol' me, Mr. Watson.

Ah know as hit's fer yer research, but might could Ah beg a hextry copy?"

It is my turn to lose the power of speech. Me, of all people! How did my words restore the old Obadiah so fast? I have never spoken to anyone in this way before. But I have been spoken to...by Flora, by Shirley and most specifically in this case, by Robby.

So this is the power of listening. I resolve to do more.

Finding my tongue at last, I promise to write up our meeting, and to bring a fair copy over for his approval. "Yer has mah say-so as we set heah, Mr. Watson. Thar's no secrets atween us. Now git y'self on back ta Flora. Yer look a mite too peckish, an' Ah want yer ta be up an' about ary ol' tahm fer a jar an' a jaw."

Chapter 22
On The Porch

Obadiah was on the right track; I feel more than peckish. It has been a morning of stressful endeavours. Granny Phipps sits in solitary splendour on Flora's porch. Flora, no doubt will be busy in her kitchen. Boldly I mount the porch, all set to show Flora how safe I have kept myself, and how ready I am to appreciate whatever she is serving today. I am more than reconciled to local produce. I bid Granny Phipps a good afternoon. She grunts. Obadiah would surely feel let down by her dispirited attitude.

"Is hit ye, Mr. Watson?" Flora calls from her kitchen. I admit it is me and that I am hungry. "Hold yer hoss. Ah'm a-comin'." Her conversational flow runs unabated as she crosses to the porch. "If 'n ye done kep' ta the road's middle, some 'un must a tol' ye 'bout Meg M'Sweeney a-cryin' wolf. Hit's the talk o' the town."

"No, Miss MacTaggart, no-one has done so, although I have, of course, been in conference with Mr. Spade, as we agreed. He made no mention of any such thing."

But enough of this small talk. Flora is empty-handed. Where is my dinner?

"Did Mr. Spade tell ye his problem, Mr. Watson?"

"Well, Miss MacTaggart, it might be more accurate to say that I divined it, and I do believe that my solution made him very happy."

"Now how might kin ary a livin' soul divine a pizen pen letter, Mr. Watson?" She glares at me as though I am the class fibber, past all redemption.

"He made no mention of any letters, either, Miss. Mac-Taggart."

"Ye 'mazes me, Mr. Watson. How kin Ah b'lieve ye was o'er ta Mr. Spade's atall?"

In a flash of inspiration, I whip out my notebook and place it face down atop the ashtray on the porch table. "This is how Mr. Spade showed me the fount of his distress. It is hardly in the nature of a letter, wouldn't you agree?" Flora reaches for her wire spectacles, anxious to peruse my evidence. Granny Phipps sneaks little looks at the drawing around the chief examiner, on whom she waits for a first opinion.

"Why this heah's no more'n a li'l chile's drawin', Mr. Watson. What ye mean by hit?"

"I myself mean nothing by it, Miss MacTagart, since it is exclusively of Mr. Spade's own execution. It shows how deeply Mr. Spade hates his work, and his heavy guilt at charging the bereaved for his services. More particularly, it showed me how he entirely discounts the immense good his receptions bring to the community. I told him each person at the reception I attended was so imbued with life by it that I felt I was seeing every one of them clearly for the first time. I don't wish to seem immodest, Miss MacTaggart, but I saw how my words restored him. Furthermore he asked for a copy of the notes which I am still writing up."

"Hallelujah! Welcome ta Caney Forks, Mr. Watson. Ah do b'lieve ye jus' mought have done arrived finely." Flora gives me a warm smile and squeezes my shoulder. Granny Phipps nods me a qualified smile of her own but skips the squeeze. It soon transpires that she was the bearer of the news about Obadiah's letter and Meg's hallucinations. In all innocence, I have upstaged her.

"Mr. Watson, we'all are at sixes an' sevens under so much news frum Granny Phipps. Now ye throws out more'n hit. Ah am a-goin' ta check mah icebox an' jelly cupboard, an' put us up a real porch picnic. Fetch y'self a chair. Set mah ashtray on the floor. Ah'll bring out the makin's an' we kin ketch ye up. Ah've pinto bean soup, poke sallet, lan' cress an' cornpone." Flora is over-excited. It must be the two news scoops in one day.

My hunger has reached crisis point by the time we can all sit down and set to. How fortunate that I have already done my talking and can focus on refueling while the two Grannies tell their news.

"Shirley come bah on thet li'l motor sickle o' mine. She had ta find what truth might could be in the rumour 'bout Obadiah gittin' nasty letters. Ah done sent her on o'er ta Granny Phipps. Shirley she done rode thar. But when Granny got heah finely jus' now, the letter bizness done got hitself clean swallered up. Meg M'Sweeney's wild tale ta ever'body done hit. Now ye know, Mr. Watson, how our Meg likes keepin' ta herself. Well, not today she don't. Did she try her story on ye bah chance?" I shake my head at once, looking as surprised as I can, walking the fine line of the white lie.

"What is this 'wild tale' of hers?" I ask Flora.

"Meg done missed me, but Granny Phipps got the whole nine yards. Let her tell ye."

"Very well, Flora. Ah was a-walkin' on o'er ta Jean Tierney ta borry a cup o' meal, mindin' mah own beeswax. All on a sudden, heah come Meg out'n the woods. She's all in a fluster, a-scatterin' pecans o'er the ground an' a-wavin thet fancy nut-catcher o' her'n, plumb pitchin' a fit. 'Red Ridin' Hood she's back thar.' she yells, 'Whar thar's she, thar's a wolf.' What am Ah ta say, Mr. Watson? Thar's no wolfs in our woods, an' sure as God made li'l green apples, thar hain't no Red Ridin Hood neither. Nor ne're was, not heah nor no place." She settles back, eyeing the apple butter jar.

Flora talk takes a malicious turn; "Our Mr. Watson, he's attached ta his nurs'ry days, Iree. He's bin singin' 'bout bars a-picnickin' in the woods. Mayhap he kin sing us sump'n 'bout li'l Red Ridin' Hood an' her wolf, too." She looks at me inquiringly. Is Flora teasing? Does she know something? Does she just want to be done with Granny Phipps' outlandish claim?

"I do recall that cautionary tale, Miss MacTaggart, but I don't believe it was ever set to music. Now, let's be reasonable. If there were to be a wolf or two in your woods, I am confident your hounds and hunters would be the first to know." That seems to settle matters. What a mercy that Meg's story, as received by Granny Phipps, is heavy on wolf and light on Li'l Red herself.

I only regret that these events make me feel rather a wolf in sheep's clothing.

Overall, and on balance, if Granny Phipps spreads the views expressed by Flora and myself, my woodland exploits should stand a fighting chance of remaining safely off the record. I breathe more easily now as I stand by for details of the nasty letters Obadiah inexplicably omitted to tell me about.

But I am momentarily nonplussed. I have never addressed Flora's sidekick directly before. I have no sense of mountain etiquette for addressing second tier Grannies. I decide to play it safe: "Granny Phipps, I am ready to hear about Mr. Spade's secret letters now, if you please."

"Well, Mr. Watson, Ah reckon Mr. Spade got hisself all too shook up ta tell ye 'bout these letters. But word done got out some wise, or Shirley 'ud ne're done rid inta town in a lather. Now Ah don't deal in no rumours, Mr. Watson. Ah done visited mah frien's ta piece together the truth on hit best Ah kin. Thar war signs a-plenny at our las' hap bee— thet's a quiltin' bee ta ye, Mr. Watson, a Jacob's Ladder--but Ah needed me more piecin' yet. Not meanin' no word joke heah, y'all unnerstan'. Jus' plain what Ah say.

"The fust puzzle piece hit was Festus fallin' out frum Obadiah. Now Festus hain't a man ta show no feelin's. They must a bin all red hot. The nex' piece hit was Obadiah a-checkin' his mailboxie way too early ever' day. So Jeppie he makes sure an' tells him if 'n thar's a cheque or a bill an' the likes ta ease his mind. But Obadiah he shows no least scrap o' gratitude fer Jeppie's kindness. The third piece was Obadiah bewailin' an' lamentin' yestiddy arter his mail done come. Eliza Jane jus' tol' me how all o' this be a surefire sign o' pizen pen letters. She once't had one all ta herself.

"Ah done mah duty. Ah done reported all mah findin's ta Shirley, Mr. Watson." Granny Phipps allows herself a look of smug satisfaction, and spoons out a generous helping of apple butter. I really shall have to find out what this substance comprises.

Chapter 23
The Green Hornet

Once again, the best policy looks to be that I lie low, like who was it? Brer Rabbit, if I remember rightly. I rise to gather the picnic remains and disappear indoors. But first, honour requires that I clear up this misapprehension about my fondness for nursery tales.

"Miss MacTaggart, you have made reference to my nursery days. I do not deny that phase of my life. But you suggest an undue attachment to those days on my part. I feel this to be unjustified for what is surely a universal human circumstance. In evidence, may I point out the reference that you yourself made to me concerning the so-called 'three bears', or 'bars', who have since so distinguished themselves at Sally Holdaway's burying? Am I mistaken, or does their nomenclature not infer the presence of the eponymous maiden Goldilocks?" Silence reigns on the porch. Have I blasphemed?

"Mr. Watson!" Shame on ye! We have spoken 'bout this afowah! Are ye some kind a lawyer? Are ye a dictionary or one o' them 'cyclopedias? What's pains ye so 'bout plain language?"

"Oh, you have me there, Miss MacTaggart. I did get a bit carried away. But let's not lose sight of the subject..."

Flora looks at Granny Phipps: "Goldilocks? *Goldilocks*? Ah cain't recall no sech Goldilocks, kin ye? 'Far's Ah know they're called Three Bars on account o' thar forever sore heads. Ah b'lieve hits them heads rather'n 'em bein' downright bear-shaped. Tho' mayhap some o' thet along o' hit.

What d'ye say, Iree?" What? Is she saying Irene?

"Amen Ah say, Flora. They hain't no Goldilocks, nor ne're was ta mah mind. What gal 'ud gaum wi' them three no-account lumps?" Her summation is mingled with a rising, high-pitched whine as a woman on a small motorbike rides up in a whirl of dust. She is wearing a big, old, green crash helmet. Glowing amber strands of hair float from under it in all directions like tiny neon signs. Criminey! It's Shirley.

"Tahms a-wastin, Dr. Watson," she calls up to me. "Grab your notebook, an' foller me on ovah ta Mr. Spade's." Her green machine has no pillion. I pick my notebook off the floor and run after her. We pause at Obadiah's double doors for an all-too-quick briefing across her hot, green motorscooter. "Flora's done tol' you 'bout the nasty letters?" I nod. She knocks. Obadiah opens up, visibly surprised to find me visiting for the second time today.

"Did yer fergit sump'n', Mr. Watson?...No, well... Good seein' ye, Shirley. Are ye gayly? Good. Why don't y'all step right on in?"

As we head for Obadiah's desk and chairs, Shirley explains that as everyone seems to know about his nasty letters, he might as well help her to find the sender and put a stop to them. Obadiah looks embarrassed: "Mr. Watson, Ah'm sorry fer not tellin' ye 'bout them letters'. Hit felt like sech a li'l thing arter ye set me up agin the way ye done".

Shirley looks at me quizzically. Me, the do-gooder in chief. "Mr. Spade and I had a heart-to-heart talk this morning, Shirley, and I believe that I left him a happier man." Obadiah smiles his reassurance to Shirley. Feeling like the cat that swallowed the cream, I open my notebook, uncap my pen.

"Well then, Mr. Spade, let's get down to fac's. Kin you tell me has Festus some ways upset you? Folks say you bin seen a-quar'lin'. Festus did a fahn job at the buryin', don't you agree?"

"Yes, he did so, Miss Shirley, but not hardly 'nuff ta earn hisself a raise."

"A raise, Mr. Spade? Has he asked for one?"

"No, not as sech, Miss Shirley, but ye might could say hit's in the air."

"In what way, Mr. Spade?"

"In the nasty letter way, Miss Shirley. Ever' durn one on 'em sings Festus' praises. Ever' other'un sets out how much more he's worth than Ah seem ta think. The nerve on hit!"

"Fust thing, Mr. Spade, let's eliminate poss'ble suspects. Might kin you reckernise Festus' han' writin?"

"Ah cain't do hit no way, Miss Shirley. Festus ne're done larn ta write. If'n he had, he might would have hisself more'n a better job 'n jus' diggin' an' fillin' fer me."

"Then we'all got us a li'l for'arder right thar, Mr. Spade. No man 'ud be happy bein' stuck so. Ah might would look glummy too in his boots. D'you see how he mus' have hisself an advocate."

"An advocate, Miss Shirley? Ah'm sure an' sartain he cain't afford no lawyer."

"Not a lawyer as sech, Mr. Spade, but some 'un ta speak on his behalf. In this case, ta write, o' course. Does Festus have any close frien's as you know of?"

"If'n ary'un ever kep' entarley ta hisself, Miss Shirley, hit'd be Festus Fraser. He's no better'n one o' them hermits."

"Then if'n nothin' else has changed, we mus' consider he has an unknown admirer." Bent over my notes, I suppress a smile, thinking how well-suited he and Meg would be. No other candidate springs to mind.

"Have you kep' any o' these letters, Mr. Spade?"

"Ah have, Miss Shirley. Ah done kep' ever' one." Obadiah pulls out a drawer and takes a handful of grubby notepaper to spread out for our review. The notes are hand-written, and quite neatly; none of your standard cut-and-paste newsprint snippets. They almost look respectable. Shirley begins to read. I look over her shoulder. There is no other way to describe their wording than polite. How can anyone call them nasty, let alone poison-pen?

Obadiah is fidgeting: "What ye thinkin', Miss Shirley?"

"Ah think Festus has himself an admirer of the highest calibre, Mr. Spade. Everwho your writer might could be, they're surely fit ta reason with, an' surely not ta be afeared. Ah b'lieve you were perfec'ly right ta keep this out'n your talk wi' Dr. Watson." While speaking, Shirley picks up a number of letters, apparently at random, and examines each from a cross-eyed close up distance. She puts each one down without comment, but sums up the outcome for Obadiah.

"We kin take this matter up momently, Mr. Spade, if 'n you'll spare me one o' them letters. It doesn't signify which." She holds out a hand for the letter of his choice, stands up and gestures me to the door.

Obadiah waves us out, looking, if anything, even more at peace with the world than at our earlier parting. Shirley interrupts my self-congratulatory reverie; "Ah am sorry, Dr. Watson. Ah hain't innerduced you prop'ly ta the newest member of our team.

This heah's Green Hornet." She pats the gray-green saddle fondly. "That name has a special meanin' heah in America, which Ah doubt y'all know in England. Our Green Hornet he's a pretend, crime-fighting vigilante, Dr. Watson. He wears a green hat an' a looong, green coat. He drives him a fancy black car, which ain't no match for Flora's hand-me-down green motor sickle heah."

Right; in addition to the nature of apple butter I must remember to find out who or what on earth a vigilante might be.

Chapter 24
Botanical Studies

Before Shirley mounts Green Hornet, she asks me if I have seen any berry patches in Caney Forks. "Do you want berries for dessert? Any particular kind?"

"Ah don't know as you 'ud reckernise our mountain berries, Dr. Watson, but Flora kin school you how huckleberries look. Hillside blueberries too. They're the both Ah aim ta locate. Thar'll be some neahabout, but not likely in plain sight."

"Do you need them for supper, Shirley?"

"Ah need 'em for mah work, Dr. Watson. Kin you take what's lef' o' the evenin' an' look aroun' for those two kinds o' berries jus' as Flora tells ta you. Thar might could be some in that ice box o' her'n she kin show you. Now remember, Ah don't need the berries as sech. What Ah need is ta know whar they're a-growin'."

"I will check with Flora right away, Shirley, and take it from there. I...er... suppose you can't tell me about your suspicions...until...all the facts are in?" I am wheedling without shame, and Shirley knows it. She is suddenly all action. She wraps her hair around her head, claps on the crash helmet, sits on the little Green Hornet, kick-starts it and howls away without a word.

Feeling rather discouraged, I head back to Flora's for my berry lesson.

Iree-Irene is still keeping Flora company in her rocker on the porch, but I don't have to interrupt. She immediately wants to know all about our meeting with Obadiah.

"I am sorry, Miss Phipps, but what transpired is fully protected by client confidentiality. Besides, Shirley won't tell me what she thinks until she has all the facts. She says it's not her style. However, to move us forward, I do need Miss MacTaggart's guidance in the matter of huckleberries and blueberries; the hillside sort in particular." Flora stares at me in something like disillusion:

"Ye surely need ta do more noticin', Mr. Watson, as Ah done tol' ye so o'fen afowah. Step inta mah parlor an' say what ye see in mah winder jar. Then take a good look at thet mat bah the door." I step into her parlor. The flower arrangement in the jar consists of some tall, broad-leaved stems bearing little black berries. I report this.

"Thet's good, Mr. Watson. They be what mah Grandaddy done called hurtle berries. Ah call 'em huckle berries, 'long with ever'body in town. Black huckle berries in truth. Hain't hit so, Iree?" Before she can answer I have to know:

"Where did you cut them, Miss MacTaggart?"

"Ah did no sech thing, *Mister* Watson. They were a-scattered in the road, like everwho cut 'em was afeared o' gittin' cotched, an' took off. Ah'm not one fer wastin' arythin', even so they hain't like ta reg'lar flowers. Now how 'bout mah mat?"

My hopes of a quick answer dashed, I look down on its well-worn, hooked surface and report: "I see clumps of little grey-blue berries depicted on entwined, small-leaved branches. I suppose they are blueberries, perhaps even the hillside kind."

"Ye reckon right, Mr. Watson. Now what d'ye plan ta do wi' mah teachin'? Are ye fixin' ta serve us dessert?"

"I may be able to do that after I have finished working for Miss M'Gonaughy. In any case, I would first need to know where I might be able to pick both kinds of berry."

Iree-Irene jumps in with both booted feet. Perhaps these berries go well with apple butter. "Ye mus' look in the woods, Mr. Watson, on up a ways, an' whar thar's sprucey pines partick'ler. Both kind a berries needs a touch o' hacid in the soil.

126

Now blue berries they grows on li'l low bushes. Ye done seen fer y'self the tall stems black huckle berries grows on. But pay heed keerful now, Mr. Watson. Bars like 'em good as wild honey. Best keep yer eyes peeled real good."

Flora has been growing visibly more agitated. "How ye a-goin' ta hunt fer berries frum the midst o' the road, Mr. Watson? Has ye plumb disremembered the promise ye made this ver' mornin'? Yer promise respectin' our prowler. Bars might kin be less'n a risk daytahm, but why'd ye go whar they go? Ye surely like ta seek out trouble."

"Why thank you, Miss MacTaggart, for your timely reminder." I have never felt comfortable on the 'straight and narrow' and I must stray from it yet again, if I am to find Shirley's answers. Or, maybe...

"Do you, or does anyone you know, possess a pair of binoculars, Miss MacTaggart? If I could avail myself of a pair, then I could survey the hillsides from the safety of the road; from its very middle, in fact." Flora, bless her, can be seen mentally reviewing the optical instruments inventory of Caney Forks. But Iree-Irene beats her to the punch. She sits bolt upright. "Cap'n Sullivan! Might could thet 'scope on his be in his sea chest yet, Flora?"

"Ah reckon hit might surely could." Ten to one Captain Sullivan lives in the woods, and we are back where we started. But I may never find out, as Flora has an epiphany: "Well, don't thet beat all! 'Member how Obadiah done borrered hit off 'n the Cap'n ta keep his eye on Festus? Jeppie Pringle done brought hit out fer him. Thet telescope hain't in the nex' holler; hit's smack dab acrost the road. Ye run on o'er, Mr. Watson, an' make y'self sure on hit. Ah b'lieve Obadiah 'ud be happy ta do ye the favor only considerin' all ye done fer him taday."

Just like that. Simple. Another new lesson in Caney Forks living.

On opening his door to me for the third time today, Obadiah shakes his head to clear it. He listens to my request and agrees to lend me Captain Sullivan's telescope without a question. But he does make me promise to return it in the same condition in which he is handing it over. I examine the instrument. Apart from the high polish of its brass casings, this is a pretty battered specimen. Knowingly I clap the thin end to my eye in true Admiral Lord Nelson fashion. Like Nelson's blind eye my eye can see nothing but a bobbing, black blur. Obadiah observes my difficulty and removes the end cap. He hands this to me.

"Hain't ye ne're used a 'scope afowah, Mr. Watson?"

"No, I am accustomed to binoculars, Mr. Spade."

"Well fust ye pulls hit all out full-length. Keep a-holt on the eye end wi' yer lef' han', an' holt the heavy end bah yer right; steady as ye kin. Now point the 'scope at ary one thing as takes yer fancy. Then shorten hit 'til what ye see sharpens up like. How big does yer hobjeck look now?"

"It's certainly big enough for my purposes, Mr. Spade, but it won't keep still."

"Thet's jus' the way on a good 'scope, Mr. Watson; the bigger she blows things hup the more she'll wobble. Jus' stiffen yer right harm best ye kin, an' look away long as ye please."

"I appreciate the lesson, Mr. Spade, and promise to have the instrument back to you before dusk, safe and sound." I turn and head for the middle of the road to begin my hillside survey.

It's a funny thing, but now that my attention is fixed upon the wooded slopes behind the settled strips lining the road, it is the nearest objects that persist in obtruding. The old, overgrown, red-rusted tractor toward Mary McRory's, much hung washing, a half fallen-in caravan by Ben Cochran's, a long-abandoned wooden hearse behind Obadiah's, hen-infested car bodies every other house, rough boarded pig pens, tall sheds no wider than their doors, a few leaning dangerously, collapsed corncribs surrounding the old Holdaway place; even nice Rosie Ross has drifts of broken implements beyond her neat garden.

It occurs to me that, as a gardener, Miss Ross might well

know the whereabouts of any berry patches in the vicinity. I hail her on her porch and put my question.

"Why, Ah don't rightly know, Mr. Watson, but 'long as ye axe, Ah seen neighbour folk passin' bah frum downtown wi' full berry buckets more'n once't this summer."

"Downtown, Miss Ross...?"

"Frum yer own way, Mr. Watson." So I needn't ply my telescope this end of town. I thank her and move off 'downtown'. I am slowly getting used to this aberration.

Once past Obadiah's I begin to swing my 'scope up and across the slopes beyond, pausing to check every potential clump of bushes and shrubs. If they ever bore berries, they are stripped bare now. Turning my 'scope on the slopes opposite I almost strike a stranger on a bike. He sports a pith helmet, shorts, heavy boots and bandolier style straps crossed over his chest. An explorer perhaps? This apparition cries at me:

"Hey! Look whar ya goin'! Watch yaself! Innerferin' in the proper hexecution o' mah 'fficial duties, everwho ya might could be."

"I do apologise, sir. I am unused to encountering any but pedestrians on this road,

"But, I digress; what official might I have the pleasure to address?" He looks uncertain.

"Ah'm Jeppie Pringle, an' Ah carry the Fed'ral mails in three hollers, Mr....?"

"Mr. Watson, here for a year to study mountain living, and most especially mountain music, Mr. Pringle."

"Don't ya need a heah trumpet then, more'n Cap'n Sullivan's tellyscope?"

"That's a fair question, Mr. Pringle, but today I am on an unrelated quest, looking for berry patches."

"Ah don't know as ary tellyscope's a-goin' ta be much help, Mr. Watson, but Ah do know whar ya mought look. Hit hain't noplace neah heah. Up behin' the McEvoy place thet's whar ya want ta be. Look close as thar's plenny o' bresh. An' ya'd do well ta swap thet scope fer a real berry bucket afowah ya start."

I can see his point, but decide to forgo the lengthy explanations that would be required to set Mr. Pringle's mind at ease about my sanity and qualifications. There is, after all, at least one other wrong-headed individual accepted by and living in the community. I thank this Federal representative, adding that I trust his back and front tires are fully inflated and that I do not wish to delay him any further in his 'appointed rounds'. I believe that is how the U.S. Post Office terms them, but for some reason he looks as though he has never heard these words before.

After staring at me for a while, Mr. Pringle peddles off, peering about him for more unaccustomed obstructions. On his back are two canvas bags, each bearing in broken, faded letters the word 'SMALL', I think it is. His bags are obviously small, so what is the point? Another mountain eccentricity I suppose.

I sheath my 'scope and wearily follow the road as far as Lyney's place, hedged in its bower of abandoned appliances and bicycles. Here I draw out Captain Sullivan's 'scope to its full extent and bring the hillside beyond into focus. Obadiah was right about the wobble. As I advance along the road for a clearer view, an outburst of hysterical barking disturbs the peace. Terry is on to me, but it is of no consequence. For once I am not transgressing any agreements with Flora, nor am I spying on the subjects of my research. I am simply doing Shirley's bidding, as facilitated by Flora herself.

Lyney or his wife have subdued Terry, and the customary mountain calm returns.

The Pringle-vouched berry patches are still playing hard to get. I back across the road for a higher view. That is when Terry's canine commentary is replaced by a stentorian shout of 'Peeping Tom'! I lower the 'scope to identify my accuser. I might have guessed that it is Peter Duffy. He stands in his front yard further up the road. Perhaps he can train the telescope on the elusive patches for me. I walk toward him to find out.

"Don't you ever work, Peter?" They say offence is the best form of defence.

"It's a down day, Tom," he answers evasively.

"Well, can I ask a small favour?"

"Ask away, s'long as thar ain't no peepin' in it."

"There is actually. I have to locate the berry patches Jeppie Pringle says are on the hillside over there, but I mustn't leave the road."

"You cain't leave our road, Tom? You sure 'bout thet? Our prowler he was no more'n a rumour, an' it ain't quite bar season yet neither."

"My reasons must remain private and confidential, Peter. I hope you will accept that fact as binding upon me." From Peter's expression, I judge that I have struck just the right note.

"Better tell me 'bout this favour, Tom."

"Could you train this 'scope on the patches so I can see them for myself?"

"Thet 'ud be aisiest done frum our place, Tom; rather'n heah. Ah don't wonder you ain't found 'em frum whar you stood. Come on up." I follow him over and into his yard, where he shows me the unmistakable berry patches, unobstructed from this vantage point by any other shrubs or trees.

"That's perfect, Peter. You have saved my day. I can go home now."

"Thet's all fine an' dandy, Tom, but what's this all 'bout? Is it all entarly private and confidenshull? Gimme sump'n ta go on."

"Believe it or not, Peter, I am as much in the dark as you. I am just doing what I have been told. By tomorrow I may know more. In any case I will be sure to let you know. Besides, I couldn't have done this without you, and that's the truth."

I turn to go, waving my goodbye. Peter is looking concerned. But it has been a very long day and I am finding it hard to think about anything more than my supper.

A supper that will also give me the opportunity to get

Granny Phipps' first name straight.

Chapter 25

Supper and a Show

I drag myself onto Flora's porch and into her parlor. The table is set for three. Then I remember that I am still clutching Captain Sullivan's telescope and creep out again to return it to Obadiah as promised. He is pleased to see it unharmed and snaps on its end cap. Unaware of why I needed to borrow it in the first place, he shows no curiosity and I am free to head home again.

As I near Flora's the now familiar howl of Green Hornet mounts from my right. I scuttle for cover, recalling that Shirley has taken no lessons and possesses no licence. She leans her little machine against the porch steps and we mount them together. Again there is no sign of Whassup?

"Does Whassup? not travel well, Shirley? It is quite a while since I last saw him, and you must surely need him with you on this case as much as any other."

"If 'n Ah sets him on Hornet he jumps smack off 'n him agin. If 'n Ah puts him in a tow sack he claws his way straight out. He scoots off afowah Ah kin hang it off 'n Hornet's handlebar. He's home, a-sulkin'. It's his own choosin', so Ah jus' let him be.

"Now, Dr. Watson, Ah'm eager ta know what you done found, but Ah want Flora ta heah same tahm as Ah do. Flora's your mainstay an' support. 'Sides, Ah owe her too; more'n Ah kin repay for this handsome Hornet." She smiles with pleasure, clearly relishing the thought of her new emergency transportation.

Flora, alerted by the sounds of Shirley's arrival, steps out of the kitchen to greet us, and indicate where we are to sit at her supper table. She leaves and returns with our plates of food; so welcome to this overworked researcher, conciliator and berry hunter.

Shirley speaks first. "Flora, Ah done axed Dr. Watson ta hold his berry report 'til you are good'n ready ta heah it y'self."

"Ah declare as Ah am curious, Shirley, but Ah lay odds not half as curious as you. Why don't ye tell us how ye done fared wi' Cap'n Sullivan's telescope, Mr. Watson?"

I tell them where the only known berry patches seem to be. I tell them how Rosie Ross, Jeppie Pringle, and Peter Duffy had all contributed. I tell them how Peter is consumed with his own curiosity as to the cause of it all, not to mention myself.

"Would you say the patches kin be seen frum inside thar homeplace, Dr. Watson?"

I have to reconstruct the relative positions of patches, yard and house in my mind before assenting to the feasibility of this proposition. Shirley looks pleased. Flora looks lost.

"What it is, we need ta keep a close watch on those patches. We need ta see who's a-pickin' 'em. Our letter writer will be one o' the pickers. We kin forget 'bout men pickers. This writer is a woman an' she's an older woman too. We kin forgit about ary young'uns. It's mah b'lief our writer's mos' likely a widder.

"Now, how kin we fix us 'nuff patch-watchin'?"

"I have met the entire Duffy family, Shirley. They might be willing to let their children take shifts in observing those patches. Especially if the job comes with Captain Sullivan's splendid telescope."

"Kin you run out thar fust thing, an' find if'n they'll play?"

"I can, Shirley, and I will. But what do the berries have to do with the letters? I am sure that Miss MacTaggart is as eager to know as I am."

"Patience, Dr. Watson. Patience, Flora. Y'all know how

Ah don't tell a theory 'til Ah have all mah facts collected up. We're close ta the answer. It's jus' one step away. So this tahm Ah done tol' Dr. Watson ever'thin' he mus' know ta help solve our case. An' y'all might kin figger the likely answer frum what Ah tol' him. Why don't y'all try?"

Supper breaks up. I carry out the dishes as usual, giving them a good rinse at the sink. Flora glares at me the whole time. "Mr. Watson, did ye go ta Duffy's arter all Ah done tol' ye?" I have to think on my feet here. No second chances.

"I was plying my 'scope nearby, from the middle of the road. Peter came out to call me a Peeping Tom. Molly came out to apologise. She said, and I quote: 'He was never like this afore we married'. After that I could hardly refuse to meet those innocent children. Can you blame me, Miss MacTaggart?" I have told her nothing but the truth. Alright; except for the actual timing of these events.

Flora sniffs. She and I each go our separate ways, figuring quietly to ourselves. Shirley is thus probably the only member of the party who will get an unbroken night's sleep, content as she invariably seems to be with just her theory.

What with everything else I completely forgot to sort out the Iree-Irene issue.

Perversely I am kept awake more by the absence of the nightly howls from Eddie's choir. I fear they will start baying at any moment, but they don't. Life is so unfair.

Chapter 26
The Duffy's Observation Post

Early, but not at all bright, next morning finds me at the Duffys again, cap in hand.

I wait while they finish breakfast, then ask if I may speak to Peter privately. This is evidently not a mountain thing to do, but Peter tells me to try him and we step outside.

"First let me tell you, Peter, that the berry patch is the last step in solving a mystery that Shirley Combs is investigating. She won't tell me why, because that's not her way. I can only tell you she needs a list of all the women who come to pick those berries. She says there's no call to record men or girl pickers.

"Do you suppose those children of yours could take turns to sit out of sight, watching the berry patches and writing down the pickers' names? If that telescope would help to engage them, I am sure I can get it again."

"Tom, let me talk ta Molly. If 'n she's for it, Ah kin promise the children's help. You know how fond they be o' stories."

I wait outside while Peter goes in to confer with Molly. In no tahm she comes out with him, smiling and excited. "It's jus' what our children need, Tom. Home work has 'em bored out'n thar skulls. This work 'ud be an adventure. When should they start?"

"Maybe one of them can start right away, unless Captain Sullivan's telescope is part of the arrangement." Molly looks at Peter, puzzled.

"Ah din't tell Molly 'bout the 'scope, Tom. Truthfully it din't seem like a needcessity. If this watchin' game lasts too long, then it 'ud surely be handy ta fresh things up a bit. Molly, let's send Tom home now, and we'll dress the job up for the children. They kin fight for who starts and who follers. Now Ah say the front bedroom winder 'ud be best. Nothin' ta distract 'em d'you agree?"

"Ah do, Peter, Ah do. Now may Ah come in an' listen ta what wild tale you goin' ta spin this tahm for our poor, innocent babes?"

Later I learn that Peter's story featured buried treasure, macaws, pirate widows and orphans. It worked like a charm, and within minutes Duffy's observation post was manned and fully operational.

Chapter 27
An Electrifying Episode

Hoping that Lyney will not have left for work yet at this hour, I walk from the Duffy's place over to his. There is absolutely no call to knock as Terry greets me with wild applause before I have even turned into the McEvoy yard. Birty opens the door to see who could be visiting so early. She looks more than surprised to find me; Caney Forks' own representative from the rarefied world of academia. Terry has no such qualms. He keeps barking his wild soprano welcome and jumping up high as my belt in his enthusiasm. I fear for my corduroy trousers.

"Why hit's Mr. Watson. Are ya heah fer Lyney?"

"If I am not too late, Birty, or too early, for that matter."

"Ah'll tell him yar heah. Ya might kin set on thet ol' trunk the while he gits hisself drest." She points needlessly to the massive fallen oak filling half of their front yard. Beyond it I see a few of Flora's old grave markers. I sit down hoping Lyney won't be too long at his toilet. I am more than ready for a nap in all this non-stop rush.

Good, here comes Lyney. "Mr. Watson is hit? What brung ya out so early?"

"I happened to be in the area," I begin lamely, unable to disclose why, of course, "I must belatedly thank you from the bottom of my heart for putting me onto Eddie's 'Hounds of Heaven'. Their singing is astonishing. Eddie has done something truly unique. And Ben Cochran too, I suppose. I would have been here before to express my gratitude but

I succumbed to a bout of brain fever which confined me to my bed.

"Now here is my problem, Lyney. No-one is going to believe my report on Eddie's extraordinary pioneering achievement without some hard evidence. Eddie himself confirmed that his performances have been banished to the hills, where indeed I heard for myself what those amazing hounds can do. I have no funds to transport them to a studio for a recording session, but I do own a portable tape recorder. In fact I was leaving Obadiah's reception to get it for recording Jess Tully and Fred White, when Eddie caught me and hauled me off to hear his hounds.

"At the reception I could have plugged my machine into any wall outlet, and at once recorded that duo for the whole world to enjoy. But how can I make it work out in the woods, Lyney? That's the question.

"I am no electrician, but I suspect that a qualified man could rig that recorder to a car battery, say, or more particularly the battery of a pick-up truck capable of going up the mountainside to Eddie's choir practice place. Can you think who might serve?"

"Fust off, Mr. Watson, Ah'm real pleased ta hear how well ya thought on them houn's. An' Ah does see why ya needs ta git 'em on record like. But ya mus' know thar's not but the one pick-up in town as works atall, an' hit's Ben's. Kin ya git 'long wi' him better'n befowah he done showed ya his part in the trainin' up o' them houn's?"

Here I am, embarrassed by my judgmental biases again, but Lyney makes a good point. I try to recall if I praised Ben specifically, or just their joint breakthrough. Probably not. So that is where I'll have to start.

"I was full of praise for their achievement, but I don't believe I singled Ben out. I do recall making both he and Eddie laugh like maniacs when I had to ask what song the hounds were singing."

"Oh, they don't know but the one song yet, Mr. Watson. The whole holler is plumb tired on the joke. Hit might could a holped ya had ta axe him. Ah reckon hit won't hurt none if 'n ya go see Ben. Tell him 'bout yer brain fever an' praise his part in the show. He ne're did set much store bah hisself. The leastest praise means more ta him'n most folks. If 'n he softens up then try him 'bout them electrics."

"Thank you for your good advice, Lyney. I shall do as you say. I hope I haven't made you late for work."

I still find it hard to decipher mountain facial expressions at such junctures as this, but at least Lyney does not seem in any way miffed.

After a late breakfast, I cross over to Ben Cochran's. His old pick-up stands in his yard, along with heaps of rusting parts. I can see nothing amongst these of an overtly electrical nature...but one never knows.

Ben is at home, looking as cross as ever, but he accepts the reason for my delay in praising him for his part in creating the 'Hounds of Heaven'. "Well, Ah does enjoy playin' mah elbow pipes, even if folks aroun' heah cain't nohow live with 'em. Eddie says mah pipin' is the one kind as works on them houn's, Mr. Watson." There; for the first time, he has acknowledged my name! I must strike while the iron is hot.

"What you and Eddie have achieved is quite extraordinary, Ben. It deserves to be heard by a much wider audience than Caney Forks alone. But we are in a tough spot for making this happen. As the hounds aren't welcome in town, and we can't afford to ship them to a recording studio, we need a third way. I have a portable machine on which we could record a performance, but since you only practice in the woods, I couldn't just plug it in and switch it on. We would need a way to power it out there. Now I am altogether ignorant about electricity, Ben. How about you?"

"Ah may could fix hit ta run off'n a batt'ry. Whar's yer gadget?"

"It is over at Miss MacTaggart's, if you want to take a look."

"Gimme a minute, Mr. Watson. Ah'll walk on o'er with ye."

Five minutes later, Ben has my recorder opened up. He is poking around inside it with gay abandon. He still hasn't replied to my question about his electrical abilities. I keep my fingers crossed that he will not put it out of service for normal use. After who knows how long he straightens up, wipes his brow and points a grimy finger:

"This heah's whar Ah might could fix a splice, an' thar's whar Ah mought drill a hole fer a batt'ry connecshun, not hupsettin' her reg'lar plug-in ways neither."

I take these generalizations to be good news. But I do keep my fingers crossed in case of entirely possible misinterpretation on my part.

"Lemme see what's a-settin' o'er thar as might could do fer this convertin'. Thar's so many places ta look Ah dursen't say how long hit might could take." If ever I heard Appalachian understatement, this has to be one for the books. I prepare for my nap.

Who knows at what time Ben returned? His tinkering wakens me, as he sorts through a collection of worn parts from a disintegrating old carton and checks their fit. He mutters as he works, reading from a grimy booklet. "Durn residual ripple..." I hear, or something like that and, "Idlin' power waste...reduce doggone losses...holt thet switch in the off." Those are clear enough to me but then he launches into a sentence worthy of Robby Burns. I know I have this right as he everlastingly repeats it to himself: "Equivalency series resistance increases with age." I am reminded of my father. Can this really be electrical talk? Is Ben going metaphysical on me?

I am not sure if Ben knows I am watching him at work, but he does at last address me directly: "She's ready ta trah, Mr. Watson. Whar's yer batt'ry?" He has completely missed the point.

"I never expected to need one," I tell him, "and Miss MacTaggart only ever had the battery in the Green...Mack's old motor scooter. Which is no longer on the premises."

"Ah've plenny dead 'uns, Mr. Watson. The only live 'un

sits in mah pick-up an' Ah hain't a-goin' ta pull hit out fer nobody."

"Perhaps you wouldn't have to, Ben. Have you ever driven your pick-up in the woods and up the slopes? I recall how unhappy you are with the way it rides, but might that not be how it got that way in the first place?"

"Mos' sartainly hit was, Mr. Watson. Ah sure hain't goin' back ta them days neither. Mah ol' sweetheartin' days as they war." He looks positively wistful.

"We are in quite different times now, Ben, and you have a once-in-a-lifetime chance to make Eddie and yourself famous. You have this one opportunity to change your life completely...if only we can make this recording. Does anyone else in town have a live battery we can borrow, or are you your only hope, if you see what I mean?"

Even a casual observer could see how deep Ben is in thought. His frown lines ripple, deepen; his hands twitch, pointing this way and that; his teeth grind with the sheer effort of his concentration as he struggles to break free of his self-imposed prison. He is the epitome of resistance increasing with age. The minutes pass, add up, caught in Ben's private web of indecision. Now he turns away.

"Ah'll do hit." His voice is choking. "Ah taken more'n Ah kin on feelin' sorry fer mahself. Ah'll do hit." He wipes a grimy sleeve across his eyes, bends to pick up my recorder, with its new ligaments trailing, and heads out to his pick-up. "Leave hit ta me, Mr. Watson," he calls over his shoulder.

I must be a born reformer; first Obadiah and now Ben, both transformed by my motivational speechifying. The 'Hounds of Heaven' recording is as good as in the can, subject only to the practical proving of Ben's electrical know-how.

As I settle down to resume my interrupted nap, I wonder idly where Flora has been, why Granny Phipps has not shown her face, and whether anyone has yet made the Duffy's list of suspects.

Chapter 28
Surprise, Surprise

Next morning a mollified Flora lets me lie in for a bit to recuperate from yesterday's stresses and strains on my feeble, foreign, flatland constitution. I contemplate the ceiling, on which I review my mental list of works to complete. Recording the hound choir takes pride of place. Then it's a toss-up between auditing Robby Burns' musical compositions and checking on the Duffys' progress. Oh, and then there is the highly recommended Miss Mary McRory still to interview. Not to mention various others who are by now thoroughly jumbled up in my mind.

But no sooner have I swallowed the last bit of my late breakfast than I hear Flora receiving a most unexpected visitor. "Why come on in, Meg," she says, louder than necessary, no doubt by way of forewarning me, "or shall we set out on mah porch?"

"Flora," says the witch, ducking the question, "Ah's heah ta holp Mr. Watson on his reesuch." I drop my fork in alarm, recover it and clear the breakfast table for battle.

Flora leads the old trout in, saying: "Meg has come ta help ye, Mr. Watson, if 'n she's tahmly." She notices the table. "But Ah see ye have yer famous notebook ready. Why don't ye set y'self down heah, Meg, acrost frum Mr. Watson. He kin tell ye how he likes ta proceed." I open my notebook in dubious anticipation.

"Proceed, is hit, Mr. Watson? Ah was jus' o'er ta Obadiah's a-collectin' mah widder's mite fer Sally's buryin'. He

The Curious Case of the Conjure Woman

was in sech good spirit Ah axed him did he win the lott'ry. He tole me 'bout how ye done set him a-right, Mr. Watson. Thet was a real kind thing ye did fer 'im. Ah come ta say sorry fer callin' ye a TV reporter, an' Mr. Clever Boots." I hold my breath, but she doesn't say a word about Red Riding Hood. Anyway, Flora is out on the porch now, waiting for Granny Phipps to show.

"Mos' folk roun' heah don't pay me no heed, Mr. Watson. Likely becaise Ah hain't ne're done holt wi' small talk. But Ah has mah troubles, like Obadiah. Ah has more'n a story fer ye than ye mought reckon". Those were pretty much Flora's own words about Meg at our first meeting. I sit up and take notice.

"Heah in Caney Forks, we'all is Pentecostal. Now ye mought think hit's a church an' a buildin', Mr. Watson, but hit hain't. Pentecostal hit's pure experience, all raw an' real. Hit comes one pusson at a tahm. Hit comes right heah at our Church of God wi' Signs follerin' fer those as practices handlin' on serpents an' a-drinkin' pizen. Ye bein' sech a perfessor mought look hup the Gospel on Mark, Chapter 16, verses 17, 18. Hit's all thar on them Signs an' those as b'lieves in his name bein' hempowered an' pertected bah God. An' a-layin' hands on the sick along on hit, Mr. Watson."

"Did you say poison, Miss M'Sweeney? This is all new to me, I can assure you."

"Ah quotes frum Mark agin: 'An' when they drinks deadly pizens, hit will not hurt them atall'. Our faith hit's innerpen'ent, Mr. Watson. We fixes all our own stuff. We has ta, fer Satan is the god on this world. He's bound ta run mos' all on the religions out thar which anywise is all confused bah folks choosin' sides. Thet's his job. Our'n is ta foller the Signs, as George Hensley done tol' us when he done started hit all hup."

"Coming back to drinking poisons, Miss M'Sweeney, I don't recall seeing any sign of such activity at Sally's buryin'..."

"Ye fergits the reception, Mr. Watson. Remember our

church hit's noplace. Hit's in each hindividual Pentecostal experience. Kin happen anyplace." Oh my God! Is this what the moonshine is all about? My notes are going all scrawly and illegible.

"Tell me the proper Pentecostal name again, would you please, Miss M'Sweeney."

"'The Church o' God wi' Signs Follerrin', but we'uns druther say C.G.W.S.F."

"Ah. I think I have right it now. The 'following' part is a noun, not a participle."

"If 'n ye say so, Mr. Watson. Ye's the scholar." I change my notes to a capital F.

"I can't help feeling doubtful, Miss M'Sweeney. Do you really mean to tell me that the relevant authorities allow snake handling and the drinking of poisonous beverages?"

"Hit depen's which State ye's in, Mr. Watson. Tennessee an' Kentucky they has laws agin' snake handlin', but we heahs they don't do nothin' 'bout 'em. Now thet Constable Collins, we'all hain't sure on his thinkin'. An' his bisickle hit's of 'en broke. Ah mahself draws the line at a couple renegade snake handlers as stick thar fingers in them 'lectrical slots. Them slots is strick'ly man-made. We'all's lucky thar's but few on 'em neahabout.

"Ah's hurt too bah the ban on female Pentecostal preachin' an' hinspirin'. If 'n Ah kin take keer on snakes atween worships, why cain't Ah handle 'em thar mahself, tell me thet, Mr. Watson? Hain't hit bad 'nuff a whippersnapper brother like Howie kin come in an' do what Ah do better an' more faithful like? Ye seed how nervous he gits at buryin's. Thet boy hain't wuth beans. Ah b'lieve they only uses Howie on account he's free."

"Things do change, Miss M'Sweeney. You ladies have far more rights now than before I was born. But if Mr. Hensley is still in charge, why not petition him for special consideration?"

"Thet's aisy said, Mr. Watson. This is a man's world. Why 'ud Ah waste mah tahm on letter writin', if 'n Ah may kin git hit a-fixed heah."

"What do you mean by fixing the problem here? How do you think that might be done?"

"Well, Mr. Watson, ye done fixed Obadiah's problem. He had his fer yeah arter yeah, jus' liketa mine. Kin ye put a word in his eah?"

"I will be happy to do that, if you really think it might help. But have you stopped to consider how much bigger your contribution is already? You keep those snakes fed and watered and safe between services, and your work hours must be infinitely longer than Howie's. Surely the community feels far more indebted to you than to Howie. Most especially after his latest performance? Have you tried asking folk? You might be pleasantly surprised at what they have to say.

"If you will start doing that, I will talk to Obadiah. Now if I may change the subject, do you have any musical interests, Miss M'Sweeney?" She bridles, hesitates...

"Yes?"

"Only if 'n ye promises not ta make no notes an' ne're tell nobody..." This is tough on a researcher. It leaves me no choice.

"I will so promise, provided that you in turn will undertake to make no mention of little Red Riding Hood, as you so diplomatically refrained from doing on your arrival today. That incident must remain forever between you, me and Jimmy Fanaghy. It was his idea, not mine, and it must never get out."

"Alright, Mr. Watson. Ah admit playin' the flute ta them snakes...jus' like they does in Hindia. Hit hain't allowed heah in snake handlin' circles on account hit takes the hedge off of 'em. Ah does hit ta keep them poor critters content in thar wee prison."

"Then it is entirely to your credit, Miss M'Sweeney. You are a far better person than I had believed until now. It is an honour and a pleasure to know you."

Meg softens and essays a shy smile. What can I say? Dale Carnegie was nothing but a novice compared to yours truly.

The bad news is that my to-do list just got longer, and what's more, Meg hadn't even been on it this morning.

Chapter 29
Comings and Goings

Her goal accomplished, Meg looks itching to take her leave.
I stand and squire her to Flora's front door. There is no sign
of Flora, and I realise I have not heard Iree-Irene Phipps
arrive. Perhaps Flora has gone looking for her associate.

I then help Meg down the porch steps and into the road.
Before I can frame an encouraging farewell to my rejuve-
nated guest, a shrill, jerky voice calls my name. It is the eldest Duffy girl, waving a sheet of paper and sprinting better
than any draft-dodging 'Bar'. She hauls up breathlessly while
Meg and I respectively give her jealous and inquiring looks.

"Why, it's er..." I stutter, lost between her two possible
names.

"Millicent," says Meg.

"Milly," huffs the girl, as emphatically as her breath-
starved voice allows. But her resentment comes through
clearly enough. At her age, I suppose it must be important
for everyone to know exactly who she is. Molly would recognise this. But what about Peter? Milly's breathing slows.
She has been thrusting her sweaty paper at me, and now
demands:

"Don't you want this, Mr. Watson? We'all figgered you
war in a hurry. It's our first report, d'you see."

"Would you please excuse me, just one minute, Milly?"

"Well, Meg, I am so glad you came over and that we
could have our meeting. I shall look forward to hearing what
other folk tell you about your invaluable services, and you can

rely on me to sound out Obadiah. But I do think it would be much the best if you can give me people's opinions first. If you do that I can present these to Obadiah in support of your petition.   Goodbye and good luck to you, Meg.

"Now we are all clear, Milly. Please step on up and let's take a look at your paper." I take the crumpled sheet from her and smooth it out on the ashtray table. Reading between smears of purpleish jam, sweat and grey fingerprints, the left hand side consists of a column of names, each separated by a couple or so inches. In descending order these read: Ian, Jennie, Milly and repeat all the way down to the foot.

"Those are our shifts, Mr. Watson. We take two hour watches. It's easier for me than for Jennie, an' 'specially Ian. He's a big fidget. But we got you some names, see."

I do see; Eliza Jane and Alice Knox, plus another name fiercely scribbled over.

"Who is the crossed-out person?" I ask.

"Oh, it was Miz Combs. Ian said she was ridin' a motor sickle, jus' like Mr. Reardon does. Daddy said she didn't count, but he wun't tell us why. He's like that some tahms. It allus makes Ian cross. That's how the grape jelly got on the paper."

"Eliza Jane and Alice Knox. Hmmm...I have only met them once. I can't really picture them. Would you call them older ladies, Milly?"

"Oh, yes, Mr. Watson, real ol' they are."

"And they both gathered berries, did they?"

"Yes they did, 'cept Miz Jane cut whole huckleberry stalks. It took her no tahm atall. Miz Knox gathered her blueberries jus' like you said. She put 'em all in a li'l bucket. I saw 'em both with my own eyes. Jennie saw Miz Knox too. She came to take over afore Miz Knox was done." So the stalks in Flora's jar may have been dropped by Eliza Jane, whatever this might mean.

"This is excellent, Milly. Please tell Jennie and Ian that you have all done very well.

Tell them to keep up the good work. I hope they still

have their hearts in it?"

"They do, Mr. Watson. P'raps we'll have more names for you tomorrer. Anywise, nex' tahm Ah'll send Ian. It'll make him feel important and keep him at it."

"You are a bright girl, Milly. One day I hope to be able to tell you what this is all about, and exactly where your contribution fits in. Now please take your tahm going home, and give your Momma a special 'thank you' from me for your efforts." I wave goodbye and turn to go back inside, but a familiar klaxon raspberry cuts the air cheekily. The hooter is Ben Cochran, parked across the way. He must have been waiting for Milly to leave. How considerate of him. What a change!

I walk on over to him. Is this the Ben I know? He looks decidedly un-Ben-like. More than that, he looks years younger. Is there no end to my gifts? Ben sits tight in his driver's seat, looking pleased as Punch. I notice my tape recorder bridging the gaps in the remains of his passenger seat. Wires run from it over the dashboard and under the bonnet. Ben doesn't say a word. He stares directly at me, closes one eye, taps the side of his nose, throws a switch on my recorder and pointedly puts both hands in his trouser pockets. Is he humming under his breath?

I jump at the sudden new blare from his klaxon. Ben's hands haven't stirred from his pockets. How the..? He is smiling now, smiling fit to bust; quite unrecognisable.

"Ah tol' ya leave hit ta me, din't Ah? What yer thunk?"

"I...er...do you mean to tell me that was a recording?"

"Hit was, Mr. Watson; more partic'lar hit was a recordin' Ah done made a couple shakes back. Jus' as Miz Milly lef' an' yaself was 'bout ta go on in."

"Then you are a genius, Ben. It's wonderful. What do I owe you for parts?"

"Ya hain't no way beholden atall, Mr. Watson. Ever' las' bit done come out'n them heaps in mah yard. Jus' don't keep me a-waitin' now, ta git our hound choir recordin' in the can, as they says. When kin ya git hit done?"

My to-do list is whirling around in my head. I feel like a helpless swimmer born along on a raging torrent. I can't afford another bout of brain fever. "Why don't you see when Eddie can set up the next performance. I will fall in with his timing, Ben. That's a promise." I make a mental note to write this commitment down.

"Now if you will excuse me, Ben, I must catch up with my note writing. It has got so far behind that I could start to forget things."

Taking his hands from his pockets, Ben cranks up and drives off with a cheery wave.

I mount Flora's porch for a deeply deserved nap. This turns out badly. My mind keeps worrying about Shirley's visit to the berry patch. Did she just want to check my location information? What other reason could she possibly have? Does she still trust me?

I do finally get my notes up to date, but I feel they suffer unduly from my distraction.

Flora returns, puts together a scratch supper and hears my summary of the day. She seems distracted too, but expresses her pleasure that Meg and I have made a peace pact. She compliments me on my further progress and abruptly calls it quits for the night. It strikes me that for Flora, a day without Iree-Irene Phipps' company counts as a day lost.

Chapter 30
Miss Mary McRory

Morning breaks. The sky is clear. Alright, here's the plan: while I wait for the new hound date and the Duffys' second suspect list, I can call on Robby Burns. No. I can't. It isn't raining. He will presumably be off up in the woods somewhere. That leaves, let's see... the elderly Miss McRory. Flora has emphasised how much information this worthy has for me, and that I shall need to call on her to gather it. Certainly Miss McRory had not looked too steady on her pins at Sally's burying, so I shall do the gentlemanly thing, and visit her.

It is so awkward having no telephones, but I was glad when Flora told me over breakfast that Miss McRory is quite the stay-at-home. Her directions are for me to pass Shirley's turn-off, then walk about a quarter mile farther, where I will see the McRory mailbox on my left. "Hit's a bluebird painted on." She is still determined I not get lost in the woods, prowler or not.

Is it my imagination, or does Flora have an unaccustomed glint in her eye? What does she know? What is she not telling me? Does she anticipate something out of the ordinary from my McRory interview? Well, I am going to find out soon enough. I stow my notebook and head out.

The day is especially humid. I find the walk to Miss McRory's quite demanding.

How ever did she make it to the cemetery and Obadiah's reception? And in her black clothes too. She must have a great store of will power. I can hardly call that a common quality in Caney Forks, always excepting Flora and maybe Eddie MaCafferty. Thus, when I reach the faded sign of the bluebird and turn in, I realise that I am looking forward to this meeting more than most.

In her cabin, shortly after my knock, Miss McRory draws aside a curtain to see who is calling. It seems that she remembers our previous meeting:

"Come on in, Mr. Watson. Flora's bin a-tellin' me ta expect ye. Ah'm real glad ta see ye heah finely. Won't ye set bah me at the winder? Ah spend mos' days in this ol' chair. Thar's few 'nuff folks pass mah way, but when they do, Ah like ta know who. Mah life is ver' lonesome, ye see, since Elmer done went ta his reeward."

"Elmer, you say, Miss McRory; would he have been your husband?"

"Yes, indeedy, Mr. Watson, an' a fine, hupstandin' man he war. Not frum these parts atall. He took sech a likin' ta me he upped stakes an' done come live heah. Ah do miss him mos' sorely."

"I am sorry to hear that, Miss McRory. I do sympathise with you. I will admit that I too feel lonely here at times, with all my friends so very far away. But at least I can remind myself that it is only for a year, and then I can return home."

"Might would ye keer fer a glass o' hice tea, Mr. Watson?"

"Yes please, Miss McRory, in fact I can think of nothing nicer after my walk here."

She rises stiffly and hobbles over to open her oak ice box, in which two glasses stand ready for callers. She brings one to me and returns to fetch her own. I take a sip.

"This is delightful, Miss McRory. It is exactly what the day requires. Now, Miss MacTaggart says you have much to tell me, so let me cede the floor to you."

"Mah late husband he was frum clear out'n state. Wes' Virginny, frum a place ye might could reckernise. His hometown was Elkins. So was his name." Mary pauses for dramatic effect. I stall in sheer bewilderment. Racking my memory, I can recall telling only Shirley about my birth name. Did she tell Miss McRory? Are there no secrets in Caney Forks? Except from flatlanders, foreigners and outsiders, of course.

"Well, I'll be damned, Miss McRory. I thought my real family name would be safe with Miss Combs. My name change is a source of continuing distress to me. I have to say I am rather disappointed to find my secret betrayed in this fashion."

"Hit hain't no way betrayed, Mr. Watson. Ye kin be sure'n sartain hit's in safe han's. Shirley knowed what a fine man mah Elmer was. She thought best ye know too. She din't think harself the right person ta tell hit. So she tol' Flora, in strictest secrecy, mark ye, an' Flora she done tol' me. Don't ye git why Flora she bin a-chivvyin' ye ta come see me? The two on us mought aisy be related." My mind staggers at this concept. How do I extricate myself from such a morass without hurting Miss McRory's feelings?

"Miss McRory, my father wanted—in the worst possible way—for me to be related to the President of the soulless IBM Corporation. Now you want me to be related to you, by marriage. Have I got that right?"

"Hit hain't so sumple, Mr. Watson. Fust off, Elmer an' me ne're could tie the knot. Ah's Pentecostal an' Elmer, he war Cath'lic. Then too, Elmer doted on mah McRory name. Thet oughta be 'nuff ta set ye straight, Mr. Watson." Wait! Flora! Flora, who strongly disapproved of the supposedly unmarried status of the Duffys. Why is she so clearly complicit in Miss McRory's never-married widowhood?

"Are ye listenin', Mr. Watson? Far's relatin', hit's more thar ain't nuthin' beats good blood. Elmer had plenny on hit. He had hisself more'n 'nuff ta go roun' an' then some.

"Elmer din't know naught 'bout his hancestors back in yer British Hisles. Leastwise, if 'n he did he ne're said one word on hit. Now Ah'd be proud bein' part o' thet mahself. Mos' mountain folks they don't want nuthin' ta do wi' thar roots. They says 'good riddance'. Ah ain't one on 'em, Mr. Watson, no sir." She draws herself up in her rickety wooden chair. The McRory jaw takes a firm set. She has me pinned right down. Her own blood must be pretty hot stuff.

"I would be pleased and honored to help trace our possible connection, Miss McRory. However, I am sorry to say that my own father signally fails to value the Elkins name. My mother is a broken reed and, as an only child, I have no other family members whose aid I might enlist. I am truly sorry, but to conduct any serious research from here, on top of my main mission, is quite out of the question." There. That should stop this misguided enterprise right in its tracks.

"Don't fret y'self, Mr. Watson. Ah know what ye come heah fer, an' Ah say more power ta ye. All Ah need is yer say-so ta git Elmer's brothers an' sister a-started on the trail. Ever' one on 'em reads an' writes. Ah know what a thrill hit 'ud give 'em workin' on mah deah Elmer's fam'ly tree. They kin start right thar at home. Elkins hit's a big railroad place an' has hits own liberry. Kin Ah say fairer?" This lady should be negotiating for the United Nations, not stuck on the outer edge of the middle of nowhere. Relieved, I draw my first easy breath and nod enthusiastically.

"You have my willing permission to do all that, Miss McRory. Shall I put something in writing?"

"Bless ye, no, Mr. Watson. Howsomever, whene're we'all is in private like now, Ah'd be so honoured if 'n Ah mought call ye by yer real name, Mr. Elkins."

"I am quite amenable to that, Miss McRory. Now is there any other information you would like to share with me?" She brightens at my invitation.

"Thet 'ud be Elmer's songs, Mr. Elkins." I rub both ears hard with my hands.

"Songs, Miss McRory? Did you say his songs? Do you mean songs that he wrote?"

"Indeed Ah did, an' Ah does, Mr. Elkins. 'Course now he's gone, all Ah has is his notes. They're heah in this drawer, ever since thet sad day o' his passin'." She rises to open a drawer in her old pine dresser. She takes out a sheaf of loose papers to hand me. "Take a good look, Mr. Elkins. Hain't nobody but me seen these papers frum the day he done wrote each on 'em."

I have made a find worthy of Cecil Sharp himself; years' old, unpublished mountain songs in the composer's original handscript. What can I say? I am too overcome to attempt any kind of response. Swarms of black dots crowd my vision. I feel all limp. I collapse into...nothing...

"Mr. Elkins! What all's the matter? Had ye a sinkin' spell did ye? Say sump'n."

Where am I? Someone is patting my face. I struggle up from the floor and ease into a chair. Did it give way? I look. No, I did. What a feeble fellow I am.

"D'ye feel more gayly now, Mr. Elkins? May kin Ah fill yer glass agin?" Oh, that quavery voice is Miss McRory's. I am sitting in her window chair, surrounded by a litter of handwritten music and lyrics. I am close to Heaven, but not yet in the company of their late lamented composer.

"Ye needs sump'n' in yer stomick, Mr. Elkins. Ah need bring ye roun' proper." She hobbles back to her handsome ice box, opens its heavy door and ferrets about inside. "This 'ull serve," she quavers. "Ah might could do wi' a bit on a pick-me-up mahself." She fiddles around some more behind the door before backing out with a tin bowl in each hand.

"Alice Knox come on bah wi' these—yestiddy, Ah think hit was. Tho' why she brung so many more'n Ah done axed her Ah plumb cain't think."

I look at the bowl before me. Blueberries; they are definitely blueberries. Delivered by suspect Alice Knox? This development can only complicate Shirley's calculations.

I had better visit her to report this, on my way back to base.

"Ah knows how good these be fer a body, Mr. Elkins. Hit's jus' plain luck they're heah atall. Thar's li'l else in mah hice box. When Elmer died he done took his railroad pension along a him. Lef' not a thing in the world fer me, 'ceptin' his writin'. Ever' day's a struggle. Ah ain't no complainer. But hit's a plain fac'."

"Then I wonder if you shouldn't put my berries back,

Miss McRory?"

"Ye's real kind ta say so, Mr. Elkins, but Ah wants ye feelin' proper when ye mus' leave. More pertick'l'ly Ah want ye 'preciatin' jus' how much yer visit means ta mah poor, lonesome soul."

I eat up gladly, like the good boy that I am evidently becoming, eager to look through Miss McRory's late consort's musical manuscripts.

Chapter 31
The Goldmine

Our berries finished, I rise to carry the blue-stained bowls to Miss McRory's big, stone sink. I stoop to gather the scattered pages from the floor, tap their edges into a neat sheaf, set this on the table and open my notebook. Here it is; the moment of truth.

The topmost sheet is clearly a continuation. I riffle through the rest until a likely first page shows. This is titled, "The Caboose". It is undated. I try my best to hum along to the written notes. Although my rendition leaves much to be desired, Miss McRory exclaims, "Why, Mr. Elkins, ye soun' liketa a train. Tuppity tup, tuppity tup, tuppity tup."

She is right. Now, what about the words? Well, to paraphrase; a train is nothing without its caboose. Just a succession of waggons and cars, full of coal maybe, but empty of meaning. Myself, I would vote for the locomotive any day, but what do I know of the American railway system? Wrong again, Tom; here is Mr. Elkins' reason. The caboose is the social centre of any train. It houses the guard and brakeman, plus an ever-changing assortment of card players and crap shooters (whoever they may be), both invited and uninvited, but born partygoers to a man. It's a red-letter day when storytellers join them, which they do from time to time. Eureka! I have found the Holy Grail!

"What you have here is a goldmine, Miss McRory; an honest-to-goodness goldmine".

"Ah's so happy hearin' ye say hit, Mr. Elkins. Ah of 'en

wunnered is they good or is they nuthin' special?" She looks suitably gratified.

"This one is very special, Miss McRory. Now let's see what's next."

I turn to the third sheet. It is headed, "The Stoker," and has no date either. This tune is harder to hum; less melodic, more percussive. But Miss McRory is waiting.

I try my best, but this time even I notice that my humming sounds more like swearing. Is this possibly the idea? Again the lyrics come to our rescue. But do we really need telling that feeding a locomotive's firebox is grueling, thankless labour? Or that it's all the worse when the air temperature is in the nineties and the world is wrapped in high humidity. Just ask Cecil Sharp. Oh, God, I hope Cecil didn't...

"When did your late husband write these, Miss McRory?"

"Well, Mr. Elkins, he done brung the most on 'em wi' him, but as ye go thru' 'em Ah kin tell ye which he done wrote heah." Alright, but did Cecil range as far away as West Virginia? How can I be sure this material is all of it unpublished? Questions and yet more questions. Some I won't be able to find answers to here in the mountains.

I look at the next page. It is another continuation, but its first page soon turns up. It is simply headed "Mary." I glance at Miss McRory. Her face is working. She is losing control of it. Out of respect I look away.

"Yes... hit's me. Thet'un...he wrote...heah." She is sobbing. I allow her time to settle herself. Have I perhaps overstayed my welcome?

"Miss McRory, I am feeling rather better now. In fact I am absolutely elated by what you have shown me. But there is no way I can review all of these sheets today. Why don't I leave you in peace for now? We can always resume later." She nods her assent wordlessly. I soon let my rejoicing self out into the noonday warmth, so much easier to take than firebox heat.

Five minutes later I turn left at Shirley's mailbox. The

Hornet is parked in her yard, so she should be home. Yes; she answers my knock, peering through her unconfined locks to see who I am.

"Dr. Watson, step right on in. Don't mind Whassup? now; he's still all in a snit." He is in fact staring at me scornfully, as though I were in league with the hated Hornet. I bend to tickle him behind the ears, but he ducks and stalks off, full of lordly disdain.

"Shirley, I want to report a complication in the berry watch program."

"Yes, Dr. Watson?"

"As of yesterday there were two qualified suspects: Eliza Jane and Alice Knox. I have just come from Mary McRory, who received a delivery of blueberries from Miss Knox; only yesterday, as far as she can remember. She told me she had requested it. I have seen them with my own eyes. I have even eaten some of them. Is that all right?"

"Ah 'preciates your concern, Dr. Watson, but it don't matter none, anymore if 'n we have us more'n one suspec'. Ah shall add Miz McRory ta mah list right away."

"Thank you, Shirley. I feel better about it now, but I do have another concern. It is of a personal nature."

"Ah hope you din't mind how Ah tol' Flora 'bout your real birth name, Dr. Watson. We both knew how much it 'ud mean ta Miz Mary. D'you see?"

"I do see now, Shirley, and I agree. However, I arrived in Caney Forks with one name and title. As of today I have three. I am starting to lose track of who I am."

Chapter 32
A Prodigal Daughter

This has been an emotional day for me. I reach Flora's too late for dinner, and too drained to contemplate my remaining to-do list. Flora is gossiping in her kitchen with...yes, that's Iree-Irene's unmistakable, fawning voice. I have to know which, but it can wait. I tiptoe upstairs and collapse on my bed. My notes can wait. I yawn. I dream a child is drowning. This child, who cannot swim, cries pathetically for help. I am paralysed. I can do nothing. The child's cries redouble. I awake. The cries do not stop. They are coming from the road. I rise from my rumpled bed and go to my open window. It is none other than Ian Duffy making all this noise.

"What's wrong, Ian?" I ask sleepily.

"Here's our new report for you, Mr. Wasson, but Ah cain't get in." He waves it at me.

"Wait a moment, Ian. I'll come and open up." Where the hell is Flora?

Down below I beckon Ian in. He is gripping his report so tightly it takes a while to release it from his sweaty palm and smooth it into legibility. Meanwhile, Ian keeps shouting, "Larkie Langmuir, Larkie Langmuir!" He seems to specialise in shouting.

"Who is this Larkie Langmuir?" I read this name writ large and crudely against Jennie's.

"Milly says Larkie lef' town years ago, an' never came back. Jennie she called for us when she couldn't figure who the picker was. Milly tol' us that's who she is, a-pickin' away an' eatin' an' eatin' like she was starvin'." Goodness gracious!

"What else did Milly say?"

"How Jennie's likely the first person ta see Larkie in a coon's age."

"And just what does that mean, Ian?"

"Ah don't rightly know, Mr Wasson, 'cept it's an awful long tahm ta be gone."

"Her's is the only name on your list, Ian. No-one else has been gathering today?"

"Daddy says Larkie may be the last, Mr. Wasson. He told us take a good look all over the patch. None of us could see a berry worth pickin' after Larkie 'ud gone. What shall we do now?"

"You have all done very well already, Ian. I don't believe you need to keep a lookout any longer, but I do think I'll walk back with you and see what your Daddy has to say. Shall we do that?" Exhausted as I am, my curiosity about Larkie Langmuir is winning out. It is a weakness I seem to share with Shirley's other assistant, the self-estranged Whassup?

Self-estranged? Come to think of it, isn't that the way I have been behaving here? At least until recently? Then I notice Ian, skipping along in front of me, all fired up with the excitement of his role in a real-life mystery, helping a foreigner from so far away. This makes me feel less of a stranger and a little less worn out. Not far now.

Ian runs ahead into his front yard. "Daddy, Daddy, Mr. Wasson's heah!"

Before I can catch up, Peter appears. "Welcome back, Tom. Ain't mah children done well?"

"As well as professionals, Peter. They seem to make a good team, too."

"'Deed they do. Now what kin we'all do for you?"

"Perhaps we should go inside to discuss it, Peter." He leads us in and we sit down.

"Firstly, do you agree with Ian that the berries are all picked, Peter?" He nods a yes.

"Then your children can presumably be excused from

keeping watch for the time being. Now what can you tell me about Larkie Langmuir, if I have her name right?"

"Well Tom, we ain't seen hide nor har o' her these five, six year. She jus' took off one day. No warnin', no note. Ah missed her a whole lot fust. We war kindred spirits, you see. She was christened Li'ly, but it warn't long afowah ever 'un called her 'Larkie'. An' not always smilin' 'bout it neither. She played so many tricks mos' folks war glad ta see her gone, though you'd find none as 'ud admit it.

"Life got so borin', Tom, Ah jus' had ta step inta her shoes. Ah know mah duty, like you know your'n."

"The big question has to be whether she is passing through, or has come back to stay.

"If she has no home here, how do we answer that, Peter?"

"You live on top o' Flora an' Iree, Tom, an' you ask me. You think they won't know in a Caney Forks blink?" He is right, of course. How long is it going to take me to become a natural member of this community?

"Well, let me get back, Peter, so I can start listening in to the porch gossip. Then we'll know if Larkie qualifies as a suspect or not."

"I doubt it, Tom. If you only knew how thet woman's mind works, you would too. Shirley's your only hope, mah frien'." He pulls out his tin whistle with a smile, and plays a brisk hornpipe to speed me on my baffled way.

Halfway back I realise I could have asked Peter if he said Iree or Irene. Hang it!

Chapter 33
Supper Is Late

I have dragged myself back, hungry now as well as weary, to find an empty porch and still no sign of Flora. I settle into one of the rockers to catch a nap.

For the second time today a voice wakens me. This time it's Flora's. She looks as fired up as Ian had.

"Ah have some big news fer ye, Mr. Watson. Jus' let me fix supper fust. Then ye kin heah all 'bout hit. An' you kin tell me what-all ye done terday y'self." I shut my eyes again. Every little helps in this exhausting place.

Flora says it's flannel cake, cornbread and buttermilk. I would never have known. Once she has set it out, Flora starts up:

"Yer likely ne're a-goin' ta b'lieve this, Mr. Watson. We got us a new resident. Leastwise she's mos'ly new."

"Don't tell me, Miss MacTaggart! Would her name happen to be Larkie Langmuir by any chance?" Flora looks quite taken aback. Uh oh...I have just spoiled her scoop.

"So ye do b'lieve me, Mr. Watson. Thet's a blessin', but Ah pride mahself on bein' fust wi' the news in Caney Forks. Ah need ta know who done tol' ye 'bout Larkie."

"It was Ian Duffy who ran over with the new berry watch report. Apparently Larkie cleared out the whole patch, clean as a whistle. To hear him tell it, she must have been absolutely starving. So I followed him back home, and Mr. Duffy filled me in on how Larkie had left town so long ago, with no warning or reason."

"Well! Larkie had reason a 'nuff. She was a real bad'un fer pullin' tricks. She use ta put folk's backs hup all the tahm. Thet Peter Duffy o' yer'n, he larned his jokin' style right frum her. Hit was real hard on us, havin' the two on 'em a-practicin' tricks an' ever huppin' thar boldness. One day Mr. Duffy really outsharped hisself—Ah hain't sayin' how—an' nex' mornin', Larkie she's gone. Hit must a bin a full blown fit on jealousy, Mr. Watson, is all Ah kin say."

"Do you suppose Peter knew that, Miss MacTaggart?"

"Hit might could be so. Ye done tol' me he said she lef' wi' no warnin' nor reason. Ah think he figgered hit all out alright. But now he's got ta be a-catawampus, ye mought say." She gives me one of her appraising looks followed by a lengthy wink.

"Now, Mr. Watson, whar d'ye reckon Larkie done settled?" Ah, so she is staying.

"I am unqualified to do anything more than make wild guesses, Miss MacTaggart."

"Ah'm glad ye say so, Mr. Watson. Ye use ta be sech a know-it-all, folks was as cautious aroun' you as aroun' thet Peter Duffy." So in Flora's eyes my reform continues unabated. This insight invigorates me. I no longer feel so much need of a third nap.

"Larkie has moved in with Mr. Reardon, perhaps. Equally in love with him and his big, muddy motorbike. Just a shot in the dark, Miss MacTaggart." Flora gives me a long, withering look. Inspiration strikes: "All right then, how about Festus Fraser? Larkie wrote those nasty letters." Flora giggles. She actually giggles! My oh my, she is showing signs of reform herself.

"Hit's no less likely nor thet, Mr. Watson. Of all the folks ta pick, Larkie took up wi' thet wrong-headed Eddie MaCafferty an' his houn's." Did she, by Jingo, but why?

For the first time I realise I have no idea where Eddie lives. You never hear his hounds voicing in the holler, and Flora would have told me if his home were in the next holler, with Jeppie and Constable Collins. She is giving me her funny look again.

"Ye ain't got no ideah whar Eddie lives, do ye, Mr. Watson?"

"I just realised it, Miss MacTaggart. Are you going to tell me?"

"Ah reckon ye 'ud dearly love ta know, but thar's a problem. Ye tol' me how he done blindfolded ye 'long the way ta his choir practice. Leastways ye did in yer fever. Why do ye reckon he did hit?" I shrug and spread my hands.

"On account his homeplace hit's a big secret."

"In that case, how do you know that Miss Langmuir is with him, Miss MacTaggart, and how did she know where to find him?"

"Ye ne're heared o' gen'ral d'livery mail, Mr. Watson?" I shake my head.

"Hit's fer folks o' no fixed address. When a gen'ral d'liv'ry hits the holler, Jeppie Pringle spreads the word. Even ye kin surely see why. The one frum Larkie caused a stir, as ye'd guess. Ah tol' Shirley. She's bin a-pokin' aroun' ever since. Ah have, too."

So that's where Flora has been. And why Eddie's secret is safe with her...for now.

Chapter 34
Dr. Watson Investigates

Early next morning I am yet again deprived of my lie-in. This time my alarm is the approaching howl of the Hornet. All this disturbance to the natural quiet of the hollow! If it's not hounds howling, it's Shirley's steel steed. I dress in haste and, unshaven for the third day now, I descend.

"We'all is on the porch, Mr. Watson."

At what unearthly hour does Flora rise? How does she manage so consistently to keep at least one step ahead of me, regardless of the subject? In the final analysis, I suppose it is no more than her being a mountain woman. What had she told me: 'It will be aisier fer ye when ye're one of us?' Something like that. So I must change my personna from academic researcher to mountain man. The idea is growing on me.

"What all is a-keepin' ye, Mr. Watson? Ye kin fergit breakfast. We need ye heah. Shirley says fetch yer notebook."

Appropriately equipped, I drag myself onto the porch. Shirley has kept her Hornet helmet on. Those strands of red-auburn hair wreath it daintily, making her look more captivating than ever. I inhale a lungful of Caney Forks morning air and rise to my full height...the one Obadiah had correctly identified upon our first encounter.

"At your service, Miss M'Gonaughy, notebook at the ready."

"Good mornin' ta you, like ways Dr. Watson. Ah trus you have slep' well."

"Well, Miss M'Gonaughy, but not long. I have just been

telling myself I need to render my life easier by adopting your mountain ways, and I am committed to that end."

"You could start bah savin' breath, Dr. Watson. Ah could a said what you jus' tol' us in half 'n the words. Shorter ones too. But Ah mus' say you're doin' well in other parts. Flora says the same.

"But Ah din't come ta tell you so, Dr. Watson. Ah am heah ta axe your help. Thar's a li'l matter you kin handle aisier'n Ah might could. Please make a note on it. Ah need a sample o' Mary McRory's han' writin'. You kin decide the bes' way ta git it, all nat'ral like. If 'n she's the letter writer, Ah don't want her a-worritin' any, d'you see?"

"Ah does, Miss M'Gonaughy...I mean I do. Leave it with me. I shall bring you a sample today, on my way back from calling on her."

"That's mah boy," says Shirley, sending a rush of blood to my face in quite the most embarrassing way.

"Ah'll git yer breakfast now," says Flora, to my infinite relief. She is a mind reader if ever I met one. The bad news is Shirley gits, I mean gets onto the Hornet and howls away, perhaps to comfort the unhappy Whassup?

After breakfast, as soon as I have cleared and rinsed the table things, I head out to Miss McRory's, hoping for a quick win, so I can beat the mid-day heat and humidity.

Miss McRory answers my knock surprisingly promptly.

"Why hit's ye back, Mr. Elkins. Ye're a welcome sight fer mah tired ol' eyes Ah kin tell ye. Won't ye step on in an' set y'self down bah mah side." The song scripts still lie on her table. Now for my cunning pitch:

"I can't stop thinking about your late husband's songs, Miss McRory. They are the biggest thing to happen to me here. You will remember promising to tell me which he wrote in Elkins, and which here. So far you have clarified three for me. Now this distinction is so important to me, I have come to ask a very special favor.

"If I sort the rest of the pile into separate and complete songs, could you please look at each, write its title on my notebook page here, and put an 'E' or a 'CF' by it. This way I shall know, now and forever, where he wrote every one of them. Could you do this for me, please, Miss McRory?"

"Jus' ye go ahead, Mr. Elkins. Pass me each 'un as hit's ready. Ah'll do jus' as ye axed. If 'n Ah gits a bit weepy, Ah hope ye'll unnerstan'."

Miss McRory plays her part to perfection. I am intrigued by the old, Dickensian, steel-nibbed pen which she uses, dipping it frequently in an equally ancient ink bottle. After many carefully inscribed entries she starts a second notebook page. By the time we are done I have counted four dozen songs. What a treasure trove!

"I cannot tell you how grateful I feel, Miss McRory. I do hope your part was not too distressing." She shakes her head, but won't look at me. Impulsively she rises shakily to her feet to visit her ice box. She takes out a little pail and divides some of its contents between two bowls. Bringing these to the table, she looks more composed as she sets them down.

"Hit looked ta me as ye enjoyed mah fust blueberry treat a whole bunch, Mr. Elkins. Why don't we'all have us a sec-on' fixin'? Like Ah tol' ye, Alice brung more'n Ah kin use on mah lonesome. Ye'll be holpin' me bah eatin' 'em hup." I don't need telling twice.

Miss McRory eats her share, but with a distant air. Then she looks straight at me and announces: "Bein' as ye're ma-kin' a speshul report on Elmer's song writin', Ah'm a-goin' ta share his secret 'bout how they war writ. Hit was Elmer's discov'ry in Elkins as he could pound up blueberries an' boil 'em down fer makin' his own hink. He kep' toppin' up his store-bought bottle as he done wen' along. These fust few songs look writ a li'l darker on account o' thar bein' some real hink lef' in his mixture yet."

My mind is working overtime at this revelation. Some-thing like this must have been at the bottom of Shirley's unspoken theory in this case. I am in at the kill, just me, all on my own. But 'kill' is an unkind word to use in any con-nection with this lonely old mountain woman, even though she has to be the prime suspect. I bring the emptied bowls to her sink, like last time, and prepare to leave.

"Unless there is any more information you would like to add, Miss McRory, I will take my leave. I can't wait to study the wonderful details you have given me. The part about Elmer's ink is very special. I have heard of Elmer's glue, but never the ink." She gets slowly to her feet and drops me a curtsey. I pick up my notebook, with it's two precious sheets, give Miss McRory my best attempt at a bow and start for Shirley's.

Whassup? is at Shirley's door when I arrive, scratching to be let in. He looks up at me, not with a baleful glare this time, but still not yet himself. Before I can knock, Shirley responds to her other assistant's resumed scratching.

"Come on in, Dr. Watson. Tell me what you done foun'."
I enter and head for the cane-bottomed chair to rest my moist, overheated frame.

"Take a look at these two pages, Shirley. Then I'll tell you about the best part of my visit." I hand her my opened notebook. For the first time I notice that she already has in her hand the letter she borrowed from Obadiah. If that isn't a solid sign of her confidence in me, then I am a Dutchman. Not Flora's forbidden Black Dutch—just regular, common or garden Dutch.

"Mary's song notes they're written jus' like her letter heah. It's the same hand for sure.

"Do you see how she has the strongest motive, Dr. Watson? She is so lonely, an' she sets out thar on the far edge o' the holler. 'Deed you mus' have felt it in your visits."

"I did, Shirley. In fact my first visit told me the whole story of her situation. But the credit goes to her, Shirley. She was so frank with me from the start."

"Well thar it is, Dr. Watson. D'you see how Ah have taken you ovah not jus' fer recordin' mah cases, but ta aid direck'ly in mah inquiries?"

There is no question that Shirley has taken me over;

lock, stock and barrel. I can only speculate why she has chosen to call me by my full title of Dr. Watson. And why we are sitting in 221B, not number one as it should logically be; how Whassup? gained his name, and why he is feeling so out of things. That old Green Hornet was only part of his problem. Well, you can't make an omelet without breaking eggs.

Enough of that. I come to my senses. "The best part is how Miss McRory learned from her late husband how to make a sort of ink by boiling down pounded blueberries. Can you beat that?"

Shirley's eyes sparkle. "Thet's not so hard ta figger if 'n you smell the letters or if 'n you notice how pale the writin' is. Ah never saw the likes of 'em befowah. They do say thar's a fust tahm for ever'thin', don't they?

"Did Mary tell you Elmer's railroad pension had no part in it for survivors? You kin add poverty ta her motives. Mary's ideah must be ta get Festus 'nuff of a raise for the two of 'em ta marry on. Did you know she an' Elmer were too far apart in thar b'liefs for marryin'? Ah kin sure see how Mary 'ud like bein' hitched prop'ly ta a man of her own b'liefs afowah she passes on. As to that, think how Festus, he's a buryin' expert.

"You did real well on this case, Dr. Watson. Let me tell you how Ah am fixin' ta settle it. We both pay Obadiah a visit. We tell him what-all you done foun' out. When he sees how it's a case of love, he'll give Festus his raise. The only problem lef' is it's Mary mus' do the proposin'. In the end, it mought be good that Festus never could be happy on his own.

"Now what d'you say 'bout a li'l dinner afowah we go on over ta Obadiah's?" I nod keenly.

I can't wait to find out how Shirley cooks, and what she cooks, or how it is to share a meal with this mountain beauty. She goes to her ice box. In no time she is setting her table with goodies and a now familiar jar of corn liquor apiece. We take our places.

"Don't you be bashful now, Dr. Watson. Jus' help y'self."

I start with the cold meat morsels. "That's rabbit, mayhap a scrap o' squorr'l." I add a long, white rooty thing, which may be parsnip. "Take good keer how you eat that 'un, Dr. Watson. It's mountain radish. Hot as you could ever want." To play safe I choose peas, and what looks to be multicoloured cabbage slivers in a thin, pale, vinegary sauce. "We call that coal slaw. Ain't nothin' holdin' you back thar." That's easy to say but what on earth can you make out of coal for eating? Maybe this kind of cabbage grows in those disused mine shafts? Wait, did she say 'coal' or 'cold'? I sample a morsel. Yes, it is cold, and tasty too. I am hungry enough to eat it all up and do.

She senses my doubting. This would be difficult if she were my wife, but of course, she is not. Then again, it would be so very wonderful if she were.

Chapter 35
We Make Our Plea

The slaw produces no adverse effects. When our meal is done I bring the plates and cutlery to Shirley's sink, and rinse them in accordance with my reforming ways. Shirley stares at me with her green eyes. And stares. Ulp. What have I done?

"Dr. Watson, you are house broken! Thar's few 'nuff men in our hollers as 'ud do what you jus' did. Ah am real glad for you. But tahms a-wastin'. Let's try Hornettin'."

Whassup? comes from wherever he has been hiding. He looks disoriented and slinks back indoors.

Outside, Shirley contemplates Green Hornet. "Let me get a bit o' paddin'," she says; to herself, I suspect. She ducks back inside and reappears clutching what looks like a bath towel, a faded green one. She rolls this up loosely and puts it behind her saddle. "Set y'self on that, Dr. Watson. Let's see if 'n Hornet kin carry the two on us." Oh boy! Trumpets sound in my head. I pray the Hornet will not balk at the load. Otherwise my heart rejoices at my luck. It's not just being spared the hot walk to Obadiah's. It's much, much, more than that.

I mount my roll of green towel and steady Hornet for Shirley, leaning back to give her room to board. We should really have done this in reverse. She brushes against me as she mounts. My heart sings. We did it the right way round after all.

"Get a holt on mah waist, Dr. Watson. Ah don't want you a-tumblin' off now, do Ah?" I most certainly don't want to fall out of Heaven, now that I have arrived.

Shirley starts Hornet with commendable ease. I encircle Shirley gently with my arms, trying to make myself as light as possible. The Hornet moves. I lift my legs. We are off. Hornet is making a throatier noise than usual, but keeps right on going.

Never in my whole life have I so much enjoyed any kind of ride. Sadly, this one ends at Obadiah's entrance. I dismount. Shirley manouevres Hornet into the shade and pulls him onto his kickstand.

"Was your ride alright, Dr. Watson?"

"I never had a finer one in my life, thank you, Shirley. Never."

"Then we better find you a helmet, han't we?" My heart jumps. There will be more heavenly rides with Shirley. But for now, we have a job to be done for Miss McRory. Obadiah must have heard us. He is standing in his doorway.

"Is thet new bike o' yer'n alright, Shirley? She soun's diff'rent-like today."

"He was carryin' a li'l extry weight, is all." I see that Obadiah has already worked the situation out to his satisfaction. He beams at me and sweeps an arm inviting us both into his cool interior. We sit on three chairs in a triangle.

"We do have news for you, Obadiah, but a couple questions fust. Did you ever wonder why you never done married?"

"Thet's all too aisy, Shirley. Folks is a-feared o' my perfession. Hit don't make no sense, but hit's Gospel. Ah soon give up a-tryin' ta court."

"Ah'm real sorry ta heah it, Obadiah. Though Ah unnerstan' all too well. Same way as folks are a-feared a me too. Now d'you reckon you kin answer the same question for Festus?"

"Ah kin, Shirley, an' Ah answer the same. Hain't no diff 'ren' atall. No ma'am."

"Well then, tell me how you'd feel if 'n Festus had hisself a willin' partner."

"Fact is, Shirley, Ah might would flat-out discredit hit. An' second, too. Hit hain't no ways reasonable."

" Ah agree as it don't seem likely, but truth is Festus has 'un, b'lieve it or not."

"Now who in thar right mind 'ud want 'im, Shirley?" He is bordering on severity.

"Obadiah, it's the woman who's bin a-writin' those pesky letters."

"How in tarnation kin ye tell, Shirley?"

"Ah know it thanks ta Dr. Watson heah. He done boiled our suspects down ta three. One is all wrong, the secon' is real unlikely, an' the third has all but confessed. He has done collected all the evidence Ah need ta point mah finger square at the culprit."

Obadiah looks long and hard at me, in a not unfriendly way. "An' who 'zackly is this crazed culprit, Shirley?" He sounds a bit impatient, as though we might be teasing him.

"Mary McRory herself. The letter you lent me is her han' writin'. The ink she wrote with is made frum blueberries. She even done tol' Dr. Watson how ta prepare it. Do you need ta know more, or are you content?" Obadiah goes all quiet and introspective on us. At last he sighs and asks why Mary would do such a thing.

"Dr. Watson and Ah agree acrost the board: she's lonely; her home is beyond the pale, an' she's poor as a mouse. Most of all, she yearns ta be truly married afowah she gets ta be one o' your customers, Obadiah."

"Hit's not hardly likely, Shirley. Ah mean, do she an' Festus git along? Ah ne're done seen 'em together, an' Ah done my share o' watchin'. Wi' Cap'n Sullivan's 'scope."

"Ah ain't sure Festus knows aught of it, Obadiah. Mary ain't goin' ta speak up less'n she thinks he's paid 'nuff for them ta marry." Obadiah drops back into his pensive mood. Probably weighing the odds of our story being true. Then running the numbers in his head to see if he can afford to be a matchmaker. He ponders on and on. Shirley never takes her green conjure woman eyes off his face 'til he jerks bolt upright.

"Ah b'lieve Ah kin do hit, Shirley, an' Ah will. Jus' gimme a couple days ta git at mah bank. Yer know hit's o'er ta Hutchins Court House." This has turned into a re-run of the hard decision I had forced him to make on his own behalf. I suppose mountain life can make people really set in their ways. Or maybe the lack of ready money is more responsible. Then again I can think of no-one more inflexible than that complacent Surbiton resident, my own father. Over here it is much easier to appreciate his difficulties.

"Ben kin fetch me ta Hutchins, Shirley. Ah'll fill his tank. An' Ah'll tell ye how much Ah kin help Festus, soon's Ah'm back."

"Obadiah, you are the bees knees, which Flora has tol' me Dr. Watson heah would tell you, if 'n he was payin' attention." I feel an electrifying nudge from her knee. Right:

"I second that, Obadiah. I can tell you that it is a great compliment." Our host softens visibly and tells us both how glad he is that we uncovered this love story. That we gave him the chance to contribute to the future couple's happiness. He brings out three jars of the local potion and we drink to seal the deal. I hope Shirley can keep her balance on Hornet, as she drives home.

But I have little such trouble, walking on air back to Flora's.

Chapter 36
Robby Burns' Turn

It comes to me in the depths of the night that I had failed to present Obadiah with Meg's plea for his petition. Of course, I hadn't been myself. I had been under Shirley's spell. But that is no excuse. I must make amends in the morning. First thing.

Now wide awake, I picture Shirley and I chatting and laughing, riding and strolling.

But where am I going to find the time? Granted that Mary's case is on hold while Obadiah hitches a ride with my chauffeur. Oh...if Ben is with him at the Court House— wherever that is—he cannot be my mobile recording studio. On top of that downtime, Eddie's plans have most likely been upended by Larkie's arrival. I have first-hand experience of this sort of upending. The delay to our joint project could be...indefinite.

That leaves Robby Burns, whose song writing has admittedly been elbowed from my mind by Elmer's. Robby, who toils somewhere and secretly in the woods all day. I rise to stick my arm out of my bedroom window. Pity. It's not raining. Excepting my Meg mission, will daylight bring my second day off? Come to think of it, my first had only amounted to a half day. But half or whole I must contrive to spend at least some time in the company of my very own conjure woman. I ponder how I might gain such a sweet success. I search in vain for a starting point. The same difficulty always rears up in my path...I cannot dissemble with my Shirley.

Even without her 'magic' powers I cannot bring myself to do such a caddish thing.

I toss and I turn. Suddenly there is a sharp rapping on my door. "Mr. Watson, ye done overslep' agin. Shame on ye!"

"Do I have a visitor?" I ask, looking for my clothes. They are not in their usual places.

"No, Mr. Watson, yer goin a-visitin' y'self. Ye'll be late less'n ye git on movin' right smart. Thar's coffee a-waitin'. Ah'm makin' ye an okry sandwich ta eat on yer way."

"Where am I going, Miss MacTaggart?" I ask as I pull on my trousers and bend to put on my shoes.

"Mr. Watson! Ah set ye a meetin' tahm wi' Robby Burns, jus' as Ah tol' ye Ah'd do. He done agreed ta take his mornin' off, but mind me well, only becaise Ah promised ye 'ud keep yer meetin' tahm in bounds. Thet's why ye need ta be quick... oh, heah ye are."

As I swallow my hot chicory water I ask myself why all the rush. Mountain folk speak slowly, live slowly, so why not me? Is it because I am not yet one of them?

Chapter 37
Robby's Revelation

The holler is no place to do the least thing unobserved. Or not do it. I have to eat Flora's okry sandwich. By the time I stand at Robby's door a digestive battle is raging within me. My host must have been keeping a lookout for me as he opens up before I can even raise a hand to knock.

"Good mornin', Mr. Watson, or may Ah say Tom?"

"You may indeed, if Ah—excuse me—kin, I mean can, I call you Robby."

"'Course you kin, Tom. We're birds of a feather don't you reckon?"

This first-name stage would take years to reach back in England. And, yes, I know I am not. I am here in the mountains. Could first names be my fast track to becoming one of them? Robby breaks my reverie:

"What you ponderin' on so hard an' far away, Tom? Kin Ah help?"

He is a good fellow. I must give him a chance. "Several of you have told me that I must become a mountain man myself to understand y'all best. Is first name usage a part of the process?"

"It is, Tom, signifyin' folks' mutual trust an' respec'. Ah once read how in England it's plumb ta the contrary. Is it true, Tom?"

"You are quite right, Robby! I see it now. Instead of winning folks' respect I has—I mean 'have'--been keeping them at a distance. Am I right?" Robby nods and keeps nodding until he slaps me on the back, grinning with pleasure.

"Considerin' your handicaps, Tom, you've come a long ways on your road. You may travel a li'l closer yet when Ah show you mah song work. Now will you have a coffee or a jar?"

"Could I possibly have both, Robby? A drop of 'shine in my coffee?"

"Sure you kin. Thet's more like it; no false front, d'you see? You spoke what was on your mind. We mountain folk 'ull do it so ever' tahm, Tom. You're a quick larner, whether you think it or not."

He wastes no time getting mugs and jars on his table, then toasting my progress with a jar clinked against mine. His sheaf of writing sits between us. He takes the top sheet and turns it to face me. I take my first look, especially curious to see what Robby means about moving me a bit closer on my way. This sheet has a dedication written across the top: 'for Ben'. The title is 'Mechanical Sorrow.' The lyrics run:

You are a model T painted black...
The choke wire hangs out of the radiator...
The crank hangs in a sling.
Starting you is not easy.

Once started you are dangerous.
You are always slightly in gear.
Your brakes are marginal.
There is a risk in riding with you.

You are not exactly comfortable.
You have leaf springs but no shock absorbers.
Your tires have inner tubes
and are not puncture proof.

You get us there.

I glance at Robby. He does not look like a man who is teasing. "That rusted truck used to be black? Did Eugene McCarthy ever visit Caney Forks? How else could he describe Ben's pick-up so accurately? Ben too, for that matter.

He is, or was, a poster boy for mechanical sorrow. Confess, Robby. Did you write this poem yourself?"

"Ah did not, Tom. Thet would of bin a real false front, an' we don't do 'em heah. Remember what Ah jus' said?" I do, but still feel that in this case my temptation was both exceptionally strong and entirely understandable.

"Ah picked this 'un for aptness ta Ben an' his ol' truck. On thet account, Ah kin see how your mistake was quite natural, Tom. Ah shall let you off with a warnin'. Thet's 'bout all Constable Collins ever tells us holler folk.

"You'll not likely guess nor believe for whom Eugene wrote the piece. Ah will tell you straight off: his fellow poet, Robert Frost." Caught clean off balance, I try to juggle the dichotomy in my mind: Ben and his pick-up versus Robert Frost and his 'road less traveled'. It's just a no go. I drain my mug and try to relax. Robby is watching me with concern in his eyes.

"Let's keep movin' along, Tom. 'Mechanical Sorrow' may be aisier for you ta follow if 'n Ah sings it." He rises to fetch his fiddle; sits down to tune it. In all this humidity I'll be surprised if his tuning outlasts his song. But it does, and how!

Robby's bowing starts in mournful vein, building toward the song's last line like Ravel's 'Bolero', but in notably slower motion. His voice reinforces the mood, bursting into gladness only at the happy ending; Eugene and Robby in easy harmony.

"I see what you're doing, Robby. It works out extremely well. But how are you going to popularise such a song? It's so very far from the mainstream."

"Thet's the way we'all are in the holler. Far from the mainstream. Mah songs aren't for the music world. They are jus' for the folk they fit. This'un goes ta Ben. It fits his elbow pipin' style. Folks do call it kinda dirgey an' Ah don't say thar wrong.

"Take a look at the nex' sheet, Tom, an' tell me who Ah wrote it for. You'll know." I pick the page up and find that Robby is right:

"Ian Duffy! You...kind man." These lyrics read:

Saturday is a whale
It swallows people
for three days
Saturday is the sphinx
It has a locked secret
Its smile is inscrutable
Saturday is a Castro convertible
It is closed all day
Saturday holds its breath.
Saturday, if it comes
could last forever

"Eugene only has the one whale in there as against five Saturdays. Aren't you leading Ian on a bit?"

"So far you jus' read it, Tom. Now listen ta the song. Most folk like Saturdays. Saturdays are the key ta this tune." He picks up his bow to play and sing. Sure enough each Saturday starts on a very low note, leaps up and plunges down again. Just like whales do. In between li'lt some amusing twiddly bits. The effect is really catchy.

"Now how d'you think Ian 'ull like it, Tom?"

"He'll love it. You know, you have a rare gift, Robby.'"

"Ah thank you, Tom. Let me show you a diff'rent one. It's for all the folks in the holler. Eugene calls it 'Wednesday.'" This time he dispenses with my reading the lyrics and jumps straight in with fiddle and voice:

Today Ah will walk all the roads,
All the paths of the woods.
Ah will work at ploughin' an' plantin'
Help with harvests.
Ah will build houses an' barns
Make hinges an' handles,
Tables an' chairs.
Ah will untangle yarn,
An' watch weavers at work,
Pick apples in ol' orchards

Bless abandoned farms,
An' all places where hollyhocks grew.
Ah will write a poem,
Before it is Tuesday.

"You said Ah have a gift, Tom. What we'all do wi' gifts heah is pass 'em on.

"Tom, is your throat parched as mine? Ah'll fetch us a refill so we kin rest up a bit. Let me give you a chance ta ask some of your reesearch questions". He brings out a large jar. His replenishing done, a few sips later he says, "Ah'm ready an' waitin'."

"What you have achieved, Robby, is so different from my expectations that not one of my routine questions applies. The pieces you have presented are so modern, so personal. I don't know how to place them. I love them but they confuse me, Robby. Where do I start?"

"Love!" sighs Robby. "You put your finger on mah hurt. Love confuses any man. Ah truly need this, Tom." He up-ends his jar and empties it, Obadiah style. It seems to take him far away. He doesn't move a muscle. Is he actually in pain? Before I can frame my question, he draws himself up in his chair.

"Sorry, Tom. Ah was some other place a minute. Are you ready for another? Another song Ah mean? Take a peek an' tell me who this'un's for." The peek he allows is so brief I can only read the first line and make a snap guess:

"Daisy Devlin?"

"Who's a genius now, Tom? Check line five on the second stanza." I do and there I find written, 'of daisies and asters'. Score two for the visitors. Robby replaces the sheet in front of me and I read beyond that first line:

Whiteness alone, not light
holds back the punctual night.
I have walked through Spring
white against green,
of anemone, laurel and thorn,

searched the pale mist of plum,
put my hands on the tangled skein
of wild cherry.

In my passing, I scattered
the scant white of Summer,
the wind drift of willow and thistle.
My knees knew the white
of daisies and asters
that spin in the wind
in the Fall.
I waded thigh deep
in the dry foam of milkweed.

Robby has coloured up considerably watching me read. "Oh how Ah want ta git mah hands in thet 'tangled skein o' hair'. Ah plain shake at the thought of 'thigh deep'."

Oh, Robby is a goner. Daisy is too much of a flirt for his kind.

"Ah kin fit a tune ta any folks Ah know. Ah kin pick a piece of Eugene's ta match, but how kin Ah tell Daisy what's in mah heart, Tom? She's sech a butterfly 'bout aught the least bit serious."

"Robby, I am too much the bachelor to be of help to you there. But your problem was all too common among my fellow undergrads at Oxford. The word they have for her type is 'flippertygibbet'."

My mortified host groans, "Mah poor Daisy Flippertygibbet, she is good as orphaned. Her 'doptive parents are in the Court House jail for larceny". He sinks his head onto his outspread arms; a complete goner if ever I saw one. There'll be no more research today, no more questions. I'll just finish my jar before I let myself out.

Chapter 38
Ben's Revelation

I haven't gone fifty yards from Robby's place when a mounting racket assails me from the rear. Swiveling in alarm I behold Ben Cochran's once black model T pick-up truck swiftly bearing down upon my defenceless, slightly squiffy person. There is the choke wire; there is the crank, both looming clearer by the millisecond. I jump for my life. Ben is standing on his marginal brake pedal. Li'l by li'l, as they pronounce it here, the brake shoes grip whatever is left to grip. The contraption shudders to a halt, no more than a foot from my feet.

"Looky heah, hit's mah new frien' Tom Watson. Hop in. Ah'll tell ya ever' bit o' news ya need know." Gathering my shredded senses, I stumble to comply. Even before I am properly seated, Ben begins:

"We has us a couple problems, Tom Watson. Ah kin mayhap solve the one. The other'un hain't no way near as aisy. Ah jus' bin tryin' ta git mah truck up whar we'all runs our houn' singin'. Them slopes hain't changed a whisker, but mah motor hit sure has. She's done lost all kind a compression since mah courtin' days. The reg'lar fix 'ud be backin' her up. Hit's the lowest geah, y'know. But how'd ya feel y'self, backin' uphill wi' all them trees ever' which way? Ah cain't afford ta risk hit." I know just what he means.

"Is there some reason why the recording has to be made in the same place as before?"

"Truth is, thar hain't, Tom Watson, but what other place

'ud serve? Tell me thet."

"Perhaps Eddie kin, Ben—I mean can."

"Well thar ya has our nex' problem. Eddie, he's in no shape fer thinkin' nomore."

"And why is that, Ben?" I think I know what's coming, but this holler has surprised me too many times already. I see why Shirley waits on hard facts.

"Hit's a woman, Tom Watson. Hit's thet Larkie woman. Folks done call her so frum the git-go. Fer good reason, too. Her whole life hit's bin a lark. Now Eddie he's all cotched up in her larkin'. He acts like he's havin' a real good tahm, but Ah hain't so sure. Fer starters Larkie's eatin' him out'n house an' home. Ah'm who's a-feedin' his houn's, or they'd be runnin' off ta hunt thar own vittles. Whar'd we'all be then?"

"There does seem to be an outbreak of woman trouble in the holler, Ben, but I am the last person to sort it out, I can assure you." Ben looks frankly dubious.

"Well, Tom Watson, Ah done heared the contrary 'bout ya doin's 'mong our women folk. Ah do b'lieve if 'n ya mought visit an' see ya'self what-all's a-goin' on, ya might could find us a way ta fix hit."

"And how am I to visit, Ben, if Eddie's home is such a secret?" Ben grins at this.

"Ah knows Eddie tied a blin'fol' on ya eyes fust tahm. Ah kin tie knots good as his. What ya say, Tom Watson?" I must have my hound choir recording, Larkie or not. I have no choice:

"I'll do it, Ben. Do I need an invitation or do we just pick the time and go?"

"Eddie ne're din't invite nobody. Hit's up ta the both on us, Tom Watson."

"Then if you'll drive me back to Flora's, Ben, I'll grab a sandwich and we can start."

Flora is visibly put out by my skipping dinner. She finally compromises by tipping my meal wholesale into a punnet and adding a spoon. In the meantime Ben begs a bit of blindfold material from her. One way and the other I feel badly for Flora.

"We are grateful for your patience with us, Miss Mac-Taggart. Two problems have come up simultaneously. I must nip them both in the bud with all possible dispatch."

"Another o' yer speeches, Mr. Watson--but short an' only two fancy words in hit. Ah am happy seein' ye so improved." I'll gladly settle for that under the circumstances. We exit with thanks all round and board Ben's Model T for the first leg of our journey. We park almost opposite Obadiah's. Ben leads our way uphill at a more sensible pace than Eddie did on Sally's burying day.

I am barely winded when, like a scout cautioning a column of troops, Ben holds his hand up. "Ya better had on this blindfol' now, Tom Watson." He takes my arm for the rest of our climb, keeping me from even the slightest scratch. Do I perhaps hear hounds whimpering, above the sounds of my twig-snapping, leaf-scuffling feet? I keep mum.

Long before we stop for Ben to restore my vision, sounds of merriment float to my straining ears. No doubt they emanate from our destination. It's a funny world; the day Eddie press-ganged me from Obadiah's reception, we left all the merriment behind us.

Eddie's abode is hard to spot until we are within thirty yards or so. Like a giant bivouac, constructed from heavy branches, stripped and clad with spreading fans of cedar, it looks a natural feature of these woods. Until, that is, a shrieking woman bursts through a gap in the cedar fans. Eddie is close behind, flicking at her with a wet towel. Like a matched pair of circus horses, they pull up together at the sight of us.

What should I do? What should I say? Where can I hide? My treacherous mind forms a perfect blank.

Chapter 39
Shrieks and Giggles

It's Larkie who takes the initiative: "This jasper, he your brother, Ben Cochran?"

"Ya knows Ah's orphaned, Larkie, neah's makes no matter. He's mah good frien' Tom Watson. Ah thank ya not ta fergit he's mah frien' an' ta know as he's Eddie's frien' too." Larkie giggles and looks me over brazenly:

"Why y'all heah? Ah don't recall sendin' no invites. Don't tell me y'all's lost."

My turn, now that I have my head straight: "Miss Langmuir, I am an English post-graduate researcher, here to study and report on the lifestyle of local mountain people."

"How 'bout thet, Eddie? He thinks Ah'm a Miss Langmuir." She bends over in a fit of laughing, too helpless to continue. But she can't help asking, between gasps, "Don't this 'un talk funny, Eddie? Funnier'n any flatlander Ah has ever heared, an' will you look at his fancy pants. How kin we'all tell if 'n he ain't dang'rous?" And I had once thought Eddie dangerous.

Eddie steps in: "Mind what Ah tell ya, Larkie. We'all owes Mr. Wats'n, a deal o' thanks. He aims ta make us all famous. Ya should treat him perlite. Don't go sendin' him off now. Do thet an' we'uns mought stay no account folks evermore."

Larkie flashes me a brilliant smile, flutters her lashes, sways and simpers...if that's the right word for her sudden display. If she's trying to disarm me, she might as well give up right now. Shirley's the only one for me.

Eddie is looking at me, distinctly uneasy. "Ah reckon ya wond'rin' when we kin git all set fer recordin', now Ben's done fixed the problem on doin' hit out o' doors. He's a thinkin' man, is Ben. Ah won't stan' ta see his work go fer naught."

"What about me?" asks the simperer. "Don't Ah count, Eddie?"

"Ah wants ya ta be famous too, Larkie. We jus' needs figger the bes' way on hit. The four on us might should be able ta plan hit out. Does y'all want ta set out heah fer a pow wow, or inside?"

Larkie takes the lead: "Let's stay heah, Eddie. Wait up while Ah fills 'nuff jars o' shine ta git us tee-totally hinspared." Unlike everyone else, she isn't shy to name our beverage. Giggling, she ducks into the bivouac. We roll a few logs into a circle and wait for our promised 'shine service. Eddie finally goes to find the cause of its delay. We hear him scolding Larkie for trying to get ahead of us in the realm of 'hinspiration.' His lecture only serves to provoke more giggles. In a perverse way I am quite enjoying myself.

There is no hiding the fact. Larkie is a champion trouble-maker. She won't take no for an answer from anyone. We shall have our work cut out to find her a part to play which doesn't ruin our quest for fame...tee-totally, was it?

Chapter 40
The Pow Wow

Eddie opens the meeting. He calls it a round-table. I sincerely hope that will be its tenor, even if the table is missing. "Larkie she needs her a part. Thet's whar we'all starts. Ben an' Ah conduc's. Mr. Wats'n runs his recordin' machine an' Larkie she jus' larks about. Thet don't add nothin' an' sure as all git out, Ah don't want her ruckus noway innerferin' wi' mah houn's singin'. Ya see the problem, Larkie? Ah don't mind ya bein' famous, but ya cain't git in our way a-doin' hit."

Larkie somehow manages to look serious. It doesn't suit her one bit. "Ah wants you happy, Eddie. You knows it. Now let's say if'n Mr. Wats'n's recordin' gits us any stage bookin's, Ah reckon Ah could lip sync for y'all."

"What's thet ya said, Larkie? What ya mean by hit?" Eddie is lost.

It's my turn at the round-table. "In filming, when your beautiful star has a poor singing voice, the studio films a good singer performing each song. Then your star watches these takes until she can perfectly mimic the body language and lip movements for every number, in exact time. Then she is filmed acting this, without making a sound herself.

"It's a hard art to master, Larkie."

"An' what's the point on hit, Larkie?" Eddie is still all at sea. Me too.

"Ah could lip sync ta your houn's singin' Eddie, don't you git it?" Quite an amusing thought, especially when it comes to the body language aspect. I suppress a giggle of my own. It's a losing battle. The noise that finally escapes me sounds uncannily like a mastiff sneezing. It's a big production. All three of them stare at me.

Larkie is the first to break their offended silence; "Thankee, Mr. Wats'n. You done made mah point." She looks pretty happy. Ben and Eddie are still frowning.

I have an inspiration. The corn liquor has done its work. "If Larkie will forgive me for saying so, as long as she is syncing her lips, she won't be able to giggle."

Ben's face lights up. "Eddie done said Ah's a sharp man, Tom Watson, but Ah hain't a patch on ya." Now it's Eddie's turn to unwind. We all look at him for a lead. This is clearly a strain on his wrong-headedness. Slowly and cautiously his words form:

"We'all kin give hit a try. If 'n hit looks liketa workin', then we'all has ta do us a whole bunch o' new practicin'. Hit 'ud be like startin' all o'er, Larkie. Ya sure better be good at this syncin' thung." Larkie looks solemn as she gives him the official Girl Guide salute. Then it hits me: she hasn't let out a single giggle during our entire debate. I take this as a promising sign which I keep to myself. Why tempt Fate?

"Thar's one more problem ta fix, Mr. Wats'n. Hit's Ben's truck. He tol' ya did he?" I nod and say:

"He did, Eddie. I suppose I should have known better than to think a vehicle of that vintage could still carry two people and a machine up your slopes here. Why, I had all kinds of difficulty myself, if you recall." Eddie smiles, nods and frowns.

"What's we'all ta do?"

We might as well be monks as another silence falls on our round-table. Again Larkie is the first to break it. "Why cain't y'all jus' push it frum behin'?" Stony silence greets her heartless solution. Time for some lateral thinking. Inspiration number two arrives:

"Is there nowhere easier than this to meet? Just for the recording session, I mean, not regularly?"

"Well," says Eddie slowly, "Ah tol' ya 'bout the complaints we gits. Any sech place 'ud have ta be far off the holler as this 'un. Any ideahs, Ben?" Caney Forks' only chauffeur is the one to know if there is or isn't any such place. I think Eddie is smarter than people give him credit for. Ben's eyes move this way and that as he mentally drives along the region's terrible roads. He is otherwise transfixed. The rest of us sip away, happy to have one problem off the table. Happy as well to top up our inspiration levels during this peaceful interlude.

As Ben remains out of it, I try to reconstruct my drive with him from Meadowview to Flora's. This had seemed interminable. Ben's mind-travel must surely be fairly close to home. But how many side roads had I seen, riding with him? I can scarcely picture one. There must have been more, or Ben would have completed his review by now. Yet he still sits there like some shrunken blue Buddha. We sip on, Larkie seeing to the refills as well as any good barmaid might. And still she refrains from giggling. Maybe she is consciously suppressing her high spirits so as not to disturb Ben's meditations...

"Ah got hit!" cries Ben, slapping his knee. Is it a mosquito or have his legs gone to sleep? "Thet ol' Fork grist mill, hit 'ud be perfec'. Think on hit, Eddie. Hit's a fair mile out'n town both ways. Hit's roof is mos'ly gone. Thar'd be no echoes ta gaum Tom Watson's recordin', an' we'all 'ud be far out a sight an' soun thar as hup heah."

The project's top man looks at once pensive and hopeful. He has been marvellously accommodating, considering his so-called wrong head. Will he keep up the good work? Either way, he'd better be pretty quick about it. I'm falling asleep on my log.

"Ah allow as thet 'ud work, Ben," he concedes at last, "but jus' the once, like Ah said. Larkie, we'all better start a-practicin' tomorrer."

Larkie's shriek is piercing enough to be audible in the holler's homes, at least at our end of town. "Y'all see how corn squeezin's brings out the best in folks? Ah' bet mah red riband bonnet y'all 'ud still be settin' at the startin' lahn yet if 'n you warn't all juiced hup. Hit never does fail."

I only hear her claims as from a great distance. Eddie jumps up to prevent me from falling off my log. They say that's an easy thing to do, and they are right. Dimly I hear Eddie suggest that I need to sleep it off. Sleep what off? What's he talking about now? You know me; I tune out...

Someone is shaking my shoulder. Why would they do such a thing? By opening an eye, I can make out a face, at an acute angle to mine. It's Ben's. But I'm shut in by branches on all sides. I must have fallen asleep in the woods. I push myself up on one elbow. "Ben? Where are we Ben? What time is it?"

"Ya at Eddie's place, mah frien'. If 'n we'all is quick, ya won't keep Flora waitin' on supper. Ah kin fill ya in on our way down, case ya done miss part on our pow wow. Now git up on yar hind legs, Tom Watson, an' let's be on our way. No call ta say 'bye ta Eddie an' Larkie. He took her way off so her laffin' 'ud not wake ya. Now let's start gittin' ya down o'er frum hup. Hit's thataway."

The next time I see Ben, he tells me that I had been so pie-eyed after the pow wow, he skipped my blindfolding. Sure enough, hard as I try, I can't recall one thing about my descent to Flora's. Nothing. How vexing. I need to be certain that Eddie's hounds still really live where I think they do. Purely for curiosity's sake, of course. Whassup? Would understand.

Chapter 41
In The Doghouse

A rackety coughing and spluttering drowns out the tree frogs, sends a stab of pain through my head. I have to see its source if I am to strangle it, but the bright light is too much to bear. Opening my eyes to a lash-shaded slit, I peer around. I am on Flora's porch, in one of her rockers. Why is the day still so bright? It hurts just to look for whatever has caused this agony. Just before I have to close my eyes tight again, I spot the culprit. Over the way, Ben is cranking hard at his model T. Unable to shout, I wave an arm at him. Once I have his attention I make the flat-hand-across-the-throat sign. He stops in mid-crank and crosses to the porch.

"Whar's yer thanks, Tom Watson? If 'n Ah'd not took charge, ya'd be lost in them woods. How ya reckon ya got ta ya rocky chair? Jus' try me. But be quick about hit. Obadiah's a-waitin' on me. We'all is a-headed ta his Hutchins bank. Remember?"

My head hurts at the least effort. "Can I deal with this when you get back, Ben? It's all too painful right now." Ben shrugs and continues cranking my headache pitilessly until his engine fires and he rolls away to Obadiah's. Eyes shut tight, I nurse my pains...

"What have ye got ta say fer y'self this tahm, Mr. Watson?" I don't need telling this is Flora, and that I am back in the doghouse.

"Can it wait 'til later? Pretty please. My head hurts, my eyes hurt, my ears hurt, and I don't know why. Besides, I can't have had more than an hour's sleep."

"If'n ye think so, A'll git no sense out'n ye afowah dinner. Fer one thing ye bin out thar fifteen hour. No drunk ne're crossed mah threshhold, Mr. Watson, nor ne're will. Shame on ye!" She is scandalised out of her mind. It hurts to think about it. I'll just do my tuning out trick...

"Dinner tahm, Mr. Watson, if'n ye've the stomick fer hit. Or ye kin wait on supper." I can only groan by way of reply. She slams her screen door. She is still on the boil. Is she going to throw me out? What a mess... The only thing that seems to help is groaning some more.

The next thing I know, Ben is shaking my shoulder... again. I am not on the ground under the trees this time. I am in Iree-Irene's visiting rocker. I still don't know her proper name. At last I can look around me without squinting, or any appreciable pain. "Ya said ya'd talk ta me when Ah's back. Well Ah is, an' Ah's a-waitin' on ya answers."

Our previous, foggy exchange filters back into my slowly recovering consciousness.

Right: "Ben, I gather you somehow got me from up there down here. How you did it I can't imagine, but I am forever in your debt."

"Is ya thankin' me, Tom Watson? Ah hain't so sure."

"I am, Ben. I thank you from the bottom of my heart for all the superhuman effort it must have cost you. And you had been drinking one for one with me too. Please tell me how on earth you managed it."

"Fust off, Tom Watson, we'all in this holler kin allus holt our likker. Ya has a long, long way ta go a-cotchin' up wi' the rest on us. As ta how, take a look at ya heels. Ya sees how Ah dragged ya downhill, far as acrost frum Obadiah's? He done lent me his cemet'ry wheely barrer an' gimme a hand a-loadin' ya. Then we'all done tipped ya onta these heah porch steps an' hauled ya hup inta thet rocky chair. Hit was on them steps ya shoes done come off."

He points down to my right where I see what is left of my only pair. Then I notice how frayed and torn are the cuffs of my corduroys, especially toward the back. If my clothes continue to degrade upwards in this way, they will soon make a passable match for Ben's own. I shake my head to clear it and offer Ben more praise: "What you did is nothing short of a miracle, Ben. I am truly sorry to have put you to all your trouble."

"Sorry 'bout them britches, Tom Watson. Ah sure hopes sech things won't ne're come ta pass agin'. Now d'ya want ta know what come out'n Obadiah's bank manager meetin' or not?' There I go again, not more of a mountain man, but less. I hang my head in shame. Flora's remonstrances are quite justified.

"Please forgive my distraction, Ben. I have never experienced such a destructive hangover in all my life. Please tell me, did Obadiah receive good news?"

"He was so goshdurn chirpy comin' out'n his bank he gimme the cash ta fill mah tank right on hup. Nobody ne're did so afowah, includin' yaself, Tom Watson." Oh! Here I should be celebrating for Mary and Festus. Instead I feel despair at my unmountainy nature and the daunting task of mending my insensitive ways. Does Ben pick this up?

"Obadiah axed me ta see if'n ya'd like ta be thar when he tells Festus 'bout his raise."

Still feeling catawampus—or is it whopperjawed?—I mull this over. Here is a chance to make amends. A chance to say the right thing: "If anyone, Shirley should be there, Ben, not me. She's the one who got to the bottom of the letters mystery. She's the one who can best judge what to do next." Ben blinks at this, looking confused. Oh. How much does he know? Try as I might I can't remember to save my life.

"If you will be kind enough to give Obadiah that message, I will somehow get to Shirley's and let her know." I am wincing to gain his sympathy.

"If'n ya kin stand, Tom Watson, Ah kin run ya far as Shirley's. Hit 'ud be wuth the doin'. Shirley has feverweed ta fix ya head." I so much want to be with Shirley but worry about her seeing me in my present condition. Seeing her wins. I struggle to my feet, sway a bit, take a step, take another and give Ben a cautious nod.

We stop at Obadiah's on the way. I keep to my seat while Ben goes in to see him. When Ben resumes our drive he stays silent. I am truly grateful for this where once I would have felt offended. At Shirley's Hornet stands near her door, so I climb out and Ben drives away. Now how could Shirley not have heard the noise of our arrival? Where can she be? I knock on her door and wait. There's no sound of Whassup's? usual scratching. I knock again and wait. At my third knock her door opens just a fraction. Just sufficient for one veiled green eye to peer at me. I wait some more. At last she opens up enough for me to step inside. Whassup? is curled up fast asleep on the table beside Shirley's chair. Something smells peculiar.

Shirley looks poorly. I am painfully aware that I probably look worse than her. But has she lost her voice? She waves me to my usual chair and I gratefully subside onto it. The musty, smothering, herbal odour is so overpowering my head swims. Am I going to vomit?

"Don't you go a-jedgin' me, Doc. Ah have ta do this at sartain tahms. Whassup? too."

"Do what, Shirley?"

"This," she says, slowly waving an untidy cigarette at me. "It's grass."

"You can smoke grass?" I am incredulous. "Why not grow your own tobacco?"

"Doc, we'all jus' calls it grass. Its real name is marijuana." Oh, this is dismal news. Shirley isn't so perfect as I had assumed. She...but am I any better in my retreating alcoholic stupor? Who am I to judge her weakness? How do...

"Ah am jus' follerin' an ol' detectin' tradition, Doc." What? This is wild talk.

"Tradition, Shirley; what tradition?"

"If 'n you know marijuana, Doc, you know 'bout laudanum." Laudanum? My mind flinches as a bell rings deep within its still tender, inflamed tissues. Wasn't it the great

Sherlock Holmes who fell into the habit of taking laudanum when his mind was overtaxed? Didn't he even frequent opium dens to get away from Doctor Watson's stern disapproval? Oh my God! Am I dreaming? Are we repeating history? Is Shirley a reincarnation of, of...a work of pure fiction? Poppycock! Piffle! Then what the blue blazes is happening here?

"We'all is human, Doc. We'all needs ta get away now an' agin. Shylock Holmes never took no vacation, an' Ah sure cain't. Are you with me, Doc?" Well, yes and no.

"You know 'bout Daisy, don't you, Doc...Daisy Devlin?" Daisy? I think back...yes,

'Lucy in the Sky with Diamonds' Daisy who said she knew that...who said I only had to check with Shirley. So there are two drug addicts in Caney Forks, maybe more. But my Shirley? There she is, admitting it freely. What has driven her to this?

A great wave of emotion sweeps over me. I haul myself up, cross to her and fold her in my arms, unable to stop myself from weeping. She weeps too. Her arms encircle me, pull me in tighter. We stay like this for a long time, but not long enough for me. My hangover returns, and I know my eyes have to be red. I part Shirley's hanging tresses and look deep into Shirley's. They are still green. She can even weep without any visible penalty. What a woman!

She picks up her mangled cigarette and offers it to me. "Doc, fer gosh sakes, take y'self one drag. Mayhap you'll unnerstan'." Yes, yes; with all my heart I want nothing more than to understand; to truly, deeply understand. I take a long pull, to improve the odds. I wait with fevered expectation. My understanding takes its sweet time in coming, but when it does, I feel her feelings. I feel as though we are one and the same.

This sensation of unity is fleeting, fades more quickly than it came. Reality bites.

"Shirley, I came to tell you Obadiah is going to give Festus that raise, and you are invited, as the author of it all."

"Jus' tell me when," she says drowsily. It is then I realize

I haven't the faintest idea.

"Shirley, can you give me one of those ciggies all to my-self?"

She gives me a long, slow, crooked smile and goes about its assembly.

I come very close to missing my third meal of the day. A man has to eat. And Flora is most probably even more con-cerned than ever for my safety.

Chapter 42
Another Doghouse Day

Have you ever tried to hurry when you're 'high', as I believe it's called? I even miss my way to Flora's. What it was I fell over I can't imagine. The dust and leaves and so forth are really hard to brush off until some man or another gives me a hand. "Owen Brien, Mr. Watson," he says. Well I never; the volunteer casket-carrier. An all-round volunteer. I offer him my hand, but he seems to keep missing it, so I give up.

"Whar ya headin' Mr. Watson?"

"I am looking for Miss MacTaggart's, Brian."

"Well let's git ya turned aroun' then. Lucky Ah come bah, or who knows..?"

My volunteer has me by the arm. Even then, it's nearly impossible to keep up with him. "Mr. Watson, if 'n ya is waited on fer supper better git a move on. We'all has a long way ta go." Funny; I already feel completely gone. Steady the Buffs. Must push on. Don't want Flora worrying about me when I've never felt better.

"What's all these stars doing down on the ground, Brian?" They are winking on and off at me in a most irregular way. I grasp for one and it's gone. It is most exasperating.

"Them ain't stars, Mr. Watson. Them's lightnin' bugs. Farflies ta ya." He is wrong. Stars are far. Flies are near. I must tell hum...him. "You're wrong, er... er...er...Brian, about...a boot...

"We'all is heah, Mr. Watson." How rude this Brian bloke is, int'rupting a perfeck'ly reasoned... I look up but can only see steps. With his help I somehow fall up them. The screech of a screen door hurts my ears.

"Jus' set the villain in Iree's rocky chair, Owen. Ye's quite the saint fetchin' him home. Ah was worried fer him, but now Ah am plain mad. He ne're seems ta larn."

"Ah be glad ta help some more anywise Ah kin, Flora, ta make things aisier."

"Well, Owen, Ah tell ye fer a fact, not but the one man 'ud no ways fill the bill. He has got hisself whar he needs a-watchin' roun' the clock. Hit 'ud call fer a team o' three ta do the job right. Ah ain't a-goin' ta ask ye fer ary sech thing, Owen, tho' Ah surely do 'preciate yer good heart.

"Now hark ta me good, Mr. Watson. Whate're ye bin hatchin' this tahm ye earned y'self one more night on the porch. An' ye kin fergit about supper. Ah need all the strength Ah kin muster wi' sech a sojourner as ye. Ah shall eat the entar meal mahself. Mayhap Ah kin starve some sense inta ye."

Where did all this hostility come from? What else can it be but a case of mistaken identity? Of course. That has to be it. I can go to sleep now with a clear conscience...if only those hound howls up in the woods would stop. They hurt my ears more than Flora's screeching door; worse than chalk on a Balliol blackboard; worse than...

Chapter 43
Rosie Nightingale

"Mr. Watson, oh Mr. Watson." Who..? Where..? Bleary eyed, I look through Flora's porch railings. Even half asleep I know this isn't Flora's voice. She's probably not speaking to me anyway. The dim figure belonging to the voice is...is... Rosie Ross!

"Please excuse my condition...Miss Ross. I've been having rather a hard time of it lately. But won't you...come up and join me?" Rosie cheerfully joins me, plonking herself down in Flora's rocking chair. She smiles at me. She holds an oddly shaped tow sack on her lap. I haven't the energy to work out what contents might bolster its lumpy contours... unless...could it be food? I have been woken, I discover, in a ravenous state. Extremely thirsty, too.

"Ah have heared 'bout yer late misfortunes, Mr. Watson. Word gits aroun' Caney Forks pretty quick. Ah reckon ye're a victim on our Southern hospitality."

"You have put...your finger right on...the heart of the matter...Miss Ross...I had not seen it that way myself. No more than Miss MacTaggart did. I thank you for...for... enlightening me...indeed for your thinking of me at all. It is I who should have...called on you...long before this. You are in fact...one of the few to say...you would be glad to...answer my questions. I have been remiss." Why am I always in the soup like this?

That insufferable porch door screeches. "Oh, hit's ye, Rosie. Ye are welcome ta sit 'til Iree arrives, but don't ye go encouragin' this cad, now. He's in the doghouse." It hurts to turn my head, so I shall never know what kind of facial mask Flora wore on stealing the word 'cad', then using it against me.

"Ah heah ye, Flora. What ye mean bah 'cad'? Ah hain't heard the word afowah."

"If'n ye done spent as long wi' mah lodger as Ah have, ye'd larn all kinds o' new words. Ah do b'lieve thet one means un-gentleman-like. He has his moments, but he's etarnally a-backslidin' on me." I mull this over. It's too confusing right now. I must revert to this strange word when I am quite recovered. The Iree-Irene thing too.

"Ah'm surprised ta heah it so, Flora, an' sorry, too. But Ah do reckon the man needs a-feedin' up. He looks more puny'n ever. Ah fetched y'all some sweet taters frum mah garden. They'll do the job, right smart." She stands to proffer her mis-shapen sack to my mentor. Flora accepts it. "Some folk is too forgivin', Rosie.

"We'all is a-tryin' our best a-turnin' Mr. Watson inta a mountain man; ta make him one of us. A-tryin' Ah says. An' very tryin' he is too, Rosie, Ah swan."

"Well, Ah have a deal o' mountain stories fer 'im. Mayhap those mought help?"

Now we are getting somewhere. I sit up. "I am delighted to hear that, Miss Ross. Would you be so kind as to fetch my notebook and pen, Miss MacTaggart?" Now I can see her, she looks hot under the collar. "Under different circumstances, I would gladly fetch both, but as you know, Miss MacTaggart, I am confined to barracks out here."

With a shake of her fine, but apparently forgetful head, Flora does my bidding. Now I'm all set for Rosie's mountain tales. "Ready when you are," I tell the good woman.

Flora withdraws bearing the sweet taters.

Keeping her voice to a whisper, Rosie informs me that Flora has always set high standards, but that after Mack's death she became more rigid, less tolerant. "Yet she has told me I need to be more sympathetic to people like Ben Cochran," I whisper back. "I don't quite..." Rosie interrupts, "Flora needs yer sympathy, along o' Ben, Mr. Watson. Ye mus' ne're forgit her own great loss." I nod and make a mental note of it.

"Ye had no chance at knowin' Sally Holdaway, did ye, Mr. Watson?" I shake my head in agreement. "Ah knowed her real close, bein' her neighbour. She was real special. She liked ta let me in on her life's secrets. Kin ye guess at her age when she done died? No, 'course ye cain't...what was Ah thinkin'? She died nigh on her hunnert third birth day. Miss Sally was born same day as Robert E Lee done surrendered ta thet Grant at Appomatox. An' jus' two years arter Wes' Virginny split off frum us real Virginians. Kin ye credit hit, Mr. Watson?

"Sally's mother suffered through our..." Rosie shifts to whispering again, "Civil War, fer a start." Who is she afraid of hearing her? Of course! The War between the States was high on Flora's list of prohibitions. "A Rafferty she was. Grace Rafferty; an' she so loved ta write. She kep' her own journal an' wrote in hit ever' day, Mr. Watson." Rosie is glancing at my closed notebook. Hastily I open it up. Now where did Flora put my damned pen?

"Thet's good," says Rosie. "Hit's whar ye come in. Sally she of 'en use ta read me frum her mother's journal. She knowed jus' how much Ah enjoyed her readin's. An' when she lay a-dyin' she done put hit plumb in mah hands. She wanted hit safe, ye see.

"Is ye alright, Mr. Watson? Ye done gone all pale."

I pull myself together and fumble for the right words. "I came here with modest expectations, Miss Ross, and you have just raised them practically out of sight. You are a wonder! And your patience with me is quite humbling." Now who else here was called a wonder? Oh yes, it was Shirley, in Jack Forsythe's eyes. Two wonder-women in a community of thirty-odd souls? Did Derek and I ever pick the right place!

"What do you propose doing with this extraordinary treasure, Miss Ross?"

"Ah bin a-thinkin' on hit, Mr. Watson. Ah do b'lieve the bes' way 'ud be ta read hit fer ye, jus' like Miz Sally done fer me. Ye kin write down in yer book what-all takes yer fancy. Mind ye, thar's plenny o' days wi' nothin' special in 'em but Ah knows ever' which one they is. Ah kin skip those 'uns ta save ye thar trouble. Is ye ready, Mr. Watson?" It is clear that Rosie's mind is made up. I give her an eager nod.

By the time Flora screeches onto our porch reading room, I have filled seven pages with notes and references. We have reached a Sunday in 1861. Glancing up, I see Flora has pushed her big, glass ashtray aside and is setting down two bowls of orange mashed potato. Each has a spoon stuck in it. But orange? "Sweet taters are orange," says Flora, reading my mind and giving me one of her frostiest looks. I oblige:

"Thank you so much, Miss MacTaggart and Miss Ross. You are both the soul of generosity." The two ladies exchange mute glances. I can only guess at their meaning.

When Flora has retired, Rosie ventures to tell me "Ye have a way on puttin' things as belongs better in them sixties'n heah an' now. D'ye know this, Mr. Watson?"

I hang my head for the umpteenth time. "You are not the first to tell me so, Miss Ross. I have been doing my best to break the habit. There are good examples around me every day, but if I catch myself using mountain words, I can't help but nip them in the bud. So far all I have achieved is choosing shorter words than come naturally to me. Please don't think I am excusing myself, Miss Ross, but in this instance I might possibly have been influenced by Miss Sally's mother's own writing style."

"Ah allow ye thet, Mr. Watson, jus' so's ye keeps yer problem well in mind. Ye cain't guess how many folks is a-waitin' on the day ye wins yer fight. Now shall we'all git back ta our books afowah Granny Phipps comes?"

Rosie is very good about pacing her reading so that I can keep up, but by 1864 the light is fading and I feel the onset of writer's cramp. We call it a day. I shake Rosie's hand warmly. To me she is so comfortable; the very embodiment of comfort. Who was that ministering angel in the casualty wards of the Crimean war? I know: Florence Nightingale she was. But I can hardly tell Rosie that. What can I say instead? "You is mah ideah o' the puffec' research 'ssistan'." My intentions are the very best. But Rosie, quite maddeningly, can't help herself from doubling over laughing and shaking.

Am I still so far from my elusive goal? How much simpler had I been born here.

Chapter 44
Exile's End

"Ye done let Rosie go, an' not tellin' me, Mr. Watson? Ah was fixin' ta fetch her in fer supper. Ta share hit wi' ye, too. Two nights outside 'ud be tahm 'nuff ta cure mos' folk, tho' ye hain't mos' folk bah ary stretch atall. Git y'self in an' wash up. Be sure an' give y'self a powerful bresh down fust. Ye've bric a brac all o'er yer clothes, Mister." She looks to the sky for help and screeches back indoors.

I have to use her porch broom to detach the debris from my unfortunate spills, then to sweep them off Flora's sacred porch floor. That done I follow her in, go to my room, wash a few blood stains from my jaw and right ear, shave and...

"Hain't ye ready yet, Mr. Watson?"

"Almost done," I call down, rushing the last stages of my outward restoration. Soon I can clatter down the stairs and, like a child, present myself for inspection. Flora only sniffs and points to my chair. She could hardly make it clearer that I am on sufferance.

I take my seat before a simple supper of cabbage and more sweet 'taters'. I mention how good it tastes. I say how badly I feel for her, after my disgraceful behaviour of the past two days. I promise to make sure no such thing happens again. She says nothing. She does not appear the least reassured.

When we are done, I bring the supper things to Flora's sink, wash them properly, dry them and put them in their proper homes. I hope that Flora notices my attempts at mending the fences I have so carelessly trampled. She is certainly keeping an eye on me. You never know.

"Mr. Watson, Ah want ye ta keep home awhiles. Ah know ye have yer work, but ye mus' find ways o' gittin' hit done heah. Do ye foller me?"

"Miss MacTaggart, I not only understand, but I deeply sympathise with you, for all the trouble I seem to keep causing. I also believe that if Miss Ross can come here each day with her historic material, I can fully comply with your wishes." I phrase this cautiously. I have no idea whether Rosie has told anyone else about the Rafferty journal. On the one hand this is Caney Forks, where secrets seem rare. On the other hand, people like Flora might think the journal belongs in Sally's estate, with its donor no longer available to confirm her gift.

"An' jus' how ye a-goin' ta fix hit this way, Mr. Watson? Rosie cain't know yer new plan kin she? Do ye expec' me ta visit an' axe her? Ah hain't about ta trust ye wi' doin' thet am Ah?" Foiled again, Tom.

We do seem to have reached an impasse. Either I am promoted to day release status or Flora must be my message carrier. I know what my choice would be.

"Let's see if 'n a one o' yer so-called frien's stops on bah. Everwho they mought be, ye kin axe 'em ta call on Rosie fer ye." Well that's one step better than a stalemate. I settle down on the porch again, regretting the lack of telephone service, listening for the approach of any footsteps or of any of the three engines in town.

When an engine does intrude on my nap, its noise is unfamiliar. Much too powerful even to be Red Reardon's big Harley. It keeps cutting out, then firing again after several minutes, in a distinct pattern. Transfixed, I await its appearance. Whatever the vehicle, it's taking its own sweet time. Caney Forks time, I suppose. And then...

A battered old brown lorry lumbers into view. Colourful packages are shelved on the sloping sides of a tent-like frame structure stretching behind the cab, under clear plastic curtains. Before I left Richmond I saw a similar lorry carrying huge panes of glass on both sides. "Miss MacTaggart," I call, "we have a visitor." She pops out to see for herself. I stand by for her verdict.

"Hit's Clarence," she says. That's an odd name for a lorry. I look to her for further enlightenment, nor does she miss my unspoken question. "This heah's our rollin' store.

"Clarence comes bah ever' week ta trade. Mr. Watson, if 'n ye hain't seen him previous, ye must a bin in one o' yer calamities. Or too drunk ta pay heed." Flora is being rather spiteful. But I forgive her, for grocer Clarence doubtless calls at Rosie's home. He can carry my message to her.

When Clarence stops at our porch, message in hand I follow Flora, purse in hand, down to be introduced to this godsent mountain Mercury.

Clarence looks me up and down, much as Obadiah did at our first meeting. But this grocer is not measuring me for funeral furnishings. Perhaps he is checking for signs of a smoker, a beer belly, a chocolate addiction. Flora opens her mouth for introductions, but Clarence beats her to it; "Ya have ta be Mr.Watson, come frum the other side ta spy on us poor, hinnersent mountain folk. What do ya fancy?" His fat, proprietorial paw sweeps the insloped shelves on the near side of his lorry, I feel a warm surge of generosity:

"Is there anything here you would call a treat, Miss Mac-Taggart? Just point it out and I will gladly buy it from Mr. Clarence. Don't hesitate. I owe you so much."

After hesitating anyway, Flora picks out a packet of confectionery quite unfamiliar to me.

I hand Clarence a dollar bill. He gives me a large selection of change. He must want me to buy something for myself in order to reveal my tastes to his salesman's mind. But no, this would not only be unfair to Flora, it would also undermine my gesture to her.

Flora steps up to bat. "Ah need mah usual, Clarence, but don't ye forgit ta size hit up agin fer this hextry mouth. Tho' Ah mus' tell ye he's bin missin' his meals a ways too of 'en since ye war las' by."

"Ah figgered so," says Clarence. "Thar ain't much mah eye don't pick hup." So that's what he was doing. In the mountains, 'sizing up' has at least two meanings.

I wince at the sight of several scoops-full of okra pouring into a paper bag. The green beans I'm not so sure about. They look nothing like Flora's 'leather britches'. Maybe hers were dried for the winter. Didn't she say something of the sort?

Happily, the rest of Flora's order looks harmless enough. I am even accustomed to her hot chicory drink by now. Flora orders the odd bottle of disinfectant, bar of soap, box of matches. No problems there. Clarence has assembled her purchases in a worn cardboard box, and is about to heft this onto the porch. I intercede: "Here, let me have that, Mr. Clarence. And I have a question if I may. Will you be calling on Miss Ross?"

"Rosie Ross, Mr. Watson? Sure as shootin'. Why do ye axe?"

"I was hoping you could oblige me by delivering this message to her."

"Ah gladly will, Mr. Watson." He takes it from my hand. "But what's amiss with our mails. Ye don't trust 'em?"

"It's not that, Mr. Clarence. This message is urgent, and I cannot leave the house."

"Now why'd thet be?" asks Clarence, looking coy. Flora stares him down, and out.

At this, Clarence climbs into his cab. The 'rollin' store', with a throaty rumble, wheels away in the general direction of Rosie and my rescue. I stagger up the steps with Flora's weekly supplies. Into her kitchen I totter with them. "Could you please show me where these things belong, Miss Mac-Taggart?" Might as well stretch my good deed all the way.

"Them vege'ables go inta mah hicebox, Mr. Watson; the soap under the sink 'long o' thet disinfectant. The day was when Ah made all mah own soap". By the time everything is in its place, Flora is looking calm, while my back feels anything but.

"Ah do 'ppreciate yer new attitude, Mr. Watson. Ah shall pray hard as hit lasts."

If my days and nights are ever to become any easier, then it's up to me to make it last. Accordingly I make my silent, first ever and rather premature, New Year's resolution.

Chapter 45
Rosie's Return

Under Flora's watchful eye, my new attitude is holding up quite well. I recall the saying that God helps those who help themselves, and work to play my part. Mainly this consists of helping around the house. When there is nothing left to do, I inhabit the porch. Will Rosie come today? While I wait, I go over the notes I took down from her yesterday's readings. Counting the pages I come up with a total of eighteen. I try to recall how far through the Rafferty/Holdaway journal Rosie had read. Unless I am mistaken, she is more than half way through its thickness. Rosie must have skipped an awful lot of 'nothin' special' days, as she termed them. That's odd. By any measure I can't have experienced more than a couple of 'nothing special' days since my arrival here. Mountain life must have been a whole lot calmer a hundred or so years ago.

I shall have to check with Rosie as to our remaining work. Is it a half day's worth, as my rule of thumb suggests? Or does the narrative heat up, shoving nothing specialness aside? I fervently hope it does. Not so much from a research viewpoint, but from my own; imprisoned lodger that I now am. But why speculate, when you only have to wait and see? To 'lie in the weeds', as someone here expressed it.

'Lying in the weeds', I have an epiphany. It answers the nagging question of how the holler's moonshiners run their product out of 'town'. Ben's tiny pick up—the only working candidate for the job—has never once gone missing, empty bottles or not, except possibly during my brain fever. That leaves...Clarence! His mobile store is the perfect cover. His retail goods are held in those insloped outside racks, leaving ample space in the 'tented' interior for a concealed inventory. What self-respecting T-man would been seen dead chasing such a ponderous vehicle? Especially one that keeps stop...if only I could stop all this yawn...

"Don't ye sleep nights, Mr. Watson?" a voice wants to know. I am getting rather the expert at waking up quickly and verifying my circumstances. No problem here:

"This is excellent, Miss Ross. I am so looking forward to resuming our reading of the Rafferty Papers."

"Hit's good ta see ye, too, Mr. Watson. But, ye jus' use up eighteen words agin' mah six? Ah say ye was doin' much better when we'all quit las' evenin'. Ye needs a kind a language class on top o' mah readin'". Dear me. More backsliding. Steady the Buffs.

"You're right, Miss Ross. I will fix that. Am I doing better?"

"Ye sure are, Mr. Watson. Kin ye keep it so?" I nod, and add my apology for having let her miss supper. Even if I can't read Flora's mind, I do owe Rosie this.

"Ah accep's yer 'pology, Mr. Watson. Supper's no account."

"Then can we start now; reading, writing and simplifying? Then you'll know."

Rosie opens the old journal and wades in. I write and write. From time to time, I put a question to Rosie, framed in the simplest possible words. Her reading voice lifts and lightens as we go. It is buoyed, I hope, by my progress in mastering the fine art of simple speech.

This is fun, even if it is a bit of an effort. We are almost through the Winter of '65 when Flora appears with an invitation to dinner. "Ah wanted ye ta join us fer supper yestiddy, Rosie, but Mr. Watson heah he done let ye slip clean away. Howsomever, Ah have us some fresh vittles frum Clarence as 'ull make hup fer his forgittin'"

"It happens Mr. Watson done 'pologised already, Flora."

Good Rosie Nightingale, tending to my psychological abrasions like the heroine of Crimea. I give her a quick smile. Mustn't get Flora's back up. But Rosie has more to say.

"Flora, Ah am happy ta say Mr. Watson is cuttin' down on his words. An' he is a-short'nin' 'em too. He done gimme plenny fahn examples this mornin'." By the look of it, Flora is reading my mind. Fair enough, I suppose, considering the number of times I have led her mind up the garden path. Does that expression mean the same thing over here? I shall have to ask Flora in private, along with the Iree thing, apple butter and vigilantes.

Dinner concludes as favorably as it started. It is a contented reading/writing team that returns to its porch rockers to finish extracting prime nuggets from the priceless, century-old Rafferty record. Later we try to work out which of us fell asleep first.

Chapter 46
The Last Lit'rary Lap

The good thing about our porch sleeping party is this. It not only prolongs Rosie's return into a third day, but seems to have caused Iree-Irene Phipps to shy away.

She is quite likely the absolute first local person on the telephone company's waiting list...waiting for whenever their lines at long last get strung to her holler.

If I had a journal of my own, it would have nothing special to report for the rest of the day. Roll on tomorrow. Roll up Rosie. Research awaits. Sleep comes slowly; stays only to the first faint light of dawn. Flora almost has a fit, finding me setting the table for breakfast, ahead of her own rigorous schedule. Only the direct evidence of my reformation counts with her. I am piling it up front and centre, fast as I can.

I am particularly keen to mine the old journal for subjects that Flora has forbidden me to ask about. Rosie has confirmed that Flora's 'War between the States' is one and the same as the Civil War mentioned unflinchingly, but hardly with approval, by Grace Rafferty. Grace's attitude was about the same for the Hatfields and McCoys, whoever they were. These people clearly weren't high on her list. So Rosie herself is probably censoring little or nothing. Even so I have heard no mention of the Pinkertons, the Blue Ridge Parkway land theft, Piggly Wiggly and so on. That last one has my curiosity all ablaze. Maybe these unmentionables all post-date Grace Rafferty's time.

Suppose they do. Rosie is adept at knowing when to

whisper. If the journal doesn't cover them, all I have to do is whisper my questions about these Florian taboos. You notice I didn't mention any trial of the 'scopes. Why should I? Whatever Flora thinks, 'scopes were invented in Italy; when her mountains and hollows housed none but Red Indians.

Today I am on full alert. I spy Rosie before she sees me. "Hi, Rosie," I call to her with a touch of mountain drawl. "What's cookin'?" She pulls up sharpish, most likely to make sure she has the right man. In no way do I resemble Flora or Iree-Irene, but perhaps I could be mistaken—at a distance say—for Peter Duffy.

Rosie resumes her advance, peering closely at my features. "Well Ah swan Ah ne're thot hit ye, Mr. Watson. Ye bin a-studyin' up on neighbour talk Ah guess. What a long ways ye come in a night."

"Truth is, Miss Ross, Ah din't ketch one wink las' night. Ah jus' lay thar a-studyin' an' a-practicin'." She mounts the porch, still staring hard at me. From the changing looks crossing her face, she is trying to decide whether I am the genuine article, or 'jus' teasin'. At last she makes her pick: "Ah am proud on ye, Mr. Watson. Real proud. See what ye kin do if 'n ye only trahs?" She pitches into Iree-Irene's rocker with a contented air.

I suppose Flora, accepting the Rosie routine, has warned off the rocker's customary occupant until further notice. This is a big deal in my eyes; a self-inflicted sacrifice to my interests, this cutting of her chief news supply line. I consider the implications. Has Flora been going out at all? Is this why she bought so much from Clarence, in lieu of bartering produce and so forth with others in the holler? But as Flora once told me: I do need to be more observant. No, I tell a lie. Her exact words were 'more noticin'.

"Is yer mind off someplace, Mr. Watson? Sure looks hit."

"Ah is tryin' ta work out if 'n Miss MacTaggart done lef' home atall the past two days. Hit's real important ta me bein' sure. Yar answer mought be fer her benefit as well." Again Rosie is stuck on hold, visibly scrutinising my request for all-round veracity , plain foolishness or who knows what all. Changing my attitude could be easier for me to accept than for other folk. A swings and roundabouts thing.

Rosie decides to be a good sport: "If 'n 'deed she done lef' the house while Ah bin heah, she must a done hit out'n her back door, Mr Watson."This information is inconclusive. Who else would know? Aha! Who else but her closest ally, Iree-Irene?

It might pay to sugar the pill. "Miss Ross, kin Ah beg one more favour afowah we starts hup?" She is still having face trouble. That's another common problem here.

"An' what mought hit be, Mr. Watson?"

"As Ah is houseboun', Ah kin only axe ya, Miss Ross, ta take mah question ta ol' Granny Phipps. Might could ya do thet fer me?"

Rosie considers, more placidly this time. "We'all is al-mos' done, Mr. Watson. Ah cain't see why not. Ah think Ah know whar ta find har when she hain't heah. Hit hain't at har homeplace neither." I realise I have never met Iree-Irene ex-cept here and during public events. But Rosie shows no sign of disclosing Iree-Irene's hideaway. You can't win 'em all.

We resume our work until good old Rosie reaches the journal's last page. She closes it tenderly. "Hain't hit sumpin, Mr. Watson?"

"Hit sure is, Miz Ross, but..." here I soften my voice to a whisper, "hit's missin' entries on three things Flora done warn me nivver ta speak on."

Rosie is so smart. She whispers her invitation to tell her what they are. I whisper the answers back. "Oh, them things war way on arter Grace's tahm, bless ye. Thet land was stole bah our own gov'ment fer buildin' a hard road 'long the Blue Ridge yonder." She points westward. "Now nobody cain't git thar frum heah no more.

"As ta Piggly Wiggly, hit's not but one o' them-new fan-gled supermarkets, over ta Hutchins Court House. Thar's no harm in hit, Mr. Watson, but Ah know how Flora disgusts the name an' disrepecks hit. Hogs rate higher'n ary supermarket in her mind". I wish I could ask her how Clarence survives its competition, but I know better.

"Pinkerton's ye said? Why they war a big 'tective agency our gov'ment done sent ta shoot down our strikin' coal miners. They war nothin' but col' blood murderers. Ah hate ta say so, but thar's still parts o' thet outfit aroun' today..." I suddenly recall sighting a chunky lorry marked "Pinkertons" as I came out of the Richmond airport terminal. It looked like a huge armoured car. But a detective agency? Could Shirley possibly be a Pinkerton's agent? I have to know:

I whisper urgently, "A detective agency ya say, an' still aroun' today. Flora she calls Shirley Combs a detective. Is she a Pinkerton's agent? Please tell me it's not so."

"'Course she hain't, but her Granny she was a Melungeon." No! That can't be true either! "Cool y'self down, Mr. Watson. Shirley's gifts they don't run ta Hoodoo. Yer worry done druv away yer new mountain talk, din't hit?" She taps her nose, grins, looks altogether too knowing. Perhaps after all it's good that we have finished our joint task.

A timely new idea percolates: "Do ya s'ppose Ah could keep up mah practice talk on Flora? Somehow hit jus' don' seem right." This time Rosie laughs aloud, before whispering: "Small wonder ye feel this way, Mr. Watson. Ah bet nor Flora nor nobody else done tol' ye how she was a school teacher fer well nigh forty year."

The screen door screeches. The retired school teacher gives us both a searching look, then checks beyond her porch railings. "What ye laffin' 'bout, Rosie Spargrass? Hain't y'all heah ta work?"

I do my White Knight thing: "We done finish this ver' minute, Miz MacTaggart, an' Miz Ross she was a-laughin' wi' wholesome relief."

"Is ye funnin' me, Mr. Watson?" Flora is furious. Rosie is placatory:

"Don't take on so. Hit's true what he done said, Flora. He hain't a-funnin' nobody. Mr. Watson is set on larnin' mountain talk. He's bin a-tryin' some on me. But we'all is done wi' Grace's journal an' Ah have ta leave anywise. Kin he practice on ye?"

Flora staggers a little. I rise to offer her my seat. Her's really. She staggers some more and falls limply onto her accustomed throne. A couple of minutes roll by with no acknowledgment of my non-cad behaviour, until she breathes. "Ah'll be blessed, y'all."

Chapter 47
A Fresh Start

Without Rosie to occupy my days now, I must find a Flora-proof reason for leaving her premises next morning. I can't go on this way. I've absolutely got to see Shirley. Hmmm. Aha! Obadiah's place is so close. Surely Flora will relent if I tell her of my promise to Meg. I will go all out on this line. I can't think up a Plan B to save my life.

Over breakfast I make my pitch: "Ah is days behin' in mah faithfull promise ta Meg M'Sweeney, Miz MacTaggart, an' thar's nothin' Ah kin do 'lessen ya allows me ta call on Obadiah."

"What promise is thet, Mr. Watson?"

"Meg she's set on takin' Howie's place but tol' me Pentecostals don't let no women folk in charge. She reckons har snake carin' tahm counts fer more'n Howie's poor efforts. So Ah done tol' Meg Ah'd petition Obadiah fer har." Flora looks quite surprised at this, then goes all pensive on me. She takes a while to adjust, but at last comes out with:

"Ah know ye have done good service fer Obadiah an' fer Ben Cochran, but ye ne're tol' me 'bout helpin' Meg. Mayhap Ah bin too down on ye, Mr. Watson. Ah noticed ye done fahn fer three days now. Alright. Go see if 'n Obadiah's thar. If 'n so, ye do yer bes' fer Meg. But don' no account let him press his squeezin's on ye. Ye men jus' cain't handle temptation, kin ye?" I hang my head. I've no need to practice that.

"Ah sure does 'preciate ya blessin', Miz MacTaggart. Soon's Ah is shet o' mah chores, Ah 'ull do 'zackly like ya jus' tol' me." It seems I shall have to blow my own trumpet more, if I am to receive lasting credit from Flora. Even for such activities as my washing up. I hope I shan't have to add laundry to my voluntary chores program. And cooking would be a disaster.

"Ah do allow as yer mountain talk hit's a-comin' along real smart, Mr. Watson. Jus' be sure yer actions match up, ye heah?" I nod my head vigorously. I know mountain life is hard, but does it have to be this hard? A providential vision of Shirley rises up in my mind, beguiles me and stops my whingeing dead in its tracks.

Drying my hands by Flora's sink I begin to relish my pending re-entry into the outside world. Free! I am free at last! I skip shaving again. Within minutes I am in the road, heading for Obadiah's. A bent figure confronts me, a dark silhouette against the sun.

"Mind ye don't knock me dahn Mr. Watson," it commands sharply.

This is Iree-Irene; the missing feature from the MacTaggart porch, guaranteed loaded to the gills with gossip and bursting to tell.

"Ah come ta give ye the fac's Rosie Ross done tol' me ye need, Mr. Watson. They're sumple 'nuff ta tell. Flora axed me not ta call on her fer three days. She said she plumb cain't leave the house, but no account am Ah ta bring her ary a thing as she's all stocked up. Ah know better'n axe her reasons, Mr. Watson. If 'n she wants me knowin', she 'ull tell."

"Ah is much obliged fer yar fac's, Miz Phipps. Ah kin answer in turn as ta what ya was a-wonderin' 'bout." A look of horror crosses the Phipps' visage. Her mouth opens and closes, opens and shuts. Air will be going in, but nothing comes out. Then I see her problem. More explanation is required than the part which her reaction had interrupted. How can I put it simply to her?

"Miz MacTaggart was jus' playin' chaperone fer Miz Ross an' mahself while we took us a look at a bunch o' vallerable research writin'. Confidential writin' hit is. But thet's not all on hit, Miz Phipps. Miz Ross done listen ta mah fust trahs at mountain talk too. Miz MacTaggart is fillin' in now bah listenin' harself." Iree-Irene totters a tad, then gets har motor functions back in order.

"O' course, Miz Phipps, ya is entarly free ta git Miz Mac-Taggart's say-so on what Ah done tol' you." She considers this at length, finally nods at me and resumes her now un-steady walk toward Flora's porch to seek its proud owner's affirmations or denials.

Perhaps this unforeseen delay will reinforce any cover story that might be required after my post-Obadiah run to Shirley's. Sniff. I have so little time on the outside.

That Obadiah is standing in his entrance doorway most certainly helps. I make a quick but thorough case on Meg's behalf. I stress how he had himself called her a pillar of faith. He undertakes to give her petition serious consideration, even first to poll the holler's residents. Bingo! My conscience is now as clear as my path to Shirley's.

I walk until I am clean out of sight from the holler proper, then break into a run, sadly out of condition. I am breathing so hard at my first unavoidable pause that Hornet's approach scarcely registers before Shirley's shout tops its racket: "Dr. Watson! Jus' the man! You'll never guess what's up." Whas-sup? did she say? Actually she did...sort of. She cuts Hornet's little motor so I can hear har better.

"Ah heard you had y'self three days of homework, so Ah held off tellin' you the bad news. It's Whassup? Doc. He done bit a new client, an' she ain't a client no more. Ah lost her in two shakes of a duck's tail, Doc. If 'n she talks we have us one big problem."

"Befowah you says innythin' more, Shirley, Ah's bin a-' practicin' mountain talk. Rosie an' Miz MacTaggart they's bin a-keepin' me straight. But Ah rather had you doin' hit fer me, Shirley, than innyone ilse in the entar world." Her face is free of horror, or doubt, or the least disapproval. It gradually lights up until it is glowing with pleasure.

"Mah oh mah, Doc! You make me so happy!" Wonderful,

but the schoolteacher's remonstrances ring in my ears. I can't be at Shirley's cabin when I'm not at Obadiah's or Flora's. So where can I be? I get another of my brain flashes:

"Ah has ta know more 'bout yar Whassup? problem, Shirley, 'cept Ah really mus' be ovah ta Flora's. Kin Ah set on yar towel agin' an' let ya fetch me back afowah she gits riled at me all over?"

"Sure you kin. Get on quick, Doc. Let's save your bacon, Giddyup, mah Hornet!" I 'git on quick' and embrace Shirley tight. I feel no fear for my safety, only a strange, unaccountable fear of losing her. We howl to Flora's. Aboard Hornet it's far too noisy for any further exchanges about Whassup's? new, depraved character. But my entrancing conjure woman has it all thought out. She stops outside Obadiah's for a council of war. I ask why Whassup? can't be cured with one or more of her potions.

"They're for folks, Doc, not animals. Tho' thar's plenny hog farmers won't take no for an answer. Ah would'n waste mah tahm on it. But Ah do want him ta meet you agin, Doc. Might could be he's a-missin' you much as Ah do." My heart leaps. My head swims. My knees turn to water. I lean against the Spade doorpost for support.

"Could you talk ta Flora, Shirley? Jus' tell her yar idea. She has me on a real short leash. Ah is like a pris'ner, 'cept Ah hain't even on day release. If 'n you kin soften har hard heart, she might could stretch out mah release tahm some."

"Ah kin sure trah, Doc. But you better walk on back an' let me come on bah later. Li'l things like that make winnin' aisier." I skip away on the instant, only slowing down to an Obadiah type funeral pace as I near the watchful, elevated figures of you know who, presiding over my porch destination. On reflection, Iree-Irene had seemed a bit warmer when we almost collided today, hadn't she? Her usual reserve was gone. She hadn't smiled, but neither had she shown any hostility. Might she be just a little bit thawed out? Might she even support Shirley's case?

To clear the way for Shirley, I greet the pair of them

warmly in my best mountain talk, give a brief, positive summary of how Obadiah received my petition and head into the stifling interior to make myself scarce. To pass the time, I attempt to compare my sacrifice with the one Flora had made for me. She wins handily. No doubt about it.

Still idling expectantly in the parlor, I have a most helpful recollection. At Grammar school, our French Master once told us we would never be truly fluent in any language until we had learned to think in it. I make a second, fractionally less premature New Year's resolution.

If 'n y'all thinks Ah's a-funnin' jus' ya listen up!

Chapter 48
Witchery at Work

I reckon an hour or more o' hidin' hupstairs done passed afowah the noise o' the Hornet is heared in the land. Mah conjure woman she has harself far more patience than Ah does. Or is she jus' dismissin' frum them hardened porch-court minds ary possible link atween har visit and mah own li'l outin'? I kin allus axe har. But only if 'n har meltin' game succeeds.

Flora she tells Shirley what a nice surprise hit is to see her. Well thar's a good start. I gits ta mah eavesdroppin' post. If 'n Shirley was ta spot me through Flora's wildflower 'rrangement, Ah sure hopes she don't bust out a-laughin'.

"How ye be doin', Shirley? Ye sure looks fahn."

"Oh Ah am, Flora, an' how y'all be doin'?"

"Gayly, considerin' mah years," says Flora, "What d'ye say, Iree?" It can't be Iree.

"Ah'm toler'ble fair ta middlin', Shirley, thankee."

"Now as ta Whassup?, it's a diff'rent story, Ah am sorry ta tell y'all." Heah hit comes.

"An' we'all is sorry ta heah hit, Shirley." Flora is out'n front on Iree-Irene in this race.

"Won't ye tell us more? We sure hope he hain't a-dyin' or arythin' too serious like."

This was not the mos' propitious moment fer Shirley to ketch mah spyin' eye. Her face hit goes all twitchy, but mah conjure woman, she's smart as a whip. Next thing Ah knows she's a-blubberin'. She hoists up her skirt front ta dry her tears. Jus' the sight on hit wrenches mah heart. She gasps a bit afowah a-statin' har case.

"Y'all cain't b'lieve how he sets bah mah door all day long, a-waitin' an' a-waitin' on that Mr. Watson. He's a-pinin' away ta nothin'. It 'mos' breaks mah poor heart in two." This is good. Har poor heart is one whole deal toughar than mine.

"Mr. Watson hain't a-missin', Shirley. Ah jus' want him whar Ah kin keep a close eye on him. Him an' his games."

"Then we have us a crossroad, Flora. Whassup? is plumb skeered o' mah...your motor sickle. Sech a li'l thing it is, too. He jus' slips out'n the tow sack Ah put him in for a ride anyplace. Ah cain't bring him ta see Mr. Watson. An' you say that poor man he's good as lock up in heah." She pauses ta let out a li'l sob, an' pulls up har skirt agin ta hide har face. A thrill runs up mah spine. Ah feels sure mah Shirley will git har way. Flora an' Iree-Irene, they're good as witched.

Chapter 49
A Royal Pardon

The silence on the porch is broke' only bah sniffs an' snuffles frum both rockers. Ah sees Flora fetch out a li'l han'kerchief an' dab har eyes. Iree-Irene she puts a sleeve ta har'n. Ah do b'lieve Shirley has done melted thar poor hearts but good.

"This heah's a better day," begins Flora, agin' all the odds, "Ah think we kin kill us two birds wi' one dornick; if 'n ye know thet sayin'. Mayhap Ah kin keep Mr. Watson out'n trouble bah a-holdin' him heah roun' the clock. Ah have ta be heah too or Ah jus' know in mah bones as sump'n real bad 'ull happen. But y'all know Ah need ta go out mahself. How 'bout ye keep him at yer place half 'n the tahm, Shirley, an' we go turn an' turn about? This way Whassup 'ull be back ta his ol' self at leas' half 'n his tahm."

Ah jus' 'bout leaps out mah skin. Flora's flower jar wobbles an' falls. Nivver in mah life has Ah moved so fast. Ah do ketch hit but hit shows me a life on hits own. Ah has ta juggle aroun' a bit afowah Ah kin set hit back safe. Thar's a deal o' water splashed about. Ah pulls out mah han'kerchief an' begins moppin' up, wringin' out inta the jar, moppin' up agin' an' sech. Thet's why Ah nivver heared how Shirley replied ta Flora. Ah'd a give mah anorak ta see har face as she was a-doin' hit.

The porch game is ovah an' won. Ah tiptoes hupstairs so's ta be ready fer Flora's call.

Hit's a long tahm a-comin'. Mebbe they're a-workin' on the fahn print. Mebbe they're a-celebratin'. Has they plumb forgot poor ol' Whassup? in all thar talkin'? Ah settles mah-self in fer a li'l siesta...

"Mr. Watson, kin ye heah me? Ah have bin a-callin' ye an' a-callin'. Shirley's come ta see ye. Kin ye...?

"Ah heahs ya, Miz MacTaggart. Ah ain't got much ta do an' Ah cain't help but keep a-droppin' off. Shirley, did ya say?" Keep it calm, Tom. Steady as she goes.

"Are ye comin' down, Mr. Watson, or ain't ye?"

"Ah is, Miz MacTaggart. Jus' let me tidy mahself a li'l fer the lady."

Ah is tidy 'nuff already, so Ah has ta figger the mos' like-ly tidyin' up tahm afowah Ah comes on down. A couple a minutes should do. Ah counts the seconds. The seconds lef' afowah Ah sees mah Shirley fer the third tahm today.

Tahm's up. Ah makes plenny o' noise on them star steps. Cain't nobody say as Ah needs remindin'. Ah joins them mixed-up three on the porch.

"Miz M'Gonaughy! How nice hit is ta see ya agin." Shir-ley claps a hand to har mouth:

"Dr. Watson! You are a sight for sore eyes. But you sounds so diff'ren'. What's up?" Thet's a good one. She sure knows how ta cover har tracks does mah Shirley.

"Ah bin tol' bah too many folk ta name, as talkin' moun-tain style hit's the bes' way fer me ta become one o' y'all. Mahself, Ah'd like nothin' better. Ah has took the plunge. Trouble is, hit's a-spoilin' mah notes like you'd nivver b'lieve. Far as spellin' an' sech."

Flora looks impatient at this stale news. Sump'n's a-bi-tin' har. "Mister Watson is hit, or Doctor Watson? Ye ne're tol' me 'bout the Doctor part, an' ye sure as shootin' cain't cure brain fever. Tell me straight which hit is." Bah now Iree-Irene's ears is almos' a-comin' off. How shall Ah put hit?

"Thet's a point as needed figgerin' afowah Ah done come heah. Ah is a graduate Doctor o' Philosophy, Miz MacTag-gart, but Ah reckoned folk heah 'ud feel aisier a-talkin' ta a plain Mister. Now Miz M'Gonaughy says she druthar call me Doctor. She ain't no ways put off bah hit, bein' mos' free

wi' har reasonin'." Ah b'lieve she 'ull call me proper now."
Shirley, bless har, nods ta reassure Flora Ah ain't a-jokin' nor
nothin'.

Flora's brow, hit's still all puckered. "Ta tell ye the flat-
out truth, Mister Doctor, Ah plumb need a break frum ye
an' yer games. Shirley heah has offered ta provide hit. She's
a-goin' ta keep ye o'er bah har place fer three days. Ah shall
have ye back fer the nex' three. Then same agin, hover an'
hover 'til all the nonsense is beat out'n ye."

Ah looks at Shirley. "Ya is mos' kind, Miz M'Gonaughy.
Ya done tol' me more on what Ah needs fer mah research
than inny other, barring Miz MacTaggart. An' she done tol'
me you was har back-up on the ver' day Ah fust arrived. Hit
soun's mos' fittin' ta me." Ah does a real slow wink at mah
enchanter.

"Clean y'self up fust, Mister Doctor. Have a shave an'
pack clothes fer three days. Ah don't want ye keepin' Shirley
a-waitin', 'specially arter har kindness ta me."

Cleanin' mahself slowly is goin' ta be hard, but hit done
give me the chance ta figger how Ah kin pack mah clothes
right fer carryin' on Hornet. Ah sure don't want 'em gittin'
atween me an' the driver. Ah calls down ta Flora; "Is thar
a satchel in the house?" Ah heahs Shirley 'splainin' what a
satchel is. Ah heahs a deal o' rummagin' aroun' down below.
Flora toils up har stairs carryin' a poke, as she calls hit, wi' a
long strap thet gladdens mah beatin' heaht. Ah thanks har
mos' sincerely. Ah packs hit, skips the shave an' reports ta
the porch. We is soon away on Hornet. Our drive is way too
short fer mah likin'.

Gittin' off 'n Green Hornet at Shirley's Ah gits all stirred
up, wunnerin' how she figgers ta fit me inta har li'l bitty cabin. Ah soon larns how. "Drop your poke bah mah door, an'
foller me, Doc."

Ah would a foller har inny place. We heads behin' har
cabin a li'l ways inta them woods. An ol' green hammock,
all shreddy lookin', hangs atween two skinny oaks. Pin oaks,
Shirley says, but nothin' 'bout all the mistletoe they hosts.

Ah pulls up short. Mah 'sperience in hammocks hit 'mounts ta nothin'. Mah mind-reader goes up ta hit, an' pushes hit aways frum har. On hit's way back mah Shirley ketches hit bah surprise, bah jumpin' in back'ards. Quicker'n Ah kin see, she done went frum sittin' ta lyin'. Ah gives har a round o' clappin'. Ah swan hit sure does look mighty comfor'ble.

"Now you try, Doc." She tips harself out in a mos' alarmin' style. Ah stands by hit, pushes hit away, jus' like she did, an' jumps inta hit. Hit ketches me face dahn. Ah cain't no ways sit up nor stretch out like mah Shirley done.

"Get y'self out back'ards," she says. "Ah'll show you slow."

But thet hammock don't like slow. Shirley finishes up a-sittin' on hits nearest edge. Most on hit is stretch all tight roun' har back. Like me behin' har on Hornet's green bath towel. "Les' trah this way," says Shirley. "Ah stay heah an' Ah holt it dahn. You try climbin' aroun' me 'til you kin lay y'self down like Ah did."

My attempts is so thrillin' Ah keeps failin' far as finishin' hup. Shirley don't seem ta mind, so Ah drags mah failin's out. The bes' part's the fust step, sittin' at Shirley's side, pushed tight agin' har bah this smart, frien'ly hammock. Las' thing, she gits a holt on me an' trahs ta git mah body dahn on har lef' an' mah legs up on over ta har right. They jus' keeps a-jammin'. We tries hit the other ways roun'. Ah swing an' Ah swang mah legs. In mah mind hit's the perfec' way. Specially when she pulls me roun' an' plants a big, warm kiss on mah lef' cheek.

"Les' quit this, Doc. Frum what Ah heahd, you won't be hurtin' for sleep a while yet. But you better practice a-hammockin' while Ah make our supper, an' you still have y'self 'nuff light. It comes on dark quicker in mah woods, Doc. Ah'll tell Whassup? 'hello'. Jus' in case he really was a-missin' you.

"Ah do b'lieve, his problem was inhalin' too much grass smoke. Mayhap Ah took more'n usual, on account o' missin' you mahself." She turns away an' leaves in a hurry.

If 'n Ah does say so mahself, 'ceptin' the hammock, Ah

do seem ta have landed on mah feet. Whassup? 'ud be mighty proud on me, if 'n he only knowed the half on hit.

Chapter 50
A New Day Dawns

A-lyin' in mah grass green string bed unner them leafy green trees in the cool on early mornin' Ah thinks me all kind a thoughts. Fust off, today is more'n a new day than inny other day in mah' life as Ah kin think on. Ah's quite happy ta lie heah a-waitin' fer hit ta start hitself up. Ah hain't in no kind a hurry.

Nex' up is thinkin' mountain style. Ah recalls how a mountain word done use ta creep in heah, an' thar, way back afowah Ah took the pledge ta think mountainy. Truth is, Ah done pushed 'em straight back inta mah own style. Hit's sad ta think on hit. Thank the Lord Ah is cured.

But Ah is still a beginin' larner. Ah knows hit. All these mixed-up tenses gits mah goat. Hit likely needs more no-ticin' like Flora done tol' me 'bout all thet other holler stuff. If'n thar's one thing Ah bin noticin' hit's how Ah has slowed right on dahn bah a-practicin' mah mountain talk. Din't Flora say sump'n' sim'lar? On account o' for'ners needin' ta unnerstan' in them early days? Slow an' consid'rate. Thet's hit. Ah is mebbe a for'ner yet, but not fer long. Ah's half ways mountainy right now, hain't hit so?

An' heah come Shirley, sashayin' 'crost them ol' leaves ta start mah day right, bless har.

"Oh, you are awake, Doc. Ah never saw you movin' one bit frum mah back winder. Ah reckoned mayhap too much fresh air done knocked you plumb out. Mah Whassup?now, he's a-waitin'. We have ta git you out'n thet hammock quick, so's we kin start our fust real day togethar. Combs an' Watson. Don't it sound good?

"Sit y'self up, Doc. Swing them legs out an' down. No, not like that, Doc. Lemme show you how."

Shirley grabs mah ankles tight, heaves mah legs up but cain't noways git 'em stickin' ovah the hammock's hedge.

"Ah b'lieve you are doin' this a-purpose, Doc. Don't you feel hungry atall?"

Ah takes mahself a big breath. All quiet like Ah says hit's she who Ah is a-hungry fer. She don't look happy so much as himpatient.

"Han't you no consideration, Doc? Whassup? is a-waitin' an' you saw me three tahms yestiddy. Now quit foolin' an' stick up your arms. Ah am a-goin' ta set this hammock a-swingin' 'til you jus' falls plumb out. Use your arms ta break the fall. Ah am low on bruise poultices." What kind a poultices kin' fix a bruised ego? The way Ah is feelin' Ah cain't b'lieve thar's inny kin do thet job. "Owww, hey!"

Ah is too blamed slow a-stickin' out mah arms. Shirley has mah frien'ly hammock swingin' 'til hit hangs straight up an' dahn. Hit pitches me face dahn on har leaf-strown ground. Mus' be broken branches in them leaves a-painin' mah palms an' knees sump'n fierce. Ah rolls ovah fer relief, mebbe moanin' a li'l. Now mah back hurts.

"Doctor Watson! What's all your fuss? You hain't hurt wuth beans. Get y'self up an' come see Whassup?" Whar's har lovin' sympathy? How kin she rate Whassup? o'er me? Ah gits ta mah feet real keerful like. Ah has ta trot ta ketch har up.

"Hey, Whassup? mah deah. Lookee who's come ta see us."

This brings mah rival ta Shirley's door. He stan's thar lookin' me up an' dahn, like Obadiah an'...Ah cain't recall who hit was no more. Then Whassup? sniffs what's lef' o' mah britches cuffs. He looks up at Shirley.

"The way Ah read him he's settled agin," says Shirley. "Now step on in an' set at mah table. We're a-goin' ta eat breakfas' if 'n you want it or not, Doc." Feelin' no more'n a worm, Ah sets mahself dahn as she done axed. Shirley gits ta work bah har li'l burner. Soon thar's bacon an' eggs afowah us. Ah'll eat mine if 'n hit kills me.

"Long as you let your true feelin's out jus' now, Doc., Ah need you ta unnerstan' our relations aright. It's for perfessional reasons Ah cain't get bah without you. Lemme 'splain. Ah bin fixin' things for neighbor folk ever since Ah was teenage. Now folks do talk, as you well know. Roun' heah word spreads worse'n a woods far.

"In 1964 the fust flatlander done come ta mah door. When Ah opened up she axed ta see mah master. Ah tol' har Ah have no master. Ah'm the only occupant an' mah name is Shirley Combs. She goes all crazy on me. She says the Shirley Combs she's seekin' he's a man. A man who wears an ol' cloak an' a funny hat. He smokes a bent pipe an' plays the fiddle. He's a great detective, she tells me. So Ah tells har how Ah bin solvin' all kind a problems for local folk, an' never a single complaint. But she pitches a fit right thar. Then she stomps out an' drives off real fast, madder'n a wet hen.

"Now that Robby Burns, he knows a lot. So Ah axed him if 'n he might could figger out this madwoman's carryin' on. It made him laugh. He tells me how he's heard of an Englishman detective called Shylock Homes, or some such. But this man's not real. He only lives in books. Mah madwoman cain't hardly a known that kin she?

"What Robby said got me curious. So Ah axed Clarence could he find me one a them books at the liberry in Hutchins Court House. He did too. Ah read all 'bout Mr. Holmes an' his frien' Dr. Watson. That's when Ah saw how Ah mus' improve mahself for flatlanders. Fust Ah got Whassup? Then Ah had cards printed up for the two on us.

"Do you see now how Ah jus' cain't live with no Dr. Watson? Now Clarence he jus' run a new message for me ovah ta Hutchins. They're a-printin' new cards for us thar. Ah need thet flatland business. Mah conjurin' trade hain't neah what it use ta be, an' our ol' folks thar a-dyin' off.

"Ah larned how your English Dr. Watson had his own place, even a wife for a while. But he lived wi' Mr. Holmes durin' cases. So you, mah own Dr. Watson, kin live heah or ovah ta Flora's, all dependin'. Three days each way is jus' a start. Flora's use ta you bein' heah, or out on mah cases. We're all set, Doc."

Ah is shook real bad by Shirley's news. Has Ah swapped mah MacTaggart jailhouse fer ta be shut up wi' mah own true love, who don't love me back? Aarrrrrgh. Surely Shirley kin see how beat down Ah is.

"Now don't you go a-frettin', Doc. Those story Holmes an' Watson they were a couple men. Men lovin' each other warn't done those days. Not even in books. But a man an' a woman, say us for example, that's diff'ren', Doc." She gives me har best green gaze. She keeps hit a-comin' 'til Ah's more'n a cooked goose'n Flora's roast hen.

Chapter 51
Back T'a Work

Soon's Ah has done mah domestic chores at Shirley's sink, Ah git set ta shave at last. But Shirley she axe, "D'you know how many loose ends you lef' hangin', Doc?"

Ah has no answer at mah fingertips, so Ah guesses an' says, "Ah do b'lieve hit's three, Shirley."

"Then afowah we do any one thin' more, les' get 'em closed up. What are they?"

"Thar's mah recordin' on Eddie's houn's. Hit's a-waitin' on Larkie larnin' ta lip sync. Ah cain't speed thet up nohow as Ah kin think on."

"Ah cain't see why Larkie 'ud want ta 'sink har lips', but Ah do know she'll be leadin' Eddie a merry ol' dance. What more, Doc?"

"Then, so long as Obadiah went ahead an' give Festus his raise..." Shirley looks impatient; "Why d'you say s'long as?" This is plumb embarrassin'. She was the one who made us miss out on Obadiah's invite.

"Ah took sick heah, an' ya done stay on a-tryin' yar healin' on me." Shirley she has the grace ta blush. How kin Ah keep har blushes a-comin'? They're so bewitchin'.

"Then we better get us o'er ta Obadiah's. Les' see how things stan' 'tween him an' Festus. That job ain't done 'til Festus axes Mary ta marry him. What more, Doc?"

Ah racks mah brains but comes up dry.

"You done tol' me you axed Obadiah ta back Meg M'Sweeney for the preachin' job. Well, Doc, does she have

it? Ah sure hain't heared nothin'. You better axe Obadiah
'bout that, too." Har look is nigh on cold as Flora's when Ah
mistakes mah promises. She jumps ta har feet. Whassup?
stirs but mus' figger he hain't in on this program. He settles
down agin' an' curls his tail close. Nex' minute we'all's aboard
the Hornet an' Ah is tight a-holt on Shirley's waist, jus' like
she done tol' me.

As hit turns out, things had gone on alright anyways.
Obadiah says he only invited us as good neighbours the fust
tahm. Festus got his raise right off, an' Obadiah, he's bin
a-droppin' hints ta him 'bout Mary. Meg's case had bin harder. Obadiah could'n find hisself no-one ta give Meg's petition. So arter he done visited his bank he went in the Court
House. A clerk done tol' him how Pentecostal is personal
as ta promotions like as ta ever'thin' ilse. The Spring Crick
preachar he'd bin a-sendin' Howie ovah on his own say-so.
Obadiah could do jus' what he pleased 'bout Meg. So startin'
nex' Sunday, he give har the preachin' job. Loose en's tied off.
Shirley acts satisfied. Amen.

On Green Hornet Shirley whispers how folks use ta figger Obadiah fer a miser. An ol' meany they'all thought him.
She tol' me Ah had done real good on account.

But thar's no let up. Back at har place arter our brief travelin' hug, she tells me Ah mus' show har my case notes. "You
know as that Dr. Watson in the book is mah model. Ah mus'
see how you measure up ta him in case-writin'. Whar is your
notebook, Doc?"

"Ah done lef' hit at Flora's, Shirley. Ya nivver said nothin'
'bout new clients, so Ah din't..." She don't let me finish;

"Les' run ovah thar right now, Doc. C'm'on!" Ah cain't
'ud put hit better mahself. Away we goes agin, me tight a-holt,
thar an' back, all too quick. Ah puts in mah two cent's worth
(Ah larned me thet 'un off 'n Ben):

"Why cain't ya drive Hornet like y'all talks in the holler,
Shirley? Ya know what Ah means. All slow an' aisy. 'Specially
fer for'ners like me."

We stand in har doorway, nice an' close. "If 'n it 'ud help

you ta slow your own talkin' down, Doc, Ah'd be happy ta oblige." She gives me a li'l peck on mah cheek an' runs inside. Ah follows har, mah notebook ready fer gradin'. Then hit hits me: this notebook has all mah research notes in hit, too. Oh, Jiminey! Ah has ta give hit har now. Did Ah put innythin' in thar mebbe Ah druthar she di'n't read? Well Ah guess Ah is a-goin' ta find out. Ah hands hit o'er, fingers all crossed.

'Long as Ah is a-waitin' heah on Shirley Ah has me one whole heap on nothin' ta do. Ah has swap Flora's nothin' fer a new nothin' off in the woods. At least Ah kin notice Shirley. Far's Ah kin tell she's doin' 'bout as much writin' in mah book as Ah ivver done put thar fust place. This don't look good. Ah twiddles mah thumbs. Hit's a hard thing when yar fingers is crossed. But what more kin a man do?

"Miaow." Thet's Whassup? a-lookin' up frum down thar beside mah chair. Does he like folk's laps Ah wunner, or is this detective cat too durn snooty? Ah tries a tickle behin' his lef' ear. He don't back off like afowah. So Ah picks him up an' sets him on mah beat-up britches. He gives me a look. Ah sure don't know what hit means, an' Shirley has har head right down. Har purty head. Har long, bright hair. Har...

"You take mind Whassup? doesn't get his claws in you, Doc, or inta your fancy pants. He hain't use ta no babyin'. You're on your own."

"Like them fust settlers, Shirley?"

"More less, Doc. But don't you go a-changin' the subjec'. You pay good heed heah. Ah am real serious. Cat scretches an' bites they're the wust. Ah done tol' you how mah potions an' poultices are runnin' low. Calls for 'em are fallin' off. Ah cain't mix up too much on ary one thing les' it go stale on me."

Whassup? has bin a-starin' at Shirley. What if'n he knows har meanin'? Kin he read har body talk well as she reads his? Mebbe he does. He jumps down soon's Shirley quits talkin' an' leaps onta har table. Fust he walks acrost mah notebook a few tahms, jus' like inny reg'lar cat 'ud do. Then he curls hisself up wi' his tail laid out ovah hit all, a-twitchin' an' a-curl-in'. Shirley has ta move hit off a couple tahms afowah she kin git back ta har readin' an' pencilin' an' gradin' an' movin' har sweet lips.

"Ah had me one o' mah new ideahs, Shirley. How'd hit be if 'n Ah gits dinner ready? Ya'd have y'self more tahm fer readin' an' writin'."

She glances up through har har curtain. "D'you cook, Doc?"

"Ah hain't nivver tried, Shirley, but Ah has ta' start sometahm. Whyn't you show me what ya fancies eatin', an' jus' leave the res' ta me." Shirley sets har pencil down an' looks...Ah don't know how she looks, but hit's differen' fer sure. Hit's a bran' new one.

"You are jus' full on surprises, Doc, an' more on 'em are gettin' ta be good surprises. Ah am real proud a you. Ah shall tell Flora so when Ah bring you back." She gits out'n har chair, crooks a darlin' finger at me an' heads fer har ol' ice box.

She points out a punnet of... "Those are chick peas. Doc. You'll reckernise them blueberries, Ah guess."

"Ya has more on 'em than innythin' ilse."

"Ah had ta run me a few li'l tests ta check mah theory 'bout the ink Mary done used on har letters. You know Ah never talks o' mah theories 'til Ah has all the fac's, don't you, Doc?"

"Ah does, Shirley, an' Ah hain't likely ta forgit hit now Ah done seen these berries. Is they dessert?"

"Sure are, Doc, but fust you are a-goin ta boil them chick-peas 'til you kin mush 'em up ready ta eat." If 'n this is our dinner, small wonder Shirley is so trim. Ah guess sech li'l meals is wuth hit. Ah draws water in a dishpan, adds them chick peas an' sets hit on thet li'l ol' one ring burner. Ah wait aroun' ta poke 'em now an' then. When they seems ready Ah strains off the water inta the sink an' axes Shirley how ta mash 'em.

"Use the foot o' this jar, Doc, but wait on mah special 'erb mix fust." She opens a cab'net, pulls out a lidded jar, opens an' waves hit o'er them chickpeas. "Now get on mashin'."

Ah does. Heah come a real tasty smell like Ah nivver done smelled afowah.

Two minutes later we'all sets down ta eat mah mash. Three minutes on we'all's ready fer them berries. Shirley fetches a jug o' milk an' pours hit inta our berry bowls. In two minutes more we'all's done, an' Ah is a-washin' up at har sink.

"How'd that milk taste, Doc?"

"Not like Ah's use ta, Shirley." Ah mus' tread keerful heah.

"Why's thet?"

"'Cos it's frum mah goat."

"Ya has a goat? Ah hain't seen hit noplace neah'bout."

"It's a she, Doc. Ah call har Mrs. Hudson. She's in the pasture yonder, whar the grass suits har best. We kin go take a look but not 'til we've gone ovah your notes. Dry up quick, Doc, an' come back ta mah table."

Soon as we'all is set, Shirley starts right in, kinda Flora-like, but still mah darlin'.

"You done wrote heah 'bout mah name. Ah want you ta add, so no-one cain't miss it, how Ah ain't nowise related ta the Perry County Josiah Combs; no more'n thet Kentucky Gov'nor, who's Bert Comb. Neither on 'em had har trouble, far as Ah knows. but thet Josiah he done 'vestigated how we'all talk in the mountains. A bit like you...hmm?

"Thar's plenny more'n your notes on holler folks you need ta fix, but mah name is jus' as important as your'n ta me. Ah have ta see that addition done right an' done now."

Mah name is important ta Shirley as har own! Mah heart does a li'l jubilation dance. Ah keeps hit ta mahself. Steady as ya goes, Tom.

Shirley pushes the notebook at me, open at the part whar she an' Ah done agree how we'll call each other. Ah adds har disclaimer 'bout non-relatives, livin' or dead, an' done push hit back fer har gradin'. She reads mah new writin' real keerful, then looks up an' give me har sweetest smile yet. Whopperjawed don't come neah covahin' how Ah feels.

"Now les' go back ta your fust day, an' start all ovah. You sure are hard on us holler folk. No-one kin please you. You come heah suspectin' a bunch o' no-goods an' that's what you got. It took all kind a scoldin's frum Flora ta turn your head aroun'. An' ever' tahm you did sump'n right you done backslid afowah the news on it could spread.

"Think on how aisy you feel now wi' Ben an' Obadiah an' Mary. Ah would love for you ta get along wi' me the exac' same way. Do you get what Ah am tellin' you Doc?"

"Ain't nothin' better in the world fer me, Shirley. Jus' tell me what Ah has ta do."

"Larn behavin', Doc. You kin start bah noticin' how folks are a-feelin'. If 'n you kin do that, your heart will tell you what ta do. Thar's nothin' in it. We'all is born that way heah. Mayhap your fancy schoolin' set you up so high, you cain't see the ground.

"Why don't you start bah noticin' mah feelin's, Doc?"

"Well ya do seem set on folks knowin' who ya is, an' who ya hain't."

"Yes, Doc, an' why d'you reckon Ah'm this way atall?"

"Mebbe ya warn't paid 'nuff heed when ya was a gal?"

"Yes, an' mah Daddy he was an' ol' reprobate. Mah family din't get no respec'."

"Oh! Is this why ya done studied at conjurin' Shirley?"

"Hallelujah! Now you are firin' along real nice, Doc. You are the sharpest man when you trah. Nex' up you kin tell me what you plan ta do for mah feelin's. Give that a trah."

Ah gits a not so good feelin'. Ah has bin treatin' Shirley all wrong. Hmmm: "Ah shall respec' ya fer yar conjurin' an' yar figgerin' as much as Ah does fer yar shinin' beauty. Ah shall look at ya wi' new eyes, Shirley. Ever' minute Ah shall 'preciate ya more'n ya kin know."

Shirley says nothin' fer once't. She looks surprised more'n anythin'. Then she pats the seat beside har. "Come set right heah, Doc. You 'bout ta get the mos' feelin' kiss on your life, 'cos you have plumb earned it. You done said what ever' woman craves."

Ah moves in close an' gives mahself up ta har warm arms, like a li'l boy.

This tahm Ah has made a promise Ah cain't nivver forgit. Far as forgettin'; hit was milkin' tahm nex' day afowah we seen how we both plumb disremembered ta visit Mrs. Hudson.

Chapter 52
A Bran' New Man

Long as Ah'm respectin' Shirley, mebbe Ah kin respec' mah-self too. Ah puts mah ideah ta the test on wakin'. Les' see if 'n Ah kin swing mah hammock high 'nuff all on mah lone-some. Gittin' har started calls fer patience. At las' Ah has har a-goin' higher an' higher. Ah's jus' 'bout set ta jump when she lets loose. Dahn Ah goes on them leaves an' broken stuff agin'. Hit don't seem ta hurt so much this mornin', so Ah don't aim ta say nothin'. Ah heads fer breakfus'.

"Have you done dropped out agin, Doc? Show me." Ah shows har. She fetches some kinda li'l packet. "Hold this on five minutes, Doc. You'll be right as rain."

Holdin' thet package puts me out'n action fer now. Ah cain't shave agin! Shirley runs aroun' gittin' our breakfus' food ready. Hit's grits like at Flora's. But Ah hain't wi' Flora, Ah is wi' mah Shirley. Ah 'preciates har an' Ah tries mah bestest at showin' hit.

"You look like a man who done slep' well, considerin'," says mah respected beauty.

Guess mah 'preciation's showin'. Hit sure feels good.

Shirley's grits taste better'n Flora's. Ah tries ta show hit. "If 'n you'd like some more, Doc, Ah kin whip 'em up real quick." She's awful good at noticin' hain't she?

Ah shakes mah head an' thanks har all the same.

"Shirley, may kin Ah see Mrs. Hudson afowah we gits a-workin'? She's bin on mah mind."

"Sooner you washes up, sooner we'all get ta visit har,"

says mah beauty. Ah picks up them bowls an' washes fit ta bust. We goes out back. Shirley has a li'l pail. She leads way beyond mah hammock. Ah sees no sign o' no pasture, but Ah does heah a lot a bleatin' way ahead. When we gits thar, Ah sees the pasture hain't much more'n a big weed lawn thet hain't bin mowed in a few months. Mrs. Hudson don't stick up much above hit but she comes a-runnin' an' a-bleatin' 'til har rope tether stops har short.

"Give har this carrot," says mah Shirley, "an' she'll be your good frien'." Ah doesn't know much 'bout goats, but Ah would'n want 'un fer a foe. "Eat up, Mrs. Hudson," Ah says but she don't need no tellin'. Thet carrot, hit's gone in a flash. Mrs. Hudson noses an' nuzzles aroun' fer more. Then Ah notices Shirley's bin a-milkin' har all along.

"Goats are all the same," says Shirley. "They'all want more'n they kin swaller. Take no notice on har." Shirley wants mah noticin' kep' fer more important things.

"Ah notices some ol', rusted stuff on o'er thar, Shirley. What's they about?"

She points ta the lef ' on the line. "Thar's mah ol' hive, then mah Daddy's gasoline drum, his ol' dirt bike, his li'l gen'rator an' mah own keepin' crate for medicine barks."

"You keeps bees, Shirley? Ah don't see none, nor heah 'em."

"Ah use ta make sourwood honey for takin' the edge off raw 'shine. That trade done fallen off, too. Folks use Kool Aid now. Them bees a-swarmed a couple years past."

"An' your Daddy rode a dirt bike?"

"He done ran 'shine on it, Doc. Li'l bitty 'shine runs they war. Off 'n the road an' through the woods. Did you reckon Ah knew how ta ride mah Hornet right off jus' bah conjurin'? 'Course not. Now lemme give you a noticin' test on it. What'all d'you see missin'?"

"Ah din't give yar Hornet larnin' no thought, Shirley. As fer what's missin', thar's no place whar other folk kin ride along." Did Shirley talk Flora out'n Hornet so we could ride him aroun' together?

"Yes, Doc. He had ta carry a big tow sack o' jars a-tween his knees. That worked fahn. 'Ceptin' those tahms he done fell off. We'all knew he had swallered a few. So thar was less ta bust. Ah allus count mah blessin's."

"Shirley, now Ah has larned ta respec' an' 'preciate ya, Ah won't be so dumb nex' tahm. Ah does truly mean what Ah says.

"If 'n Ah may change the subjec' kin we talk some tahm on makin' an' runnin' 'shine? Flora warned me off, but she din't once deny hit don't happen heah."

"She don't want trouble, Doc, an' Ah don't neither. But Ah might kin tell you 'shine tales frum way beyond Hutchins County as 'ud curl your toes." Thet thar hit's a right hoot. Flora done tol' me how Shirley 'ud curl mah toes. "Ah promise you Ah ain't goin' ta forgit. Right now tahms a-wastin'. Race you back, Doc."

Shirley wins aisy. She knows whar all the roots is an' them broke branches an' all the weed tangles an' mudholes. She has ta gimme a couple more'n 'em packets ta hold on mah ankle scrapes. Then she gits down ta work.

Ah is lef' ta mahself agin'. Ah uses the tahm 'preciatin' Shirley. How she pushes har har back. How she moves har lips ta holp har thinkin'. How she sets up real straight 'til she forgits an' bends down ovah mah work agin. Is thar a better way on 'preciatin' har other'n ta respec' har methods? Ah has no trouble keepin' awake. What a cure mah li'l beauty is fer all mah failin's...

"Stir y'self, Doc. Come ovah heah. Ah want ta take you through ever'thin you done missed or mistook.

"Ah put in all the points you lef' out on your report 'bout the Jack Forsythe case. An' thare are a lot on 'em. Lemme show you. Now be sure an' tell me if 'n you cain't foller any part of it."

Fust thing Ah notices Shirley done used a reg'lar pencil. No red, nor blue noplace. Hit takes longer ta figger out how mos' on what Ah done missed is whar Whassup? put in his oar. A lot on 'em misses was when he was cleah out a mah sight. Fust when Shirley sat me behin' har screen fer Jack Forsythe's visit. Nex' when Ah was out back on thet Marion house. Ah puts this ta Shirley in the nicest way...

"Back then you were on trial. From now on in you'll be at mah side, Doc. What you see heah is jus' how Ah expec's you ta notice an' write down. Whassup? will do what he's always done. Now you're number one." She's lookin' at me as she says this. "Ah may kin axe Clarence ta take that Shylock Holmes book out agin if 'n you want ta study up on his Watson."

"Ah b'lieve Ah kin see him an' his ways clear 'nuff in mah mind, Shirley. If 'n ya thinks Ah needs improvin' inny tahm atall, then Ah'll read hit cleah through. In a whole new way, o' course."

"You have y'self a deal, Doc. Why don't you read mah Beatrice case comments nex'? Ah will fix us dinner." Ah pulls mah notes for'ard an' gits 'em set so Ah kin study frum whar Ah lef ' off, stuydin' Shirley's pencilin' an' 'preciatin' har cookin' moves.

"Hit's sech a pleasure ta read you," Ah tells har. "Ah cain't forgit a word you done put down heah." Ah kin tell frum har look she knows hit's the flat-out truth. An' Ah begins ta see how hit's more aisy tellin' the truth. No more pretendin', no skulkin' in the woods, no gittin' cotched, no more lyin', nor gaumin' up mah li'l improvements.

Arter Ah has cleared up har dinner things, Shirley tells me how well Ah is doin' but then says, "Bring your notebook out ta the hammock an' finish your studyin' thar nice an' slow. Ah mus' tend ta mah house."

Ah has one li'l problem 'bout har plan. Ah has ta git inta thet hammock on mah own agin'. Arter all kinda tryin' Ah figgers out a way, an' lays back ta ketch mah breath. Now Ah kin study nice an' slow, like mah Shirley done tol' me...

Chapter 53
A Li'l Rain

Drip...drip...drip...like Chinese water torture. Hit's too dark ta figger whar Ah is, but Ah feels all trussed up. Drip...drip... drip. Mah face is wet, mah har is wet, mah clothes is wet, an' still those drips keeps a-comin'. Ah wants ta escape but mah feet they won't run, won't even move wuth beans. Is this a nightmare? No hit cain't be 'cos Ah realizes now how Ah is trapped bah mah hammock. Mah wet green hammock. Hit hain't no water torture; hit's plain wet rain. Now hit don't rain much in this holler so why is Ah allus out in hit? Ah's got ta git at the groun' someways.

The way Ah figgered fer leavin' this hammock done worked in the dry...sorta. A wet hammock hit's a whole dif-feren' ball o' wax (Ah owes Peter fer thet 'un). No matter what Ah does, hit acts more like a hoctopus--the hammock, not the wax. Ah gits plumb tuckered out, an' nothin' ta show fer hit atall.

Nex' thing Ah knows Shirley's a-shakin me. Hit's day-light, an' Ah is a-steamin'. "You are soakin', Doc. Why din't you come in out'n this rain? Mah eaves would a kep' you dry. Now you'll likely ketch cold."

"Flora done tol' me how rain don't bother nobody much. But now Ah thinks on hit, she has me carry an umbrelly ovah har. Yar hammock don't have one, Shirley."

"Quit your ramblin', Doc. Les' see how we'all is goin ta get you down. The wet will make it harder. Mayhap if 'n Ah get har swingin high 'nuff, Ah may kin pull you out an' stay you frum fallin'. Ready?" Shirley sets ta swingin' an' jus' as Ah is gittin' real narvous she grabs a-holt an' pulls me onta har. This is a whole lot better'n pointy twigs an' ol' leaves. Ah hates ta break our clinch. Ever' second Ah don't Shirley gits more on mah rain on har. Ah steps back out'n mah respec' fer har an' mah 'preciation.

"You are quite the gen'leman, Doc, an' comin' along real nice. Now walk on in an' get y'self dried up." Ah follers har, trailin' water acrost har floor, a-feelin' real dumb. Whassup? cain't take his eyes off o' me. Cats is a-skeered o' water. Shirley drags out a tin tub she calls a hip bath. How is Ah goin' ta dry up in a tub? She sets hit in front o' har sink, neah bah har one-ring burner. Nex' she moves thet screen on hars fer hidin' note takers. Ah gits hit. This tahm she wants ta hide the note taker frum harself.

If'n Ah is quite the gen'leman then she's quite the lady. A born lady. Mah respec' an' 'preciation climbs another notch or two. No, les' make hit three.

Shirley's bin a-clearin' out har sink, an' settin' a pot o' water on the burner ta boil. She drapes a towel o'er the screen. Hit's mah Hornet ridin' towel. She han's me a big, rough bar o' soap. "Made it mahself, Doc. Now we're all ready. Put your clothes in mah sink. When that pot's boilt, you pour it in the bath. Then be sure'n draw as much cold water as you need for a-climbin' in an' not scaldin' y'self. Pay heed ta what Ah'm a-tellin' you, Doc. Mah poultices for scalds they're all use up ever' last one.

"Las' night Ah did as much house tendin' Ah done felt like. This mornin' it's mah yard is due for tendin'. Weedin' is borin'. Ah kin put mah mind ta figgerin' how you're ta dress 'til your clothes are all dry."

By the tahm thet pot's a-boilin' Ah is a-shiverin'. Ah strips off ever' bit'n mah clothes an' drops 'em in the sink. Ah is real keerful 'bout pourin' thet boilin' water inta Shirley's hip bath. Ah cools hit down wi' plenny more cold potfuls. Ah gits in an' works out how best ta fit. Ah starts feelin' better. Hit's too good to las' an' hit don't. They're no way ta lie back.

Mos' all on me is above water no matter which way Ah sets. So soon's Ah is soaped an' rinsed Ah climbs on out. Mah ridin' towel is kind a thin an' smooth. Ah cain't dry off tee totally. Damp as hit is Ah wraps hit roun' mah middle. Ah waits fer Shirley ta be done wi' har weedin' an' thinkin'. Ah waits some more...

"Are you done an' decent, Doc?"

"Ah is, Shirley. Hit's safe ta come in." Safe fer har. Not so sure 'bout mahself.

Fust thing Shirley does is wash har hands at the sink. She's wearin' a funny kind a smile. "Ah figger Ah might ought know mah own clothes, Doc. Thar ain't so many. An' thar ain't none as suit a man. 'Specially a gen'leman. You keep behin' that screen. Ah shall toss you ovah the best Ah kin find. Ah have seen it done in some outdoor movie ovah ta Hutchins Court House. Cain't recall me the name on it for beans."

Har voice gits quieter an' louder as she goes into har li'l sleepin' space an' returns.

With a swish an' a whirr a cloud o' colour spreads o'er the screen top. Whatever hit is, hit's green an' yeller. Ah pulls hit keerful off 'n the screen an' holds hit up. What kin Ah say? Heah's another fix. Ah cain't offend Shirley. Ah has ta do sump'n wi' this dress. But what?

Hit's good an' long. Mebbe Ah kin put hit on like hit's meant fer, then pull up the skirt part an' tuck hit inta the neckline. Ah gives mah ideah a try. The doubled-up dress rides too high. Hit's too drafty. This gives me one o' mah best ideahs. Mos' folks in the holler has Scots ancestors. Scotsmen wind a long tartan blanket roun' thar midriffs. Hit was the draft give me thet brainstorm. Hit was a good brainstorm too. Hit works real well. Les' see if 'n Shirley agrees.

"Ready or not heah Ah comes." Ah strides forth an' strikes a pose. "Like mah kilt?"

"What ya laughin' at, Shirley? You want me ta wear hit like you does or sump'n?"

"No, Doc, but you're 'bout ta lose it." She jumps ta pull

on the loose end an' tuck hit inta mah kilt top. Ah cain't find no words ta tell y'all how thet felt. Ah mus' keep loosenin' hit 'til she git's wise ta mah li'l game. No Ah mus' not. Ah kin 'preciate har all Ah like, but Ah cain't direspec' har. No sir Ah cain't. An' Ah won't.

Shirley she's lookin' respec'ful too. "Doc, Ah reckon you never done heard on the Arkansas Traveler Tartan." Ah shakes mah head an' waits ta find what she has up har sleeve this tahm. "It's mos'ly green an' yaller. Thar the same nat'ral colors in them Ozark Mountains. All you need is a li'l blue an' a touch o' red. Les' see what Ah got."

Hit don't take har no tahm a-comin' up wi' a blue scarf an' a red belt. She passes the belt aroun' me. Ah steps up mah respec' quick as Ah kin. Now she's fixin' the scarf an' standin' back. Then she's a-fixin' hit an' a-fiddlin' 'til Ah's plumb dizzy. Ah b'lieve hit's har sweet breath done hit; she's up so close. Mah respec' is fightin' wi' mah nat'ral feelin's. Ah has ta tell har, "Stop. Ah cain't take no more."

What do Shirley's look mean this tahm? Does she like bein' so close? Is she one o' them women who has ta dress jus' so? Ah cain't b'lieve thet. So what is Ah ta...

"Doc, you ain't y'self. Don't think Ah ain't a bit catawampus mahself. The las' man Ah had ta dress was mah Daddy." She looks so sad Ah has ta give har a quick kiss an' a hug... an' back right off in a hurry. Who cares what the scarf looks like? Ah done remembered thet lookin glass on har'n an gits me close 'nuff fer peekin'. Ah busts right out laughin'. Mah laughin' breaks Shirley's spell. We is both so bust up we has ta lean on each other. Ah is nothin' now but pure 'preciation.

"Ah mus' tell ya, Shirley, how ya bringin' up yar poor Daddy makes me think on mine. He's the one who done changed mah name. If 'n he hadn't Ah'd be two thousan' mile an' more away. How would Ah ivver met you? Ah better sen' him a pos'card. You kin help write hit if 'n you like."

"Oh, Ah would too, Doc. Ah sure 'nuff would." Heah comes har meltin' smile agin. Ah is bein' tested ta mah limit. Mah respec' hit's goin' all weak at the knees. As usual Ah has ta change the subjec'.

"We done forgit mah notebook out thar in the rain, Shirley. We cain't open har an' not do har no harm 'til she's all dry. Kin you tell me those 'shine stories ya promised?"

"Wait up a minute, Doc. Wait while Ah hang your clothes out ta dry." She wrings each piece ovah the sink an' hops outside. She's back in less'n a minute.

Chapter 54
'Shine On

Shirley sets bah har table. Ah sets at the mos' respec'ful distance Ah kin an' still keep in har cabin.

"Even so you don't have your notebook, Doc, don't you go writin' down what Ah tell you anyplace, anytahm." She's bein' loyal ta Flora Ah guess. Mebbe mountain folks is all this way. If 'n so thar's no way Ah is ivver goin' ta git at the truth. Mah respec' fer Shirley keeps right on a-risin'. Now hit's someplace up among har saggy rafters.

"Les' start wi' the makin' on it, Do.. Folks who call it farwater done gotten 'em a bad batch, bah accident or bad feelin's. Real 'shiners say they allus throw out the heads an tails. Now what do you reckon they mean bah that?"

"Ah guess they're talkin' distillation talk, Shirley. The fraction they wants is the middle part." Shirley claps har delicut han's.

"You're right, Doc. They calls that middle bit the heart. Thar's mountain talk for you. Bet you never heard any such name in your borin' ol' chemistry classes, did you?" Well no, Ah din't, an' mountain life hain't nivver borin'. Hit's all Ah kin do ta handle hit.

"Now as ta names. Moonshine means all the ways frum rough corn squeezin's ta mah own fav'rit mountain dew. Hit's the dew Ah give you. All others burn mah mouth.

"D'you know why folks think 'shine's illegal, Doc? They heah 'bout T-men raids an' their bustin' up stills--they're Treasury Department men, Doc. What 'shiners don't think on is how they cheat on tax-paid ABC store liquors. All they have ta do is pay thar Virginny alcohol taxes. No more'n that. Then they'all kin quit a-worryin' an' a-hidin' an a-sneakin' aroun' ta make an' deliver thar batches. Doc. you know we mountain folk are way too independent ta think on that. We'all don't pay much thought ta gov'ment."

Shirley looks up at the sound o' some kind a soprano owl. Ah nivver does heah many birds in our holler. This 'un mus' be real rare.

"You'll not guess what that's about, Doc; not in a coon's age." Ah has worked out as owls is night birds, so Ah jus' shrugs. "That's how the McEvoys whistle for Terry when he runs off. Leastwise Lyney sounds liketa hoot owl an' Birty more like a screech owl." Ah has ta think who Terry is. Uhh... yes. He's the dancin' dog at Obadiah's reception. He's the one who chased them Three Bars inta the woods at Sally's buryin'. He's sump'n is Terry. Ah'd make crazy noises too if 'n Ah was wearin' McEvoy boots.

"Don't go botherin' your head any, Doc. They always find him. Mos' tahms he's a-waitin' on 'em when they get home.

"Now Ah done tol' you how mah Daddy done run his tow sacks o' liquor. They were real small 'taters 'longside what them big boys use ta do. Mos' had big-engine cars they ran on nitro. A few peppered 'em too. No T-men could ketch 'em for speed. Sooner nor later they done laid ambushes for ever' car they knew was runnin' liquor.

"The smartest runner on 'em all was way south a heah, close bah the Tennessee line. He had him a car dealer brother-in-law. This dealer 'ud lend him a diff'ren' car for ever' run, 'long as he kep' on bringin' 'em back. After he retard they made a movie on him. He died well-off, frum nat'ral causes. How 'bout that, Doc?

"Over ta Harriman use ta be a man folks called the Flyin' Milkman. He'd a made a consid'rable runner. But he was smarter'n 'em all. He got paid deliverin' milk. He got his fill o' racin' on the side, in stock cars. He done raced ever' dirt track Ah ever heard on. Tracks in Roane County, at Crossville an' Cookville an' more yet. He was a good family man too. A man as lived an' died in peace, cravin' nothin' more'n that.

"You could say runnin's bin all downhill since more'n twenny year back, when some Frenchman took a fancy ta runners racin' for fun. Those boys were real hot. Folks say he figgered thar was more money in the racin', than the runnin'. So he set up a racetrack . Afowah folks knew it, he had him an outfit. 'Deed he done discovered NASCAR. Now Junior Johnson he was the mos' famous bootlegger, an' the fust inta thar Hall o' Fame."

"Bootlegger, did ya say, Shirley?"

"Yup. Our Civil War soldiers they use ta smuggle whiskey flasks inta camp stuck in thar boots, or strapped under thar leggins'."

If 'n only Shirley warn't mum as Flora on local 'shine action, Ah might could axe har 'bout Clarence bein' our runner. Hit's real detective stuff fer sure. Ah reckon hit's why thar's not but the one set a wheels on the road heah anymore.

"Heard 'nuff, Doc? Feel like gettin' dinner agin'?" Ah does an' Ah do. But whar'd breakfast go? We must a bin havin' us sech a good tahm hit plumb got away.

Dinner is slow an' aisy. Now Ah's done readin' ever' word Shirley added, we has all the tahm in the world.

"Doc, you ain't axed me all that Ah'd want ta know 'bout grass, if 'n Ah was you."

"Ah hain't so sure what Ah should axe, Shirley. Ya done tol' me how ya smokes hit ta help yar stress. Ah has already seed what hit done fer Whassup? What more kin ya tell me?"

"It's allus bin a Southarn habit, Doc. Sometahm back in the seventeen cent'ry our fust House a Burgesses made a law. It requared ever' planter in Virginia ta raise grass. Mah kind a' grass. Thomas Jefferson he planted o'-plenny at Monticello. They knew how folks need ever' medicine they kin lay thar han's on. Them Burgesses done called it hemp rope, Doc, but it's the spittin' same weed as mah own.

"Now this ain't Monticello. Mah patch is off in the

woods, fenced in an' noplace neah whar Mrs. Hudson might could help harself. Whassup? doesn't stray far on his own. It's entarly mah fault when he gets high. See how Ah ain't bah no means perfec', Doc?" If 'n she's a-tryin' ta put me off, she mought well quit right now.

"Don't go direspectin' y'self, Shirley. Has yar smoke done inny harm ta Whassup? as ya knows on? In mah eyes you is closest ta perfec' Ah ivver done seed in a woman." Ah cain't holp mahself if 'n tellin' the truth makes har blush. Hit works ever' tahm.

"Doc! Ah ain't sech a country gal as Ah don't know a flatterer when Ah heah one. Now Ah don't like pushin' you, Doc, but is your notebook dry yet?" Jiminy...Ah nivver done brung hit in. But Shirley's way ahead a me agin. "Why don't you check it, Doc? Yonder, on that shelf ovah mah burner." Shirley, she don't miss nothin'. Ah has so much ta larn.

Sure 'nuff she's dry, 'ceptin' right thar in the middle. But mah writin' hain't reached them pages yet. Ah tells Shirley this. "Heah's what you do, Doc. Tear out the pages with mah notes on 'em. Flip the book ovah an' start copyin' 'em new. Your writin' an' mah writin' togethar." Hit's mah turn ta blush.

Ah do as she says. Now Ah has a pile o' torn out pages, an' a notebook cover drawn special bah Obadiah. Hit hain't like research notes no more. Hit looks all mountainy.

"Quit your day-dreamin', Doc, an' get dahn ta writin'. Ah want you clean done afowah Ah bring you back ta Flora. Pizen pen letter case an' all." This hain't fair. Ah cain't a bin heah three days. But Shirley's got har green eyes on me. Ah better start.

The light is fadin' as Ah finishes the pile. "You done good, Doc. You done real good. Ah shall miss you.

"Now put your clothes on quick. Ovah that kilt, quick as you kin. Heah's your towel all dry. Come hop on Hornet. Flora'll feed you tonight." One more tahm on the green towel—a bit damp still—a-clingin' ta Shirley like she's a life saver. Well, she is. Fer me.

Chapter 55
Flora Frosts Up

We pulls in bah Flora's porch. Ah hangs onta Shirley a shade longer. Ah don't have mah sea legs tonight. The porch door screeches, an' Flora does purty much the same:

"A li'l Birty done tol' a tale on ye two. 'Bout all Mr. Watson's clothes a-hangin' in the trees behin' yer place, Shirley. Is hit true?" All red an' shoutin', she looks like as she might could axe Constable Collins ta arrest the both'n us heah an' now.

Shirley takes the fust shot at bailin' us out: "Dr. Watson he's bin a-sleepin' out in mah hammock, Flora. Jus' like we done agreed. Ah figgered if 'n a rain comes on he'd have 'nuff sense ta move under mah eaves. But he din't. Ah guess he sleeps too heavy. An' Ah find he cain't no ways get hisself out a that hammock on his own..." She pauses, perhaps ta git Flora sympathysin' wi' mah poor helplessness:

"Yessum, thet's jus' how hit was, Miz MacTaggart. Ah woke up so slow Ah done got plumb soaked." Flora's eye be sharper'n Shirley's. Hit's so sharp on me hit hurts.

"Tell me this, Mr. Watson. What was ye wearin' while yer clothes was a-hangin' out a them trees? Ah see yer has a blue scarf, but thet don't cover nothin'." Shirley's turn agin. Ah cain't trust mahself not ta snigger, case hit warn't no joke Flora jus' made.

"He's sharp, Flora. He made hisself a kilty get-up. An' he set behin' mah screen all the while, clear out o' sight. He's modest an' respec'ful like no other man Ah ever met."

"Ah feel real badly Ah done missed the kilt, Shirley. What kind o' tartan was hit?" She don't care 'bout mah bein' a true gen'leman. She's hot onta the fashion side.

"It was the Arkansas Traveler, Flora. Green, yaller an' a li'l bit o' red. But it lacked the blue." Shirley waves har han' at mah scarf. The one Miz MacTaggart had scorned. Ah 'ud like ta meet the person who kin best mah Shirley. An' she hain't even done yet.

"Flora, did you mean for me ta join you at supper? Ah know you want ta heah how mah guest done behaved. You tol' me so." She has Flora boxed in real tight.

"Ah b'lieve we kin stretch the vittles atween three. While Ah lays 'em out, Shirley, kin ye drive on o'er ta those libelin' McEvoys. Tell Birty how she done got the wrong end o' the stick? Ah have mah good name ta keep hup, lettin' Mr. Watson back in mah home." Well, at least Ah kin show mah face in the holler agin, if 'n Ah gits the chance.

Supper is boiled taters an' sump'n like suckertash. Ah thinks thet's how Flora said hit.

But Ah knows fer sure what Shirley said. She done praise mah respec'ful nature up one side an' dahn the other'n. She done said how Ah gives thought whar the gen'ral run a men nivver does. She says how Ah kin neah read har mind when sump'n needs doin'. She tells Flora how Ah is domesticated right up.

"Ah know all thet," says Flora," Hit's how he carries on fer hisself as worrits me." Ah trahs ta shrink out a sight.

"If 'n he gave me one li'l consarn in three days Ah cain't recall it, Flora. That's the flat-out truth, mah deah." She's right, of course, but Ah has ta keep pretendin' Ah hain't at the table. Flora is lookin' like a hangin' judge heahrin' an extry tough case.

"Hit's Ben Cochran bothers me too, Shirley. He stopped bah ta say Eddie an' Larkie are all set fer the houn' recordin'. How could Ah sen' him on ta yer place arter what Birty done tol' me? So Ah tol' him Mr. Watson took sick agin an' cain't see no visitors. 'Specially them. Thet Larkie kin twist any man ta do foolish things. An' ye know how Eddie's allus bin..." Is Flora goin' ta cry on us? Shirley will know what ta do.

"Now Flora, Ah see your fix plain. But Ah kin tell you Dr. Watson he's a new man entarly. This houn' recordin', it's the biggest thing in his life." Shirley's layin' hit on a bit thick heah. Hit's the secon' biggest. Hit's a-trailin' way behin' harself.

"Why don't Ah bring him on out ta the recordin' place an' stay thar right through. How 'ud that be, Flora?" No matter what Miz MacTaggart thinks, ta me hit's a genius ideah. Ah waits fer the hangin' judge verdict...

"Ben b'lieves Mr. Watson is too sick ta see folk. How kin we say he got better in the blink on an eye, Shirley?" In mah opinion, Flora done set thet problem up all on har own. Why's she want another ta fix hit? Shirley is wearin' one a har conjure looks.

"Have you lost your faith in mah' healin' powers, Flora? Din't Ah fix the Doc's brain fever? Nobody cain't do nothin' 'til tomorrer anyway. Ah kin see Ben in the mornin'. Tell him the Doc. had him jus' a li'l backset so Ah done dosed him same as afowah an' he's a-rarin ta go..." She is starin' Flora dahn fit ta bust. Flora cain't look neither at har nor me. She is plumb stuck. But not fer ivver:

"Ah bin a-wond'rin' how Ah kin finish up mah house reddin' wi' thet man ever under mah feet. Havin' him out all day 'ud answer jus' fahn, Shirley. Les' do hit yer way."

Ah tries ta look respec'ful, but cain't no ways look at Flora. Hit's too much ta axe a man who wants ta cheer an' laugh all in the same tahm. Ah wunners how Shirley keeps har face so private. Ah has so much ta larn frum mah darlin' conjure woman.

Bah risin' ta cleah the table an' wash up, Ah loses Shirley. She says hit's high tahm she went. Whassup? he's bin on short commons what with all the readin' an' writin' an' dryin' an' gradin' an' dressin' an' modesty an' sech. Shirley don't want Flora forgitin' what a model man Ah is now. A man ta be trusted.

Chapter 56
Recordin' Day

No sleepin' in terday. No razor tahm neither. If 'n Larkie don't spoil the performance an' if 'n Ben's sound fix is still workin', terday mought make Caney Forks world famous. An' Shirley she'll be bah me all day long. Life is good. Ah is good. No more itchin' ta run off of mah rails. No more divils a-whisperin' in mah eahs. Not when Shirley's face an' voice is takin' up all the space.

Ah is dressed afowah Ah heah's inny soun's below. Now whar's Shirley's green an' yeller dress ta go? Cain't have Flora findin' hit or the sky 'ull fall. Thar hain't many hidin' places. Under mah mattress looks best. Ah folds hit real keerful an' stows hit away. Ah straps Shirley's red belt on under mah cord'roys. Ah stuffs the blue scarf inta mah shirt front. Ah is all set ta face Flora.

She's still Mizin' when Ah gits ta har kitchen corner. Breakfast is the same mos' days so Ah gits hit all ready.

Flora don't come dahn. Good manners or not, Ah better had eat mah vittles. Ah sets Flora's whar hit kin keep warm. Ah washes mah bowl an' spoon. Ah dries 'em. Flora mus' heah me fer sure. Har ears is too sharp fer comfort. What should Ah do?

A clatter soun's frum the porch. Ah nivver looked out thar. Sure 'nuff hit's Flora.

"Mr. Watson, Ah done gave Ben a good talkin' ta. If 'n Shirley cain't keep ye straight he will. Ah have his solemn promise." Flora kin look at me this mornin'. "Did ye eat already, Mr. Watson?"

"Ah did so, Miz MacTaggart, an' yer breakfast hit's a-warmin' o'er ta heah." Ah pulls hit out an' sets hit on the table in har place. She hain't sure what ta do wi' har face 'til she cracks a li'l smile.

"Thet was a good, thoughtful act ye done, Mr. Watson. Ah warn't sure how Ah might should take Shirley's praisin' on ye, but hit seems ye might could a earned hit true."

Soon's she done eatin' Flora tells me how Ben an' Shirley is set ta call at nine. She says Ben mus' fust run Eddie an' the houn's ta the mill an' then Larkie. Shirley's ta tail 'em on Hornet actin' escort in case on houn's escapin' or Larkie doin' sump'n' wild.

All Ah kin do is wait. Ah waits a lot. Flora starts lookin' sorry fer me.

'Bout twenny a ten Ah heahs Hornet. Shirley says she's sorry. Larkie done trahd ta bring Terry along, an' got in a fight with Eddie an' the McEvoys. But hit's all squared up now an' ready ta go, she says, pattin' mah arm. Shirley gits on Hornet's saddle. Ah gits on mah frien'ly, drah, green bath towel. Ah gits mah fust reeward as we pulls away.

Our ride on ta the mill hit's way too short. Li'l but good, as they says. Hit's all thet.

We kin heah the racket out'n the mill afowah we ever gits close. Hit almos' hurts mah ears arter Shirley cuts Hornet's engine. The houn's sound like they're a-partyin'. An' Larkie she sure is. Eddie don't soun' none too happy. Ben hain't makin' no noise atall as Ah kin heah. Likely still skeered bah Flora's talkin' ta 'im. They'all sure seems ta need 'em a manager.

"You really wants ta go in thar, Shirley? Hit looks 'bout ready ta fall smack dahn. An' all thet ruckus hit cain't help none."

"Mos' o' them walls is sigogglin', Doc."

"Sigogglin', mah deah?"

"They're leanin' out, Doc, an' half a the roof done clean finished its fallin' anymore."

This Ah mus' see; a roof on the floor. Ah goes in, a-treadin' real keerful. Hit's noisy, uphill work. You gits thet frum a tin roof on a floor. Ah hain't too steady on hit. Ah has both han's o'er mah ears ta cut the racket. Ah is glad ta see what roof is lef' angles up o'er us kind a like Ah has seen in concert halls. They holps the music soun' better.

Ah keeps lookin' aroun' doin' more noticin' on this speshul day.

Fust off Ah notices Larkie She's standin' on a slantin' millstone a-wavin' a stick. Eddie sees whar Ah is lookin'. "Larkie thinks she's a-goin' ta conduc' 'em," he says, all tuckered out. "Ah done tol' har a hunnert tahms she don't know when ta wave an' when ta stop. Hit's Ben an' me as does. She jus' gits mah houn's all shook up. She has 'em confused all ta pieces. Now they're so far off key she cain't lip sync neither.

Kin ya have Shirley talk ta har? Git har ta button up? Ya bring har outside thar, Mr. Wats'n. Mayhap she'll listen if 'n she heahs hit tol' bah some'un new."

Ah exits stage lef' ta do what he axed. Larkie follers.

Shirley sees straight off what hit's about. Larkie, she's still a-figgerin'. "Why we'all out heah?" she wants to know.

"Jus' stay heah 'til Ah has mah recorder workin' good 'nuff ta ketch yar lip syncin', Larkie. Then we'all's off ta the races. We'all kin be world famous afowah ya knows hit." Larkie cain't be none too bright if 'n she thinks mah sound recorder kin make har lip syncin' famous anyplace. But hit works. Mah darlin' is havin' major face trouble agin. She done squeeze mah arm long an' hard afowah she lets me go back in.

Ah sees whar Ben done set mah recordin' machine on top of a big, denty ol' gas drum.

The wires go...dahn ta the roof on the floor...out through a gap in the wall, then whar?

Ah realize as his pick-up truck is noplace in sight. "Ben, whar's yer..?"

"Hit's out back, Tom Watson. We doesn't want ta draw no attention... An' we'all din't afowah Larkie she started har cuttin' up. Hit's all connected. Jus' check hit an' ya kin see how so." Ah does an' Ah do.

"Whar's the..?"

"I hung ya mic off 'n thet droopy cable strung atween the side walls." Ah sees hit now. Ah looks at the mill's doorway. "Kin Ah record what them gals is a-sayin' out thar?" Ben nods. Ah gives hit mah bes' shot. Ah plays hit back.

Larkie comes o'-runnin'. "Ah heahs what you means, Mr. Watson. Les' git this show on the road."

The sorely tried Eddie lines up his houn's a bit past whar the mic hangs, in front a thet millstone. They sure is a motley group 'longside yer av'rage trio. He gits 'em set dahn on their haunches, well spaced. They looks aroun'; a-waitin' an' a-wond'rin' Ah'd say.

"Has they bin heah afowah?" Ah axes Eddie.

"What-all Ah mought a said, we'all had us twelve practices heah, but Ah guess they din't see yar machine afowah. Nor yar mic neither. Once't they're a-singin' Ah b'lieves as they'll settle dahn good. They'll do ya proud. Alright, Larkie. Tahm ya got on yar 'stone. Stan' up straight now. Fol' yar han's on yer belly an' smile sweet at the mic up thar yonder." Larkie's hooked. She's behavin' good as gold.

Shirley has followed har in. Ah gives har my bes' smile. Ah remembers how she has ta keep me in han' or face a new round wi' Flora. Ah doesn't want mah Shirley in no trouble as Ah kin holp.

Ben wails on his elber pipes. The houn's perks up like Larkie done. Is we off? Mebbe so, arter Ben puts his pipes dahn an' picks up his not-throwin' stick. Now we is. Eddie draws his stick back. Ben does the same. Ah hits mah 'record' button. All on a sudden we is smack dab inta a whole new number. Ah jus' cain't figger the words yet, but Larkie knows what they look like. She's a-syncing away like inny big pop star.

Blue's voice still soun's like Ben's pipe wails. Red's barks booms better'n ivver in heah, an' Ah jus' loves his color. Walker's buglin' voice hit's a real treat hindoors. Only Walker the English-American foxhoun' cross seems off his game. No matter what Ben said thar's a li'l echo. But they does all soun' way stronger in this mill 'un in the open.

Now Ah gits the tune; "The Ol' Mill Stream." Hit's so durn ketchy Ah has ta stop mahself frum a-singin' right along. But, hey, under mah machine is thet denty ol' drum. Ah jus' beats the measure on hit. Them conductin' sticks goes back'ard an' forrard, back'ard an' forrard. No houn' ivver takes his eyes off of 'em. An' no houn' makes a mistake far as Ah kin tell. Larkie is a-smilin' an' a-swayin' an' a-steppin' an' a-tappin' har feet. Har han's nivver leaves har tummy. Har eyes nivver leaves mah mic up thar.

Eddie said nothin' 'bout endin'. Ah tries ta recall how they done hit in the woods. As things turn out hit don't signify one bit. A bisickle wheel noses through the doorway, runs smack dab agin' our roof. Hit's Constable Collins. He gives a whoop an' a holler. Soon's he's all in he's a-tappin' his boots on thet roof. Bein' as the roof is tin an' lyin' on the floor hit makes a real innerestin' soun'. Hit's good Mike's musical or he mought a spoilt the whole blamed recordin'.

But Eddie he ain't so sure what's a-goin' on. He stops his not-throwin'. Ben ketches on quick an' stops too. Thet Walker he starts whinin'. Eddie tells 'em, 'hush yer noise.'

"Mike, Ah hopes we hain't..."

"Eddie MaCafferty, ya's a genius. Fust ya had me spooked fer fair. Then Ah seed how yer done hit. Whar'd ya git the ideah?" Eddie's relief shows plain. He gives Mike the same fac's he done give me thet fust choir practice. Mike he looks plumb whopperjawed. He runs acrost the roof in his hurry ta shake the han's o' both on our conductors. They looks so pleased an' happy hit does mah heart good.

"Now, Mr. Watson...Mr. Watson hain't hit? What ya got thar?"

"Oh, this is a machine ta record the houn's, Constable."

"An' me," says Larkie. We needs a new subjec' real quick.

"This heah's 'lectric. Ben done rig his Model T so's hit works anyplace he kin drive." Ah sees Mike's eyes light on the 'lectric wires an' foller 'em ta the sidin'. He steps out, ta see whar Ben parked, Ah guess. When he come back he axes; "When y'all is done, Eddie, kin Ah ketch a ride home? We have us a flat tire agin."

"If 'n ya don't mind a-waitin' fer two more numbers, Mike. But fust off Mr. Wats'n has ta check the one ya heared the end on."

Ah goes ta hit 'play'. Durn hit; thet button is still dahn. Did Ah press hit agin arter playin' back the girls' talkin'? An' now hit's Mike an' Eddie talkin'. How much tape is lef'? Looks like jus' 'bout none. Ah tells Eddie the bad news. He done looked brave as he kin. Ah notices Mike tryin' not ta look too happy 'bout this new twist.

Ah is thinkin' fast. If 'n Ah plays the fust session back, Larkie's goin' ta find out how har lip syncin' don't show. Nor all har smilin'. Nor all har sashayin' neither. Jus' har feet a-tappin' on har millstone, wi' Constable Collins' shoutin' an' roof tappin' a whole bunch louder.

"We'all is in one big fix, Eddie. Take mah word on hit. Mebbe Larkie kin drive Constable Collins home an' his bike while we sorts hit out. Other ways the Constable he mought be waitin' on us evermore." Ah gives Shirley a big stage wink so's she don't offer ta drive. Ah gives Eddie an' Ben one a thar own. Eddie looks confused. Ben looks flat-out desp'rit.

"Kin Ah show ya sump'n 'bout mah pick-up, Tom Watson? Afowah we decides what's best?" Ah nods mah head an' we is out'n the door. Turns out Ben don't need ta show me nothin'. But he sure wants me ta know how Larkie she's the wust driver in the world. Ah tells him why Larkie musn't heah the playback yet. Ben thinks on his feet:

"Les' pull the recorder wires as we'all's heah. This way we kin call hit a recordin' breakdahn. Larkie won't know frum beans. Ya kin give Mike his ride if 'n ya likes. Ya makes a new frien' an' ya sees a new holler, too. What d'ye say, Tom Watson?"

Ah says yes. Ben's right. Ah'll feel like a true mountain man, a-drivin' a Model T.

We leaves the wires a-hangin' dahn the mill wall an' gits us back hinside.

"Ben has 'ppointed me ta fetch ya an' yar bike home, Constable. Ah is at yar service." Ta the rest on 'em Ah says, "Ben kin hit the 'play' button, so's ya kin heah the recordin' while Ah's gone." This seems ta satisfy Eddie an' Larkie, but not Shirley. She gits harself another fat wink.

Back a the mill ya cain't see no water fer mist. But ya kin sure 'nuff tell hit's thar, a-swishin' an' a-gurglin'. Ah axes Mike an' he says all the racket be frum two cricks. Hit's the fork whar Spring Crick an' Caney Crick joins up he says, an' gives the mill hits name. So right heah's the wet Caney Fork! Robby warn't a-funnin' me. No false front he done tol' me. Ah feels bad jus' thinkin' on hit. Ah should a knowed.

Mike loads his bisickle onta the pick-up bed, cranks fer me, an' off we drives. He talks an' talks 'bout Eddie's singin' houn's an' naught else more. Ah gits no chance ta axe 'bout the places we shakes an' rattles bah 'long the way. Ah notices how his holler looks durn nigh same's our'n. Ah drops him off an' turns fer the mill.

Hit's like when Shirley an' Ah done fust arrive. All shoutin' an' wavin'. They soon figgered mah machine won't play if 'n Ben's truck is Mizin'. Now hit's back Ben makes a show on tryin' ta git hit a-workin' agin'. We's all a-watchin' him. He looks up at us. "Hit's no good," he says. "Hit's busted." Ah notices hit hain't so much busted as mah ol' plug is on the wire. If 'n innybody trahs ta connec' hit they'll git no joy out'n hit atall. No siree.

Ah pulls Eddie aside. Ah tells him how ta settle Larkie when we does heah the tape. "Hit's job is sellin' the houn' choir singin' ta music agents. The nex' step 'ud be a live test. Larkie has ta be good as the houn's fer thet. An' all har practicin' has made har so. Mebbe ya wants ta break hit thet way afowah the playin'." Eddie he's a-thinkin' on hit. Ah kin tell.

Ah leaves 'em ta pack up mah recordin' geah an' truck the houn's home. Eddie rides wi' Ben fust, ta do his 'splainin'. Them houn's kin listen all they wants. An' Larkie, she jus' jumps aroun' some more on har millstone, makin' faces, dreamin' har dreams a fame an' fortune.

Mah own fortune is tight in mah arms as Green Hornet heads fer Flora's an' house arrest. But thet hain't the way our ride sugars out—not bah a country mile hit don't.

Shirley stops neah Robby Burns place an' switches off. "Doc, Ah jus' had me an ideah as might could help Robby court Daisy. He's a-hurtin' for har so bad an' his Daisy song ain't a-goin' ta help him none. Robby has brains on both sides o' his head. Daisy ain't got but half o' one. Kin you lay low a minute for me, Doc?" She's gone afowah Ah kin git mah feelin's straight.

Hit's takin' Shirley more'n a minute gittin' Robby ta har way o' thinkin' 'bout courtin'.

Ah needs no convincin' on thet score. Ah is soft an' meltin', but Robby mus' be resistin' har ideah no end. When she comes back Shirley she's a-dustin' off har han's. Surely they hain't bin a-fightin'?

"That Robby, he thinks too much. He kep' fallin' ovah hisself figgerin' why mah plan 'ud only land him in the briar patch. Ah had ta promise as it only wants the one chance. We need ta talk it ovah in private, Doc. Grab a-holt on me." Ya bet Ah does.

In private? Is she expectin' those McEvoys agin? Any case, whar's private in Caney Forks? Noplace.

"We're a-headin' for the bone yard, Doc. Hang tight."

Afowah we arrives, Shirley done shet Hornet dahn. We coasts in quiet an' sly. We jus' makes hit undah them cedars. Sure 'nuff heah's the privatest place Ah kin think on.

"It's this way, Doc. Robby's bin a-pinin' for Daisy ever since she done turned sixteen. But he's shy an' wrong-headed as all get out. Now, you've heard on 'des'prate measures', ain't you?"

"Ah has, Shirley, Ah has. Ah has done more des'prit thungs in Caney Forks than Ah kin rightly recall. Mos'ly frum thinkin' too much. Far away, mah conjure woman." Shy an' wrong-headed hain't mah style no more.

"Remember Ah tol' you how Daisy was tellin' you true 'bout har grass smokin'? What it is she smokes right along o' me. At mah place. Ah know she tol' you Molly Mulcahy is a-teachin' har the tambourine. Now poor Robby he needs ta get his stress way dahn low, an' he plays the fiddle like me. You ketch mah meanin, Doc?"

"Ah b'lieves Ah does, Shirley. But why's ya tellin' me?"

"On account we mus' do this proper an' respectable like. Two women an' two men, Doc. Hain't nothin' less 'ull serve. Not in this holler." Ah sees now how Ah din't git har drift tee-totally.

Ah cain't back out on Shirley. But how kin Ah do this thung an' not set Flora hot on mah case agin? Well, Ah should a knowed mah darlin' 'ud be way ahead on me jus' like allus.

"Mah cabin has the 'lectric, Doc. Remember mah Daddy's ol' gen'rator? You bring that recordin' box ta our li'l party, an' treat us ta the houn's singin'. Daisy she'll go crazy for it, an' Robby he should be slap behin'. If 'n you keep a-playin' your tape, we three kin fiddle an' beat right 'long. We kin light up, puff an' play an' puff some more 'til thar's no stress lef ' in nobody. An' not noticin' neither if 'n you don't keep up with our puffin' an' sech. Think you mought stan' the strain?"

Ah'd be some fool if 'n Ah cain't. So Ah tells har 'yes'. "That's mah boy," she says. Now Ah feels in mah bones thet's fer sure who Ah is. At last an' finely.

"Walk me ovah yonder fust, Doc? Ah mus' pay mah respec's ta Daddy." She stops by a li'l flat stone in the grass. 'Johnny M'Gonaughy RIP' is how hit reads. Mah love pulls a li'ly out'n har dress front, an' lays hit acrost the stone. "Ah done pick it bah the weep willow on the mill bank," she says, kind a chokey. Ah takes a-holt on har trembley han' wi' mine ta keep har poor heart steady. She looks at me frum under har helmet. Ah sees tears in har eyes. Ah drops har han' ta grab the whole on har afowah she falls ta the grass. We stays like thet fer longer'n inny Hornet ride we has took.

Arter a deal o' blinkin' Shirley gives me a shy li'l smile. "You are jus' so good ta me, Doc.. Flora doesn't get how good you are. It's all dahn ta har jealousy. Ah jus' hate ta carry you on back thar, but Ah done promised." Jealous? Flora?

We turns ta head fer Hornet, slow like an' a-holdin' han's agin. "Did Ah tell you the party's tonight, Doc? Leave Flora ta me on this 'un."

Who knows what mah conjure woman done tol' Flora? Ah gits an evenin' pass. An' a ten pee em curfew.

Right arter supper, settin' on the porch, Ah heahs Hornet. But he stops short an' cuts out. Ah sits up ta see what's gone wrong. Mah eye kin jus' ketch Hornet standin' thar bah Ben's place. He'd make three men. What is Shirley doin'?

Then Ah sees the light. She'll be axin' Ben ta bring mah recordin' box bah. Ah had figgered on clutchin' hit all the way ta Shirley's cabin 'stead a clutchin' har. Mah own Shirley. Heah she is on the porch bah mah side a-lookin' inta mah eyes. Thet helmet. Hit suits har so well, but hit makes har hard ta kiss 'hi'. Or 'bye'.

"C'mon, Doc. We mus' move mah gen'rator afowah the show starts." Ah has ta rush an' climb on arter har or Ah'd a plumb Mized the boat. Shirley's in a fever. Ah has ta grab har extry tight. Specially when she gits us a-bouncin' thru har woods, on past a skeered lookin' Mrs. Hudson an' right on up far's har Daddy's ol' gen'rator.

Ah trahs a li'l heftin'. Hit's too heavy fer the two on us. Don't want Shirley sprainin' no part a har bewitchin' body. What kin we do?

Shirley always knows. "Pull that dirt bike out'n them weeds, Doc. Roll har on ovah heah. We kin set this 'lectrifier whar mah Daddy use ta holt his liquor sacks."

Gittin' thet bike loose frum all them weeds hit's a heap harder un hit looks. An' when she's out, Ah sees the tires is all flat. "We needs Constable Collins." Ah tells Shirley.

"Them tires won't matter none for this job," she says. "Now lemme holt the bike, an' you tip thet gen'rator onta the runnin' boards." Ah is gittin' all mah huffin' an' puffin' in way ahead a our guests' own share. Shirley's lucky Ah doesn't lose a-holt inny tahm or she 'ud be needin' a poultice or three harself.

Ah begins ta see how she leaves the bad news right 'til the las' minute, but Ah works at savin' har inny harm frum hit.

Then she pulls the same kind a stunt agin'. "Kin you shake har some, Doc? If 'n we cain't heah no gas we better roll har on ovah ta Daddy's drum." Shakin' this bike-load jus' don't work none. We drags har ta the drum an' leans har agin' hit. Sort a sigoggly. Thar's a li'l tube a-hangin' out'n this drum. Shirley picks hit up an' screws the fuel cap off of our 'lectrifier. She puts thet grubby tube in har sweet mouth an' draws on hit. Ah jus' shudder thinkin' 'bout what she's doin'. On a sudden she nips hit atween har sweet fingers. She pops the end out'n har mouth an' inta thet fuel tank. Ah heahs the petrol pourin' in. Shirley nips the tube agin. She holds hit straight up an' let's hit dangle bah the drum whar hit started.

Ah gits mah breathin' almos' normal. "Shirley, why ya done did sech a nasty thung? Ah 'ud a done hit if 'n ya'd a tol' me what ya wants."

"Ah sure 'preciates your kindness, Doc. but Ah have bin doin' hard things all mah life. On account o' bein' on mah own." Har green eyes nivver leaves mine frum under har pesky green helmet. "Push, Doc, push, or we's a-goin' a be behin' on our guests."

Bah the tahm Ah has the gen'rator in place under Shirley's back winder, Ah has worked out why she din't want Ben's truck this evenin'. Ben he'd a had ta walk home. The code o' the mountains done tol' har what ta do. Or what Ah had ta do, more like.

Soon's we's inside, Shirley gits a long, cool drink fer me. Ah should a axed what hit is but Ah is so parched Ah don't. Ben has set mah recorder on the table. Whassup? he is paddin' aroun' hit a-rubbin' hisself on the corners. Ah checks hit out quick an' rewinds the tape. Jus' in tahm, too. We heahs Daisy closin' in. Robby too, 'cept he's leavin' all the talkin' ta har. Whassup? has his ears all pricked up. Shirley stan's bah har door a-waitin'.

"Come right on in Daisy an' Robby. We have a real treat heah. Dr. Watson made a mighty special recordin' for y'all ta enjoy. An' y'all will soon see whar your instruments come in." She's shiverin' wi' the fun o' hit all. "Mah reefers an' match-box are in the jar on that shelf ovah thar. Like allus, Daisy. Ah shall fetch the 'shine when y'all are ready. You better set on this chair, Daisy an' you on that 'un, Robby." Ah notices them chairs hain't partic'ly close. Ah wunners why. Shirley don't make no mistakes.

"Far har up, Doc." Ah pushes the 'play' button. The sounds o' Shirley sortin' out Larkie fills the room. Robby looks at Shirley. "You said nothin' 'bout this, Shirley. What do you mean by it?"

"Truth is, Robby, Ah din't know nothin' 'bout it 'til jus' now." Shirley is lookin' at me. "When do we get ta the mu-sic?" Ah fast forwards the tape 'til the fust screech tells me we'all's at the houn's. Ah backs hit up a couple a secon's. We's off an' away.

Daisy she's takin' a fit jumpin' up, beatin' an' shakin' har tambourine, a-dippin' an' a-twistin' ever' which way. Robby he stares at har like she's a puppy dog in a winder. Then he sets a li'l box on the floor, gits out his fiddle an' pitches in. He's soon on his feet, bendin' an' swayin' an' a-tappin' away. All loose an' excited. Them two is doin' jus' fine without no grass atall ta holp.

But Ah notices Whassup? lookin' right skeered. Hain't no other word fer hit. Soon's them houn's stop singin' he lets out a primal yowl, deep an' long an' dahnright spooky. He runs at the door, a-scratchin' hit like he's a wildcat

Shirley runs ta let him out. "Ah am so sorry, mah deah. Ah never thought... Ah will make hit up ta you." She looks like the party's ovah fer har. But thet Robby he's lookin' charged up. He picks his li'l box off of the floor. Now Ah kin see what hit is. One o' them li'l carry-round recorders as runs off 'n torch batt'ries. He presses a button.

Heah comes the houn's agin. Jus' the houn's. No Shirley. No Larkie. But Mike's boots is thar a bit. The sound hain't so good as mah recorder, but... All on a sudden the singin' stops an' thar's Whassup? tellin' his fear ta the world. Robby looks like he's on far. "Ah jus' love the houn's singin' but Ah love hearin' your cat's opinion 'nuff ta beat the band, Shirley. You have a smash hit heah. We kin..."

"Oh, Robby, a smash hit! Ah never thought you'd be like this." Daisy has har han's put togethar like she's a-prayin'. She looks adorin'. Har eyes is shinin'. But they hain't green. "Sorry, Robby, Ah broke in on your tellin'. What was you goin' ta say?"

Ah knows what Robby's a-feelin'. He cain't recall what he was goin' ta say. Sump'n more important has come up. C'mon, Robby, tahms a-wastin'. Ah knows now why Shirley keeps tellin' me so. Robby gits mah message somehow. He's on his feet. He's smilin' at Daisy fit ta bust. Daisy falls inta his arms.

Shirley an' Ah tip toes out ta comfort Whassup?

Hit takes us a whiles a-findin' him. He's a-layin' under mah hammock, fast asleep.

"See how he don't jus' Miz you, Doc., he needs you. Better get up thar. She helps me climb in. Thet leaves har stanin' all alone... Ah remember 'bout har Daddy. This ain't right. Kin Ah help you in, Shirley?"

"Ah do reckon you might could. Ah still feel real bad for what Ah did ta mah poor Whassup? Ah do need a li'l comfortin', Doc." So long as she axed, Ah is happy ta 'blige. So long, did Ah say? Hit turns inta a couple hours. No sign on Robby nor Daisy yet. Ah settles back beside mah Shirley an'...shoot far, mah curfew! Ah has no watch...

Shirley stirs, readin' mah worry. "What moonlight's lef ' says we have us a half hour more o' comfortin', Doc.. It's tahm Ah tol' you 'bout mah Momma.

Chapter 57
Journey's End

Wi' jus' a half hour more in the hammock Shirley she's in a moony fit, carryin' on 'bout her Momma.

"Celie her name was. She had har like mine. She had a cuttin' tongue an' a hard han'. She may bin a beauty but she was a real witch. It was her done drove mah Daddy ta all his hollerin', an' drinkin', an' fightin'. Ah cried wi' joy the day she run off. She never tol' Daddy she was a-goin'. She lef' no note. We never done heard frum her agin. Daddy took a whiles ta quiet hisself down. When he did, he was a bran' new man, Doc. That's why Ah misses him so much."

Shirley is grippin' me so hard hit hurts. But hit's in a good cause. Ah kin handle hit.

Ah grips right back. "Ah feels fer ya, Shirley. Thar's no way Ah kin fit in his shoes, but if 'n ya wants ta tell me inny partic'lar thung ya misses mos', Ah will try mah best an' mend hit." Shirley grips me tighter yet.

"You are doin' good right now, Doc. Don't go a-changin'. It's mahself Ah worry 'bout. Ah am afeared ta become like her an' drive you away. You unnerstan' me, Doc?" She mus' be real skeered. She's a-tremblin'.

"Ah does, Shirley, an' Ah doesn't. Ah loves yer har, jus' like yer Daddy must a loved yer Momma's. Ah loves yer green eyes. Was yer Mama's eyes green?" She shakes her head far as our closeness allows.

"Then we mought have us jus' half a problem, Shirley. Ah reckons hit makes things twice as aisy fer us two." She goes all limp an' soft an' Ah remembers all thet mistletoe.

We'all is quiet an' still. Ah watches the moon movin' acrost the branches above, wishin' Flora's curfew 'ud go way. Hit don't work. Shirley gives a li'l twist an' she's back on the ground, pullin' me inta her arms. "If 'n we make 'nuff noise, Doc, them two lovebirds 'ull know ta pack up an' leave. They cain't stay the night or all them gossips 'ull run me plumb out'n town."

We stamps acrost ta Hornet. Shirley revs him up real loud an' we'all is on our way.

Holdin' her waist seems sech a li'l treat now arter bein' like sardines in her hammock.

Flora she's a-keepin' watch on her porch. "Ah see ye have larned good behavin' Mr. Watson. Ah thankee, Shirley, fer holdin' him ta his promises." She heads in an' Ah almos' gits past Shirley's helmet wi' a goodnight kiss.

Ah cain't git no sleep. But Ah hain't really tryin'. Thar's too much ta think on. Bah dawn Ah is itchin' ta be up an' movin'. Mah kitchen work is goin' well 'til thar's a soft li'l tap at the door. Hit's Robby. He beckons me out inta the road an' along over bah the cemet'ry. "Ah'm on mah way ta Shirley ta thank her for changin' mah whole life. She sure is one wonder."

"Ya be the third man ta say so, Robby. The fust was one a her clients. The second was me. But why is you callin', Robby?" His eyes is a-glowin' considerable.

"Tom, Ah meant what Ah said last night 'bout the hound singin' bein' a smash hit. Ah know a few big music producers who might launch it national for you an' Eddie."

"An' fer Ben an' Larkie an' ya, if 'n so," Ah correc's him. "But, Robby, ya done tol' me ya don't want no mainstream fer yar music. How 'ud ya know sech folk?"

"Easy, Tom. They came ta me for it. Ah told 'em no. No way. But Ah can give 'em a diff'ren' answer now, d'you see? All Ah need do is find whar thar cards is hidin'."

"Ah cain't b'lieve this, Robby. Hit is wunnerful news. Kin

Daisy help ya dig out them cards?"

"You bet, Tom. She'll be hotter on it than me. Now b'lieve me or not, Ah haven't been thinkin' 'bout her all night. Ah have been thinkin' too 'bout our recordin's. Ah have ta know can you get Whassup's yowl out'n mine onta your'n. Ah reckon at the end on every verse, whar it 'ud really get folks a-laughing. Do you know how that's done?"

"Ah thinks Ah might could swing hit, Robby. Mah tapes is big an' yar'n hit's small. Splicin' is out but re-recordin' mought work. Let me know when ya has tahm."

"Ah has plenny tahm now so long as Daisy is in on hit. You name the day."

"Let me git this all straight wi' Flora fust. Why don't ya stop by arter ya done seen Shirley?" Robby agrees an' takes off. Plumb out'n tahm ta shave agin, Ah goes back o'er fer kitchen duty. Breakfast is ready when Flora comes down.

"Ye are keepin' up yer himprovin', Mr. Watson, Ah mus' say. Mayhap Shirley is good fer ye arter all. An' yer cookin' is passable...fer an Englishman."

"Ya is kind ta say so, Miss MacTaggart, but Ah'd say Ah is way more mountainy than English now." Flora sets a-thinkin' 'bout mah claim. If 'n innyone kin judge, hit's her.

"Don't let yer grits git all col'," Ah tells her.

"Thet does hit. 'Deed ye are a true mountain man, Mr. Watson, jus' so yer beard gits a deal longer. Ah better call ye Tom heah on out. An' Ah am Flora ta ye, Tom." Well this is one big day all roun'. We'all trod us a long road an' we'all are home at last."

"Flora hit is then, Flora, an' Ah has big news fer ya. Robby knows folk as kin make Eddie's singin' houn's famous. We jus' has ta do a bit on re-recordin' afowah we makes our pitch ta 'em. New music gits not but the one chance. Ever inch on hit mus' be jus' so. We kin do hit heah if 'n ya want or..."

"Oh not heah, Tom, fer the love o' Moses. Ah'm still a-cleanin' house. Ye pick what-all other place ye want an' git right on wi' hit. Ah'll thankee."

The rest is history.

The producer Robby picks out'n them cards is a Floyd Z Folsom, of Nashville. We'all has ta rent us a car ta bring us thar. Obadiah puts up the cash in return fer a one tenth share on the takin's. Floyd neah falls out'n his fancy chair when we plays him our fixed-up recordin'. Later on he visits Caney Forks an' a photographer too. When he meets Larkie she cain't stop gigglin'. Floyd loves hit an' wants her gigglin' spliced inta the verse breaks. Fust Whassup? then Larkie, then the nex' houn' verse is how hit goes.

Ah agrees wi' Floyd on his gigglin' ideah. Ah tells him 'bout the laffin' policeman record in Britain. Hit was nothin' but non-stop laffin' an' hit done sold thru the roof. Come to think on hit, thet's the last tahm England hit come inta mah new mountain life.

Floyd sees Larkie lip syncin' an' wants her syncin' at all our concerts. He wants six more numbers too, afowah we cuts our fust album. Robby an' Eddie works on these new 'uns. Larkie keeps on a-larnin' 'em. Floyd keeps a-crackin' the whip. He's aimin' ta have us in the stores fer Thanksgivin' trade. Robby has no tahm ta be in the woods. But he is a-goin' ta git hisself fat checks, like Eddie an' Ben, an' me too. We'all kin take turns a-ridin' inta Hutchins Court House wi' Ben ta put 'em in thet bank on Obadiah's.

Robby an' Daisy is talkin' 'bout gittin' spliced at the Courthouse right arter Jeppie brings 'em thar fust Folsom Records check. Flora wonders will Mary an' Festus beat 'em ta the Jedge.

Ah hain't so busy as them others. Shirley gits most o' mah tahm. Ah larns how best ta stan' in fer her Daddy. Ah keeps larnin' more conjurin', mountainy ways frum her.

Ah doesn't mind which is which. We talks 'bout all the marryin' goin' on. Fer now she don't want me tied dahn like her Daddy was. Since she 'fessed up, folks 'preciates her more. An' me? Ah hain't bothered one li'l bit if 'n things stays jus' the way they is.

Acknowledgements

Linda Goodman, of Waxhaw, NC, deserves my special thanks. A professional Appalachian storyteller of Melungeon descent, Linda gave me crucial insight into mountain dialect and speech patterns. The heaviest belong to the oldest generation. Dialect, speech patterns and colloquialisms lighten or disappear with each new generation. Linda expects all such remaining traces to be gone in twenty years. I therefor set this story in 1968, to permit speech with more character and color, and to record that for posterity, no matter how amateurishly (I am an Englishman).

Jean Koon, Morattico basket-maker extraordinaire, deserves recognition for her passionate belief in mountain holler authenticity, and for naming its best exemplars as my muses. Fellow Morattican Mary Byrd Martin, as general editor, gave the MSS her best attention and expertise, and we both speculated on the possible origin of Melungeon as Mélange' un. You never know.

On Virginia's Northern Neck, members of the Rappatomac Writers critique group have been generous with their detailed dialect examples, the more surprising as most are definitive flatlanders. I thank them too, especially for the inevitable ensuing laughter.

I cannot thank Margaret, my wife of 51 years, enough for putting up with those endless hours when, like any busy writer, I was living in my head.

The actual Green Hornet, not the scooter, is a property licensed by Green Hornet, Inc.

Confessions

In writing this book I grew increasingly conscious of three prime influences: Kingsley Amis' "Lucky Jim", which I knew long before emigrating from England; the Foxfire book series, which I read avidly soon after arriving in America; and Jeeves, the stately and erudite butler of P.G. Wodehouse's comic tales in his Bertram Wooster series.

Googling 'Lucky Jim', I was startled to discover that, like Kingsley Amis, I had written a picaresque novel. A picaro is an engaging rogue who lives by his wits among humble strangers and, within an episodic structure, points up the hypocrisy and corruption of our world. In uncovering the admirable qualities of holler life, the character Tom Watson does this for England's academia.

It has been said of the picaresque novel that its hero (or anti-hero) takes the reader, happily perched on his shoulder, on a wild ride. Tom Watson does this in spades.

The earliest picaresque novel is generally accepted to be Cervantes' 'Don Quixote'. Apart from 'Lucky Jim', the best loved are probably 'The Adventures of Huckleberry Finn', by Mark Twain; 'Pickwick Papers', by Charles Dickens; 'Tom Jones' and 'Joseph Andrews' by Henry Fielding, and 'The Adventures of Roderick Random', by Tobias Smollett. All promote a good measure of social reform.

Chapter Notes

Chapter Two: Nowhere
Don't plan on losing weight in the Bosphorus Steam Baths. They don't exist.

Chapter Four: My New Tutor
Jack Forsythe's case is freely adapted (and much abridged) from Sir Arthur Conan Doyle's short story entitled "The Adventure of the Yellow Face."

Chapter Eighteen: Peter's Invitation
Peter's stories about the whale in the well and his own preposterous longevity are the inventions of Will Parsons, Elizabethton, TN, proprietor of Parson's Mandolins. As you might expect, Will has many more tales, untold here.

Chapter Thirty Seven: Robby's Revelation
These poetry excerpts are the true work of the late Senator Eugene McCarthy. The whereabouts of the quoted source of authorization to reproduce is no longer known to USPS, and the original publishers untraceable, even on Google. Eugene's prose is, if anything, better. I heartily recommend his local book, "From Rappahannock County".

Chapter Fifty Four: Shine On
The "Flying Milkman" was Rubben Burgess, who drove for the Norris Creamery of Harriman, TN. His daughter, Wanda, kindly supplied the details recorded here.

Chapter Fifty Seven: The Journey's End

As Shirley could hardly have put the mistletoe in the pin oaks, she must have chosen to sling Tom's hammock beneath it. "Li'l things like that make winnin' aisier", is the principle she espoused to Tom before winning his freedom from Flora. Shirley always made therapeutic use of the white berries; originally for alleviating circulatory and respiratory ailments, and latterly to emulate the cancer curative extracts 'Iscador' and 'Heliodor', pioneered by Rudolph Steiner.

The Missing Chapter

This chapter missed the train at Meadowview, and got left out. If there had been a chapter fifty-eight it would have told how Eddie became CEO of HOH Corporation and lives in a new hilltop mansion named 'Hound Heaven'. He has purchased three burial plots in Colbert County, Alabama, where on Labor Day, 1937, Key Underwood buried his beloved coon hound 'Troop'.

The best publicised occupant is still 'Hunter's Famous Amos', Ralston Purina's 1984 'Dog of the Year.' This will change as Blue, Red and Walker move in. Of course you must never point at this graveyard either, but it's only necessary to do so in heavy mist or darkness.

Larkie wasted no time in taking over Floyd Z Folsom, whose wife never did make him laugh.

Ben bought himself a brand new, shining, black T-Bird convertible right off the showroom floor in Roanoke. To this day he remains partial to Ford Motor Co. products, the colour black and the letter 'T'.

Made in the USA
San Bernardino, CA
18 November 2015